THE
DOCTOR'S
CHILD

DANIEL HURST

Published by Bookouture in 2024

An imprint of Storyfire Ltd.
Carmelite House
50 Victoria Embankment
London EC4Y 0DZ

www.bookouture.com

ISBN: 978-1-83525-605-3
eBook ISBN: 978-1-83525-604-6

For all my readers who have supported me on my writing journey so far – thank you and I hope you enjoy this story.

PROLOGUE

Lots of things can come from an affair.

Heartbreak. Scandal. Divorce. Forgiveness.

A child.

I was just one of the consequences of the affair between Doctor Drew Devlin and his mistress Alice Richardson, an affair that became so notorious that it spawned its own true crime documentaries and countless newspaper articles. I was the unintended result of two people being together – two people who never should have met, two people whose liaison caused the loss of several lives. A child is usually a source of joy, but in my case, I'm connected to a dark history and will forever be linked to one of the most notorious women in England, a woman the police force are still searching for to this day.

The doctor's wife.

Being the child who was born out of that fateful affair has meant I have grown up hearing all about the rumours and news stories surrounding Fern Devlin, my father's wife, as well as my late father Drew, my mother Alice, a detective and everybody else whose lives intertwined in the resulting investigations and court cases. The impact on an innocent child like myself, who didn't ask for any of that, has been huge. But how much will it shape me now I'm an adult? Only time will tell, but like all things connected to Fern Devlin, the infamous doctor's wife who remains on the run, the consequences surely promise to be two things.

Explosive.

Unpredictable.

Then again, there was usually one thing that could be counted on when Fern Devlin was involved, and it was that death followed her wherever she went. I was warned about what would happen if I ever tried to find her, and those warnings came from people who knew exactly how dangerous and deadly the doctor's wife could be.

But like many youngsters, I ignored the warnings from my elders and thought I knew best.

Revenge really is a powerful motivator.

Unfortunately, I've realised far too late that I am out of my depth. I simply want to go home, but after the terrible thing that has happened recently, that would be difficult, as I am now in just as much trouble as Alice and Fern.

I thought I was better than the two women who came before me, but quickly realised that I am not.

I've made mistakes. I'm not perfect. My future is now as clouded as my past.

It's me.

Evelyn.

The doctor's child.

ONE

FERN

PRESENT DAY

Can a child inherit the bad parts of their mother as well as the good? I have to assume so, although it doesn't please me to think that. My daughter might have some of my more appealing physical characteristics like hair colour, height and a fast metabolism that lends itself to a slender appearance, but what does she have inside? Does she have my darkness – my penchant for wicked acts – the part of my soul that is capable of not just dreaming up crimes but carrying them out too?

I suppose what I really want to know is this: could my child take another person's life like I did?

In eighteen years of motherhood, I haven't had any reason to believe this yet and I hope I never will.

I pray that I remain the only killer in the family.

Needing some relief from my intrusive thoughts, I find it in the sunlight that filters through my bedroom window of this chateau in the French countryside. The vitamin D is welcome, but not unexpected. That's because the weather is usually fine in this part of the world and that is just one of the many things that I relish about living here. I also appreciate the scenery, particularly the rolling green hills that I can see if I look out of my window. They are the hills that surround this village I call home, the ones that are populated with vineyards where wine is produced, bottled and sold to connoisseurs all over the planet. I love the melting pot of people who call this village their home too, some of them French locals but many of them people from abroad, from countries like Spain, Portugal or Switzerland, people who came here once on holiday and enjoyed it so much that they returned to buy property. My reason for coming to this village was very different to theirs, but I've blended in as easily as they have and, just like them, I expect to live out the rest of my days in this quiet, rural retreat.

I also adore the house I now reside in, a two-floor stone property that dates back to the sixteenth century and was once home to a French aristocrat and his merry band of maids, at least if the history books are to be believed. I was sceptical at first and thought it was just our estate agent spinning us a story to make this house seem even more enticing, but it turned out to be true. This house really was once occupied by French royalty, although now, it's just home to a three-person family who have very normal jobs and spend their spare time doing very normal things.

The house is big, but not so big as to feel like I could get lonely as I potter around it whenever I'm here by myself. All the floors are stone, which gives this place a rustic feel and also helps keep it cooler during the heatwaves that are frequent between May and August. I initially missed the feeling of carpet on my bare feet, but now I am soothed by the coolness of the stone whenever I pad around without shoes. The kitchen is my favourite room, the long wooden table in there the scene of many happy family meals in recent years, though the study is a close second – the room with two large bookcases full of all sorts of gripping stories I like to lose myself in during the colder months of the year. Outside, the garden is sizeable – a sprawling lawn encircled by tall trees that offer shade from the summer sun and privacy from my neighbours' homes nearby. I love spending the middle months of the year out in the garden, tending to the flowers and developing a healthy glow on my skin that lasts long into the tougher months, when the trees shed their leaves and the ground is as cool as the stone inside. But the thing I love most about this place, and a thing that will never be topped because it's easily the most important out of all the aforementioned things, is that I've been able to live here for almost eighteen years without anybody knowing who I really am.

My husband, my daughter and the other two hundred or so people in this village simply know me as Teresa Brown, an expat who left England and moved to a small French village, seamlessly blending into life in her new country.

None of them know the real me.

None of them know that I am Fern Devlin, the doctor's widow, and the woman who every police officer in the UK is still on the lookout for.

I'm sitting at my dressing table in front of my mirror and, as the sunlight continues to pour into the room, I am warmed both by the added heat and the fact that, despite my advancing age, I still look pretty good. I'm fast approaching sixty and the wrinkles that have grown in number and strength over the last few years will vouch for that, but unexpectedly, I feel fine about it. I wasn't aware of it until I reached my fifties, but I quickly realised there is a calmness that comes with ageing, one that the folly of youth doesn't appreciate. I almost cringe now when I think back to some of the other big milestones in my life, like turning twenty-one or thirty, and how I would feel like I was already old and over the hill at that stage. Back then, birthdays were almost something to be feared rather than celebrated, as if getting older was a hinderance rather than a help. But now I see that there is a beauty that comes with age, as well as a wisdom, and the older I get, the calmer and more confident I seem to feel. I might never have lacked confidence in my life but I certainly appreciate that calmness, particularly as I'm still on the run from the law and will be until the day that I die.

As I comb my dark hair, the hair that I have dyed once a month to cover up the greys, I think about one milestone in particular, one that stands out more than all the others because of what happened that night and what came after it. My fortieth birthday is one I'll never forget, but mostly, for all the wrong reasons. That was the birthday when my boyfriend at the time threw me a surprise party, but the real surprise turned out to be when, at the end of that night, I discovered he had been lying to me and was not the man he said he was. Rather than being Roger, a guy I had met in a bar and the guy I was looking to build a life with after the death of Doctor Drew, my late husband – who I helped put in an early grave – it turned out my boyfriend was really Greg, Drew's old friend. And the guy who was trying to expose my hidden secret. I killed Greg that night, marking my fortieth with a dead body, which was apt as I had already arranged the murder of my cheating husband Drew. But the consequences of that night are what drove me to be here, many miles away from all my family and friends back in England, in rural France, living a quiet life, because that's the only life I dare to live now.

That night was also the night I conceived my little girl.

My daughter, Cecilia, was born as a result of mine and Greg's relationship, and if her arrival seems like a long time ago, the fact she is almost eighteen now only serves as a reminder of that. I can't believe the little baby I gave birth to in Cornwall – the baby I fled with overseas – is officially going to be an adult soon.

I also can't believe I've had to keep so many secrets from my own child.

Over the years, as Cecilia grew, I knew only two things with any certainty. One, that I would love her and look after her for as long as I lived. And two, that she could never know who I really was, who her father had been, and the real reason why we were living in France. I've managed to achieve that, although it hasn't been easy. Lying never is. As far as my daughter knows, we left England and moved here to escape her dangerous father, my abusive ex-boyfriend who was known for drinking a lot and putting his hands on women even more. That fictitious cover story is one that has made it easier for Cecilia to not feel any love for her absent father or make her want to go looking for him but, crucially, it is also one that prevents her from doing such a thing. That's because I've told her that my ex is so dangerous that if he was to ever find us, he would most likely hurt me and possibly even hurt his daughter for leaving him, so we can never risk him knowing where we are.

That means we can never go back to England.

Of course, the real reason we can't go back is because I would be arrested, but I needed a way to make sure my daughter never wants to visit the country where she was born. So my fictitious ex was my solution. It's a terrible lie, but it's far better than the truth. Imagine if Cecilia knew that I had actually killed her father after he exposed my own lies? Not only that, but what if she discovered that I was already guilty of being involved in two other deaths as well as that of my first husband Drew – of Rory, my accomplice in Drew's murder, back in Arberness, and of Greg, her own father. My daughter would hate me, and quite rightly so, and I doubt I would ever see her again. That's why she can't know the real me. I simply can't risk losing the love of my baby.

But I'm not just being selfish. Like any good mother, I also have my child's best interests at heart. I'm aware that keeping her from the truth is the best way to protect her mental health and save her from drowning in a sea of shame. If she knew the chaos that she really descended from, what kind of life would she have then? It certainly wouldn't be a normal one, not a healthy, thriving life where she reached her potential and found true happiness with all the people she encountered. The past would affect everything from her personal life to her professional one, and that's even before any journalist tried to get to her to tell 'her story' in the national news. None of it would be her fault, but that wouldn't be much consolation as she tried to navigate through life with one deceased parent and the other one in prison for his death.

Cecilia can never know the real me.

And neither can the new doctor in my life.

I finish combing my hair just in time to see the man I share this bedroom with walk in behind me, looking dashing in his smart suit, his hair already perfectly in place, in time for him to leave the house this morning.

'*Bonjour ma belle,*' my sexy Frenchman says as he leans over to kiss the top of my head, and I smile as I always do when Pierre greets me in the morning by calling me beautiful.

'*Bonjour mon bel homme,*' I reply, my customary reply, to let my husband know just how handsome I think he is, before he leaves the house to start another day of work. But I don't just say that to be kind to him. I also say it because even after all these years of living here, I still get a kick out of the fact I can speak a language other than my native tongue.

As Pierre picks up his briefcase and leaves the room, I call after him to wish him a good day, though I know it will be because it always is. Like my first husband, Pierre is a doctor, but unlike my first husband, he is an honest, decent man. That means he'll go to his office, treat patients with love and care, and then come home to me and treat me in the same way. Not like Drew, with his affair and his lies and with his ability to use his career choice to make him feel superior to others. I used to worry about where Drew was and what he was up to when he wasn't with me, but I don't have that problem with Pierre. I trust him.

I started dating Pierre when my daughter Cecilia was five years old, and our love has continued to grow over the years for many reasons. I love Pierre not just because he loves me, but because he loves Cecilia too. She might not be his daughter, but he has helped to raise her like she is his, giving her a strong, dependable male presence in her life when my actions in the past could have easily meant that she never had a father figure to look up to as she grew. He's a good man, a better man than I deserve, though of course, just like my daughter, he can never know who I really am.

My cover story of an abusive ex just waiting for me to return to England is how I have managed to stop Pierre suggesting we take a trip back home to where I grew up, and why he believes me when I tell him that if we never leave this village for the rest of our lives then I'll be happy. But there is a problem there. While Pierre and I have no plans to leave, somebody in our family does. Cecilia wants to move to Paris when she turns eighteen, seeking adventure in a big city alongside her best friend, Antoinette, who she has known since her very first school day in this village.

I can't stop my daughter. She's almost an adult and free to make her own choices. But I am afraid. Her going out into the world means I can't control the narrative as much, if at all, anymore. She's free to explore, forge her own path, and possibly, find her own truth. It's a day I've been dreading since she was born. I could keep my secret safe when Cecilia was small, but now she's bigger, what's stopping her from figuring it out on her own, especially with information on the internet so freely available at her fingertips? I did consider making this a Wi-Fi free home at one point, but anyone with a teenager will surely know that's not a realistic thing.

As she gets older, maybe it's only a matter of time until she figures out the truth about her upbringing. It's a massive problem, though I know I'm not the only one seeing their baby become a grown-up. Alice will also be going through the same thing. The woman Drew had his affair with had a baby too, and it's the baby I saved the life of before I fled to France. If I hadn't done that then I'd be in prison now, though at the time, I was simply trying to save an innocent life rather than make it all about me.

Alice's child, Evelyn, must be eighteen already, as she was a little older than Cecilia.

I wonder how the doctor's mistress is coping as her own child turns into an adult.

If she is even coping at all, that is.

The last time I saw her, I had just saved little Evelyn's life on a clifftop in Cornwall and, eternally grateful to me, Alice allowed me to get away again, despite spending so long trying to catch me before that. It's weird to think that the woman I have to thank for the life I lead now is the same woman I once hated with a passion and framed for murder. Life sure has a funny way of working things out... although I do sometimes wake up in the middle of the night and wonder if Alice has ever had a change of heart.

Does she still forgive me for what I did, and live her life in peace these days?

Or does she think of me as often as I think of her. If so, what is on her mind?

TWO

ALICE

It's a typically wet and blustery day in Arberness, the village in the far north of England, where the beach overlooks the southern tip of Scotland and where tourists like to make a stop-off to take a few photos and sample some of the local pub food before moving on. But I haven't moved on from Arberness and, with so much time having passed since I first moved here, I don't think I ever will now.

This village is more than my home, it's the place where I've had some of the best and worst days of my life. Other people might be weighed down by that history and run from so many memories in favour of finding peace elsewhere, but I have remained. I decided this was not only the best place for me but for my daughter, Evelyn, too, which is why I have raised her here for the past eighteen years. Despite some tough times, I feel like I did a good job of that. But unsurprisingly, now she is an adult, Evelyn has decided she wants to see more of the world.

'How's it going?' I ask my daughter after coming downstairs to find her where I usually do these days, which is sitting at the dining room table surrounded by travel guides for all sorts of interesting destinations in Europe.

'Fine,' is the curt reply from Evelyn as she keeps her head down, the pen in her right hand moving across the piece of paper she has in front of her, which tells me she is taking notes based on whatever she has just read in one of these books.

I wasn't expecting a monologue from my daughter, but something a bit more substantial than a one-word answer would have been nice. That's just the way it is between us most of the time. It's been that way since she became a teenager, if I'm honest, although I can't blame her hormones for the fact that she doesn't talk to me as much as she used to when she was smaller. What I can blame it on is the fact she grew up and got to the age where she could find out about my past by reading all sorts of salacious news articles online, as well as reading the articles where she was summed up in one very succinct way.

While I will always be known as 'the doctor's mistress', Evelyn will always be 'the doctor's child'.

'Where are you reading about now?' I try again in the hopes of a conversation being struck up between us.

'Somewhere far away from here,' Evelyn replies, again without looking up at me as she speaks.

'Don't be like that.'

'Like what?'

'You know what I mean. Making out like you can't wait to leave me behind.'

'I can't.'

'Evelyn…'

'Shut up. I'm trying to work here.'

'I will not shut up! How dare you talk to me like that in my own home!'

'Urgh,' Evelyn groans and she starts picking up some of her books, which suggests she is going to go and carry on working in her bedroom. But I don't want her to do that because, as much as it can cause conflict, I'd rather have her downstairs with me than upstairs where I can't see her.

'It's okay. Stay there. I won't interrupt you again,' I say before she can get up and go, in the process letting my daughter off lightly for the way she just spoke to me, but anything to try and keep the peace around here.

I leave Evelyn to her travel-planning and go into the kitchen to make myself a cup of tea, staring out at the wet, windswept field at the back of my house and feeling a little sorry for the one lonely sheep I see standing out there, bearing the full force of the elements. I don't know where the rest of his flock is, but he or she is all by themselves and it makes me feel sorry for them. And as the kettle boils, I know I am going to be like that sheep very soon myself, all alone with no company to brighten my long, slow and repetitive days. That's because Evelyn is planning to go backpacking in Europe, hence all the travel guides currently littering my house, and once she's gone, there'll be nobody living here but me.

As I take the teabags from the cupboard, I feel guilty and more than a little selfish for not wanting my daughter to leave home. I should be happy and excited for her and the adventures that await her beyond the borders of this tiny village, and I am sometimes, but I'm also very sad too. I'm sad not just because my little girl is spreading her wings and flying the nest, but because we're hardly on the best of terms. I can't help but feel that once Evelyn has gone, she will never come back here again.

It's not unusual for children to move out of the family home when they reach adulthood. They might get a job and a place of their own, or go to university, or travel. As the decades go by, more and more options open up to the youth of today that might not have existed for previous generations. And that is a good thing, not just for the youngsters but for their parents too, who only want their children to thrive and follow their dreams. But it does mean that while Evelyn will be away doing just that, I'll be left with nothing but the memories of the past eighteen years, hoping that I'll get the chance to make new memories with her in the future. But that's not a given because all the one-word answers she gives me, as well as the slamming of doors and tutting whenever I try and make an effort with her, is proof that my daughter can't stand me and can't wait to get away from here.

And if I'm honest, it's not her fault.

I'd probably hate me too if I was her.

As I linger in my kitchen and sip my tea, not daring to go into the other room where Evelyn might be dismissive towards me again or, worse, ignore me completely, I think about the journey we have both been on to get to this point. It all started when I had that stupid affair, and I fell for the charms of Doctor Devlin. In the process, I incurred the wrath of his vengeful and resourceful wife, Fern. Drew died, though not before impregnating me, then I was framed for his murder soon after. Then the real craziness began. It was a craziness that culminated in me having my baby before eventually tracking Fern down to a village in Cornwall with the help of my ex-boyfriend, Detective Tomlin. If it hadn't been for the fact that baby Evelyn had been snatched and taken onto a clifftop by Fern's disturbed next-door neighbour, then Fern would be behind bars now because I had caught her and was ready for her to finally face justice. But Fern saved Evelyn's life that day. I was so grateful to her that I had to let her go.

I don't know where Fern is now and what became of her and the baby she had.

All I know is that Evelyn hates me for allowing the woman who killed her father to get away.

How does my daughter know what went down on that clifftop in Cornwall eighteen years ago? I told her, that's how. I thought I was doing the right thing at the time, by being as open and as honest with my daughter as I could be, though in hindsight that was definitely naïve of me. But I'd simply wanted to give Evelyn the full story of what had happened with Fern and Drew, not just half a story or, worse, the story that journalists wrote about at the time because they didn't know the full facts, only I did.

Evelyn was four when she started asking about her daddy, no doubt because she had seen other children at her nursery being picked up by men as well as their mothers. Back then, I told her simply that her daddy was in heaven with the angels and, while she was sad, she left it there. It was in primary school when the teasing started, a few unsavoury little boys and girls in her class picking on her because they knew she was different. She was the only one without a dad, though thankfully, at that age, the bullies didn't really know why.

It was during secondary school when that changed.

I'd always feared the day when Evelyn, and all the other kids at her school, would figure out that her father was the infamous doctor who had died on the beach and made national news. I tried to pre-empt it by broaching the subject with Evelyn myself, sitting her down when she was ten and telling her that her daddy had been killed by another person, but that he hadn't been in pain, and it was a very long time ago. Evelyn had been upset, and very confused. I'd tried to answer her questions as best I could, although there was one that was hardest of all to answer.

'Did the person who hurt him go to prison?'

I had wanted to say yes, because that should have been the answer, and it would have been the only response that might have made Evelyn feel a little better about the situation, but I couldn't. I had to tell her the truth: that the person who plotted the murder got away with it. I had to tell her because she'd only find out by reading news articles online when she got older anyway. I told Evelyn that Fern was still out there, which was the truth, and the reason every police department in the UK has her photo on file, and unsurprisingly, my daughter was not happy about that. But rather than risk having my child go her whole life filled with vengeful hate towards the woman who got away, I tried to offset some of that anger by telling her that Fern had saved her life once.

I'd hoped such a revelation would make Evelyn feel a little less hatred and, in turn, make her life a bit easier as she grew, and for a little while, it did. But the bullying Evelyn suffered at secondary school was intense; once she was old enough to read things online and get her information from other sources beyond her mother, she couldn't believe that I had allowed Fern to get away.

'She killed Dad!'

'She framed you for his murder!'

'She was evil!'

I've lost count of how many times I heard Evelyn say those sentences once she was a teenager, and it carried on all the way until she was fifteen. By then, Evelyn had become much more reserved, a shadow of her former self as a child, not just from the bullying she had endured but because she had made her mind up about everything.

She had made her mind up that she hated me, and I was at fault for the life she had.

I want nothing more than to have a normal relationship with my daughter. I'd love to go into that dining room now and sit down beside her and ask her all about the travels she is planning. I want to engage with her properly, have a long conversation, see the light in her eyes when she talks about her plans, but also see the love in her eyes when she tells them to me, her mother. But that won't happen. If I was to sit beside Evelyn now then she would just get up and go to her bedroom, and if I followed her in there then she would leave the house entirely. At least if I stay away from her then I can pretend like we have some semblance of a normal mother–daughter relationship.

Evelyn feels like justice hasn't been done for her dad, which is understandable, but it's more the way she feels about me that hurts. Thanks to the news reporters who spun their stories about me, the mistress that caused the doctor's wife to go on her killing spree, Evelyn has a fixed idea of me as being some sort of man-eater who got involved with another woman's husband and set the whole chain of events into motion. She's called me some awful names over the years, though she's most likely only been repeating what she's heard people at school saying about me. It's been tough. Tensions have eased recently, but only because Evelyn is on the verge of leaving home, which is hardly a cure for our problems. But what can I do?

I really don't want Evelyn to go away for an undetermined amount of time, especially when things between us are so fractured, although at least if she gives me her travel itinerary then I will know where she is.

That's better than not knowing, which has happened before.

Despite everything I've been through, the day Evelyn went missing is still the worst day of my life...

THREE

ALICE

They say being a parent is the hardest job in the world, and I can attest to that, but I've also found something else that can be tough too.

Being your own boss.

When I decided to set up my own business, I thought it would be a breeze. Set my own hours. Work at my own pace. Give myself permission to take an extra day's holiday here or there. However, if anything, I'm working harder now than I ever have before, but I had little choice if I wanted to keep sustaining myself as a single mother.

After my break-up with Tomlin – the detective who helped me navigate the first few stressful months of Evelyn's life by providing not just moral but financial support too – I had to survive on child benefit payments. I never saw any of Drew's money, because there was no will that said I or any child he might have in the future would be entitled to it in the event of his death. It wasn't beneath me to be on benefits, mainly because it was a matter of survival, and I took advantage of a few precious free hours of universal childcare that the government offered to new parents until Evelyn was old enough to go to the free state school in the village. But despite the occasional bit of respite, there were some long years of being cooped up at home with my daughter, unable to have a real break or go out and earn the kind of money that would have made a difference to our lives. Once Evelyn reached the age of five, I started working in the local butchers, which was messy work, to say the least, but it gave me a solid income. But there's only so long a woman like me can come home covered in animal blood. I made the decision to do something a little more suited to my personality, and that's how I had the idea of making my own greetings cards. I liked the idea of being creative and producing things that people could gift to each other on occasions like birthdays and anniversaries, so I watched a few videos online and then jumped right in. I've been doing it ever since and, slowly but surely, I've built up enough of a customer base online to ensure I can keep doing it for as long as I want to.

It's much better than working at the butchers, that's for sure.

The only time I get blood on me now is with an accidental paper cut.

The house is quiet, allowing me to work easily on my next card, and it will stay this way until I've picked Evelyn up from school and brought her back here. I collect her every weekday at half-past three, making the ten-minute walk from here to the school gates, where I join the rest of the mums in the village – although by join, I mean stand near them while they gawk and gossip about me.

I had been hoping to make some new friends during the school drop-offs and collections, expecting to find some common ground with the other mothers, but while we share having a child in common, it seems that's the only way we can relate to each other. The other mums have never made much of an effort to talk to me and I know why. Many of them either dislike me because of the part I played in the suffocating drama that enveloped this village for several months, back when Fern Devlin was the talk of the nation, or they dislike me for another reason.

They think I might end up trying to sleep with their husbands.

I only had one affair, an affair I tried to end myself on several occasions, I might add, yet every female under fifty in this village seems to think of me as a threat who will sleep with any man I can if given half a chance. That's laughable for several reasons, not least of which because I haven't even been with a man in years, not since I ended my relationship with Detective Tomlin after I discovered him kissing another woman just before I went to Cornwall and confronted Fern. The last thing I want in my life is another man, but that hasn't stopped those at the school gates from keeping their distance from me, as if making me their friend will only lead to them coming home one day to find their husband under the sheets with me. Some-times, when I've been feeling particularly lonely or hurt by their standoffishness, I almost feel like trying to seduce one of their partners, just to prove them right, but that would be stupid.

There's no way I'd ever dare get involved with another woman's man again.

The last thing I need is another Fern Devlin on my case.

But while I can handle my problems with the mums in the playground, I'm not sure how well my daughter is handling her problems with the kids in it. Several of them have been teasing her about the past and, in particular, her father in that often overly honest and hurtful way that children can be, and I know it's getting to her. She's come home in tears a few times and, while I've spoken to the headmistress, it's not been nipped in the bud yet. I just hope today has been a good day for Evelyn, for both our sakes; but just after lunchtime, I get a phone call that tells me things are not good at all.

'Hello Mrs Richardson,' the headmistress at my daughter's school says, an air of nervousness in her voice. 'I'm sorry to call, but we were wondering if Evelyn is with you?'

'With me? Why would she be with me? It's the middle of a school day. She should be with you.'

There is a brief pause from the other end of the line then, which is another bad sign.

'What's going on?' I demand to know. 'Where the hell is my daughter?'

'It seems she snuck out of the school during the lunch break, and she hasn't come back to her class yet.'

'Snuck out? How could she sneak out? Weren't you watching her?'

My chest is starting to tighten as I think of my eight-year-old daughter roaming around the village on her own, crossing busy roads, going in and out of places she shouldn't be going. But then I have an even worse thought.

'What if she was taken?' I cry, my heart rate increasing by the second.

'Oh, I'm sure that's not the case. The school is very secure,' the headmistress assures me, but that's not much good after Evelyn has already got out.

'Secure? You have a missing child!' I shout down the phone as I begin to panic. 'Have you called the police?'

'Well, no, we were just trying to find out if she had gone home. If a child sneaks away then it's usually to go back to their house.'

'I just told you she isn't here!'

This can't be happening. Where is my daughter?

After telling the headmistress to keep looking, I end the call and instantly dial the number for the village police station. It's only tiny because there is never any crime here, not since Fern

Devlin's actions, but it's a start and they can bring in reinforcements from Carlisle, the nearest city, if need be. But I'm praying it won't come to that and I rush to the window, hoping I'll see Evelyn walking towards the front door with her school bag. I wouldn't even be mad at her for leaving school, I'd just be glad she's okay. But I don't see her outside, so I have to tell the police officer who answers my call that there is a missing child in the village.

If it was an adult then there would be far less concern but, given Evelyn's age, action is taken immediately, and I'm assured that everybody who can help will be looking for her around the village. But as I put on my coat and run from the house, desperate to join the search myself, I feel like I need to do more. My support network is limited, not much larger than the people in this village – and most of them just feel sorry for me – and doesn't extend to my old friends, all of whom gradually stopped replying to my messages, no doubt because it was awkward and I was the 'taboo' subject in the group. It's been a similar story with my family too, though I have to take some of the blame. The shame I feel about not just embarking on an affair but going to prison, even if I was framed, means it's easier for me to avoid familiar faces from the past and stew in my own self-pity than face whatever judgements they have of me. But there is someone who might be able to help me now, so I make a call to a person who has come to my rescue before. It'll be the first time we've spoken in years so it might be awkward, but at a time like this, there's far more important things to worry about.

'Hello?' the gravelly voice says when they answer, and this man sounds worse than I remember him being.

'Tomlin? It's Alice,' I say, letting my ex know it's me in case he had deleted my number at some point since we split almost eight years ago. I'm not sure why I kept his number if I'm honest, though maybe part of me knew having a detective on speed dial might come in handy one day, although based on what I read in the newspapers a few months ago, it's ex-detective now.

'Alice?' Tomlin says, suddenly clearing his throat. 'How are you? Are you okay?'

'No, Evelyn's gone missing from school, and I have no idea where she might be!'

'I'm on my way!' Tomlin says without skipping a beat, which is incredibly kind but also incredibly sad, because I can already hear in his voice that he hasn't moved on from me, even after all this time. Then again, I knew that already after reading about how he had been dismissed from the police force recently due to alcohol problems. The journalists who scavenge around in the gutters of society for a story that sells were quick to latch onto the news that the detective who had famously believed Fern Devlin's lies and botched the doctor's murder case so spectacularly had fallen on hard times. I was sorry to hear Tomlin had been struggling but, right now, I just need his help.

While he's on his way from Carlisle to Arberness, I go everywhere in the village I think my daughter could be. My first stop is the sweet shop, followed by the park, followed by the beach, but there is no sign of her. It's troubling to not find her at the first two places, but it's almost a relief that she's not at the beach; it would be too dangerous for her on her own by such a large body of water. Then again, I had wondered if she might be somewhere on the sand, in particular in the area where her dad was killed, because she has asked me a lot of questions about that place recently in that morbidly curious way kids do when death is involved. Unable to find her, I have no choice but to just run from building to building in the village, asking pedestrians if they have seen her and knocking on doors and trying to recruit residents inside to help. I get aid in the form of Dorothy and Ethel, two women who were regulars at the coffee mornings I used to organise at the community centre; further help comes as a couple of police officers and two teachers from the school lead the search, as well as the sheepish headmistress. Then Tomlin arrives, having made the hour-or-so journey through the country roads from Carlisle, looking like he needs a good wash, a change of clothes, a haircut and a shave. When he speaks to me, I can smell alcohol on him. Has he driven here under the influence? I don't get time to ask him because one of the teachers calls out that she's found Evelyn's schoolbag on a bench near the village church.

It's evidence that my daughter was here, so after checking the bag to see if there's anything in it that might offer clues as to her whereabouts, I run around the cemetery part of the church, calling out to Evelyn and hoping to spot her somewhere amongst the headstones. But she's not there. So I go into the church. While at first I think the old stone building with the stained glass windows is empty, I hear a creak and assume it's from the rows of wooden pews. A quick search of them all yields nothing, and I'm just about to go back outside again when I hear another sound.

Crying.

I find my daughter crouched inside the pulpit at the front of the church; the place where the vicar delivers his Sunday sermon is Evelyn's selected hiding place after she fled from school. I feel my shoulders sag and the tightness in my stomach loosen once I know she is safe, the curse of a parent forever resigned to worrying about their offspring. This has been just one of a number of tense times in my life since I became a mother.

It takes me a while to get her to stop crying and tell me what is wrong and, when she does, it turns out that it was more bullying that caused her to run away. I'm just glad I've found her, as is Tomlin, the police, the locals and, of course, the head-mistress who might have been fearing for her job only a few minutes earlier. But, despite the panic being over, I know the underlying problem is not solved. Will it ever be?

I just want Evelyn to be a normal child and have a normal childhood, but how can she, given who her parents are and their connection to the doctor's widow? Maybe it was a mistake to stay here but, with the story being national news, she could be bullied about my past at any school. At least we're familiar with Arberness, so we're somewhat comfortable in our surroundings during trying times. Better the devil we know, and all that.

But this is still hard. I don't want to say it to any of the people in the village who smile at me as I take my daughter home, but I'm clueless as to how to stop what has happened in the past affecting Evelyn's future.

I'll try my best, but I guess I'll only know if it has worked when she is older.

I'll know because one of two possible things will happen.

Either she'll love me.

Or she'll hate me.

FOUR

EVELYN

I'm glad Mum hasn't come and sat with me or asked me more questions about the trip I'm planning. I hate how she insists on the pair of us having a forced conversation that always ends in an argument, either because I get annoyed at her for talking to me or she gets annoyed at me for not talking to her. Better for us both to just do our own thing and only talk when we absolutely have to. But soon, we won't even have to do that, because I'll be out of here, many miles away from Arberness, and I cannot wait.

I put down my pen and look at the notes I've just made. I've jotted down a list of things worth seeing in Madrid, in preparation for when I eventually make it to the Spanish capital and have time to explore the city. The travel guide I have for Spain tells me there is a lot to do there and I can't wait to see it for myself, but it'll be a while until I do. I have many stops to make before Madrid, including Paris, Amsterdam and Brussels. But my first stop is London, which is where I will take the train to begin my journey.

I'm so excited to be a backpacker. I've dreamt about it for the last couple of years, ever since I found out it was a thing that people could do. The thought of just throwing a few belongings into a bag, putting that bag on my shoulder and then hitting the road is an enticing one and perfect for someone like me, who feels like they'd be happier anywhere but home. I know that it's not just a desire to see more of the world that is driving me, it's also a desire to escape Arberness and my family's horrible history in this place, but so what? I want to get out of here and, pretty soon, I will get my wish.

I pick up the travel guide for Greece and flick through a few of the pages, my eyes taking in the wonderful sights of ancient ruins and sun-kissed beaches. I plan to end my trip in Athens, although I'm flexible and could end up anywhere, depending on how long my finances last and what happens to me along the way. I might find a job en route, working in a bar for extra funds that could keep me away for longer. I might even meet a man on my travels and move in with him, which would be ideal – then I might be able to stay away forever. I'd happily never come back to Arberness if I can help it, and I think Mum knows that, which is why I think she gets so upset whenever we have one of our arguments and I end it by telling her I can't wait to leave home.

But can she blame me? She has no idea how hard I've had it for the last eighteen years. Everybody I've ever met has already known who I am since I was a little child. I'm the offspring of the doctor who was murdered and the woman he had an affair with. I'm a consequence of an affair that saw a doctor's wife go crazy and kill several people; she remains at large to this day, which is insane. I presume she fled to Europe, which might be another reason why I'm interested in going there. I might see something in the news about a woman matching her description on my travels and somehow bring her to justice. It's a little fantastical, but stranger things have happened. Fern certainly made enough headlines in this country – maybe she's already up to her old tricks elsewhere.

But mainly I want to get out of here and spread my wings because none of it is my fault. I didn't ask for any of this to happen. Why would I? Because of what happened before I even existed, I've been bullied for years and have no real friends in this village despite living here my whole life. Sure, some of the older women say hello to me when they see me out on the street, but no one here my age wants to hang around with me.

That's why I can't wait to leave. I can have a fresh start, reinvent myself, free myself from the shackles of the mistakes people made before me, mistakes that have followed me around since I was born. I plan to use a different name when I travel, a fake name that I'll make up and sounds cool. Maybe I'll go by a different name in each country I go to, introducing myself to other backpackers in the hostels with a new identity each time until I find the one that I like the best. Whichever one makes me most popular will be the winner. I definitely won't use my real name, Evelyn Richardson, because all anybody has to do is type that name into a search engine and the internet will give them my whole past.

'You're the doctor's child?' some of them might ask before they stop wanting to be my friend, instead seeing me as a great bit of gossip they can share when they meet other backpackers, ones who have had normal lives and don't have a dad who was murdered and a mother who was framed for it. I want to avoid such a scenario at all costs, so I'll make sure I do that by going under an alias.

I pick up my pen and write down the name Tiffany. I like that. Maybe I'll start out as a Tiffany.

Deciding that I've spent enough time looking through all my travel guides today, I gather them up and leave the dining room table, carrying them all to my bedroom where I dump them on my shelf, beneath which sits the backpack that I will soon fill when I start my travels. But I'm not quite ready yet, mainly because I could do with earning a little bit more money from my job at the village supermarket. Stacking shelves is what I have done since I left school at sixteen. While it's been boring beyond belief, two years there while living at home rent-free has allowed me to save up a nice chunk of cash and, as long as I don't go too crazy when I travel, it should last me a long time. Then there's the money Mum has offered to give me, although I'm still not sure if I'll take it. Sure, it'll be nice to have extra funds and see a few more places, but accepting it might make her think that I'm grateful to her and I'm not sure I am.

How can I be grateful to the woman who let my dad's killer just walk away?

The evil bitch who killed my dad is still free, out there somewhere living her life, well away from here. It seems like I've been punished instead of her and that is not fair, but I can't do much about it. If the police can't find her then I won't be able to, not that I've ever spent too long looking. I don't want to torment myself by thinking about that woman any more than I already have done. She doesn't deserve it. But I find it unbelievable that Mum had the chance to have Fern arrested and didn't take it. If she had, maybe I'd be feeling slightly better about things. I don't know, maybe not, but I surely wouldn't be feeling any worse. As it is, that woman is still out there and, because she is, the newspapers will occasionally mention her, speculating on where she might be, and that only helps keep her and, by extension, me and Mum in the headlines, which is the last place I want to be.

I'm glad I didn't see Mum as I moved through the house; I'm hoping I won't see her as I head for the front door. Fortunately I don't, which spares us both another uncomfortable moment. Once I'm outside, I'm already feeling a little better.

Imagine what I'll feel like when I'm thousands of miles away. Like a new person, hopefully. But before that, I am still very much me, just a lonely, confused young woman who never got to meet her father, and has only read what other people have written about him online.

I take a walk on the beach in Arberness every day, whatever the weather, because the fresh air and sea view usually lifts my mood, even though this place is where Dad lost his life. I tend to avoid the exact spot on the sand where he died, sticking to the other end of the beach, because that's better for my mental health, but whenever I'm here, I do feel closer to him. I'm not sure I'd go as far to say his spirit still lingers here, but knowing I'll never actually meet him means this place is the next best thing. If he was really here now, in flesh-and-bone form rather than just spirit, I would have so many things to say to him. Unlike with Mum, where I'm practically mute, I would ask him a million questions.

'What were your hobbies?'

'Did you like travelling?'

'What was your childhood like?'

'Do you regret having that affair? Why did you start it?'

'What would you do if you had more life to live?'

So many questions, and while I could get many of the answers to them from Dad's parents, who have reached out to me in the past, I've never felt ready for that. I want to speak to Dad, not them, but that's impossible. I'll never get the chance. Fern Devlin denied me that. I've never wanted to meet them, which isn't their fault, it's mine. But what good can come from me being around more people who Fern hurt? I've been having a hard enough time dealing with my own grief, let alone anybody else's. But maybe I'll meet them one day, ideally when we have something to be positive about.

I'd love to be the one who catches Fern one day. I would finish what Mum started and actually hand her over to the police, or maybe I'll go even further than that. But I guess I'll never get that chance.

I'll never be in the same place as her.

Maybe that's for the best.

Or I might end up a murderer like her.

FIVE

FERN

The big day has arrived. It's the day of my little girl's birthday party, although she isn't so little anymore, as the large number eighteen on all the balloons in this room remind me. But rather than dwell on where all the years have gone and how I'll never have Cecilia fall asleep on my chest again, forcing me to carry her upstairs to her bed, I will focus on how this is a happy occasion that is to be celebrated and enjoyed.

I know my daughter is certainly excited about it.

This party was her idea.

As I look around the lavishly decorated room and see all the people who have come out tonight to celebrate with us, I know Cecilia is more than happy with the effort me and Pierre have put into this event. There is a long line of hungry guests queuing at the buffet table, the bar is busy and there are several movers and shakers on the large dancefloor, in front of which a DJ plays some pop hits that I am far too old to know the words to. I spot my daughter in the middle of the dancefloor, her arms stretched above her head and a big grin on her face as she loses herself in the music alongside some of her best friends. Antoinette is beside her of course, just like she has been for the last thirteen years. They became firm friends at school and vowed to do everything together as they grew up. They've stuck to that youthful promise, and soon they will both leave here and go to Paris where they each have jobs lined up. Cecilia has an internship at a fashion house in the city centre, which has always been her dream line of work, while Antoinette is getting a start with a recording label, which is perfect because music is her particular dream. How wonderful it is to see two youngsters going after what they really want in life. I'd say they remind me of myself, but it's so long ago I can't recall what it was like to be young and do what I want. I'm not even sure I was ever so carefree.

'I still think that dress is too short.'

I turn to look at the man who has just sidled up beside me and smile when I see Pierre, easily still the most handsome man in the room, despite there being many males in here under half his age. But Pierre is ageing as well as any of the fine wines that are produced in this region, and he must be happy enough with my appearance too – he has his hands around my waist, and he gives me a kiss on the cheek as we watch Cecilia continue to dance.

'The dress is fine,' I tell him, although I did have reservations too when I first saw what Cecilia planned to wear to this party. The black dress she spent most of her birthday money on is made of a wonderful material, it's just a shame there isn't a little more of it; but like my daughter reminded me, she's old enough to decide what she wears now, and soon I won't even get to see what goes on in her wardrobe. Paris is only forty miles away from this village, but it might as well be four hundred. It feels like a huge chasm between me and the little life I so carefully raised. But I am happy for her and know she will have a wonderful time in the city. This village is better suited to people like me and Pierre, those looking to gradually wind down in life, rather than those just starting out in it, but still, she's my baby.

I will just have to visit her as often as I can.

Pierre realises that we are both out of wine and struts away to the bar to get us some more. While he's gone, his spot beside me is quickly filled by Marion, a good friend I've made since moving to this village. Like me, she moved here from elsewhere, but unlike me, she isn't on the run, or at least I don't think she is. She's just a normal woman, and normal is exactly what I needed when I came here, which is why I guess I find her company so soothing.

'It's a shame they have to grow up, isn't it?' Marion muses as we watch the dancefloor. 'It's hard when they're a baby, but I'd give anything to go back in time to when my girls were small again.'

'Yeah,' I say as I gaze in awe at Cecilia and the woman she has blossomed into. That's despite the fact she spent the first few months of her life living in very abject conditions, back when I was a struggling hideaway in Cornwall with barely two pound coins to rub together. 'I don't know where the years have gone.'

'Instead of focusing on what you'll lose when Cecilia moves, try to focus on all the things you've got to look forward to,' Marion says, using her own experience of being a mother of two adults to help cheer me up. 'You'll get to visit her own home one day. You'll see her on her wedding day. She might become a mother. There are so many adventures still ahead for you both to experience together.'

I appreciate Marion's words, and I appreciate the drink Pierre hands me when he gets back to the bar. I certainly need a few gulps from my glass a moment later because the music cuts out and as everybody stands around to see what is going to happen next, Pierre reminds me that it is time for us to make our speeches.

As I follow my husband to the stage where the DJ has a microphone ready and waiting, I can see Cecilia frowning because she has no idea what is going on. Pierre and I made sure it was that way; she would only have tried to talk us out of it if we had told her that we planned on saying a few words. As it is, Cecilia is powerless to prevent the pair of us speaking to the gathered guests, and as my husband takes the microphone first, I smile at my daughter to let her know that yes, the next few minutes might be a little embarrassing for her in front of all her friends, but it's going to be fine and, when it's over, she'll appreciate what we have to say. Hopefully.

'Thank you all for coming,' Pierre begins, before adding a little French where he thanks the staff who have been catering for us all this evening. Then he switches effortlessly back to English, not just for my sake because I still find my native language easier, but because everyone we have invited can speak English too, so it's no issue for him to converse in that tongue.

'It's a wonderful evening to celebrate the milestone of a wonderful young woman,' Pierre goes on, smiling at my daughter as he speaks. 'As most of you will know, Cecilia, and her mother, came into my life thirteen years ago. Back then, I thought I was happy enough living here, fulfilling my duty as a doctor and imbibing several glasses of wine in the village bistro every Friday evening, which totally contradicted the advice I'd spent all week giving out to my patients.'

A few people in the room laugh, including the owner of the bistro himself, a man who has profited greatly from my husband's custom over the years.

'But then I fell in love with the woman standing beside me here tonight, and only then did I realise what true happiness was.'

I roll my eyes at Pierre's soppy show of affection, and he winks at me before he goes on.

'However, I fell in love twice when I came to be around Cecilia, and discovered what an absolute joy she was. I met her when she was just five years old, and if you think she is cheeky now, you should have seen her back then.'

Laughter around the room. Cecilia still looks like she'd prefer the speech to be over, but there's a little way to go yet.

'I just want to say that it's been an honour and a pleasure to be around to witness you grow into the woman you are today,' Pierre goes on, looking slightly misty-eyed as he speaks, which tells me just how much affection he has for my daughter. But he didn't have to make this speech to tell me that; he's more than proved it over the years since I made the big decision to introduce him into my daughter's life when she was younger.

'I know you're going off on a wonderful adventure in Paris soon and we're going to miss having you around every day, but we wish you the best and can't wait to hear all about your adventures. Speaking of which, your mother and I have got you a little something to kickstart those adventures.'

Pierre reaches into his suit pocket now and takes out an envelope before inviting Cecilia onto the stage to join us. She's reluctant but her friends quickly nudge her in our direction and, once she's beside us, Pierre hands her the envelope.

'Happy eighteenth,' he says with a smile as Cecilia opens her present, and when she sees what it is, her smile couldn't be any bigger.

'Front row seats to a fashion show in Paris,' Pierre declares triumphantly as Cecilia beams widely. 'I think she likes it!'

Everybody cheers, well aware that for somebody as obsessed with fashion and glamour as my daughter, this is the perfect present. I take in how happy Cecilia is before giving Pierre a kiss, because it was he who was able to afford such an expensive present. I'd been saving for a long time for this day but would still have been way off affording something like this, but my husband had secretly been saving too.

Doctor wages to the rescue, and not for the first time.

Then Pierre hands me the microphone and I guess it's my turn to say a few words about the birthday girl.

'Where do I start?' I say as the room falls silent. The tears I had been hoping to keep at bay until the end of this speech already threaten to overwhelm me. 'My baby girl. All grown up. It only feels like yesterday when I was holding you in my arms in the hospital.'

Everyone in the room smiles at that moment, except Cecilia who just blushes, but while I am smiling too, the memory I have just mentioned is tinged with the fear I had at the time. I was still relatively new to being on the run then and living under a fake identity, so was praying that I wouldn't be exposed or my baby would have been taken away from me. As magical as the moment I first met my child was, I will never forget the extreme paranoia I felt as I lay in that hospital bed and tried not to imagine several police officers swarming onto the ward. I feared that the hands I was using to feed, swaddle and soothe Cecilia would soon be restrained by handcuffs, and it was terrifying to think about the little life I had just given birth to having to fend for herself in this big wide world without her mummy around to look after her. But the police never came and, eighteen years later, I'm still waiting for them to find me.

'We've been through so much together, you and I,' I go on as no one in the room, including Cecilia, can possibly know what I'm really talking about. 'I'm just so glad that despite not really knowing what I was doing, I've somehow been able to help you grow into the wonderful person you are today.'

Cecilia doesn't look quite as embarrassed now. Instead, she just looks emotional, which is sweet.

'I just want you to know that wherever you go and whatever the distance between us, I will always be thinking of you and will always be here for whenever you need me,' I say as a tear rolls down my cheek. 'Have fun in Paris and follow all your dreams, but don't forget me. Promise?'

Cecilia laughs before she moves in for a hug, and the pair of us embrace as everybody in the room applauds. As we separate, tears in our eyes and smiles on our faces, we have a quiet moment amidst the applause where Cecilia thanks me for everything I have done for her, which means a lot. But there's no need for her to do that, and now it's all about looking forward, which is why I say what I do next.

'I know you'll love Paris and have the best time,' I say, excited for her. 'But just remember, and you know I hate having to remind you, but I'm your mother and you know I worry. You'll see lots of signs for the Eurostar while you're there, but don't be tempted to get the train to London. I mean it, Cecilia. It's too risky. Your dad might find out if you went to England and we can't have that. Okay?'

'Yes, Mum,' Cecilia replies, rolling her eyes because she's heard this all before.

'I mean it. Promise me.'

'I promise.'

I only end the conversation once I'm convinced Cecilia has got the message again. I think she does so now she's free to rejoin her friends on the dancefloor, and as the DJ starts the music again, the party is back underway. I watch my daughter dancing and it looks like she doesn't have a single care in the world at this moment.

Oh, how I wish I could say the same...

SIX

ALICE

I'm making the drive from Arberness to Carlisle, a route I have taken many times before, but today's trip is not an easy one to make. That's because I'm on the way to the train station and, when I get there, I will be saying goodbye to the person currently sitting next to me in the passenger seat.

'Can we turn the music off and just talk for a minute?' I suggest to Evelyn after she has turned the radio on to try and avoid any awkward silences between us.

Evelyn sighs before reaching out and turning off the music. Now the car is quiet, which is how it has been for most of this journey so far. But this time, I'm determined to say what I need to before I no longer have the chance to converse with my daughter.

'Look, I know things have been hard between us for the last few years,' I begin, as Evelyn folds her arms across her seatbelt and turns her head away from me to look out of her window at the passing countryside. 'But I hope you know that I've always tried my best to do what's right for us and I hope that one day you can appreciate it.'

'Whatever.'

'Evelyn, come on, talk to me.'

'What do you want me to say? That I can't wait to get out of here? Because I can't.'

It hurts to hear it, but I can't say it's shocking news.

'I know you're excited to go travelling and I'm excited for you too. But I hope that you understand that I'll be worried about you, so it'll be nice if you keep in touch with me and let me know that you're okay.'

Evelyn doesn't say anything to that, which suggests that her plan was to completely cut contact with me once she gets on that train to London.

'You don't have to message me every single day and you don't have to send me lots of information, but just a short message every now and again to let me know where you are and that you're safe. That's all I ask for. Can you do that?'

'Fine,' Evelyn says, her head still turned away from me.

That's all I really needed to say, but as we're talking now, or at least one of us is, I keep going before Evelyn turns the radio back on.

'One day, if you have a child of your own, you'll understand how this is for me,' I say, feeling emotional as I grip the steering wheel tightly and focus on the quiet road ahead. 'How it feels to spend eighteen years of your life loving someone and caring for them only to have them grow up and be so distant.'

'So it's my fault now?' Evelyn says, finally looking at me.

'No, I didn't say it was your fault. I'm just telling you that you probably don't understand the sacrifices I made for you—'

'Sacrifices for me? Yeah, it must have been really hard for you to have an affair and then let Dad's killer walk away because you were too much of a coward to stop her.'

'Evelyn!'

'Just leave it, Mum.'

'No, I won't just leave it! Not when you talk to me like that!'

Evelyn lets out a deep sigh and turns away again, clearly

ready to get out of this car and onto the train. Maybe I should just leave it before we both say things we'll regret, although I doubt there's much more Evelyn can say that she hasn't already at some point over the last few years.

'I haven't told you this before but screw it, I might as well tell you now because who knows when I might see you again,' I say as Carlisle comes into view in the distance. 'When I first had you, I struggled badly. You were a terrible sleeper and cried all the time. I couldn't cope. The doctor thought I had depression.'

'Great, you were depressed when you had me, that's lovely to hear,' Evelyn says, shaking her head as if I'm making this worse, but I've not got to my point yet.

'You don't know how hard it can be to have a baby and I hope that, one day, if you do become a mother, things will be easier for you. But it was hard for me, damn hard, and I am not ashamed to admit that I was struggling to bond with you.'

'Even better!'

'Listen to me!' I cry as Carlisle train station comes into view. 'What I'm trying to say is that if things hadn't gotten easier when they did, I might not have been able to cope and, if I hadn't, I don't know what would have happened to you. You might have been taken away from me and, if you had, you might not have had the life you've had.'

'I might have had a better one.'

That stings, but I ignore it and move on quickly.

'What I mean is look at the opportunity you have here now. You're getting ready to go and see the world. Do you know how lucky you are? But if you'd gone into care and ended up with someone who didn't treat you well, you might not have had this chance now you're all grown up.'

Evelyn doesn't say anything to that, so I keep talking while I have the chance.

'I'm saying this because I know you're hurting and feel filled with hate and anger, for both me and Fern, but my point is, when you were taken from me that day in Cornwall and that disturbed woman held you on that clifftop and threatened to jump off it, that was what snapped me out of the mess I was in. But by then, I thought I was too late and would never get the chance to love you properly. Then Fern saved you and, thanks to her, we've had these eighteen years together, and now you're going to go and have the time of your life.'

I think Evelyn gets my point. Both me and Fern, the two women my daughter hates the most in this world, are big factors, if not the biggest, as to why she is alive and well and in a position to make the choice to go travelling and live her life.

'I want you to enjoy yourself, darling,' I say as I bring the car to a stop in the station car park. 'Don't let your heart be filled with hate, for me or for Fern or anybody else. Try and be happy and try and see that I love you more than anything, and I'll miss you like mad, and any message you send me while you're away will be the best thing that happens to me that day.'

Evelyn is just staring ahead out of the windscreen at all the other people scurrying into the station to catch the next train southbound, but then she finally speaks and, when she does, it's all I needed to hear.

'I'll message you whenever I get the chance,' she assures me quietly. 'I need to go.'

I thank her before we get out of the car and, after she has put her heavy backpack onto her shoulders, I take in the sight of my daughter as she prepares to leave me behind and branch out on her own for the first time.

'I love you,' I say as I give her a tight hug, and I'm saying a silent prayer that I'll hear the same words back any second now.

'Bye, Mum,' Evelyn replies before she turns and heads for the station door, and I keep my eyes on her the whole way in until she disappears from view. Once she's gone, I have a thought about how I hope her train gets randomly cancelled so that I get to spend another hour or so with her, but despite sitting in the car and waiting, I see a southbound train come and go and know that she'll be on it now, whizzing down to London and further away from here by the second.

I'm aware that the drive back to Arberness is going to be a lonely one and I will feel even lonelier when I get to my house and walk in to hear the deafening silence inside it. I'm sure I could do my best to keep busy when I get there, finding clothes to wash and dusty surfaces to clean, which should help kill a little time. Then I could go and sit down at my desk and start putting together a few more greetings cards, pouring myself into work to help me forget the aching void in my heart now that Evelyn has moved out. But before that, I decide to make a stop-off on my way home, parking at a motorway service station to grab a cup of coffee and some sugary snacks to lift my mood.

As I walk through the doors and see dozens of other motorists who have stopped off like me for refreshments, I am struck by the memory of the time I used a service station to get revenge on somebody who had wronged me. It was back when I was driving down to Cornwall almost eighteen years ago, to try and catch Fern. I was in the car with my boyfriend at the time, Tomlin, and my friend from prison, Siobhan. With the knowledge that the pair had recently betrayed me by kissing each other when they thought I was asleep, I saw an opportunity to get my own back on Siobhan, abandoning her at the service station by the side of the motorway, driving away and leaving her to figure out how to get anywhere without a car.

It made me feel good at the time and I presumed I'd never have to see that woman again.

But I was wrong and, in hindsight, I probably shouldn't have messed with a woman as dangerous as that...

SEVEN

ALICE

The first year of Evelyn's life has been a blur but her first birthday party came and went in a flash, and now it's time to put away all the balloons and banners. Yesterday was a lovely day, the few people I call friends in this village accepting my invitation to come to my house and indulge in a slice of cake and some soft drinks to help celebrate my daughter's first milestone in age. But today is all about the village fete, and me and Evelyn are going to check out the colourful stalls and see if we can spot something either of us might like.

It's a fine day in Arberness, a blue sky hanging above the village and bathing it in much-welcomed sunlight, and that makes for a pleasant walk from home to the high street, where all the stalls are set up and music can be heard coming from the band on the stage at the back.

I smell sizzling sausages and catch sight of multicoloured cards on display for sale and think about how, one day, I'd love to make my own cards and maybe have my own little business, but there's no time for that at the moment. There's no time for anything with a one-year-old, so I've done well to just get out of the house.

I smile at a few familiar faces – while ignoring some of the frowns I get from those in this village who disapprove of my past and the fact I still choose to live in Arberness – before coming to a stop at a stall that sells all sorts of lotions and potions for skincare. Tempted to pick something up to help me battle the bags under my eyes, I browse the selection and I'm just about to make my choice when the band finishes playing their latest song and the singer announces it's time for the raffle to take place. I bought a ticket for the raffle last week, so I reach into my purse to find it while hoping my number is called, because it's always nice to win things, isn't it? Then again, maybe not for me. I wonder if I would get booed by some of the people in this crowd who don't like me if I went up on stage to claim my prize. But as I find my ticket and look up to the stage to watch the singer make the announcement, I catch a glimpse of someone in the crowd that I did not expect to see. In fact, I never expected to see this person ever again, or at least hoped I wouldn't.

But I'm sure it was her.

It was Siobhan.

I could have sworn I just spotted the woman I used to call a friend. The last time I saw her was when she was walking into a service station by the motorway before I sped away and left her behind. Because she betrayed me... But was it really her? I can't confirm it because I can't see her anymore. I've lost that woman in the crowd and, despite looking everywhere, I can't find her again. I'm unsettled now – what if it was her?

What the hell would she be doing back in Arberness?

Isn't it obvious, my paranoid brain says to me. *She's back here to get revenge on you for leaving her.*

I try not to entertain that thought but the worries come thick and fast.

She is a killer, remember. She tried to murder her old boss. That's how you met her in prison. She's incredibly dangerous. What did you think would happen when you made an enemy of a woman like that? She'd just laugh and forget about it? Of course not. She'd take action. She'd come back and make you pay.

Unable to relax and appreciate my surroundings any longer, I push Evelyn's pram away from the busy street, totally ignoring the raffle ticket number that is called out. I have far more important things to worry about now.

No sooner have I got home and made sure Evelyn is safe than I call my ex-boyfriend. Detective Tomlin answers my call on the first ring and asks me if everything is okay.

'I think I saw Siobhan. I think she's in Arberness,' I say in a rush, afraid that I am right, and it wasn't just somebody who looked like her.

'Really? What's she doing there?' Tomlin asks; but the answer to that is obvious to me.

'She's come to get her own back on me, hasn't she!' I cry. 'I never should have left her at that service station.'

'Calm down, I doubt that's what it's about.'

'Why else would she be here? I invited her here last year, so she knows where I live. She's come back to see me again, except we're not friends this time.'

Tomlin keeps trying to get me to calm down, but it's no good and now I am angry.

'This is your fault! If you hadn't kissed her then we never would have fallen out and she wouldn't be here now trying to hurt me.'

'We don't know if she's going to try and hurt you. You could be overreacting.'

'What am I supposed to do? What if she hurts Evelyn? How can I keep her safe?'

Tomlin reads between the lines and tells me what I'm hoping to hear.

'I'm on my way,' he says. 'Just stay in until then and don't answer the door unless I tell you it's me outside.'

———

By the time Tomlin gets to my house, I've calmed down slightly but it's still good to have him here to protect me and my daughter. But as soon as he enters the home we once shared together, I get the sense he'd been hoping for a call like this for a while, as evidenced by the way he looks at both me and Evelyn once he's back in the same room. That's when I get paranoid again.

'Wait. Have you done this? Have you orchestrated Siobhan's return here so you can worm your way back into my life?'

'Don't be ridiculous. I haven't seen or spoken to Siobhan since that day you left her,' Tomlin assures me. 'I'm here as a friend. I just want to help.'

'Fine. You can help by looking around this village to see if you can see her anywhere. Check everywhere. The pub. The park. The butchers. The supermarket. But start with my back garden. She might be hiding out there, waiting for her chance to come in.'

I can see that Tomlin thinks I'm crazy, but he does as I say and begins conducting his checks, knowing exactly what the woman I have tasked him with finding looks like. But after ninety minutes, he returns to the house to tell me that he has looked everywhere, including at the busy fete, and asked several people he passed on the street, but there is not a sign of Siobhan anywhere.

'What about the beach? Did you check down there?' I ask him, and he tells me that he drove past the stretch of sand and didn't see a single soul out there today, not even a dogwalker, which is rare, but then everyone must still be at the fete.

'She's biding her time,' I say, thinking out loud as I watch Evelyn sitting in her highchair with the food I tried to give her earlier mostly around her mouth rather than inside it. 'She's clever. She's a schemer. She told me that when she tried to kill her boss, she plotted it for months.'

'Look, I don't think you have anything to worry about but, just in case, how about I stay here tonight?' Tomlin suggests before quickly adding, 'I'll sleep on the sofa! Not upstairs. Don't worry, I'm not here to do anything but be a friend.'

I take Tomlin's word for it and agree that him staying the night is a good idea. It's likely the only way I'll have a chance of getting a wink of sleep, because otherwise I'd just sit up all night listening for any sounds downstairs. But with him watching over us, hopefully everything will be okay.

———

'Alice! Wake up! We have to get out of the house right now!'

Tomlin's desperate pleas stir me from my slumber. When I open my eyes, I see him standing by the side of the bed holding Evelyn, who is wriggling and on the verge of tears. But I see something else too.

Smoke.

And lots of it.

'What's going on?' I ask as I pull off my duvet and rush out of bed while Tomlin goes to the bedroom door, looking out into the dark, smoky hallway.

'I don't know. I woke up and smelt smoke and realised the house is on fire,' he says. 'Come on. We have to go now!'

I can't argue with that and, as I follow him out of my room, I am wondering why my smoke alarm didn't go off to warn me. But as we pass under it, I can hear it faintly bleeping away, though it's not very loud. It takes me a second to figure out why it's so quiet. It's because it can't compete with the sound of the flames roaring away below us on the ground floor.

'Oh my God!' I cry when I look down the stairs and see nothing but an ominous mass of black smoke sitting heavily above the steps – visibility is reducing by the second. 'How the hell are we going to get out?'

It looks to me like our escape route is blocked and I'm now imagining me and my daughter perishing in a fiery inferno. But Tomlin isn't giving up just yet and his police training quickly kicks in. 'Cover your mouth,' he says as he pulls at the top of my night dress. I follow his instructions and use the fabric to act as somewhat of a shield from the plumes of acrid smoke threatening to enter my lungs. I watch as he puts Evelyn inside his shirt, shielding her from the smoke too, as well as any flames we may encounter on our way out of here. Then, while keeping one strong arm wrapped around Evelyn, he uses the other to reach out to me and pull me down the stairs with them.

We descend the staircase at a frightening speed and I'm afraid we might trip and fall at any moment, but we make it down. Once we do, I get a true sense of the heat down here. It's unbearable and, between the sweat pouring down my face and the smoke stinging my eyes, I'm struggling to see where I'm going. But Tomlin just keeps pulling me along, that is until a wooden beam comes down and I let out a scream, fearing it is going to strike him and Evelyn – terrified my daughter will surely not survive the blow. But just before it hits, Tomlin twists his body and takes the brunt of the blow on his back, which keeps Evelyn safe, though the loud cry the detective lets out tells me he has just been hurt. But he pushes on past the flames that envelop us on all sides, probably fuelled by pure adrenaline, before a door opens and I see beautiful, brilliant darkness beyond. It's the back garden and, a second later, all three of us are out in the safety of the fresh air, where the fire and the smoke can't hurt us any longer.

Tomlin collapses to the ground, and Evelyn rolls onto the grass beside him, crying out for me, and I waste no time in picking her up and making sure that she is okay. She seems to be unharmed, but the same can't be said for the man who just saved our lives – he is clearly in a lot of pain. When I get a glimpse of his left arm, I see why. He is badly burnt and is in agony from the injuries he must have sustained while ensuring we all made it out of the house.

The house.

I turn back and see my home disintegrating before my eyes, the flames devouring every single part of the building where Evelyn and I should have felt most safe. By the time the fire engines arrive, there isn't much to save, but at least the fire is put out before it can spread to any of the neighbouring homes, and the main thing is that no one has died here tonight. But Tomlin is in a bad way and is taken away to receive urgent medical attention, while a couple of paramedics check on me and my daughter too. I'm happy for them to check Evelyn, but I tell them that I'm fine and don't have time for going to the hospital because I need to speak to the police.

'I know who did this!' I cry to the first police officer who comes my way.

It has to be Siobhan.

I might know that, but as I watch my home being consumed by the fire, I don't know the answer to another question.

Where is she now?

EIGHT

FERN

PRESENT DAY

I move around my quiet house with only the sound of the birds chirping in the trees outside my kitchen window for company. Pierre is at work and Cecilia is in Paris. I guess this is my new normal now. No longer will I hear pop music blaring from my daughter's bedroom or find her dirty plates and cups in the sink instead of in the dishwasher, where I constantly reminded her to put them. Nor will I find her shoes lying by the front door after she got home late from another night at the village bistro with Antoinette, or see her enter my bedroom in one of her hungover states and watch her flop down on the bed beside me before asking if I fancy ordering a pizza and watching a movie together.

Cecilia is in the French capital now, currently 'living her best life', as youngsters like my daughter like to say, and I'm here, pottering around by myself, checking my phone every five minutes to see if she has sent me a message or uploaded anything new to Instagram that might give me a clue as to what she's up to.

Her last message, sent to me yesterday afternoon, told me that she was preparing for a night out with Antoinette after they had spent the day browsing around the many retail stores that Paris has to offer. They haven't started their new jobs yet and are taking the opportunity to have some fun before getting a dose of reality, and their city life experience starts to include commuting and deadlines as well as happy hours and window shopping. I then saw a couple of photos of her on Antoinette's Instagram account, Cecilia holding up a colourful cocktail to the camera in the first image before being pictured posing beside a large neon sign in a nightclub.

My daughter is having fun, and I couldn't be happier for her. I also can't blame her because Paris is an incredible place to visit, never mind live in, and I know that for a fact because I have experienced the city myself in the past.

As I step outside into my sun-kissed back garden and occupy myself by clipping a few dead flowerheads, my mind is on the first time I went to Paris. As far as my current husband knows, I had never set foot in the French capital until he took me there himself a few months into our relationship, but in reality, I had been there many years before.

I'd been when my first husband whisked me away for a romantic weekend.

The memory of being in Paris with Drew is not one I should dwell on because it's not fair on Pierre, who over the years has treated me to a lovely trip there not just once but several times since we have been together. But I can't help it because, while the second doctor that took me there did a great job of spoiling me with luxurious hotels, magnificent meals and shopping sprees, the first doctor managed to outdo him with the treats he laid on for me.

It feels bad to even compare the two in my mind – Pierre is far more of a decent man than Drew ever was – but I can't deny that when Doctor Devlin took me to Paris it was incredible. We stayed at a hotel with a breathtaking view of the Eiffel Tower from the bedroom, we dined at rooftop restaurants that overlooked such iconic landmarks as the Arc de Triomphe and the Louvre, and we even sailed along the Seine after Drew had paid somebody to row us down the river on a fine summer's day. Back then, I thought my husband was the best man in the world, a guy who doted on me and would give me anything he could to make me happy, and it sure was a blissful state of ignorance to live in. The trips I've taken with Pierre have never quite matched the heights of that first city break I took with Drew. But then again I've never had to be told Pierre is sleeping with another woman, nor have I had to stand outside a window and listen to the sound of lovemaking and betrayal coming from his doctor's surgery.

So, swings and roundabouts, I suppose.

I must be feeling a little guilty for thinking about Drew, which I often do when he enters my thoughts at various intervals during each and every day, because I put down my clippers and send a text message to Pierre telling him that I love him. He doesn't reply, probably because he's with a patient, but I know he'll smile when he sees it. Then I send a message to Cecilia too, telling her that her favourite tree in our garden is looking wonderful and I take a photo of it to show her. My daughter has loved the pink petals of the cherry blossom that has bloomed every year since she was a little girl. I have so many pictures saved from over the years of her standing beside it with a big grin on her face. Oh, how I wish she was here now so I could capture another image, but it's just me in this garden. Not even the little squirrel that hops across the trimmed lawn in front of me can give me the kind of company I am longing for at the moment.

I receive a text message a few minutes later and wonder who has replied to me first – Pierre or Cecilia. But it turns out to be neither – the message is from Marion. My friend is checking in on me to see how I am getting on since Cecilia left, bless her, and it's a nice thing to do. She must know how I'm feeling, and she is right.

Hope you're not feeling too blue. You'll come to enjoy the peace and quiet again soon, as well as having a tidier house. It'll just take some time.

It's a nice gesture from my best friend in this village, and I reply to thank her before letting her know that my garden is keeping me busy. As I put my phone away, I'm glad that I didn't let my paranoia ruin what has turned out to be a great friendship with Marion. That's because, when I first met her, I was terrified she knew who I really was.

My main reason for thinking that was because Marion asked an awful lot of questions when we first got talking properly on my wedding day to Pierre, which took place in this quaint French village. I feared she was prying when she asked me about my former life in England, or worse, feared she was taunting me and pushing me to keep lying while she already knew the truth and was just taking pleasure in making me squirm. I remember ending our conversation, making up an excuse about having to go and talk to a few other guests, and after that, I tried to avoid her as much as I could. But it's impossible to avoid anybody in a village this size, so we predictably kept crossing paths and, every time we did, I felt like every stare she gave me or every sentence she uttered was done with something sinister in mind. That was until I realised she was like that with everyone. She is chatty, she asks a lot of questions and she likes to know everyone's life story. She's not shy in telling hers either, and gradually, over time, I relaxed around her until the point where I realised what a valuable friend she could be. Now I don't harbour any worries about Marion knowing my dark secret because, if she did, she's spent several long years keeping it to herself, so why would she suddenly blurt it out now?

She doesn't know.

Nobody knows.

Well, nobody except some of the wildlife in my garden, who I have occasionally confessed my sins to whenever they have been playing on my mind a little too much. Thankfully, the birds and the squirrels can't speak, so my secret is safe with them.

I end up spending a little too long out in the sunshine. By the time I go back indoors, I fear I have suffered a bit of sunburn on the back of my neck. I'm sweating too and my nails have dirt under them. I also have backache, but that's just part of the joy of approaching sixty, so I can't blame the hot weather for that one.

Deciding I need to both freshen up and soothe my bones with a bit of hot water, I run myself a bath in the spacious bathroom that Pierre delighted in paying for because he knows how much I like to relax in my own space under a few soapy suds. As the hot water runs and the tub slowly fills up, I undress and crane my neck as I look in the mirror and try to see just how sunburnt I am. It's not as bad as first feared, so I've been lucky there. Far luckier than last week when I took a shower and almost lost my wedding ring down the plughole. There's not as much of a risk of that happening again now that I'm taking a bath, but I'd rather play it safe, so I slide my diamond ring off my finger and place it beside the sink. It's a beautiful ring, it really is, and while Pierre never told me how much it cost, I did some snooping around online to try and find a photo of it and when I did, I got an idea of the price.

Let's just say Pierre probably couldn't have afforded it if he hadn't been a doctor.

But the sight of the stunning piece of jewellery just sitting there on the stone sink makes me think back to the day Pierre first put that ring on my finger.

Our wedding was unforgettable for many reasons.

It was the day I married the man I love.

It was also the day I went back to being the woman I swore to myself I'd left behind.

NINE

FERN

I stare at the woman looking back at me in the mirror and can't believe I am her. The woman in my reflection is wearing a white wedding dress, yet I swore I'd never marry again, so it can't be me, can it?

'Are you ready, Mummy?'

I look away from the mirror and down at my daughter who is wearing her own pretty dress, this one a pink floral number, which is perfect because she is the designated flower girl at this wedding. Soon, she'll be walking down the aisle ahead of me, sprinkling pink petals all over the floor.

'I think so,' I reply as I beam at Cecilia and I'm not sure who is more excited here – her or me. It might be my big day, but to my eight-year-old daughter, this is the stuff dreams are made of. She has already told me that I look like an angel in my white dress, and I know she has spent the last few weeks practising for her big moment with the petals, taking the job I have given her very seriously, which is incredibly sweet. If I'm honest, I'm almost going through with this as much for her as for me, because I know that getting to be a part of a special event like this is something Cecilia will remember for the rest of her life. I'm also doing this because, despite my previous belief that I would never fall in love with another man again after the disasters that were Drew and then Greg, I have met a man that fills my heart with happiness, and now it's time to make our love official.

Pierre will be waiting for me at the altar, so I better get moving, and that's why I tell Cecilia to pick up her basket full of petals and join me by the door. She does as she's told, I've been blessed with an incredibly well-behaved child, and as we take our positions, the door is opened and the music starts to play.

I get a glimpse of the church ahead of me and see our guests from the village standing in the rows of pews, their heads turned back to get their first glimpse of the beaming bride. I see Pierre's family too, sitting up at the front just behind where the groom himself stands and waits. The only thing missing is my family, but I've already had to make my peace with never seeing my parents ever again. As far as Pierre knows, they died many years ago.

I see the smile spread across the face of my handsome groom when he sees me, and I smile back at him before I give Cecilia a gentle nudge to let her know that she is to begin. I see my little girl take a deep breath before she strides forward and, as she begins to pass the rows of guests, she starts throwing out pretty petals around herself, which only makes everyone witnessing it smile and whisper to each other about how cute it is.

Then it's my turn to get moving, so I set one foot in front of the other and slowly begin the walk to the altar, trying to ignore the photographer at the front who is snapping several images of me as I get closer. When I had finally relented and agreed to marry Pierre after his very unexpected proposal six months ago, I insisted on this being a very small and private affair. That wasn't just because small and private affairs are best for a woman on the run like me, but because I've already done this before, and I didn't care to be reminded of that first time by having all the things I had then. My wedding to Drew was a decadent occasion, so by making sure this one was much smaller, it was my way of separating them in my mind and giving them as many differences as possible. Thankfully, Pierre was happy to keep this occasion small, even though he had no idea about my real reasons for wanting it. I just told him I was shy and didn't like having a lot of attention on me, and he said he was happy enough to do whatever I wanted, as long as I agreed to be his wife.

So I did.

And here we are now.

The vows Pierre and I exchange are short and simple, classic lines that most couples who wed share, and the ceremony ends with the two of us kissing once we have officially been declared husband and wife. Cecilia sneakily saved one last handful of petals for this moment because she throws them right up in our faces as we turn to celebrate with our gathered guests, and everybody laughs before we all leave the church, crossing the street to the village hall where the reception is due to take place. But first, Pierre, Cecilia and I must pose for several photos, and it's lovely to be able to have them taken outdoors where the sun is shining and the weather is warm. My new husband is so composed that there is not even a single bead of sweat on his forehead despite the rising temperature. He always tells me that he grew up in good weather, so he doesn't get sweaty, unlike me and my English upbringing. My lack of experience in hot climes has me melting every time the mercury in the thermometer goes up just a tiny bit.

After the photos comes the food and we all feast as if food is going out of fashion, gorging on generous portions of French cuisine, all washed down by hearty measures of red wine from the local vineyards, of course. As day turns into night and the music begins to play, Cecilia is on the dancefloor with some of the other children from the village. I am busy enough chatting with our guests, including a new resident here called Marion, who I feel like I might have to be wary around – she asks a lot of questions and I wonder why she is so interested in me. It feels weird to have people here at my wedding who I barely know but, because this village is so small, we felt like we had to invite everybody or risk having a very awkward time in the future seeing all the people who didn't make the guestlist. Thankfully, not every single person accepted our invites, but it was important that we gave everyone the chance to be here. Village life is just like that.

You'd think I'd have learnt my lesson after living in Arberness and fled to a city instead of a place like this, but apparently not.

The party goes on late into the night, far later than Cecilia should be staying up, but how can I tell her to go to bed early on her mother's wedding day? By the time the music has stopped and the guests are filing outside to take in the spectacular sight of the starry sky as they walk home, Cecilia is fast asleep on me and I'm going to have to carry her weight all the way back to her bed. But she's getting too heavy for me to carry these days, plus my feet are aching badly after so many hours in tight-fitting shoes, so Pierre offers to carry my daughter for me. The fact she doesn't even stir and looks so comfortable on my husband's shoulder is just one of the reasons I know it was the right thing to do to marry him. Cecilia adores Pierre and he adores her, so I didn't have any reservations there.

By the time we make it back home and get Cecilia to bed, it's well after midnight and all I want to do is collapse onto my bed and sleep. But Pierre seems wired, or at least he is running on all the red wine he's consumed today, and he has the idea that we open some of the cards we received from our guests during the course of the day. I was quite happy to leave them until the morning, but Pierre makes an eager start. As he opens a few and I see some of the kind messages that have been written to us, as well as several Euro notes falling out of the cards and onto the bed, I decide it might be fun to open a few cards myself after all.

Picking up the nearest one, I tear open the envelope and admire the beautiful card with the cute illustration of a wedding chapel on the front before savouring the nice message that is written inside by two of the guests at our big event earlier. Then I open another one and I'm wondering if this one will be just as sweet. It seems like it at first because the front of the card features some lovely words and another nice illustration, but when I open it, my heart skips a beat and all I can think is how I have been incredibly lucky to pick this up before Pierre had the chance. That's because the message written inside is hugely troubling.

Instead of it saying something nice about us as a wedded couple, congratulating us and wishing us many happy years together, it just has eleven terrifying words scrawled across the page.

I know who you are and what you did.

Hello, Fern.

TEN

CECILIA

PRESENT DAY

'I can't believe they advertised this place as having a view of the Eiffel Tower,' I say as I stare out of the window at the tip of the famous landmark; the tip is all I can see of it, as the bulk of the building is obscured by other buildings in front of it.

'Technically, we can see it, so they weren't lying,' Antoinette says from her position on the sofa behind me, where she is flicking through one of my fashion magazines.

'We can only see the top of it, that's it. It's false advertising.'

'What are you going to do? Sue our landlord?'

'I don't have the money to sue anyone. I've already spent half of my savings since we've been here.'

'Well, shut up and sit down then,' Antoinette replies with a laugh, and I can't help but smile as I leave the window and slump down onto the sofa opposite her.

I'm not really that bothered about seeing the Eiffel Tower from the window of our new flat, because I can just walk outside and be right at the base of it in ten minutes if I wanted to. But it was more than a little cheeky of our landlord to advertise this rental property in the way he did. He made it sound as if we would be looking out at one of the most famous buildings in the world every day as we sat and ate our breakfast or entertained friends with a few drinks in the evenings. As it is, there's not much of the tower to see, although at least the rest of the flat is exactly as advertised.

Antoinette and I are sharing a two-bedroom flat in the Beaugrenelle region of Paris, and while it's small and expensive, it's a perfect base for us to explore the city as well as commute to the jobs we are soon to start here. Other than the two tiny bedrooms that are barely big enough to fit in a bed and a wardrobe, there is the miniscule bathroom and then there is the 'largest' room, which basically consists of the kitchen, dining room and living area all in one open-plan space. It was already cramped when we first got here, and that was before we even unpacked all our dresses, shoes and make-up accessories, but as Antoinette keeps reminding me, it's better to be in a small home in Paris than a large home back in our tiny village.

It's easy to agree with her because since we've been here, I can safely say I've had nothing but a good time and I'm not missing home one bit. Okay, so I do miss Mum a little, as well as Pierre, but it's not as if I've been moping around staring at these four walls and allowing myself to get homesick. That's because Antoinette and I have been out every night in Paris, partying until the early hours of the morning, hence my rapidly depleting funds. We've also shopped on the Champs-Elysées, which has only ensured my bank balance has diminished even quicker. But it's not all been about spending money. We've also sat in the park by the tower and soaked up the sun, as well as strolled along the Seine and paused to admire all the street artists at work, and it feels like each day has been better than the rest, even with a few hangovers added into the mix. I know the holiday can't last forever, not least because we're both due to start work in a couple of days, but I'm hoping that work will also be enjoyable and, even if it's not, there'll still be lots of sight-seeing and partying to do in our free time. Even better, we'll soon be getting paid.

Still feeling the after-effects of a late night last night, I tell Antoinette that I'm going to go for a lie down and she laughs and calls me an 'amateur' before I enter my bedroom and close the door. This room is a fraction of the size of my room back home when I lived with Mum and Pierre, but it feels good to be independent and have my own place, although I bet it won't feel as good when the next rent payment is due and I have frittered most of the money for that on drinks in some Paris super club.

Collapsing onto my bed, I am aiming to get some much-needed sleep but, before that, I use my phone to scroll mindlessly through social media for a while. There's not much of interest for me to see online, barring a few updates from the celebrity accounts I follow, and that's because I don't have that many genuine friends whose updates I can look at. Antoinette is my best one, and I have a few more friends back in the village, all of whom made my recent birthday party very special, but it's a small circle and not just because I grew up in a tiny village.

It's because it's been tough for me to make friendships when I've always felt like I stuck out.

Being the only English girl at a school in France meant it was easy for me to feel different, and it was also easy for a few bullies to pick on me, highlighting my differences to make themselves feel better and me feel worse. I never asked Mum to move me to a different country when I was small, and even though I have spent most of my life in France and speak the language fluently now, all it took was a few of the nastier kids in my classes to find out that I was originally English and they saw to it that I had to be teased tirelessly every day.

Mum always told me that it would get better, and she was right because it did, eventually, and it certainly helped when

Antoinette started sticking up for me and the two of us became close. I've barely left her side since, which is why it was a no brainer for me to come to Paris with her when she first floated the idea a couple of years ago. I can't complain and say I've had a bad upbringing – that wouldn't be fair on Mum and Pierre who did their best to give me everything they could – but there have been times when I have tried to talk to Mum about the reasons why we moved here and also about the things we might have left behind. I have no grandparents, cousins, aunts or uncles, because when Mum made the decision to move abroad, she cut ties with every single one of them. She tells me it was because we were in danger from my father, who was abusive towards her, she had no choice, and I guess she wouldn't lie about something like that, but still, how am I supposed to feel about having practically no family?

How am I supposed to feel about never getting to meet my dad?

I could tell from an early age that Mum got quite defensive whenever I broached the subject of him, so I learnt not to upset her too much by pestering her for more information on him. The way I see it is if he hurt Mum, to the point where she felt she had to flee, then he didn't love her, or me, so that has made it a bit easier to try to forget about him and the huge hole he left in my life. But again, it's just another sign of me being different. Without a dad to pick me up from school the meaner kids were quick to latch onto that and tease me even more; at least they were until Pierre came on the scene.

I know things must have been hard for Mum in her life, but I don't think I've ever really told her how hard they have been for me too, and I probably never will because I don't want her to feel guilty. It's not her fault she was abused and had to run away with me to keep us both safe. I'm sure she'd have preferred to stay in England and have a stable family unit, but it wasn't meant to be. But should one man's actions keep us from so much?

Moving to Paris was a big dream of mine, but I'd be lying if I said I hadn't dreamt of moving to England too. I want to see where I was born and learn about English culture, because it is my heritage after all. But more than that, I want to find out if my grandparents are still alive, as well as if I have any other relatives that I could talk to and help me form a better understanding of where I come from and what my life might have been like if Mum hadn't moved us when she did. But I'm not allowed to do that – Mum says it's too dangerous for me to go back there. She is afraid that her ex will find me or her again and hurt us, and the fact she has drummed that fear into me so many times over the years tells me that she really is worried about it and needs me to stick to the rules. That's why I always have done, but it was easy back when I was living in the village. There, everywhere else feels like a million miles away, England included. Now I'm in Paris, I see signs for the Eurostar all the time and, as well as the relatively cheap ticket prices that are advertised, it's also the fact that I can be in London in just over two hours.

It would be so easy for me to just take one of those trains and end up in the English capital, where I would be free to walk around and see the sights. I could do it one day and Mum would never have to know. I could come back that same day, making it a quick stop-off, so at least I can say to myself that I have been. I could go with Antoinette and I'm sure we'd be fine because how would Mum's ex find us? He could be anywhere in England. He might already be dead.

Maybe I'll rebel one day and go to the UK.

What's the worst that could happen?

According to Mum, it would be disastrous.

But she's surely just exaggerating.

Isn't she?

ELEVEN

EVELYN

I've been in London for three days now and, so far, I have mixed feelings. In a sense, it's been predictable. No sooner did I get here than I felt the best I've felt in years, and I know that is all to do with me getting out of Arberness and stepping out of Mum's shadow. It's also been predictable in that I've been to see all the famous sights that any tourist goes to see while here.

Buckingham Palace. Big Ben. The Tower of London.

Tick.

The reason for my mixed feelings is that some things have been unpredictable and the biggest one is that it has been incredibly hard, if not impossible, to make any friends to share my travels with.

Loneliness has been the story of my life, but it was a story I expected to end when I hit the road and began backpacking, not add a few more chapters to. Yet despite my eagerness to make friends out of the other backpackers I have met in my hostel, it's not gone well so far. Maybe I've been overeager and that has put them off. Nobody wants to hang around with a desperate person. But I don't think I've been desperate. At least I hope I haven't, anyway.

I'm staying in a hostel near Waterloo, which is very cheap and, as a result, very crowded. But that was exactly what I wanted because one, I need to make the most of my money and two, I want to have the chance to meet as many people as possible. There are all sorts of people here, from English and Irish, to German and French, and of course several Americans too, and I was very much looking forward to chatting to as many of them as I could as I entered my eight-bed dorm room and dropped down my backpack onto my personal bed. But the first few people I met clearly didn't speak a word of English, and while I had imagined conversation might be tricky with a few foreign nationals, I hadn't expected it to be downright impossible. Then I met some travellers who did speak the same language as me and, after asking them where they were from and where they were headed next, I suggested we all go out to see a few things together and maybe get some food afterwards. They seemed unsure and told me they already had plans and that they'd see me later. It turned out I never did see them later because they were out all night and, by the time I woke up the next morning, they had already checked out and moved on.

I'm not going to let my slow start to friendship-making put me off. The main purpose of this trip is to see more of the world and friends will come and go along the way, so I just have to let it happen naturally. As tough as it has been to spend the last three days by myself, wandering the streets of London and wishing I had somebody to take a photo of me instead of just posing for yet another selfie, I know this is a marathon not a sprint. I also know that no matter what happens, this is still better than being in Arberness.

I'm currently lying on my bed in my otherwise empty dorm room in the middle of the afternoon, and I'm here instead of out in the city because I know this is check-in time. I'm hoping the door to this room is going to open at any second now and one or two backpackers who I might get on really well with will walk in and be open to a conversation. Then I'm hoping that I can go out and have a good night with whoever they are, because as amazing as sightseeing has been, I'd also like to check out some of the pubs and nightclubs that this city has to offer. That's not really the kind of thing I can do alone unless I want to be the sad girl at the bar with nobody by her side.

For now, I'll make do with lying on my bed and looking at my phone, although I wish I wasn't doing that when I see another message come through from Mum.

Hey! Just checking in! Are you having fun in London? I know you must be busy but just checking you're okay. Have you made some new friends? Miss you. Mum xx

This is the fourth message Mum has sent me since I left Arberness and, as of yet, I have only replied once. I sent her a quick text to say that I had made it to London and hoped that would keep her satisfied and off my case for a while. But she just replied instantly and, even though I haven't gone back to her since, there has been a steady stream of these types of messages popping up on my phone.

I should reply now and then I can go back to ignoring her for a while again, but there's something about her most recent message that has caught me off guard, and suddenly I have tears in my eyes. It's not that it's caused me to feel homesick, it's more that she has asked me about friends. She's probably imagining me surrounded by people now, laughing away and having the time of my life, yet that couldn't be further from the truth. I only have to roll over on my bed and look around this empty dorm room to remind myself of that.

But rather than go back to Mum and tell her that, pathetically, I have been by myself so far, I leave it. With a renewed determination to change my circumstances and make things happen – so I won't have to lie when I eventually do reply to this message – I get off the bed and prepare to go out into the common area where I expect several backpackers will be hanging around.

Entering the common area, I do see some people, most of them lounging on beanbags or sofas, all of them on their phones and a few of them with headphones over their ears. I ignore the seemingly anti-social ones and head for the ones without headphones, and I'm doing my best to feel confident as I sit down beside a friendly looking woman who is watching a video on her phone.

'Hey! How's it going?' I ask as I notice the video she is watching is of her and another female on Tower Bridge.

'Oh, hey,' she says in an American accent, briefly looking me up and down before returning her gaze to her screen.

'Where are you from?'

'Oklahoma.'

'Cool. You like it here?'

'Yeah, it's cool. We're leaving tomorrow.'

'Oh, right. What are you doing tonight?'

'Nothing. We have an early flight in the morning.'

This isn't going well and I'm wondering if I should abort and find somebody else to try and entice into an evening out in London, but just before I can make my excuses and go, another American approaches and starts talking to my 'new friend'. It's clear they do have plans tonight and the woman with the phone in her hand was just keeping them from me.

'Come on, let's go,' the second American says, and the backpacker I was talking to is quick to get out of her seat, saying that they should get some food first because she can't go to another nightclub on an empty stomach. That suggests to me that she does plan on having a late night after all, despite what she told me about her early flight, and I'm hoping she might remember our brief conversation and ask if I'd like to join them. But that doesn't happen and, as I watch the two Americans walk away, chattering loudly as they go, I just shake my head and think about how much easier this would have been if I had travelled with a friend from home like they clearly have done.

Looking around the common room, I don't see anyone that gives me hope of having a better interaction than I've just had, so I cut my losses and leave the hostel, walking outside to get some fresh air. I find myself on Waterloo Bridge looking down at the boats sailing by on the Thames, and all around me people rush by, talking to companions or to other people on their phones, and once again, I feel like I'm the only one who has nobody to talk to.

I could call Mum but I'm not going to do that. So what should I do?

Feeling like I've already had enough of London, I make my mind up that it's time to move on.

I'll check out of the hostel tomorrow and head to St Pancras station.

That's where the Eurostar goes from.

Next stop for me – Paris.

TWELVE

FERN

Having spent the whole time since Cecilia left for Paris either cleaning the house or maintaining the garden, I am at the point where there's not a single job that needs doing around the home to help occupy my mind and keep me from missing my daughter. That's why I'm sat at my laptop now and am currently checking hotel prices in the French capital.

It's time to book a trip.

'What are you doing? I thought we weren't going to go to Paris until Cecilia said she was settled and had some time off work,' Pierre says as he enters the bedroom and notices what I am up to.

'I'm just browsing,' I say, even though I am actually very serious about booking something, today if possible, so we can be in Paris sooner rather than later. But my husband knows me all too well, which is why he closes the laptop screen.

'Hey, what are you doing?' I cry, surprised he just did that but, when I look up at him, he is smiling.

'I know what you need. Follow me.'

Pierre leaves the bedroom. I'm not sure what he is talking about, but I do as he says and, as I go downstairs, I find him in the kitchen putting the finishing touches on what looks to be a picnic basket. I see baguettes, packets of meats, a few salad items as well as a bottle of red wine and two glasses. Yep, sure looks like a picnic to me. But if it is, it's an unplanned one.

'The taxi will be here any minute,' Pierre tells me as he places a tub of olives into the treat-laden basket.

'Taxi? Where are we going?'

'We're getting you out of the house where you've been cooped up ever since Cecilia left. So we're going to have a lovely afternoon outside in the fresh air where I'm going to show you the benefits of it just being the two of us now.'

We hear a car engine outside. Pierre picks up the basket and tells me to grab a blanket from the cupboard under the stairs as well as a bottle of sunscreen if I know where one is. Five minutes later and we are both sitting on the backseat of the taxi as it whizzes through the countryside. As I look out at all the green fields passing my window, I can't say I'm annoyed about the surprise that has been sprung on me. I'm certainly not annoyed when we reach our destination, which is a vineyard about a dozen miles away from our village. We've been here before and it's one of my favourite vineyards to visit because the views across the valley are incredible, particularly on a fine day like today, and Pierre has clearly planned this well.

After getting out of the taxi, Pierre tells me he is going to buy some cheese in the produce shop as well as pay our entry fee into the vineyard, and suggests I go and find us a nice area to sit where we can enjoy our picnic. I know exactly where to go and head for the part of the vineyard where I can see some of the fruit trees as well as a few of the workers who wander amongst them, checking on the quality of the produce they are picking.

It's wonderful here and, by the time Pierre returns, there is only one thing I have to say to him.

'Thank you. This is just what I needed.'

Pierre already seemed to know that as he smiles and he takes his seat on the blanket beside me, before reaching into the basket and taking out the bottle of wine. After opening it and pouring us each a generous amount, we clink glasses and toast to what should be a lovely day. But it's not just today that is on my husband's mind.

'Here's to doing more things like this,' he says, still smiling as a gentle breeze blows through the vineyard and lightly sways some of the trees in the distance. 'I know it's been hard seeing Cecilia go. I've struggled with her not being around myself, so I can't even imagine how you have been coping. But she's having the time of her life in Paris, and it's important we have some fun too now that we're free from the shackles of parenting on a daily basis.'

'You're right,' I say in agreement. 'This is just what the doctor ordered.'

I wink at Pierre before taking a refreshing sip of wine as he gets out the food and we start to sample all the calorific treats he has packed for us. I'm almost finding it hard to believe that a woman like me who has done what she has done in the past could be having such a wonderful moment like this one. There are hundreds of police officers back in England whose blood would literally boil if they could see me now, because the only view I should have is the inner walls of a prison cell. Yet here I am, looking out over these fields, and I can see for miles.

'What's on your mind?' Pierre asks, and I guess I've been daydreaming for longer than I realised.

'Huh? Oh, nothing,' I say quickly. 'Mmm, these olives are good.'

But Pierre doesn't buy that. 'Are you thinking about Cecilia again?'

'Not quite.'

'What is it then?'

I'm not so stupid as to suddenly blurt out that I'm thinking about how I should be in an English prison right now, because my husband has no idea about any of that and I'd like to keep it that way. But he does have an idea about something dark in my past, and while it wasn't on my mind just then, it has been something I've been dwelling on for the past few days, particularly whenever I look at my wedding ring and remember that period in my life when I was a newlywed. It should have been a golden time, yet it wasn't for me, all thanks to that threatening wedding card.

I didn't show the card to Pierre that night, so he never knew what was written inside it, but that doesn't mean there were no more repercussions. That card was just the beginning of a nightmare that would involve both me and the man I had married.

'I promised never to talk about it,' I say to Pierre in answer to his question about what I have been thinking about, and he instantly knows what I am referring to.

'Okay, let's not talk about it then,' he says rather predictably. It's predictable because he was the one who first suggested that we should never mention what happened again. I've tried to honour that promise ever since and have done a pretty good job of it but, recently, it's been playing on my mind far more than usual, and I really think it would help me if we could discuss it just a little bit.

'Do you still think about it?' I ask Pierre nervously, ignoring his wishes.

'Stop it. Let's not ruin this picnic.'

'I'm not trying to ruin the picnic. It's just that you asked me what was on my mind, so I'm trying to tell you.'

'That conversation is off limits,' Pierre reminds me, no longer eating or drinking, just staring into space.

'Come on, it's not healthy to keep it bottled up forever. We can talk about it for one minute. I think it's because our wedding anniversary is coming up soon. That must be why I'm thinking of it more.'

'It happened years ago, and we've got this far without any problems because we've never mentioned it since, so drop it, please.'

I can see how anxious Pierre still is about it all based on how wound up he looks, so I decide to leave it, at least until we have had a little more food and wine. But another half an hour passes by and the combination of the alcohol and the warm sun emboldens me to broach the nervy subject one more time during the course of the picnic.

'I just want to make sure you're okay,' I say to Pierre. 'I mean, if it's on my mind it might be on yours too.'

'On my mind? Of course it is! I can't just forget what we did!' Pierre cries, almost knocking over his wine as he suddenly sits up straighter.

'Pierre, relax, it's okay.'

'No, it's not okay. It'll never be okay. The only way it was reasonably okay was when we promised to never talk about it again, but you're ruining that now.'

Pierre gets to his feet and I fear our lovely afternoon is over. But he doesn't grab the basket or any of the items strewn around it on the blanket. He just marches away across the field, towards the tall trees in the distance, and he takes the bottle of wine with him.

I guess he needs a break. A bit of time by himself. I'll leave him to it then.

I never should have brought up the secret from our past, but I'm foolish and I'll have some apologising to do whenever he comes back.

But even though I can't talk to him, I know what he'll be thinking about now.

He'll be thinking about the same thing as me.

He'll be thinking about that awful crime we committed together.

THIRTEEN

FERN

Most people spend the first days of marriage basking in a warm glow of love and contentment, reflecting on their wonderful wedding day and feeling excited about the next step in the adventure that is their relationship with the person they adore the most. I certainly had that experience the first time I got married, back when I was with Drew. But my second time has not been like that at all. Instead of being blissfully happy the first few days since I said my vows, I've been anxiously waiting to see if the person who sent me the disturbing wedding card is going to send me anything else.

I have no idea who in this village knows my secret, but somebody does and I know that for a fact – they used my real name in their message. Somebody here knows I am Fern, not Teresa, but the question is, what do they intend to do with that information? So far, they have only tipped me off that I have something to worry about. As far as I know, they haven't told anybody else yet, certainly not the police, or I'd be in handcuffs already and possibly back in England by now. I don't know why they are teasing me, and they are certainly tormenting me, but I am grateful that they seem to be giving me a chance.

The problem is, I can't do anything about it until I know who it is I am dealing with.

I've spent every second since my wedding night trying to work out who sent that card. Every person in this village is a suspect, but there are a few people who stick out to me more than others. One of them is Marion, the nosey woman who seemed to be asking me a lot of questions on my wedding day. I haven't seen her around the village since, but I am looking out for her. When I do see her, I will have to approach her cautiously to find out what she has to say next. It could be her, then again, it might not be. I'm also thinking it might be Ed and Maureen, the English couple who retired here two years ago. They would have heard all about the doctor's death in the news back home and the hunt for his widow. When they first moved here, retiring to the sunnier climes of France, I was terrified that they would recognise me instantly. But that didn't seem to happen and, while I've always kept my distance from them the few times we have passed each other in the street, we have always just smiled and wished each other a good day. So is it them or is it someone else?

I'm driving myself mad by not being able to trust a single person in this village besides Pierre and Cecilia, and I don't know how long I can go on like this. Pierre has already noticed that I'm distracted, and it even got to the point last night where he asked me if I was having second thoughts about the wedding. He was worried that I'd been regretting marrying him because I've been so distant since that first night but, of course, it's nothing to do with him and I reassured him of that. I just spun him a lie about the wedding making me think about my family and friends back home who I'll never see again, and how I was feeling more down about that than usual, and he believed me, thankfully. But that was only a short-term fix and, unless I can solve this mystery, then my long-term future is looking very bleak indeed.

I've just dropped Cecilia off at school, spending the ten minutes at the gates nervously looking at all the other parents and wondering if any of them could have been behind the card. But nobody seemed to pay me much attention, beyond the two mums that told me they had a great time at my wedding and were thankful for being invited. I smiled politely, but I've just been thinking about how I wish I hadn't bothered getting married and inviting everybody in the village, because it made me the centre of attention for a day. That could have been what spurred on my mystery threat to step out of the shadows and send me that ominous message.

Maybe I need to move. Leave this village and start again elsewhere. I even suggested such a thing to Pierre last night over dinner.

'Would you ever leave here?' I asked him as we tucked into a plate of seafood and salad while Cecilia slept upstairs.

'The village? No, it's our home. I love it here, you know I do. I've spent most of my life here, barring that time I worked in the city, which I hated. Why?'

'Just wondering. You've never fancied a change of scene again?'

'No, not really. Do you?'

'I'm just thinking out loud. Maybe it would be nice to live somewhere else. This village is nice, but it can be a little suffocating at times, don't you think?'

'I thought you loved it here.'

'I do! I did. I mean, I don't know... Never mind.'

'You have friends here. Cecilia has friends too. She likes her school. We've put a lot of work into this house. I thought you were happy.'

'I am happy. Never mind.'

I'd been able to change the subject quickly enough then and

neither me nor Pierre have mentioned moving since, though I do wonder if things would have been easier if he had told me he was open to the possibility of uprooting our lives and starting afresh elsewhere. If he had said that then I'd have probably started packing right away, but it hasn't come to that, which is probably a good thing. I know Cecilia would hate me if I told her I was taking her out of school and away from Antoinette, who she doesn't stop talking about whenever I pick her up after another day's classes.

So, if I can't leave, I have no choice but to find out who the person is who sent the card, and then I'll have to do something about it. I wish they'd make it easy for me and just tell me who they are.

I'm five minutes from my house when a miracle happens, and I get my wish, very quickly bringing to mind that age-old adage about being careful what you wish for.

'Hello, Fern.'

My blood turns cold at the mention of my real name, and it's far scarier to hear it spoken out loud than it was to read it in that card. As I spin around, I see a man I don't recognise looking right at me. He has dark hair, slightly longer than most men have theirs, just past his ears, and he has dark eyes too. But the most unsettling thing about him is the way he stares into my soul with a sense of pleasure about the power he holds over me, and what he could do to my life if he only had the inclination to destroy it.

'Excuse me?' I try, feigning ignorance, but this man clearly knows who I am, not just because he said my real name but because he is smirking like he has something all the police officers in England don't.

Me.

'Congratulations on your wedding. Did you like the card I sent?'

I don't know what to say and all I do know is I'm frozen,

unable to attack or defend myself. Right now, the carefully
constructed life I have made in this village seems to be falling
apart, and my first thought is who is going to pick up Cecilia
from school if I'm in prison by then? I guess it would be Pierre,
but if he already knows I've been lying to him by then, why
would he help me anymore?

'What do you want?' I'm finally able to say, relieved that I
know who my enemy is now, but despondent because I can
hardly do much about it out here in broad daylight. There's no
one around, but even I'm not stupid enough to risk retaliating
out here in the wide, open space where anybody could wander
along and see me. At least that night on the beach when Drew
died was under the cover of darkness, and when I killed Greg it
was in a hotel room. But to do anything drastic now would carry
too much risk, and that's even before I consider whether or not I
even have it in me to kill one more time. This well-built man has
strength on his side, so my one chance of overpowering him
would be with the element of surprise. Unfortunately, he's the
only one doing the surprising so far.

'You can probably tell by my accent that I'm from Engand,'
the man says calmly. 'Like most people there, I was gripped by
the huge news story about that doctor who was murdered in
Arberness. I was even more gripped when it came to light that it
was his wife who had been behind it all, and she ended up
going on the run. I'm not ashamed to admit that I have watched
all the documentaries about the case, so please forgive me if I
appear a little starstruck. It's not every day a person is in the
presence of such an infamous figure like yourself.'

'What do you want?' I repeat, not caring for all the unnecessary background story as to how he came to know who I am.
He's from England, and he knows who I am, despite the passing
of time and the change in my appearance, and that's all there is
to it.

'However, while I claim to be from England and sound like

I am, I actually spent the first fifteen years of my life right here in this village,' the man goes on. 'I was born here, and I went to school here, the same school your daughter is at right now.'

'Don't talk about my daughter,' I warn the man, and he seems to take that on board.

'My point is, I'm no stranger to this village, even though it has been over forty years since I originally left it. No one here would recognise me now, but I know a few of the faces and one of them is your husband. That's because Pierre and I were class-mates at school.'

'Why are you telling me this?'

'So you understand the reason behind what I am about to ask you,' he says coolly. 'Back in school, Pierre was the man, if you know what I mean. The popular kid. The one who was the best player on the sports teams and the one all the cutest girls in class wanted to be with. No one could compete with him, least of all me, but Pierre didn't take his good fortune grace-fully. No, he used to tease and taunt kids like me. I'll never forget him laughing in my face after he told me he had just kissed the girl who I had nervously asked on a date only ten minutes earlier.'

That doesn't sound like the man I have come to know and love, but then maybe that's to be expected, because Pierre wasn't a man at all back then. He was just a boy and probably did plenty of foolish things his older self would look back on and frown at. Unless he still has another darker side to him, but I hope not – my secrets are more than enough for the both of us.

This man and his recollection of childhood memories shouldn't be my problem, but it is, and I still don't know what to do about it.

'I don't like Pierre. Never have and never will,' he goes on. 'But I do find it amusing that he is now married to such a dangerous woman as yourself. I imagine he has no idea. The police certainly don't. So I am going to give you a chance, Fern.

I will not tell anybody about your secret if you give me the opportunity to get my own back on Pierre after all these years.'

'Get your own back?'

'Yes. I want to get the girl this time. His girl. Sleep with me and then I will leave you alone.'

I'm baffled by the proposition, but the man is deadly serious and seems confident that he can get what he wants. He's presumably lonely too, if he's suggesting such a thing, or maybe he is just driven by a simple need to one-up Pierre, or at least the version of Pierre he remembers from school. It's an awful proposition that he has made me, but part of me is somewhat grateful. That's because at least he has given me a chance to get out of this.

'That's your house in the distance, isn't it?' he asks, and I don't have to turn and look at it to let him know that he's right. 'How about we go back there and have a little entertainment while Pierre is busy being the village doctor? Then I'll leave you alone and you can carry on living a peaceful life here with your daughter.'

I have no other choice, no time to think of a Plan B, so I agree to the proposal and start walking to my house, the man following behind and chuckling as we go. But I'm not finding any of this funny and, by the time we get inside my house, the darkness that my tormentor possessed earlier has now transferred itself to me. That's the only explanation I have for what happens as soon as we have entered my bedroom, because the real me returns to the surface, the woman who has spawned dozens of documentaries and countless conversations.

The doctor's wife strikes again.

Grabbing my hair straighteners off my dressing table, I hit the man over the head with them before wrapping the cable around his neck and then pulling him backwards, down onto the carpet with me. As I see blood pouring from the side of his skull, his legs kick and arms grab for the cable, but I refuse to loosen it, using a strength that frightens me to keep him trapped in his perilous position.

It takes several long and awful minutes that he spends writhing around and gurgling while I simply grit my teeth and keep straining before he stops moving. But just to make sure he is actually dead I stand over him and hit him three more times with my weapon until I'm satisfied that my latest threat is safely neutralised.

Then I go and throw up in the bathroom sink because, despite my past, that was horrible and I'm disgusted both at what I've done and the fact that even now, at almost fifty, I clearly still have it inside of me to end another person's life.

As I step back into the bedroom and look at the body, I know I have to get rid of it before Pierre and Cecilia come back here. But then I hear the front door open downstairs and my husband calls out to me.

'Hey! My first two patients cancelled, so I thought I'd come back and have a late breakfast with you. Is everything okay?'

It's funny but, for the second time this morning, I have no idea what to say.

FOURTEEN

ALICE

It's been four days now since Evelyn left Arberness and, barring a couple of very short messages, I haven't heard much from my daughter. I guess she's been busy, but I haven't had many details to go on, only a couple of facts like her location.

She was in London but now she is in Paris.

The distance between us grows even further.

The aching in my heart grows only stronger.

I've decided to take up power walking as a way of dealing with my despair and loneliness, mainly on the recommendation of Audrey, a villager here who has been doing it for years and is always quick to extol the benefits of it. I guess it must have worked for her because she's in her nineties now and still as fit as a flea.

'Much easier on the joints than actually running, but still enough to get your heart rate up and give you a good workout,' she said to me the other day when I saw her on the high street and said I was thinking of starting some form of exercise. 'Plus anybody can do it. You just walk like you always have done, only try to do it faster. I've had to slow down now at my age, though I still get out and walk every day. But you'll have no trouble!'

I decided to give it a go yesterday and found it slightly more refreshing than I was expecting, so I'm back out again today to do it again, and I'm currently making my way along the pavement that runs alongside the beach, feeling the wind in my face as my heart rate gradually quickens. Healthy body, healthy mind, is the mantra, and I'm hoping that consistent bouts of power walking will make me feel better about missing Evelyn and everything that has gone before.

As I carry on my way, swinging my arms and shuffling my legs, I am enjoying it enough to the point where I think this is something I could feasibly do for many years, or at least as long as my health permits. I've not lived in the healthiest of ways ever since my life began to unravel, the traumatic effects of what I went through meaning that these days I prefer a take-away over having a toned body, but if I can't try and improve my ways again now at my age, when can I?

I think about messaging Evelyn and telling her about my new hobby, but now she is in a different country I'd probably be better off emailing her rather than texting, as I don't know what the charges would be for either of us. I don't want her getting annoyed at me that a message I have sent her has ended up costing her money, so I'll stick to email from now on. But I am eager to hear from her, even more so now she is in Paris, because I bet it's incredible there. I've never been, and am not likely to go anytime soon, seeing as it's the city of love and I have no one to love me, so I'll rely on my daughter to paint a picture of what that place is like in her messages.

If she ever replies, of course.

As I turn towards the beach and consider going down onto the sand to continue my power walk, I think about how Evelyn would probably be quicker to respond to me if she knew half of the things that I had done in my life to keep her safe. Being near this beach is a reminder of one of those things, and it's something only I know about, as I experience a flashback to that time, seventeen years ago.

It's the time when I had to do something very drastic to make sure Siobhan could never try and hurt me and my child again after that fire.

––––––––

SEVENTEEN YEARS AGO

I leave my temporary accommodation, although sadly only for a short while because I'll have to come back here soon with Evelyn, and I have no idea when we'll be able to live somewhere better. I'm getting us both out of the house we are currently sharing with Audrey, the kindly villager who offered to give us a place to stay after our own home burnt down in the fire that turned out to be arson.

It's been three weeks since Tomlin ran into my bedroom and roused me from my bed before he heroically pulled Evelyn and me out of that burning house, but so far, the police have not been able to catch the culprit, despite me telling them exactly who it was. I know Siobhan started the fire that almost killed three people, and I have given the investigating officers her name and her photo, but they haven't been able to trace her yet. I'm not even sure how hard they are looking for her because I don't think they even believe my theory that she is the arsonist they are looking for. They just think it's another dramatic story from the woman in the village who always seems to be involved in dramatic events.

With my house in ruins, most likely needing to be knocked down and rebuilt, I was praying that the home insurance money would help me out. But that's being withheld while the investigation is pending, so it could be a long time before I see that money, if ever. That's why it was incredibly kind of Audrey to ensure we had a roof over our heads and a warm bed to sleep in.

It feels weird to be staying at the house right next door to where Fern and Drew lived during their time in Arberness, but this isn't a time for letting things like that get in the way of me keeping my daughter safe, so I've just been getting on with it. It's not been easy living with Audrey, despite her hospitality, because having lost everything we owned in the fire, Evelyn and I have struggled to adjust to our new surroundings. Evelyn misses her favourite toys, and I don't even have the money to replace them at the moment. I miss my home comforts, but in the grand scheme of things I shouldn't complain. At least we're alive and at least we were unhurt, barring a little smoke inhalation that gave me and my poor daughter a cough that lasted for a few days after the fire. That's more than can be said for the man who saved us, because Detective Tomlin did not have such a lucky escape.

He suffered extensive burns to his arms in the fire, wounds that have required surgery and will leave deep scars. He is currently under heavy medication in hospital. It'll be a while before he's discharged and able to return to his normal life, so I shouldn't complain about the upheaval I've had to suffer over the past few weeks, as it's nothing in comparison to how bad things could've been.

I'll forever be indebted to the bravery of Tomlin and will visit him in hospital as well as continue to check on his recovery, and generally check on his wellbeing for the rest of our lives. That doesn't mean I want to rekindle my romance with him though, nor do I pity him, but it's just the least I can do after he fought so hard to keep us safe.

Evelyn is in her pram, though she has taken some steps recently, and I am encouraging her to practice standing on her own two feet more and more. My plan is for us to get to the beach and then I will let her have a play around on the sand. It's a dry day and, when we make it to the beach, it's a surprise to see it so quiet. But that just means more space for me and my daughter to roam in. We make our way across the sand, Evelyn still in her pram but her little legs kicking away, eager to be set free.

I am on the lookout for Siobhan again, nervously glancing over my shoulder as well as peering into the distance to see if she might be around. Ever since I spotted her at the village fete, and even more so since the fire, I've been on edge. But there's no sign of her, which shouldn't be a surprise. I imagine she is lying low after the serious crime she committed that could easily have ended in murder charges. She must have seen the news and learnt that everybody in the house survived the fire. I wonder how that made her feel.

Like she has done enough now?

Or like she needs to do even more?

I push the pram down to the water's edge and then unstrap Evelyn, lifting her out before placing her down on the sand, where she quickly runs her hands through all the grains around her. Then she attempts to get up and, while she is very wobbly, she does manage to get to her feet before tumbling back down and giggling loudly as she goes. I keep a close watch on her as she scrabbles around on the sand, but that means I'm distracted. I'm not doing what I have been doing for the last few weeks.

I'm not looking over my shoulder.

That's how I fail to realise Siobhan is there until she's standing right behind me.

I only see when Evelyn points and, as I turn around, my heart skips a beat at the sight of the woman I'm afraid of being so close to both of us. My first instinct is to pick up my daughter and run, but before I can do that Siobhan reaches out and grabs my arm.

'Bet you wish you didn't leave me behind at that roadside

now, don't you?' she says with a smirk. 'Did you really think I'd let you get away with that?'

'Get off me!' I try, but Siobhan feels stronger than me and that's a worry – what if she goes for Evelyn? Will I be able to fight her off?

'I thought we were friends,' Siobhan goes on, keeping a tight grip on me. 'But I'll admit I made mistakes. I guess you knew about what happened between me and your boyfriend. How is he doing by the way? Hope his burns are healing.'

'You bitch. You could have killed us!' I cry, hoping my voice will carry across the beach and into the village, where somebody might hear me and come for help. But nobody seems to be nearby, and unlike the last time I was put in danger by this woman I don't have Tomlin around to save me.

'Do you have any idea how hard life has been for me since I got out of prison?' Siobhan says, clearly only thinking about herself here. 'I can't get a job, I can't get a man to stick around, family and friends have cut ties with me. Why do you think I was so quick to come here and visit you when I did? It's because I had no one else. I have nothing else.'

'You kissed my boyfriend! That's not what friends do!' I try, but Siobhan just shakes her head.

'You guys were having problems! I thought you were over,' she says, but she's just making excuses. Not that I care. I really don't give a damn about the past; I just want to get me and my daughter away from this dangerous woman. But I can't because she won't let go of me. Her grip tightens.

'Maybe it's right what they say in prison,' Siobhan goes on. 'People like us don't change. We can't change. We're broken and, even if we get out, we're just destined to make the same mistakes again and again. I'm sorry, Alice, but I don't know what else to do with my anger.'

A second later, I'm on my back on the sand. Siobhan had pushed me down hard and now she's coming for me again, so I try to scramble back to my feet but I'm not quick enough, and now she's on top of me.

We roll on the sand and then I feel wet on my back, telling me that we must have rolled down to the water. I can hear Evelyn crying but I'm just glad she isn't being hurt, yet. I see a white flash of light as Siobhan hits me hard in the face. It stirs something inside me, bringing out a side that I need to unleash if I am to survive this. I scoop up a handful of sand before throwing it in Siobhan's face.

While she is temporarily blinded, I get on top of her and slam her head into the sand. The wet, sticky surface isn't hard enough to hurt her too much, although when she rolls onto her side, I sense an opportunity and now I'm on her back.

With my whole weight on top of her, she can't get up and I push her head down into the soaking sand as the water rolls over her again and again.

She keeps fighting, Evelyn keeps crying and I keep my weight where it is.

Two minutes later and only one of those things has changed.

Siobhan is no longer fighting.

Only once I'm sure she is dead do I get off her and, as I stand, I look down at her lifeless body, face down in front of me. I'm on the verge of being sick because of what I have just done, but then I look at Evelyn and feel grateful that she is safe.

I'm grateful for one more thing, too.

My daughter is far too young to remember her mummy killing somebody right in front of her.

With no one else around besides my daughter to see what I have just done, I drag the body out into the water, before returning to the beach to take a few clumps of sand, which I stuff into Siobhan's pockets to weight her down. I wade out with her deep enough for her to slowly start sinking below the surface and far enough for the current to take over for me.

As the corpse disappears, I make sure it's far enough out so as not to wash up back on shore anytime soon and, with a bit of luck, it will be carried out to sea, and nobody will ever know what happened here. That, coupled with the fact I know Siobhan had few people who might miss her, makes me feel hopeful I'll get away with this.

Of course, I'll always know what I did and have it weigh heavily on my conscience, but I'll deal with my guilt privately.

The main thing is that my daughter is safe.

The things a mother has to do for her child.

FIFTEEN

EVELYN

Paris is pretty but, so far, I'm having the same problem I had in London.

I'm still all by myself.

I disembarked the Eurostar yesterday and went straight to the Eiffel Tower to get the obligatory selfie there. Then I checked in to my new hostel, hopeful that this would be where my luck would change, and I would meet one or two people who I would be able to hang out with so that all my memories of my trip wouldn't be solitary ones. But, once again, I've encountered nothing but backpackers who seem happy to stay in their own groups and not allow a stranger like myself into their inner circle. I'm not going to do what I did in London and just lie on my bed rereading Mum's latest messages and wondering if I made a mistake in getting away. I am going to take some initiative. If I can't find somebody to hang out with, I'll just have to go out by myself.

I've spent the past hour in the hostel bathroom applying make-up to my face to complement the sparkly dress I'm wearing and my hair, which is looking the best it's done in several days. I'm ready to hit the town, or the city to be more precise, and I'm going to drink and dance the night away and at least act as if I am having the time of my life. Surely that will be more achievable if I go to a place where alcohol is flowing freely, and social lubrication presumably will make things easier when it comes to making new friends.

A very loud German backpacker enters the bathroom and frowns when she sees me before going into one of the cubicles. I decide to hurry up so that I won't still be at the sink when she comes out to use it soon. I get a few more strange looks from some of the other backpackers I see as I return to my dorm room. It's probably because they are scruffily dressed and lounging around with nothing to do and no money to spend, but I won't let their low vibe bring me down. I make sure I have what I need in my handbag before I head for the door. I'm not going to be like them, and if they won't make the effort with me, I will leave them behind and go and find some people who are more fun.

———

It feels good to get out of the hostel and, after having a drink in a bar on the corner, I head to a nightclub I have read good things about online. It proves to be popular because there is a long line of revellers waiting to get in and I take my place in that queue, feeling nervous and excited in equal measure. As the line slowly moves and I get closer to the security guys guarding the entrance door, I wonder if I should have had a couple more drinks, not just because I need the extra confidence but because it's probably very expensive in here and I am on a budget. But it's too late for that now and, after showing my ID, I am granted access into the club and head down the stairs before laying eyes on what is a very large dancefloor.

It's so crowded in here, but I tell myself that's a good thing because once I've joined the crowd, it will be harder for anybody to tell that I'm by myself. First I need a drink, so I find the bar and once again I'm queuing. As I wait to catch the attention of one of the bartenders, I check my phone and see that I have another email from Mum. I told her I had got to Paris yesterday but haven't sent her anything since, and now she's asking for a photo. I could send her the one of me in front of the Eiffel Tower, but screw it, maybe tomorrow. For now, I put my phone back in my handbag and focus on where I am rather than where I have come from.

By the time I place my order with the barman, I seem to have attracted the attention of a creepy older guy who is trying to speak to me in French despite me telling him that I don't speak the language and therefore cannot understand him. Thankfully, I'm able to get away from him and his grabby hands and lose him on the dancefloor. As I sip my drink through my straw, I try to lose myself in the music. It takes me a little while to stop feeling awkward, but I eventually find my rhythm and, half an hour later, I'm feeling like I'm having a good time. The problem is that I'm not having a great time. Whenever I see groups of friends laughing and joking together, I wish I was part of them.

I consider going up to one of the groups and trying my luck, introducing myself and seeing if they'll be receptive to me. Maybe I will have more chance here when everybody is inebriated, as opposed to at the hostels where everybody seems like they are either moody because they have run out of money or only interested in talking to the person they have gone travelling with from home. I will do that, but first, one more drink.

I return to the bar and it's even busier than it was the last time I was here, but I bide my time and eventually make it to the front where I can speak to a bartender again. Just as I go to place my order of vodka and orange, a young woman wearing an even shorter dress than me tries to give her order at exactly the same time as I do.

'Oh, I'm sorry,' she says when she realises she has just interrupted me, possibly out of line.

'No, it's okay,' I reply, smiling because she looks to be the same age as me and is obviously polite, so I can't be mad. She's also very pretty too, and I wonder who she is here with. A boyfriend, perhaps, though I can't see anyone who seems to be here with her.

'No, you were first. You go,' she says, and I thank her before repeating my order to the bartender. Before he can turn away and start making my drink, I decide to offer to buy a drink for the woman beside me.

'What would you like?' I ask her with a big smile to show it really is just a friendly gesture on my part.

'You're buying?'

'Yeah, why not?'

'Wow, thank you. I'll have a vodka soda and my friend is having a rum and cola.'

I make sure to pass that on to the bartender, and as he gets to work, I try not to think about how much those three drinks are going to cost me in a place like this. Maybe it will be worth the investment because I might have just got myself a friend.

'You're English?' she asks me, and I confirm.

'You?'

'No, I'm French. Can you not tell by my accent?' she replies, but I can only just hear her over the music, so detecting an accent is tricky.

'This club is cool,' I say as the bartender works in front of us.

'Yeah. I was here two nights ago, but it's way better tonight. So, who are you out with?'

The question is one that I'm nervous to answer because I wonder if I'll be judged negatively if I say that I'm out by myself. But I might as well be honest and see where it gets me.

'I'm actually on my own,' I say. 'I've only just got here. I'm backpacking and don't know anybody in Paris yet.'

'Oh wow! That's so cool,' she cries, and while it hasn't actually been that cool so far, I smile and agree. Then she says something that is music to my ears.

'You have to come and party with me and my friend! Get your drink and come with me!'

I thank her for the invite and try to play it casually as I agree, as if I have any other options available to me, and once the bartender hands over our drinks, we are on the move.

I follow her across the crowded dancefloor to a table at the back of the room where I find another woman around my age sitting. She looks very pretty, far prettier than most of the other women in here, but before I can talk to her, the friend I made at the bar introduces herself properly.

'I'm Antoinette,' she says, and this is my first big test. Do I give my real name, or do I use one of the fake names I've come up with because I want to make sure I cut all ties to the old me?

'I'm Tiffany,' I say, proving which option I went with.

'What a beautiful name!' Antoinette cries, clearly having no idea that it's fake, before she turns to her friend to introduce us.

'This is Cecilia,' she tells me. 'She's originally from England too. I think you guys will get along!'

SIXTEEN

CECILIA

My feet are aching from all the dancing I've done, and my throat is sore from having to shout over the loud music whenever I wanted to talk, but that doesn't detract from what has been a brilliant night. Antoinette and I always have a good time when we go out together, but this was something else, this was epic, and our night was even better because we had an extra person to share it with.

Antoinette came back from the bar with a total stranger, but once we'd been introduced, it was clear that we had the same interests in life. We love to drink, we love to dance and we love the fact that neither of us are from Paris yet we'd made it to the glamorous city. Not bad for a pair of eighteen-year-olds.

But while the three of us have had a great time in the hectic club, we haven't had much of a chance to talk properly because it's so loud. That's why, as the clock strikes two o'clock in the morning, I suggest we leave and go and get something to eat.

Antoinette and Tiffany are keen on that plan, so we make our way out of the club, dodging the advances of several drunken male revellers who try to persuade us to stay with bad chat-up lines or suggestive stares.

'Tonight was *épique!*' Antoinette cries once we're back out on the street, and it's nice to be able to hear my friend properly again, although I can also hear ringing in my ears after spending so long near those booming speakers.

'I need chips and I need them now,' I exclaim, and Tiffany agrees that chips would be perfect, so we look around for somewhere to get some food.

'Over there!' Tiffany shouts when she spots a takeaway, and we head across the street, the three of us giggling as we sway and stumble, euphoric from the potent combination of alcohol and endorphins.

Entering the takeaway, we quickly claim ourselves a table before we task Antoinette with going to the counter and placing our order. She's less forgetful than me so it's better that she does it, and as she goes to get us the food that our stomachs crave, I sit down across from Tiffany who is smiling widely.

'Thanks so much for letting me hang out with you guys,' she says as I take off my heels and give my aching feet some air. 'It was so much fun.'

'It's been lovely to meet you,' I reply, meaning it. 'Thanks for all the drinks. I'm pretty sure we owe you some money.'

'Don't worry about it,' Tiffany says, batting the air in between us. 'I've not spent much since I've been travelling, so it's fine.'

'How have your travels been going?' I ask, glad I can have a proper conversation with our new friend now rather than just a few snatched sentences in between dancing to the next song.

'Not great if I'm honest. I mean, it's been interesting seeing the sights here and in London, but travelling alone has been harder than I thought it would be.'

'Oh no, sorry to hear that. Did you not have any friends at home who wanted to go with you?'

Tiffany shakes her head. 'Nah, they're all boring,' she says quietly before looking away, but I get the impression that she might not have had that many people to ask.

'So how long are you here for?' is my next question. 'Because if it's a while then we should do this again!'

'I'm not sure yet. I haven't really got a plan. I've just been taking it as it comes.'

'How adventurous!'

Antoinette returns, the orders placed, and now all we have to do is wait patiently for our names to be called when the food is ready. But there are a few people waiting ahead of us so it could be a while yet. That's fine though, because I want to know more about Tiffany and where she comes from. I like to learn more about England any chance I get, especially because I might never get to go there and see it for myself.

'So whereabouts in England are you from?' I ask curiously.

'Oh, it's a tiny village. You'll never have heard of it,' she replies.

'We're from a tiny village too,' Antoinette chips in. 'It's boring, isn't it?'

'Hell yeah,' Tiffany says, rolling her eyes. 'I like Paris a lot more. Plus my mum isn't here so that helps.'

'You don't get on with your mum?' I ask.

'Let's just say we have a complicated relationship.'

'I know exactly what you mean,' I reply. 'I love my mum, but I had a bit of a weird childhood and sometimes I feel like she hasn't always told me the truth about it.'

'That's exactly how I feel!' Tiffany cries, looking amazed that she has met somebody else who she shares this problem with. I'm amazed too because growing up in the village, it seemed like I was the only one with an unusual upbringing. I love Antoinette, but she comes from a very stable home where both parents were always around for her, so that's always been the one area where we haven't had something in common. The same goes for the other kids I grew up with in the village. But now I've met somebody who might know how I feel.

'What about your dad? Do you get along with him?' I ask her now, but she just shakes her head.

'I never met him,' is all Tiffany says, but it's enough for me to get the sense of how upsetting that has been for her. I try to cheer her up by letting her know that she's not alone there either.

'We left mine behind when we moved from England, and Mum tells me it's too dangerous to go back and find him,' I say. 'Sucks growing up without a dad, doesn't it?'

'Sure does,' Tiffany confirms as Antoinette leaps out of her seat to go and collect our food order that has just been called out.

As I see our delicious food being brought back to our table, I watch Tiffany and see how vulnerable she looks, like she is a little bit damaged and needed something like tonight to make her feel better about herself for a while. Maybe it's because we seem to have had similar issues growing up in our families or maybe it's just the way she looks. Despite all the make-up and the wild dancing back at the club, now we're in the bright light of a takeaway, I can see the real her and I sense a loneliness. That's only enhanced by the fact she was all by herself when we met her in the club earlier, and I hate the thought of anybody feeling like they don't have someone to call a friend. That's why, once we've had a chance to eat a few chips, I have an idea.

'Antoinette and I have jobs here in Paris,' I say in between mouthfuls of greasy food. 'Why don't you try and get one too? You could stick around for a while. I think we need more nights out like this one.'

'Yeah, you should stay!' Antoinette cries, more than happy to have Tiffany join us for future adventures.

'I'd love to,' Tiffany replies, looking touched that we are so enthusiastic about seeing her again. 'But do you think I'd find a job?'

'Sure,' I say confidently. 'It depends what you want to do. But you could do anything. Bartending. Waitressing. Office work. You name it.'

'I probably do need to get a job if I stick around for a while. It's so expensive here,' Tiffany says, and I agree with her. Then I have another idea, possibly one fuelled by how much I've had to drink tonight, but I'm sure Antoinette won't mind when she hears it because she's just as sociable as me.

'You could always stay with us. We have an apartment nearby. It's only got two bedrooms, but we could figure something out. It's quite expensive for two of us, but if we could split the rent three ways then that would make it cheaper.'

Tiffany seems genuinely appreciative of my suggestion that she comes and lives with us rather than heading off elsewhere on her own. I check with Antoinette if she agrees with my suggestion.

'Yeah, that'd be cool,' my best friend says. 'As long as our landlord doesn't find out there is an extra person staying. But I'm sure he won't.'

'Are you serious?' Tiffany asks.

'Yeah, why not?' I say. 'Isn't travelling all about making new friends and taking chances? I mean, I get it if you'd rather carry on backpacking around Europe, but it sounds like you're not on a strict schedule and in any rush to get back home, so why not live in Paris for a few months and see how it goes?'

'I'm definitely not in a rush to get home,' Tiffany confirms. 'And Paris is so pretty, I'd love to see more of it.'

'Plus who wouldn't want the chance to hang out with two crazy cats like us?' Antoinette cuts in, and we all laugh before Tiffany agrees to the idea.

'Great!' I say with a smile as I pick up another chip. 'Here's to new friends!'

SEVENTEEN

FERN

I love waking up next to a strong, dependable man and I just wish it was the weekend rather than a weekday, then Pierre wouldn't have to get out of bed and go to work. But I'm out of luck and, after he kisses me to say good morning, he slides out from underneath the duvet and heads for our ensuite bathroom, his bare feet padding across the carpet as he goes. If I could have picked something else to wake up to then it would be a new voicemail message from Cecilia, and I'm pleased to see that there is one waiting on my phone for me.

As I stay snuggled in the duvet, feeling glad that I don't have to get up and go to work myself, I open the message to see what my daughter has been up to recently. I can see that her voicemail was left at four a.m., which could be a cause for concern – it might mean that she was in trouble or had a problem so big that it was preventing her from falling asleep. But I quite quickly hear that I have nothing to worry about because when I press play, it's obvious why she left me a message at the time she did.

'Hiiiii Mummmmm. Just letting you know that I had the

best night. We made a new friend! Tiffany. What a cool name! She is going to be living with us now. Anyway, just wanted to say I love you and miss you. Say hi to Pierre for me. Byyyye!'

I smile at the sound of my daughter's drunken voice and laugh at how she has a new friend to live with, because the plan was always for just her and Antoinette to live together. But that's my baby, spontaneous and adventurous, and I'm sure Tiffany is lovely. I guess I'll meet her when we go to Paris, and as I type out a reply to Cecilia, I'm excited for when that time will come.

> *Morning, darling. Sounds like somebody had a good night! Glad you're having fun. Maybe don't stay up quite as late when you start your new job though. The sun is shining here. Hope it's nice there. Love you xx*

I don't expect to get a reply for a while, mainly because Cecilia is most likely sleeping off a terrible hangover right now, so I put my phone down and roll over, glancing towards the bathroom door. When I do, I see Pierre emerge, his trousers on but his upper half still topless, and while he reaches into the wardrobe for a white shirt, I tease him by telling him that I think his current look is already perfect, and he doesn't need to add any more items of clothing.

'Actually, on second thoughts, some of your female patients have high blood pressure, so maybe seeing you half-naked might not be the safest thing for them,' I add, and Pierre laughs as he buttons up his shirt and then finds a tie to complement it.

'I'll save the state of undress for the weekend,' Pierre says with a wink, and I tell him that sounds good to me.

As he finishes getting ready, becoming smarter by the second, I try not to see flashes of Drew in him, though it's hard. I spent so many years lying in bed, watching my first husband getting ready to go and be the good doctor, that it's hard not to be reminded of that now I have another handsome man in my bedroom wearing a smart suit. But as Pierre kisses me goodbye and tells me to have a good day, I get flashes of something else too, and it's the thing we almost talked about during the picnic the other day. We haven't broached the subject since, but it's still very much on my mind. As my husband leaves the house, I lie back on my pillow and, while I might regret it, I allow myself to think back once again to ten years ago, to the most difficult period of our relationship.

It was the time, yet again, when a dead body almost cost me everything.

———

TEN YEARS AGO

I can't believe this is happening. Not only have I killed again, but my new husband has come home unexpectedly, and now he's only seconds away from figuring out what kind of woman I really am.

But I had to kill this man. He knew who I was, and he would have continued to blackmail me into doing all sorts of things unless I took action. He was a problem so I dealt with it, but I have an even bigger problem now.

Stepping away from the body on my bedroom floor, I go to the door and look down, seeing a flash of Pierre's suit as he moves under the staircase. I can't have this. I need to get Pierre out of the house as quickly as I can so I can then focus on getting the body out of the house. But my husband is in the kitchen now and I guess he's not going anywhere for a while.

Closing the bedroom door so that the body won't be clearly seen if Pierre comes up here, I head downstairs and find my husband rummaging around in the fridge.

'Everything okay?' he asks me as he takes out some bacon and eggs.

'Okay? Yeah, everything's fine. Why wouldn't it be?'

I'm probably fortunate that Pierre doesn't look at me as I answer, still far too preoccupied with finding more food, because otherwise he would surely see how bad a liar I am and that things are not okay at all. He'd also surely see what a mess I currently look – all sweaty and shaky – and while I manage to keep my voice steady, it's about the only thing that is right now.

'I'm starving,' he says as he turns on the cooker, and within minutes there are two pans being heated, one frying bacon, the other cooking eggs. It should smell delicious and, ten minutes ago, I would have been hungry enough to gobble all of it up, but not after what I've just done. Killing that man has left me feeling sick, and the smell of the cooking breakfast is only adding to my nausea. But of course, Pierre is totally unbothered because, as far as he knows, this is a great morning. He's got less work to do than he thought and soon he will be tucking into a tasty meal.

I know that my secret is safe upstairs as long as my husband stays down here, so I tell myself that this doesn't have to be so bad as long as he just eats his breakfast and goes again. Pierre is surprised when I tell him I don't want anything to eat myself, but I just say something about starting a new diet, and he doesn't ask any more questions. I watch him as he sits and eats his meal, taking his sweet time, totally oblivious to the horror that sits just above our heads. Finally, after what feels like forever, he puts his knife and fork down on his empty plate and says he better be making a move as he has a patient to see in fifteen minutes.

'I'll tidy up here. You get yourself back to work,' I say, ushering him towards the door, and it seems like I'm going to get away with this after all. That's until Pierre suddenly stops and turns back towards the stairs.

'I'll just use the toilet before I go,' he says, sending a shiver down my spine, because the only two bathrooms in this house are upstairs.

'Can't you wait?'

'No, I'll just be a minute,' he says before he heads up the stairs, and I feel weaker the further up he gets. At least I closed the bedroom door, so he won't see anything as long as he doesn't open it.

'Use the main bathroom,' I say as I follow him up.

'Why?'

'I'm cleaning the ensuite,' I reply, pleased with my quick thinking, and he does as I say, heading into the bathroom that isn't connected to our bedroom.

I wait outside the door for him, like a guard standing on duty, but I simply can't allow him to move around up here without keeping watch. When I hear the toilet flush, I hope that's the end of this unnecessary drama and he'll finally be on his way now.

'Damn it,' I hear Pierre cry a moment later.

'What is it?'

The bathroom door opens now and, when it does, I see why he just got so annoyed. There is a green stain all down the front of his white shirt.

'I spilt mouthwash down myself,' he says with a huff. 'I'll have to change now.'

That's the last thing I wanted to hear because all his spare shirts are in the wardrobe in our bedroom.

But he cannot go in there.

'Wait!' I cry, stepping in front of him and putting my hands on his chest before he can go any further. But I fear I've been too desperate to keep him out of the bedroom and now he knows something is going on.

'What are you doing?'

'Erm. I'm cleaning the bedroom too. It's a mess in there. Just wait here and I'll get you your shirt.'

Pierre frowns, but I tell him I'll just be a second and then I quickly open the bedroom door, but only enough so I can slip inside and not an inch more. Then I close the door again and, ignoring the corpse on the carpet, I rush to the wardrobe to grab Pierre another shirt and I think that somehow, as crazy as this is, I am going to get away with this.

And then I hear the bedroom door open behind me.

My breath catches in my throat as I spin around and see my husband standing in the doorway, looking down at the body of the man I killed before he came home.

This is it. My marriage is over. I've just lost the man I love and, when my daughter finds out, I might lose her too. I certainly will if Pierre goes straight to the police. But will he?

'Wait! I can explain!' I cry, dropping the shirt I was holding and rushing to Pierre, but he just recoils and keeps his distance from me, clearly unsure if he can even trust me.

Does he think I'm dangerous? Is he scared of me? It's hard to tell – his eyes are only on the dead body.

'Please, let me just tell you what happened!' I beg, praying Pierre doesn't run out of the house because I won't be able to stop him.

'Who is that?' he asks me. 'What have you done?'

I'm lucky that Pierre doesn't seem to recognise this man as being one of his former classmates, but it was a long time ago, so deciding to use that bit of luck to my advantage, I begin to weave another lie as quickly as I can.

'It's him,' I say quietly. 'My ex.'

Pierre looks even more horrified than he did two seconds ago, but I nod my head, leaning into the lie.

'I don't know how he found me, but he did, and he was making threats. Said he was going to hurt you and take Cecilia away from me. I didn't know what to do so I tried to calm him down. I told him I'd missed him and that you were out at work. I said I was sorry for running away from him and that I wanted to make it up to him, so I brought him back here. Then I killed him.'

It's possibly the worst lie I've ever told, although a few other people might disagree, but I've told it now and I just have to hope that Pierre believes it.

But does he?

'How did he find you?' he asks, suggesting he does believe me after all.

'I don't know! But he did and I panicked! I'm sorry. I didn't know what to do! I couldn't risk him hurting you or Cecilia. I had no choice! You have to believe me!'

I try to hug Pierre and this time he doesn't back away. Maybe that's because I'm crying now as well, the emotion of not just the past half an hour spilling out of me, but the emotion of keeping all my secrets from him for so long.

But I think he does believe me with what I've just said. Then he proves that he does as he takes out his phone.

'Who are you calling?' I ask him nervously, fearing it's the police.

'My receptionist. I'm telling her to cancel the rest of my patients today. We need to hide this body.'

Pierre steps out of the bedroom and makes his call, explaining to his receptionist how he feels ill and needs to take the rest of the day off.

I can't believe it.

He's going to help me sort this mess out?

I love him so much. But I'm not quite out of the woods yet, so while Pierre's back is turned to me, I quickly kneel down and search inside the dead man's pockets, desperately looking for his wallet. I pull it out when I find it and hide it in the drawer on my bedside table. With that out of the way, there's no chance of

Pierre checking this man's ID and recognising the name of his former classmate.

He thinks this is my abusive ex.

As long as he keeps thinking that I should be okay.

I just have to remember the extra lie I have told. As if I didn't already have enough of those to remember.

EIGHTEEN

ALICE

PRESENT DAY

I smile as I pass the nurse sitting behind the desk of this particular ward of Carlisle Hospital. She presses the button to electronically unlock the doors for me so I can make it to where the patients are. I've been here a couple of times before, so I know which bed I am looking for, and as the other people who have arrived here at the same time as me for the beginning of visiting hours reach their respective patients, I find the person I am here to see.

'Hello, Tomlin,' I say as I stop beside the bed of the man who I used to be so close to. But there's a huge distance between us now, not literally, but emotionally, and while he turns his head and looks at me, he quickly turns it back and returns to staring out of the window at the grey sky beyond.

'I brought you some chocolates,' I say, placing the snacks I picked up on my way here down on the table beside his bed. 'I thought you might be running low on supplies.'

Tomlin doesn't acknowledge me or the chocolates, so I take a seat and give him a moment to hopefully become more receptive to me. As I do, I can hear the voices of the other people on this ward, patients and their visitors, all of them chatting and catching up, though I can't see any of them. I can't see them because the curtains are drawn all the way around Tomlin's bed, as they always are whenever I come here. I know why that is and, as always, I feel guilty because of it, mainly because Tomlin's need for privacy is borne out of the scars he got while saving me and Evelyn from that fire so many years ago.

His badly scarred arms have not just caused him to be self-conscious though, they are responsible for far more than that. Like the addiction to painkillers that he developed as his burns were healing – the addiction that almost saw him lose his job in the police force before he was given help. But while he was able to reduce his dependency on the medication, he increased his dependency on alcohol and, eventually, his employers had enough and there was no saving his job at that point. While he has been able to live off his pension since he was let go from the police force, 'live' is not exactly the right word to describe it. He's been an addict for years, barely leaving his house and now, after such a long time of punishing his body, it is failing on him and, sadly, the staff here don't think he has long left.

Why am I here to see him when we broke up such a long time ago? It's not just the guilt of how he got his burns that drives me here. It's simply because I recognise that he doesn't really have anybody else. Since we broke up, he hasn't dated again – and neither have I – so there's no partner to sit by his bedside, nor are there any children to pay him regular visits. Not even his former colleagues come to see him, although that's just because Tomlin is still bitter about how his career ended up and he has shunned a lot of them, not just because they remind him of Fern and the investigation that he messed up but because he still thinks that people blame him for it now.

Things might have been different if I hadn't let Fern get away in Cornwall. If she had been sent to prison, Tomlin could have put the whole sorry tale in the past, but with her still out there somewhere he has never been able to rest, and over the years it has eaten away at him little by little.

'You're looking well,' I try, wondering if Tomlin will believe my lie or at least laugh and tell me to stop talking nonsense. But he doesn't do any of that, choosing to keep ignoring me instead, and I'm starting to think it was a mistake in coming here. However, with Tomlin's days numbered, I thought I should make the trip one last time, though if I'm honest, I thought my previous trip here would have been my last. I'm surprised he's still hanging on because he looks so ill, deathly pale, extremely gaunt and despite the food the nurses bring him – as well as the chocolates I try and tempt him with too – he isn't taking in much food these days. He's on the verge of death, but stubbornly living on, as if he is waiting for something before he goes.

But what?

I reach into the bag I brought the chocolates in and take out the other thing I bought on my way here. It's a newspaper and I brought it because I thought Tomlin might like to hear about some of the stories currently dominating the headlines. That investigative mind of his must still be in there somewhere, so I wonder if he would want to hear about a few of the unsolved cases currently keeping the police busy and see if he has any theories on them himself. But it turns out that it was a bad idea, because no sooner have I started talking about one of them than he tells me to stop.

'Aren't you interested in the news?' I ask him, but he just shakes his head.

'The only thing I'm interested in is if that bitch has been caught yet.'

I know he is referring to Fern, which only makes me feel worse – he's clearly getting increasingly bitter about her still being on the run. Maybe if he had been like this back in Cornwall, all those years ago, then I wouldn't have been able to stop him arresting her, but on that day, after she had saved Evelyn, he was just as happy for her to walk away as I was. Because she saved Evelyn. But time has hardened him and he's clearly back to wanting her caught, though there's little either of us can do about that now.

I decide to give up with the newspaper, but leave it on his bedside table just in case he wants to look at it after I've gone. I'm thinking about giving up on being here at all but, before I can say my goodbyes, Tomlin speaks up again.

'How's Evelyn?' he asks me, and I'm touched because, despite his cold, withdrawn demeanour, he obviously still cares about my daughter; he spent a lot of time with her when she was a baby.

'She's great, thanks for asking,' I say. 'She's gone travelling now. I think I told you she was planning it.'

'Travelling?' Tomlin says as he stares vacantly out at the same view he's had for months.

'Yeah, she went to London first and she's in Paris now.'

'Does she message?'

'Every now and again. I think she's having too much fun to want to talk to me every day.'

At least that's what I'm telling myself.

I wonder if Tomlin is going to ask me next how I've been, but he doesn't do that. As an uncomfortable silence falls between us, I consider telling him that I'm sorry. For everything. For breaking up with him, which maybe I regret a little because these years have been lonely. For letting Fern get away when we had her. For him being in my house when Siobhan started the fire, and for what has become of this man who was once such a hardworking, dedicated detective. But I don't, mainly because I fear he might get angry at me if I do.

'Goodbye, Tomlin,' I say as I stand up and gently touch his shoulder before waiting for him to say goodbye to me. But he doesn't, and I'm not sure if that's because he thinks he'll still be alive long enough for me to make another visit, or if he simply doesn't wish to end things between us on a civil note.

Making my way out of the ward, I pass a nurse I recognise and smile at her before asking her how long she thinks he has.

'Honestly, it should be any day now,' she says sadly, and it's hard to disagree with that based on how the ex-detective looks sitting forlornly in his bed. But as I leave the hospital and prepare to make the long drive back to Arberness, I realise there is something that both myself and the nurse looking after him have failed to take into account.

Yes, Tomlin is gravely ill.

But he isn't going anywhere.

He is clinging on until he has closure on the one case he has never been able to finish.

The one who got away...

NINETEEN

FERN

A coffee morning with my best friend in the village is just what I need to rid myself of the daily anxieties that rattle around in my brain and will do so until the day that I die. As I walk into the café and see Marion already at the counter getting ready to place her order, I am glad that the most demanding thing I'll have to think about for the next few seconds is whether I opt for a cappuccino or a latte. That's certainly better than thinking about anything from whether or not Pierre and I will ever face the consequences of hiding that body, whether the police in England will ever figure out I'm hiding here in France and whether Cecilia will one day disown me and I'll die all by myself in a windowless cell with nobody to come to my funeral.

'Hi!' I say, putting on a brave face, and Marion smiles when she sees me.

'Hey, I've just ordered. What are you having?'

'Can you get me a latte? I'll find us a table.'

Marion can handle that. As I find us the one table in here that isn't littered with empty cups and cookie crumbs from previous patrons, I try to relax. It helps when I check my phone and see that Cecilia has just sent me a message, letting me know that her first morning in her new job has gone well. I text back to say that I'm pleased to hear it, as well as very proud of her beginning the career of her dreams. From spending eighteen years worrying that social services would take my girl away when they knew what kind of a murderous mother I was, to being excited about my baby entering the work force and building a life of her own.

What a wild ride.

'One latte,' Marion says as she places my drink down on the table, and I quickly put my phone away, ready to give my friend my full attention.

'Thank you,' I say before reaching for a sugar sachet, and once we have both made sure our drinks are exactly to our liking, we begin catching up.

'So, on a scale of one to a billion, how much are you missing Cecilia?' she asks me, and I laugh before answering.

'Two billion, I'd say.'

'Sounds about right. Is she enjoying Paris?'

'Loving it. Her new job seems to be going well and she keeps talking about the new friend she has made. Tiffany.'

'That's a nice name.'

'Yeah, I thought that too.'

'How did she meet her?'

'On a night out, apparently.'

'Party animals.'

'Yep. It sounds like they've been inseparable ever since.'

I think about how that might be a bit of an understatement, because almost every message I receive from Cecilia now seems to mention this mysterious new friend of hers. But it's not long to go now until I get to meet her and be in the same room as my daughter again.

'Pierre and I are going to Paris next week,' I exclaim with a huge grin spreading across my face. 'We're going to stay for three nights. I can't wait.'

'How wonderful! You'll have an amazing time.'

I sure hope my friend is right, but I can't see why she wouldn't be. Catching up with Cecilia, seeing where she is living now as well as getting a bit of time to do a few romantic things with my husband can't be anything but enjoyable, can it?

The rest of my catch-up with Marion goes well, and we plan to do the same thing again when I get back from my trip so I can tell her all about it. But just before we depart, my friend says something that instantly takes me back to the time when I used to be paranoid about her and whether or not she knew my secrets.

'Be careful in Paris. Lots of tourists around, including plenty from England.'

She gives me a knowing nod before walking away. Gripped with fear, I call after her to see what she meant. Is she referring to the fact that I'm a wanted woman in my home country and somebody in Paris might recognise me and have me arrested? If so, I can't believe she has pretended to be my friend all this time while knowing who I really am. But she just shrugs as she stops.

'I'm talking about your ex. You don't want him or anyone he knows recognising you, right?'

'Oh, yeah, of course.'

Marion gives me a wink and heads on her way, and I watch her until she disappears from view, an unsettled feeling in my stomach. No, don't be paranoid again, I've got enough to worry about, I tell myself before I turn for home. But I've barely gone on my way before I get a call from Pierre and when I answer it, he asks me if I'm still at the café with Marion.

'No, she just left. Why?'

'I was wondering if you could pick me up a slice of chocolate cake and a coffee?'

'Chocolate cake for the doctor? What would your patients say if they knew you were eating unhealthily?'

'Try and smuggle it into my office the best way you can,'

Pierre says, and I laugh before telling him that I'll be on my way.

———

I pick up what my husband has requested and then head for the building in this village where the locals go when they have something to worry about health-wise. Fortunately, I've not been here much myself, not just because I have my very own doctor at home to consult with on a daily basis, but because I've been fortunate enough to not have many issues or ailments since I've lived in this village. But while I've been okay, I do often wonder how my parents are back home. They'll be into their eighties now, if they're still alive, and I wonder what sort of life they might be living. But as usual, I can't dwell on that without feeling on the verge of tears, so I do what I always do and tell myself that they're both still perfectly healthy and enjoying their retirement and will continue to do so for many years to come. Better that than imagining one of them at the funeral of the other and their only daughter nowhere to be seen. The media might have enjoyed making me out to be some selfish person with a heart of stone, but I'm not and I miss my family terribly. The problem is, I can't let anybody else know that, because sitting down with a journalist and 'telling all' is hardly an option for me.

'Bonjour,' I say to the receptionist as I walk in before asking if Pierre is currently with a patient or not. But the waiting room is empty so I'm hoping not, and she tells me he is free, so I can enter his office. I knock twice before doing that and find Pierre sitting at his desk and writing something on a notepad, but he looks far more thrilled when he sees me than he did working away a second ago.

'You're a lifesaver,' he says. 'I'm falling asleep in here, so I need sugar and caffeine and I need it fast.'

'Just what the doctor ordered,' I say as I hand him his treats. He gives me a kiss.

'How was Marion?' he asks me, and I say she was fine, obviously not mentioning her slightly ominous words to me as we parted.

'Good, good,' Pierre says before sipping his hot coffee. 'I bet she's jealous about Paris.'

'Yeah, I guess. That reminds me, I need to start packing, so you'll have to get the suitcases down from the attic for me tonight.'

'Will do,' Pierre says before telling me that he better get back to work.

I give him another kiss and am just about to walk away when I notice what he was writing on his notepad when I walked in. I had presumed it would have been something about a patient or a note to remind him to do something before he finished for the day, but it's not that at all.

You are not a bad person.

'What's that about?' I ask Pierre, and when he realises I've seen the notepad, he quickly covers it with another one.

'Oh, that? Nothing. Just patient stuff. Sorry, you shouldn't have seen that.'

Is it really to do with another patient? Or is it about my husband?

'Are you sure?' I ask. 'Is everything okay?'

'Yeah, fine,' Pierre replies before telling me he has a phone call to make so I better go.

I'm still not convinced that Pierre is being honest with me and am concerned there is something troubling him, but decide to leave it, for now at least. There'll be plenty of time at home for me to ask him about it again.

'I love you,' I say to him as I open the door and prepare to leave.

'Love you too,' he replies quietly before turning back to his desk, and I guess that's all I needed to hear.

Pierre's fine, right? He's always fine. At least I hope he is.

After all, he's usually the strongest one out of the pair of us.

He proved that on the day he helped me bury that body.

TWENTY

PIERRE

I really wish my wife hadn't seen the stupid scribblings I had made on my notepad. I don't even know why I bothered making them because they don't even work. Despite what some studies say about writing affirmations to make yourself feel better, I can categorically state that it does not work, at least for me anyway. I should know because I've been writing them for a while, several years in fact, on and off, but I don't feel any better about myself or what I did in the past.

I still feel guilty about burying that body.

And I still live in fear that I'll go to prison one day for doing it.

Sipping my coffee and nibbling on my brownie does stop me from feeling as tired as I was before my wife came and brought me these things, but fatigue is the least of my problems. Guilt and paranoia are far higher on that list, and those aren't quite so easily dealt with. A person might think that someone with my skillset and knowledge would know of a medication that might help with processing a troubling event in the past, but all I do know is that none of the medications work. Pills are only good for certain things and, while they can ease physical pain, they can't remove the memory of a dead man.

Wine can help things, but it's only a short-term fix.

There's no long-term escape from the torment I have inside me.

Trying to get back to work, I wonder why my actions ten years ago are playing on my mind so much again now. Some days are always worse than others, and sometimes there are a few magical days when I almost go the full twenty-four hours without thinking about that hole I dug or the person I put into it. But today is not one of the good days and it's been more bad than good recently.

When I discovered that my wife had murdered her horrible ex-partner and he was lying dead on our bedroom floor, it was an awful lot to process. Unfortunately, there is not a lot of time to process things when a dead body is involved. You have no choice but to move quickly, at least you do if you want to stay out of prison, so I sprang into action that day before I really had time to think about what I was doing. Even now, it's hard to know if I was more fuelled by a desire to avoid the police or desire to keep the woman I loved safe, so I like to think it was 50/50 and leave it at that.

On that day, ten years ago, after excusing myself from work for the rest of the day due to a fake sickness bug, I went downstairs to the kitchen to find some items that could help me with what I needed to do. I found a couple of pairs of rubber gloves under the sink as well as several cleaning accessories, and I returned to the bedroom with them all before telling my murderous wife what we had to do.

'We need to put the body in the back of my car, but we can't do that until it's dark in case somebody sees us. So let's just move him downstairs and clean up in here as best we can and then we'll take him out of the house after sunset.'

I had almost been surprising myself with how composed I

was being, but one of us had to be like that. It was no time for panic, and while it was a shock to find out that the woman I married was capable of killing another person, I knew she had only done it because her loved ones had been threatened, so she really had no choice. Of course, I wished she had just found a way to call the police rather than resort to such drastic action, but I know she wouldn't have done it if there was any other way, so I couldn't be mad at her, or love her any less.

After putting on our gloves, we began to move the body, which was no mean feat because it literally was a dead weight, and it took a while just to drag it to the top of the stairs. Afraid of getting any more blood and fibres on the floor than we already had, I then returned to the bedroom and took out several bed sheets before laying them out down the stairs so they would catch any incriminating DNA. Far easier to wash a few sheets than scrub the entire house.

It took a lot of struggling before the body was downstairs, and I covered it in a sheet as it lay behind the door, where I presumed it would be well out of view if we were to get a surprise visitor at any point before we had chance to remove it. Then, already sweating, not just because of the exertion or the heat outside, I started cleaning, joining my wife in the bedroom and working our way systematically back along the route we had dragged the body, looking out for any drops of blood and praying that we were cleaning away any incriminating evidence.

It took hours, mainly because I insisted on being so meticulous, and the only time we spoke was to give the other one an instruction.

'Move that.'

'Don't forget to wipe that part there.'

'Help me clean this blood up here.'

But even when we were done, it was still several hours until sunset. I wasn't going to risk carrying the body to the car and bumping into the postman or some villager, so I insisted on waiting until after dark and, with some time to kill, I tried to figure out if there might be anybody out there who would miss this man who we were about to try and hide forever.

'Family members or friends of his back home,' I had said to my wife. 'People will be looking for him. Will anybody have known he was coming here?'

'No, I doubt it,' she'd replied, but unconvincingly.

'Are you sure? Because this is important! If anyone knew he was coming here then they will know where to look when he fails to turn up again!'

'Yes, I'm sure!'

'How can you be?'

'He told me he was here by himself. He tracked me down by himself and nobody knew about it. I swear.'

I took my wife's word for it then because what else could I do? I had to hope she was right. The long length of time that has passed since suggests she was – nobody has ever come to the village to look for him.

With that additional bit of anxiety cleared up, and one more time asking my wife if she was sure we could get away with this, I had gone to the garage where I kept several tools that would help me with the disposal of the body, a spade being the main one. I'd put them in my car, making sure to leave space for the body that would soon be in there too, and then I waited for the sun to go down.

By the time we'd transferred the corpse from the house to the car, I guess the shock of what had happened had worn off, because I'd suddenly been struck by an urge to call the police. Maybe I shouldn't have allowed myself to have been talked out of it, but I was. If only I had called the authorities then I might have saved myself so many years of stressing about the past coming back to bite me. In the end, I did what I felt was best to keep my family together. That meant not allowing my wife to go to prison and not allowing Cecilia to see her mother in handcuffs.

With the body in the back and my wife in the passenger seat, I drove us out into the countryside, getting over fifty miles away from home before I felt like I was ready to park up and do some digging. I probably didn't need to go as far as I did, but I felt like I wanted to put a considerable distance between myself and the corpse when I got back home, as if his ghost might want to haunt me but not bother when he realised how far it would take him to get back to my place. By the time I finally started digging, it was almost midnight and I'd fully come to terms with what I doing by then. I accepted that I had crossed a line and there was no going back, no matter what happened in the future, and I just had to accept my life choices and get on with it.

I didn't say any words after I had rolled that man into his grave, not feeling like offering any comment whatsoever, not just because he surely didn't deserve it but simply because I was too exhausted to even speak. It took what little energy I had left to fill in the hole and then drive back home, my wife in the seat beside me as silent as I was behind the wheel.

Before we re-entered our home, we both made a vow that we would never talk about what happened again, and while it seemed a silly notion at the time, we have successfully managed it, for the most part. Nobody has discovered that body, so I guess I did a good job, not that I ever feel like giving myself a pat on the back. I would check the UK news online from time to time over the years, searching to see if there were any articles about a missing person, looking for photos of the man I had buried, trying to find out if there was a police investigation into his whereabouts. But I never found anything. He literally vanished in all senses of the word. While that is very strange, because surely someone in England missed him, it was good news for us.

Here I am, all these years later, still a practising doctor, still getting to help people and have everyone in this village think I'm a good guy who would never do anything awful, let alone cover up a murder. That's the illusion I must keep up and it's the same illusion my wife keeps up too.

Have I ever had my doubts about what really happened in that bedroom before that man lost his life? Sure, but there's not much I could do to ever find out if what happened differed from what I was told. I just have to take my wife's word for it.

She has been honest with me, hasn't she?

I hope so.

One skeleton in the closet is more than enough for any marriage.

The best thing about it all, even better than the police not finding out about what happened, is that Cecilia has no idea either. That means she still retains the idea that the two people who helped raise her are innocent, good and honest people.

That's very important to me.

I'd hate for her life to be screwed up by other people's actions.

Thankfully, it seems it's not going to come to that.

TWENTY-ONE
EVELYN

I stroll right past all the shops that I'd love to stop and browse in, and I don't even glance up at the Eiffel Tower in the distance or pause to take another photograph. That's because I'm no longer just in Paris as a tourist. I'm potentially here now as a resident, although that will only be the case if I can find myself a job that will support my stay here.

After making two new friends in the club the other night, they have persuaded me to stick around and spend the entire summer in Paris. It didn't take much to convince me, not just because this city is an amazing place to live, but because it feels brilliant to have companionship after so much time on my own – not just on my travels but growing up back home too. Cecilia and Antoinette are lovely, really genuine, friendly young women who have been incredibly kind to me in many ways, and while I do feel a little guilty about giving them a false name when I met them, meaning they still think my name is Tiffany, it's hardly the worst thing in the world. If I ever do tell them the truth one day then I'll just say I was trying to reinvent myself, which is true, and hopefully, they won't mind. Besides, I do like my new name much more than my old one.

It was nice enough of Antoinette to invite me to party with her and her friend, when she met me in the nightclub and realised I was all by myself, but their generosity hasn't stopped there. After we got food together that first night, they told me about their place and how I could potentially live with them if I wanted to. It might have seemed a bit of a rush and, if I'm honest, I thought it was only something they were saying because they were both very drunk. I presumed they'd wake up the next morning, regret it and withdraw the invitation or possibly not even message me again at all. But that didn't happen. My new friends were clearly being genuine when they suggested I come and live with them in their apartment, and so I sprang into action, looking for a job, any job, as quickly as I could, so I could stay and contribute to the rent with them.

So far, my search for work has been fruitless, which is frustrating, but it's still early days. Fortunately, I budgeted for a long trip around Europe, so I have more than enough funds to last me a while. That's why Cecilia and Antoinette have been happy for me to move in with them and start contributing already. It was a joy to check out of my overcrowded hostel and move into their airy apartment, and while my new accommodation is obviously going to be a lot more expensive than my old one was, it's well worth it. The apartment is in a great location, and I can even see the Eiffel Tower from the window of it, albeit just the top of the tower, but it still counts. As for sleeping arrangements, while there are only two bedrooms in the apartment and they are both rightly claimed by Cecilia and Antoinette, there is a very comfy sofa bed, plus both girls have said they're more than happy to let me sleep in their beds from time to time, and especially if one of them ends up staying elsewhere like at a guy's place.

This is going to be so much fun. Three eighteen-year-olds, living away from home, in the city of love, free to party, date and laugh as much as we want to, without parents around to watch over us and tell us what we can and can't do. I'm so lucky that I met my new friends because, if I hadn't, I'd probably already have left Paris and moved on to the next city, as lonely as ever and on a certain path to ending up back in Arberness with Mum again. But now I have an amazing summer to look forward to and who knows how long I'll end up staying here for. But I do need a job to fund it all, so I walk into yet another restaurant, my eighth of the day, and smile widely at the first person who greets me. They clearly think I am here for a table, but I let them know that's not the case.

'I was wondering if there were any waitressing jobs going?' I ask with a smile. 'Or any jobs working behind the bar. I can do either.'

'Do you have any experience of working in a restaurant?'

This already sounds far more promising than the first few places I tried because, by this point, they had already told me that there were no vacancies and I had to scuttle away out the door in disappointment. At least it sounds like there might be a chance here.

'Yeah, loads of experience!' I say, bending the truth some-what. 'I've worked in restaurants before, back in England, as well as in a pub.'

They are lies, but needs must, and there surely isn't anyone who got a job without telling a few fibs to get it.

'Do you speak French?' is the next question and my heart sinks because while it was easy to lie about my previous work history, it's going to be impossible for me to pretend like I can speak another language when I don't.

'Erm, French? I know a few words. Enough to get by in here, I'm sure.'

But that answer doesn't go down well.

'You'll need to be fluent,' I'm told. 'Our customers aren't just tourists, we have many locals as well, and they won't be happy if they have to order in English all the time.'

'Oh, I see.'

I can feel this potential job slipping away and, sure enough, after being unable to convince that I can carry off speaking French to any diners in here, I am politely told that there are no jobs available at the moment.

'Damn it,' I say to myself as I step back out onto the street that is bathed in sunshine.

That's so annoying, but I mustn't be deterred. This is a huge city, and somebody will hire me to do something, and I don't really care what it is as long as I can stay here and keep having a great time with my new friends.

———

Deciding to call it a day, I head back to the apartment that I now call home and use the key that Antoinette lent me to get inside. She said I can have it all day as long as I'm home when she gets back from work so I can let her in, so I make sure I always do that. Entering the apartment, I pour myself a glass of orange juice before taking a seat on the sofa. Checking the time, I am pleased to see that I'll have company in the next ten minutes or so. It's just gone five o'clock so my housemates will be back soon, and it'll be nice to hear about their day at work, even if it will slightly remind me of the fact that I'm still currently jobless.

I expect Antoinette will be back first because she works closer to the apartment, but it ends up being Cecilia, and I smile as I see her enter the apartment.

'Hey! How was your day?' I ask her as she immediately goes for the fridge and takes out a soda can.

'Busy,' she replies. 'My boss took us all for lunch at this really fancy restaurant by the river. I had a couple of cocktails because everyone else was drinking, but I regretted it when I got back to my desk because could I concentrate on my work then? Nope.'

I laugh as Cecilia slumps onto the sofa beside me and cracks open her can of soft drink before taking a thirsty sip.

'How was your day? Any luck on the job front?' she asks me.

'Not yet. Came close a couple of times.'

'You'll get there. Just enjoy not having to get up early for a while yet. I'm exhausted.'

'Are we still going out tonight?'

'Hell yeah. I'll sleep when I'm dead.'

We both laugh before Cecilia takes out her phone, and I see her checking a few of her messages. I should probably do the same, but it'll only be Mum who has been in touch with me and I'm not in a massive rush to reply to her. I haven't even told her that I'm living in an apartment yet with some people I just met, so she probably presumes I'm still in a hostel or moved on already.

'Guess what? My mum is coming to see me this weekend,' Cecilia suddenly says. 'Her and my stepdad. I guess I better book a table for us to go for dinner.'

'That's nice,' I say, not expecting that it will involve me, but I'm wrong.

'You'll have to meet her. Come for dinner with us. Antoinette will be coming.'

'Oh, erm. Are you sure?'

'Yeah, of course!'

It's so nice of Cecilia to keep including me in things, and I guess this is what I've been missing by not having good friends all my life in Arberness. But then Cecilia says something that I'm not quite as happy about.

'Why don't you invite your mum to Paris too? We could get all the family visits over with in one weekend. It might be nice for our mums to hang out. That way, we could probably escape earlier and go out ourselves, leaving them to it.'

'My mum? Erm, I don't know.'

'You could ask her?'

'I could. I'm not sure I want to.'

'Just an idea,' Cecilia says. 'I guess if you're staying here then she'll want to come and visit you at some point. Might be less awkward if my mum's here too.'

I think about it and it's not a terrible idea, but I'm still not sure I want Mum coming here. Things are going well for me in my new life, so why drag my past into it?

'I'll think about it,' I tell Cecilia before we hear the buzzer to our apartment blare out, telling us that Antoinette is outside and needs letting in.

I get up to open the door for her and, as I go, I consider Cecilia's suggestion some more. Things have been hard with Mum, but maybe here, in a whole new setting and with so much excitement to be had, it might actually make things easier between us. It's either that or I carry on just ignoring her messages. I suppose I could ask her and see what she says. It's probably too short notice, but never mind. I'd probably prefer it if she said she can't come, and I'm sure she won't, so what's the harm in asking her?

TWENTY-TWO

ALICE

It's another long and lonely day in Arberness with nothing but the greetings card I am working on to keep me occupied. I'm designing a new anniversary card that I'll display for sale on my website soon, but I'm not feeling very creative today and it's showing in the quality of my work. Maybe it's because it's been a grey, dreary day here and that is causing my low mood. Perhaps it's because my recent visit to see Tomlin is still fresh in my mind and I'm feeling sorry for him. Or it could simply be because Evelyn is still not messaging me back much – we're becoming more and more distant by the day.

When I hear my phone bleep I pick it up and see that my daughter has just got in touch; my spirits soar and I'm feeling happy again.

I feel even happier when I open the message and see what she has sent me.

> *Hi, Mum. Just to let you know that I've made a couple of new friends in Paris and I'm living with them now. They're my age and both really nice. I'm looking for a job for the summer. Anyway, one of the girls has her mum coming to visit this*

*weekend and I was wondering do you want to come too? You
don't have to. Hope you're OK. Ev x*

There's a lot to make me smile in that message, not least the
fact that my daughter has said that she hopes I'm okay and
added a kiss at the end. But it's the fact that she has invited me
to go and see her in Paris that is the most heart-warming.

Is she serious?

I check the time, wondering if Evelyn might be drunk now.
Why else would she send me a message like this? But it's only
the early evening, so she might not be. If I woke up to this
message then I could put it down to her sending it after a late
night at a club, but it's been sent at a respectable hour and there
is nothing in the words that suggests she has been drinking. So I
have to assume she genuinely means it.

As I continue to get excited about my daughter possibly not
hating me anywhere near as much as I fear she does, my mind
starts racing with ways I could accept this invitation and be in
Paris this weekend. It is short notice, but I work for myself, and
my social calendar is hardly full, so I can easily find the time to
go. Why shouldn't I? I've never been to Paris, and could do with
a holiday, but it's not even about that. It's about going to see my
daughter and potentially healing a few wounds now she has left
home.

After so many years of the pair of us having arguments in
this tiny village, I am thrilled by the thought of us having some
mother–daughter time in a new city. Maybe a change of scene is
all it will take for us to settle our differences, and it sure seems
that way if Evelyn is already being more receptive to me.

Deciding not to overthink it any longer and risk my
daughter regretting it and changing her mind, I type a reply to
her as quickly as I can.

Hi, love. I'm well, thank you. So glad to hear you have made friends. Good luck on the job hunt! I'd love to come to Paris! Thank you! I'll have a look at flights now and see what time I can get there and let you know. Love Mum x

The fact that I'm almost shaking as I send that message is proof that I've hardly ever had the type of relationship with my daughter that required me to send nice messages like this one. But it feels good to be able to express my love and genuine happiness for her, and I'm just praying now that she doesn't reply by saying it was a mistake, or worse, that one of her friends had her phone and sent me the message themselves as a prank. But that doesn't happen and five minutes into me checking flights to Paris, I get another message from Evelyn.

Great. Let me know x

It's much shorter than her first message was and it's hardly full of enthusiasm, which suggests that my daughter is a little tentative about this whole idea, but it's not a withdrawal of the invitation, so that's the main thing. With the trip very much on, I get back to checking flights and see that there is one that could get me into Paris in the early evening on Friday, which would be perfect for the start of the weekend. I guess I'd come back on the Sunday or maybe I could extend my trip for a few days, seeing a little more of the city, even if Evelyn isn't free to be with me the whole time. I might as well make the most of this opportunity and I'm excited to look for hotels once this flight is booked.

The problem with being based in a place like Arberness, or at least one of the many problems, is it can be a bit of a hassle to travel abroad. There's obviously not an international airport here, nor is there one reasonably close, so I have to travel quite a way just to get to the point where I can even show my passport to somebody. I guess I'll be flying from Manchester, so that's a journey before the actual journey begins, but it's not as if I've got loads to do here. This greetings card can wait, so once I've booked the flight, I hurry into my bedroom and pull out my suitcase, keen to make a start on my packing.

I'm so out of practice when it comes to going away that I'll probably forget half the things I need, but I make sure to pack the essentials and figure I can manage if I fail to pack something that's not as urgent. The main thing is that I have my passport. There is a brief moment of panic when I open it up and fear that it might have expired, but I see that it's still in date and useable at border control.

After making a good start on the packing, I see my flight booking confirmation has come through via email, so I take a screenshot of it and send it to Evelyn so she'll know exactly when I land. Then I message her to say not to worry about meeting me at the airport – I'll just get a taxi to my hotel and then meet her wherever she is from there. It might be a little presumptuous of me to think that she was going to bother to come to the airport to greet me, but I like to imagine she would have done. But Evelyn just replies to say that sounds good, so I guess she probably wasn't going to be at the arrivals gate holding up a big sign saying: *'Welcome to Paris, Mum!'*

I spend the next hour booking the other parts of my trip, including my train from Carlisle to Manchester and also my hotel for my stay in France. I decide to book for four nights and see how it goes. I've got money saved up from doing very little over the last few years, beyond making sure the bills were paid and Evelyn had a full fridge to explore, so I'm not too worried about the cost. Besides, a trip like this is priceless and I can't wait to get going.

I can't believe I'm going to Paris.

It's going to be amazing.

A trip I'll never forget...

TWENTY-THREE

FERN

We're packed and on the road, and as the music plays on the radio and the wind blows in my hair from my open passenger side window, I can't take the grin off my face.

I'm on my way to see my daughter.

Next stop, Paris.

I send a quick message to Cecilia to let her know that we're en route and she replies to wish us a safe journey. It should take us just over an hour to get there. It would be quicker if we had some motorways to go on, but coming from the village it's all narrow, winding country lanes until we get to the city's edges, not that it is necessarily a bad thing. The view on both sides of the car is lovely, all green fields and tall trees, so I'll make the most of that before the densely packed buildings of the French capital come into view.

Pierre is at the wheel and rigidly sticking to the speed limit here, which is unsurprising because he's always been a very sensible driver, although he has to slow down when a tractor pulls out into the road ahead of us.

'Still not as bad as rush hour in Paris,' I say jokingly, but he doesn't smile as he keeps his eyes on the road ahead. He's been a little distant with me all day and I know why that is. Today is the anniversary of when we buried that body together and he's always distracted at this time of year. Not even me turning up the radio and singing a song can snap him out of his sombre mood, but I dare not mention it in case it makes him feel even worse, so instead I talk about what should be a brilliant weekend.

'Cecilia has booked a restaurant for us all tonight,' I say. 'It looks really nice.'

'All of us? Who else is going?'

'Antoinette, obviously, and their new friend Tiffany.'

'Oh, right. I thought it would just be the three of us.'

'I told you it wasn't. Weren't you listening?'

The look on Pierre's face lets me know he clearly wasn't listening, but given how distracted he has been lately, I will let him off.

'I guess this Tiffany has made a good impression on Cecilia and Antoinette if we're getting to meet her so soon,' I say.

'Yeah, I guess,' Pierre replies as the tractor continues to trundle along in front of us, and it's a relief when we see it turn off the road a few minutes later, allowing us to get back up to speed.

'So what else do you know about this Tiffany?' Pierre asks me as the countryside zips by again.

'Not much really other than they met in a club and now she is living with them.'

'Is she from Paris?'

'I don't know. I presume so.'

'They've allowed a stranger to live with them?'

'She's not a stranger. Like I said, Cecilia and Antoinette must really like her if they have been spending all this time together.'

'It's just you don't seem to know much about her, that's all.'

'Well, I can only go off what Cecilia tells me in her

messages, and she's never been the chattiest when it comes to those,' I remind my husband. 'I'm not sure why you think this is a problem.'

'I just don't like surprises, I guess.'

'It's not a surprise.'

'Fine.'

I study my husband's expression and see that he is still very distant, clearly worrying about the past, and I guess that is why he is anxious about surprises. People with secrets like us like to know exactly what we are getting ourselves into and with who, but he's being even more paranoid than me. Or maybe I just have more experience at handling my nerves than he does. After so many years of quite literally getting away with murder, I am not as on edge as I used to be, not as fearful of meeting new people and certainly not thinking everyone I do meet somehow knows my secrets. But Pierre is still there, even after years of dealing with this himself, and I bet he only feels settled when he's at home in the village, keeping his head down and going about his usual routine. Routine breeds comfort, but I want him to know that breaking our routine now isn't going to mean we end up in handcuffs.

'How do you do it?' he asks me now, breaking the silence that had fallen between us.

'Huh?'

'Live your life as if you didn't do a terrible thing? I've been wanting to ask you for years, but didn't want to dredge it all up again. But if I'm honest with you, I'm really struggling lately and I'm afraid it's going to get worse as I get older.'

'I don't live my life as if I have never done a terrible thing,' I reply, glad Pierre only knows about one of the terrible things I've done and not about all of them. 'I just live it as best I can day to day, which is all any of us can do, right? Nobody's perfect, but we get up and try and make today better than yesterday was.'

'Nobody's perfect? That's true, but that doesn't mean every-body has dug a grave and put a body in it either,' Pierre says as he turns off the radio, clearly not in the mood for music at a time like this.

'I understand that, but we did what we had to do,' I say clearly. 'What would you have preferred? Trying our luck with the police? If we'd done that then I doubt we'd be on our way to Paris now. We'd still be finishing our prison sentence.'

'Our prison sentence? I didn't kill him.'

'No, but you helped me get rid of the body.'

'Maybe that was a mistake.'

'Really? Helping your wife was a mistake?'

Pierre's silence answers that question and we say nothing more for several long minutes. I don't dare to put the radio back on, but I am worrying that the tension between us is going to carry over into our time away and spoil what should be a great weekend with Cecilia and her friends. I also get the sense that I need to nip this in the bud sooner rather than later, for fear it could have consequences for our relationship even after this weekend is over. That's why I choose to say what I do, in the hopes that it will make Pierre feel better before Paris comes into view.

'You're the bravest man I've ever met,' I say, meaning it. 'What you did for me that day was truly heroic, and you know I'll never forget it. You kept our family together. Without it, Cecilia wouldn't have the life she does now. Maybe none of us would. You're free because you helped me get rid of a horrible man who threatened us all. Remember that.'

Pierre seems to take on board what I have said, and I hope it's worked, though not everyone is like me. I've told so many lies and kept so many secrets that it's just a part of my identity now, and I often wonder if there is anything I wouldn't do to keep me and my family safe. I just really hope I never have to be put to the test ever again so I don't have to find out. As we near

Paris and the Eiffel Tower comes into view, I am anticipating nothing but a relaxing weekend filled with laughter, good food and wine, and a little pillow talk with Pierre as we lie in our luxurious hotel bed.

That's all this weekend will be about, right?

Nothing else can happen.

———

If only I'd known then what was awaiting me in this pretty city I'd have screamed at Pierre to hit the brakes and turn the car around, before urging him to speed away as quickly as he could in the opposite direction. I'd say don't stop until we get back to the village, and then I'd stay there for the rest of my life, hiding in my house and enjoying what little freedom I had left. But I wasn't to know the horrors that awaited me there, not one of us did – not me, not Pierre, not Cecilia and certainly not the people she was about to introduce me to.

We all just thought this would be a memorable weekend, and it was.

Just for all the wrong reasons.

By the time it was over, my carefully cultivated life was in ruins, and I wished I had listened to my husband's paranoia.

He's right.

The past can't stay hidden forever.

The truth will always come out and, when it does, good luck.

TWENTY-FOUR
CECILIA

'I think this is as tidy as we're able to get it,' Antoinette says as she finishes plumping up the cushions on the sofa, and as I look around the apartment, I guess she's right. Between the three of us, we've spent the last few hours trying to make our living space as clean and uncluttered as we can, so that my mum has no idea about all the junk food and drinks that have been consumed here since we moved in. This place looks almost as good as it did on the day we got the keys to it, and there's no hint of the empty pizza boxes, empty wine bottles and discarded clothes that were littering the carpets not so long ago. We even have a few scented candles to mask the smells of our recent meals, and they seem to be doing the job.

'We've done well,' Tiffany says as she admires our work, and I have to agree with her.

'It actually looks like a girl's apartment again,' I say with a laugh, as opposed to it looking like one where a group of unruly guys live. But if one thing has become clear over this past week, it's that we can make just as much of a mess in our living space as our male counterparts.

'They've checked in at the hotel and are on their way, so

they should be here any minute,' I say in relation to Mum and Pierre and their whereabouts. 'How's your mum doing?'

I look to Tiffany then and see her checking her phone, and when she does, it's better news than the last time she looked.

'She's just boarding her flight,' she tells me.

'Great, better late than never,' I say, referencing the two-hour delay Tiffany's poor mother has already endured.

'It's only a short flight, so she won't be too late,' she says. 'She could just meet us at the restaurant when she gets here.'

'I'm happy to push the meal back so we can wait for her,' I suggest, but Tiffany doesn't want to do that.

'No, it's fine. She can come and find us. I'm hungry and everyone else probably is too, so we'll stick to the plan.'

The plan is for us all to go to the restaurant around the corner, where we have a reservation for seven o'clock; it's the kind of place we wouldn't go without our parents, mainly because it's expensive, so it will help that they can cover some, if not all, of the bill.

The buzzer sound makes us all jump, as it has an annoying but hilarious habit of doing, and that must mean Mum is here.

I hope she doesn't say or do anything embarrassing, I think to myself as I go to let them in, but that remains to be seen, because parents are as unpredictable as their children at times.

'Hi!' Mum cries when she gets her first look at me in weeks, and she pulls me in for a hug before giving my arms a squeeze to make sure I haven't lost too much weight since I moved out of home, which I haven't, but she has to be sure.

'Welcome to Paris,' I say, feeling grown up that I get to say that to them, before giving Pierre a hug too.

'So this is where you're living now, is it?' he says as they follow me to where my friends are waiting in the living area. 'Great location.'

'Yeah, it's perfect,' I say before they see Antoinette and give her a hug too, happy to see my best friend is thriving here alongside me. That just leaves my new friend for them to meet.

'This is Tiffany,' I say, and Mum and Pierre keep the smiles on their faces as they greet the newest person in my life. But for some reason, Tiffany doesn't smile at first. She looks unsure, but it could just be shyness, which is sweet, if not a little unexpected, because she certainly hasn't seemed shy since I've known her.

'Lovely to meet you,' Mum says, not self-conscious at all, and she goes to embrace Tiffany too.

'And you,' Tiffany replies as they hug before Mum pulls back slightly, looking a little surprised.

'You're English?'

'Yeah,' Tiffany replies, smiling a little now, but still not looking quite as happy as she normally is.

'Oh, okay. Sorry, I just presumed you were from Paris,' Mum says before Pierre offers his greeting.

Now Mum is the one who looks awkward, and I have absolutely no idea what is going on, but it's probably just the initial stage of people getting to know each other. I'm sure everyone will loosen up when we're at the restaurant and enjoying a glass of wine.

'Let me show you around before we go for dinner,' I say, gesturing for Mum and Pierre to follow me so I can give them the guided tour of the apartment, not that it will take long.

As I head for my bedroom, I glance back over my shoulder and see Mum frowning slightly, and while Pierre looks okay, Tiffany is standing behind him and she looks pensive too. Fortunately, Antoinette is her usual self and suggests we all have a drink here before we go.

'There's a bottle of wine in the fridge,' she says breezily, and I tell her that sounds good as I show Mum and Pierre my room.

'Cosy,' is my stepdad's opinion of it, which is a polite way of saying it's tiny, but it's more than enough for what I need, which is basically a place to crash out after a night of partying. I look to Mum to see what she thinks, but she's still looking weird, like she isn't herself. She seems to have turned when she found out Tiffany was from England. Is that what it is? Is Mum worried that somehow, having this connection to the country she ran away from with me is going to be a problem for us? If so, her paranoia is in overdrive, because not every English person is a threat, only one, my dad, her ex, and he's got nothing to do with Tiffany.

'Are you okay, Mum?' I ask her.

'Yeah, fine,' she replies, seemingly snapping out of it, and she looks around my bedroom properly now. 'This is nice. Tidier than your room at home.'

'I'm a grown-up now,' I say with a laugh before we leave the room, and after I've shown them the bathroom, which is currently gleaming after we scrubbed it all and soaked almost everything we could in bleach, we rejoin my friends on the sofas.

'Here you go, guys, you must be thirsty after your drive,' Antoinette says as she hands Mum and Pierre a glass of wine. I see Tiffany already has hers, so I pick mine up and then toast to what will hopefully be a great evening.

'To tonight,' I say happily.

Everyone's glasses clink together, but not everyone seems as enthused as I am. Tiffany is still being very quiet and has barely said a word since she first met Mum. Why is that? I want to ask her if she's okay, but I don't want to put her on the spot in front of everyone else and draw more attention to the fact that she seems a little withdrawn, so I leave it. I decide to update Mum and Pierre on the part of this evening that they aren't aware of yet.

'Guess what? Tiffany's mum is on her way to Paris too, and she's coming out with us tonight as well,' I say. 'Isn't that right, Tiff?'

'Yeah,' she replies before taking a swig from her glass, and I was kind of hoping she might elaborate a little more with her answer, but it's not to be. As it is, Mum quickly fills in the silence.

'Why didn't you tell me?' she asks me, looking slightly annoyed, which is strange.

'Tell you what?'

'That Tiffany's mother is coming. That they're from England. Any details would have been helpful to know.'

'Okay, sorry. It's not a big deal, is it?'

I frown at Mum because I'm confused as to why she is seemingly annoyed at me. Antoinette clearly senses a little tension between the two of us because she asks Pierre how the drive to get here was and that breaks the ice a bit better. But there shouldn't be any ice to break, surely?

Why is there a weirdness in the room?

As we carry on making small talk, Mum seems to relax a little and that's a relief. Maybe she was just tired from the drive, or who knows, but she seems okay now. Tiffany has said a little more too, opening up as she drinks her wine, and I guess it was just nerves on her part. Maybe meeting my mum was a bigger deal for her than I thought. She probably wanted to make a good impression but felt nervous because Antoinette already knows our guests well, whereas she doesn't.

Everything seems to be going better now and, as we finish our drinks, Tiffany tells me that she has just got a message from her mum to say that she has landed.

'Great!' I say as I collect up the empty wine glasses and put them by the sink. 'Shall we make a move to the restaurant then and she can meet us there?'

'Sounds good,' Tiffany says, and we all go to leave but, just before we do, Mum excuses herself to go to the bathroom.

'It's usually you who is waiting for me,' I say jokingly as we all stop by the door to wait for Mum. Pierre chuckles, and I expect Mum to as well, but she doesn't.

She just goes into the bathroom and quickly closes the door, locking it behind her.

Is everything okay with her?

TWENTY-FIVE

FERN

Why did they have to be from England? I silently ask myself, cursing my bad luck, because what I thought was going to be a great weekend has now turned me into a nervous wreck. Tiffany would have been a baby when my story was in the British news, but my photo still occasionally gets recirculated now in the media, particularly on the anniversaries of my crimes, so she might be getting the sense that she's seen me somewhere before. And what about her mother who has apparently just landed at the airport and is on her way to meet us for dinner? Will she recognise me from the news, even after all this time has passed? Do I look different enough? Will she get a sense that I bear a resemblance to the infamous doctor's wife she recalls seeing in all the news bulletins, and if she does, what will she do about it?

I have no idea who this woman is and whether or not she will recognise me, but I'm extremely anxious and don't really want to hang around and find out. What if I make up an excuse to get out of this dinner? I could say that I'm sick, would that work? Pierre probably won't buy it because he's been with me all day and I've been fine, but I could say it has come on suddenly. I could make up some story that I feel nauseous or have a bad migraine or any other ailment that could cause me to have to miss dinner tonight. Then I could just go back to the hotel and relax there, and not have to meet Tiffany's mum or worry about whether or not she remembers seeing my face in the British tabloids almost two decades ago. Or am I overreacting? Maybe I could go to dinner, and everything will be fine. I won't be recognised as that woman who went on the run and it will just be a nice evening.

What shall I do?

I have no idea.

'Are you okay in there, Mum?'

Cecilia's question followed by her knocking on the door tells me I've already been in here too long and should come out if I don't want to make this weird for everybody waiting outside for me. As I look at my reflection in the mirror, I try to tell myself that it's impossible to be recognised after so many years, so I'll be fine. My hair's a different colour and length. I've put a little weight on, thanks to all those French pastries I can't stop eating in the village. And I've aged, the wrinkles of time adding another layer to my disguise. I'm the same woman, but I look very different, and I can't act like this every time I'm around someone from England, I try and convince myself. It just isn't healthy.

But as I turn away from the mirror and go to unlock the door, I'm still not sure what I'm going to do. It's only when I open it and see Cecilia standing on the other side of it with an excited grin on her face that I realise I can't ruin tonight. My daughter is excited to have me in Paris and show me a part of the life she is building for herself here, so I don't want to ruin that for her. I want to hear all about her new job, and what she is doing in her free time, as well as get to know her new friend a little better. Plus, I promised Antoinette's mother back in the village that I would catch up with her daughter so I have lots of news when I get back. Bless her, Antoinette's mum is not very well, so she couldn't make the trip with us, and she'll be disappointed if she finds out I didn't go out for dinner with our children while I was here.

'Sorry. I'm ready to go now,' I say, forcing a smile onto my face, and Cecilia rolls her eyes before telling everybody that we can get going.

I follow everybody out of my daughter's apartment, hoping that I'm not making a huge mistake in going ahead with this dinner. But the closer we get to the restaurant, the more I have a sinking feeling in the pit of my stomach that I can't explain or shake off.

Call it a sixth sense.

But I feel like something terrible is about to happen.

TWENTY-SIX

EVELYN

As we make the short walk from the apartment to the restaurant, I discreetly glance at Cecilia's mum a few times along the way, because there is something about her that is troubling me. I'm not sure what it is, but she seems vaguely familiar, like I've seen her somewhere before. But I surely haven't, not that it helps me shake off the sense of déjà vu that surrounds her.

It's not just me that is feeling weird. She seems a little 'off' too, like she's not quite settled. She spent an awfully long time in the bathroom before we left the apartment and, at one point, I was wondering if she even wanted to come out for dinner with us all tonight. She is still here, so I guess she does, but she did seem to lose a bit of enthusiasm around the time she found out my mum was coming.

The mention of England certainly seemed to spook her, but maybe there's just a good reason for that. Cecilia has told me all about her upbringing and how her and her mother fled home to get away from a dangerous person back there, so it's possibly just a bit of residual tension whenever she is reminded of where she came from. I'll put it down to that, although as we carry on to the restaurant, I'm still not sure what to put my sense of tension down to.

'Almost there,' Cecilia says breezily, clearly feeling fine herself about tonight – and why wouldn't she? Antoinette seems happy too, chatting away with Pierre about something to do with the village. I'm glad Mum is coming after all because I could easily end up feeling left out amongst these four who all have so much history. I'm the new one, the one that everyone is still getting to know, and I'm getting to know them, so I guess it will be nice to have a familiar face at the table.

A text from Mum says that she got through customs quicker than she anticipated and is now in the taxi headed for the restaurant. She's probably about twenty minutes behind us, but it will give us time to get seated at the table and perhaps order the first round of drinks, so I text her back to ask what she would like me to get her. I figure it'll be nice of me to have a drink waiting for her when she gets here, and it's just one small part of trying to make the effort with Mum this weekend. It might go disastrously but I should try if she's coming all this way to see me, I suppose. Maybe the distance that I created between us with my travelling will help once we're back together again. It would be nice if I had a better relationship with my mum, and maybe the key to getting that is for us to only see each other sparingly, and somewhere a bit more uplifting than Arberness.

Mum replies to tell me she fancies a glass of red wine, so I commit that to memory as we reach the restaurant doors and are welcomed in by a grinning maître d' who probably has all sorts of fancy qualifications in hospitality and fine dining. I get that impression from the way he carries the menus as he shows us to the table, as well as how he points out several things on the way like the fish tank full of lobsters, the piano where a musician will soon perform and, of course, the view from the large glass windows at the back of the restaurant that overlooks Paris and the famous tower. Then he's straight into a well-rehearsed speech about the wine options available to us, as well as the soup of the day, the chef's special and what he would personally recommend if he was dining here himself this evening.

'Thank you,' is the least we can say after listening to all of that before we are left alone for a few minutes to savour both the extensive drinks menu and the wondrous view of Paris in front of our table.

'This is amazing,' I say, meaning it, and Pierre agrees with me.

'Well done on booking this,' he tells Cecilia. 'Was it hard to get a table?'

'I have my contacts in Paris,' she replies with a wink. 'But don't get too excited. We should probably brace ourselves for when the bill comes.'

'I'm sure it won't be that expensive,' Pierre says before looking at some of the prices on his menu and raising his eyebrows.

Beside him, and opposite me, his wife sits there quietly perusing her own menu, not looking up, not saying much. I get the chance to really look at her again. It's so bizarre but I'm still getting the strangest sense that I have seen her somewhere before. But where?

Another message arrives on my phone, and I probably break one of the rules of dining in a place like this by checking it at the table, but I have to so I can see where Mum is.

'Mum's ten minutes away,' I tell the table as a waiter arrives to enquire about our drinks, and we place our orders just before we hear the first sounds coming from the piano this evening. We all turn to look in the direction of the music and see a silver-haired man in a tuxedo sitting at the keys, his eyes shut and his fingers moving from memory, as he plays a song that only adds to the ambience of this venue.

This was certainly not the kind of place I expected to find myself in when I set off on my travels. I thought I'd be eating packet noodles in a grotty kitchen surrounded by dozens of international travellers, not waiting for my wine to arrive at this immaculately set dinner table where a classical musician serenades us. I certainly didn't expect Mum to be joining me on this adventure, but she must be no more than five minutes away now and, very soon, she'll sit down in the empty seat beside me and get to know the other people we are out with this evening.

I wonder what she'll make of my new friends. She'll probably think I've landed on my feet considering the place we're eating in and the apartment I'm living in. It certainly feels quite glamorous. The longer we are here, the more Cecilia's mum seems to be relaxing. She seems to know quite a lot about several of the wines on the menu, as well as which wine would go well with the main course that her husband is thinking of ordering, and that suggests to me that she isn't entirely unaccustomed to eating in places like this. Then again, she's married to a doctor, so I bet that has given her a nice life, or at least a nice one since she got away from her ex in England.

There's something about the thought of a doctor that suddenly sends a chill through my body.

Is it because my late dad was a doctor, just like Pierre is, and it feels a little close to home? Or is it something else? I don't know, but I find myself staring at Cecilia's mum again, only this time, I get caught.

'Are you okay, Tiff?' Cecilia asks me, clearly having noticed me eyeballing her mother.

'Erm, yeah, fine,' I say, but it's no good – it's been too obvious that I'm not fine and my friend knows it.

'What is it?' she persists, and everyone at the table is looking at me now, the only noise the sound of the perfectly played piano in the background.

'It's just...' I begin before wondering if I shouldn't say it. But everyone is still looking at me, waiting for an answer, including

Cecilia's mum, so I look at her again and tell the truth. 'Well. It's just that I think I recognise you from somewhere, that's all.'

'You recognise my mum?' Cecilia asks as she looks between the two of us before laughing. 'That's weird.'

Antoinette laughs too. But Cecilia's mum isn't laughing. She just looks down at the table and then puts a hand to her stomach.

'Oh no. I felt a bit queasy back in your bathroom,' she says. 'I have a bit of an upset stomach and I'm afraid I'm not going to be able to enjoy the food tonight. I might have to go back to the hotel.'

That just seems like very bad acting to me, but both Pierre and Cecilia seem to buy it and ask if she is okay. She says not, but she seemed fine to me a minute ago, at least until I said that I recognised her. But before anyone can say anything else, Mum arrives at the table.

'Hi!' she says when she sees me, and I get up quickly to give her a hug, which should help her feel more at ease around all these other strangers. It should also make it look like we have somewhat of a normal relationship, because I don't want Cecilia's family thinking we're weird.

It is nice to hug, which is a rarity, and as we separate Mum says what a nice restaurant this is before looking at the rest of the people I'm with.

That's when her face drops in horror. She's now staring at the same person I was just staring at, except there is one crucial difference.

I only thought I recognised Cecilia's mother.

But it's clear my mum knows exactly who she is.

TWENTY-SEVEN
ALICE

How has this happened?

'Fern?' is the only thing I can say as I stare at the face of the woman who I never thought I'd have to lay eyes on again.

It's a face that has changed since I last saw it, but that's just what the best part of twenty years will do. It's still her, of course it is. I'd recognise those features anywhere, even with a few wrinkles and a new hairstyle. I'd recognise her face even in this unusual setting of a fancy restaurant in the middle of Paris. We are a hell of a long way from Arberness, or Cornwall, the places I associate this woman with, but there's no denying it is her; although, bizarrely, it seems that is what Fern is going to try and do now.

'Excuse me?' she says, looking puzzled, but I can also see the shock in her expression, and she is as caught off guard by this as I am. She isn't doing a very good job of pretending like I have made a mistake. She must recognise me too – there's no way she can't. We have far too much history.

'Who is Fern?' the man at the table asks now and, to be fair to him, the confusion on his face does seem genuine. I'm guessing Fern has a new man in her life and has been keeping secrets from him, but that's hardly a shock. What is a shock is the fact that I'm confronted with my past again and, more specifically, I'm face to face with the doctor's wife once more. She's been on the run for so long that I'm convinced the police back in England have given up looking for her. Maybe they've even forgotten about her by now. *But I never did.*

'You know it's me,' I say to Fern. 'Alice.'

Fern hears my name but still pretends like she has no idea who I am, unlike the others at the table who genuinely don't know.

'Evelyn, we need to go,' I suddenly say to my daughter, still feeling utterly clueless as to what I have walked into, but feeling like the only thing that is best for my child is to remove ourselves from this situation as quickly as possible. But not just best for us, best for everyone at this table, because besides Fern, how much do they all know about her, if anything? I can see two other young women sat at this table with my daughter, though I have no idea who they are. Fern had a young daughter of her own with her the last time we were together, so I guess one of these women must be her. The other might be a friend, or maybe Fern has two daughters now. Whatever the case, Fern's entire family is at risk of blowing up if this gets any worse, and despite the past, Fern still saved my child's life. I'm willing to walk away again, especially as walking away is the safest thing anyone can do in Fern's presence.

'Evelyn?' one of the young women says. 'I thought your name was Tiffany?'

That only confuses me even more and I look to my daughter, but she isn't getting up out of her seat yet and leaving like I suggested we should. She is simply staring at Fern before looking back to me, seemingly for confirmation.

'Fern?' she says in an inquisitive tone before realising she doesn't need me to even answer. She already had a feeling something was wrong about this woman. 'Oh my God, it's you! I knew I recognised you from somewhere! You're the evil bitch who killed my dad!'

Evelyn does get out of her seat now but only to lunge across the table at Fern, who quickly gets out of the way, aided by the man beside her who puts an arm out to keep Evelyn at a distance. But the noise she has made disrupts the entire restaurant and, as the piano stops playing, we become the main source of entertainment for the other diners.

'What the hell are you doing? That's my mum!' the nearest young woman to Fern says, so I guess this must be Cecilia, the baby I met briefly so many years ago in Cornwall. 'Are you okay, Mum? What's going on?'

Cecilia looks at Fern, concerned for her wellbeing, because Fern looks like she is going to pass out. She's gone as white as a ghost and looks like she would collapse to the floor if it wasn't for the fact that her partner and her daughter are holding her upright.

'Evelyn! Let's go,' I say, fearing this is only going to end badly if my daughter keeps pushing Fern; every time this woman is backed into a corner, she always gets away, but not before somebody else has died.

But Evelyn is in no mood for doing what I did so many years ago and allowing Fern to walk away. To make that point most dramatically, she picks up a knife from the table and points the sharpest edge towards Fern.

'I know it's you and you're not getting away this time!' Evelyn cries.

One of the waiters rushes over to try and defuse the situation. I don't envy him – if he had any idea what was really going on then he would know that defusing it is impossible now. I already know that, which is why my only hope is to drag Evelyn out of here before she can use that knife and end up in a Parisian prison, or worse, before Fern gets hold of it and uses it to defend herself.

'Evelyn, please!' I try again, grabbing her arm that holds the knife, but her strength surprises me, though maybe it shouldn't. My daughter has gone her entire life hating the circumstances in which she grew up, and now she has come face to face with the cause of all of them. She's never going to back down, and I think Fern understands that at the same moment as I do, because she suddenly turns to leave.

'We have to go now!' Fern cries. 'These people are dangerous!'

It's hard to argue against that when Evelyn is holding a knife, so her partner and daughter quickly follow her, though the other young woman just stays in her seat, seemingly frozen in fear or just stunned into staying seated. We watch the three family members leaving the restaurant. But at least they're leaving. I am stunned by how randomly my path just crossed with Fern's again; I also know we're lucky that no blood was shed like the previous times.

And then Evelyn goes after Fern with the knife still in her hand.

'No!' I cry as I try to catch my daughter before she is past me. But it's too late, so all I can do is chase her as she chases Fern and her family out of the restaurant. We hurriedly leave behind all the gawking diners and the horrified wait staff who can do nothing but watch us go.

'Evelyn! Stop! She's dangerous!' I cry out as I chase my daughter out onto the street, but she's not slowing down, and as several pedestrians hastily step out of her way, I realise it's going to be impossible to stop her using that knife on Fern because I simply can't catch her. But I can't give up either, so I keep running and calling out to my daughter as we move onto another street and more pedestrians dart out of our way.

I hear a car horn up ahead and see Fern narrowly avoid getting struck by a vehicle in her desperation to get away, but it allows Evelyn to make up some ground on her. Now I'm just hoping that the man Fern is with can stop my daughter from causing devastation with that knife.

We're onto a bigger street now and, as I see Fern and her family run across the road, several cars have to slam on their brakes. I fear that Evelyn is about to be knocked down by a speeding vehicle when she attempts to cross. And then I hear a sickening thud – that's when I realise that one of the cars wasn't able to slow down quickly enough to avoid the people running out in front of them.

At first, I fear that my daughter has come to harm. But it's not her who has been hit. She has stopped right on the edge of the pavement. I wonder if it is Fern, the woman who has caused all this, and I think about what it would feel like to see her dead body. But it's not her either, because I can see that she has made it across the road and is standing opposite, although she has turned back to the accident too. Then I see Cecilia is with her, which means there is only one person missing.

That's when I see Fern's partner lying face down in the middle of the road.

The car that hit him has a damaged front bumper, and the driver of the vehicle has got out from behind the wheel and is holding his head in his hands as he tries to come to terms with what just happened. It seems as bad as it looks because the victim isn't moving. I'm not the only one who knows it. As my eyes meet Fern's across the busy, crowded road, where so many motorists and pedestrians have stopped to stare too, I see that she knows that the man she was just with is no longer with us.

That's when I grab hold of Evelyn and tell her that we need to get out of here now, before the police arrive, or worse, before Fern does something in retaliation.

This time, finally, my daughter agrees with me.

TWENTY-EIGHT

FERN

'Pierre!'

I rush back onto the road to get to my husband, not worrying about being hit by any traffic myself because everything has come to a standstill around me. The road is totally blocked, because the man I love is lying on the tarmac, and since he got hit by that car, he hasn't moved yet.

'Pierre! Can you hear me?'

I reach him and check for signs of life, hoping to see him move or hear him make a noise, but when he doesn't, I check for a pulse on the side of his neck. I can't feel one, but that could just be because of the awkward position he is in. He's currently face down, though I know better than to try and roll him over on to his back, as that could make whatever injuries he has sustained even worse. I am desperate to get just one sign of life from him so that I can at least feel like the emergency service workers who will eventually come here will have something to work with. But as I stare at Pierre's unmoving body and see blood on both his head and his back, I fear for the worst – and I'm not the only one.

'Is he dead?' the frightened voice behind me says, and I turn around to see Cecilia looking down. Behind her, I see somebody on their phone, and I presume they are calling for help. Then I look around and see several other faces just watching me, waiting to see what happens next. But the faces of Alice and Evelyn are not amongst them, though it remains to be seen if that is a good or bad thing.

I have no idea how this could have happened. How my daughter ended up becoming friends with Alice's daughter and how we all came to be at the same table in a restaurant in Paris, with my real identity revealed and the person whose life I once saved then chasing me through the streets with a knife. But right now, the most important thing is protecting my daughter, and that means helping her as she tries to process the fact that the man who she has known since she was just five years old is now lying bloodied and bruised before her.

'I don't know. I mean, no, he's not dead. He just needs help,' I say before raising my voice so everyone else around here can hear me. 'He needs help! Call for an ambulance! Please, help him!'

The doctor on the ground urgently needs care himself, and the sound of sirens in the distance tells me it is on the way. That was quick, but I suppose if there is anywhere to have an accident, the middle of one of the busiest cities in the world is the best place – it'll never take long for aid to arrive. Until it does, I can only sit with Pierre and tell him that he's going to be okay while praying that he can not only hear me but that I am telling him the truth.

Cecilia doesn't say anything more, simply standing and staring at me on the ground in front of her. An ambulance arrives and the paramedics disembark before quickly getting to work. I get out of the way so they can examine the patient, and I am hoping there is going to be some positive news in a moment. Miraculously, I seem to get my wish, because they don't confirm that the patient is dead, instead looking to safely try and move him as quickly as possible, supporting his neck before he is put onto a bed and carried into the back of the ambulance. I quickly follow and am allowed in, as is Cecilia, and the pair of us watch on in horror and hope as Pierre is worked on. The ambulance doors slam shut and we are on the move.

As we race through the streets of Paris to get to the nearest hospital, I watch as a pair of paramedics do all they can to give their colleagues at the A&E department something to work with when they deliver the patient there. My husband is hooked up to a heart monitor, given oxygen and, terrifyingly, revived once with a defibrillator. He's clinging on to life, but is clearly in a bad way, and the paramedics seem to know it because whenever I ask them what is going on or if he is going to be okay, they either tell me that they're trying their best or they tell me to be quiet.

Cecilia is still not saying anything, so it's hard to know exactly what she is thinking. I am guessing, or maybe hoping, that her only concern is for Pierre's health, but I'm aware that after what was said at that restaurant, she might be thinking about the thing I was accused of and the name I was called. Alice called me by my real name of Fern, a name that Cecilia has never known me by, while Evelyn said that I killed her father.

What does Cecilia make of all that?

I tried to emphasise that we were in danger, that we had to leave that restaurant, and was able to make it to that road with Pierre and Cecilia seemingly on my side before my husband's accident. But now, I fear it's over, and whatever happens to my husband, I'm going to have some tough questions to answer from him and my daughter. But I'd rather have Pierre alive to ask me those questions than have him die without ever getting to tell him that I'm sorry and I really do love him despite my lies, so I push all the frightening thoughts of the future out of my head for the time being and just keep urging the paramedics to save him.

Unfortunately, by the time we make it to the hospital, the heart monitor has stopped showing signs of life and the repeated usage of the defib is not working like it did before. I hear lots of hurried sentences in French, and my understanding of the language is enough to decipher one of them, though I wish I couldn't when I hear it.

'We're losing him.'

'No! Keep trying!' I cry with tears running down my face, and now Cecilia is crying too. But despite the best efforts of the paramedics, as the ambulance doors are opened and somebody else comes in to assist, it's obvious that the rush to get him inside is over.

Pierre has gone.

His death is confirmed to me by a senior doctor at the hospital half an hour later, but his words are just a blur of noise to me, although one thing he says does stick out more than the rest.

'Police.'

Of course they will be involved, because there will have to be an investigation into how a man came to be struck by a car and died. I'm sure the driver of the vehicle involved has already been spoken to at the roadside, and I imagine he has told them the truth, which is that Pierre ran out in front of the traffic along with two other people. A few witnesses might also have spoken to the police and backed up that account, but possibly mentioned that the people they saw run into the road were being chased. The police will want to speak to me and find out why we were running, and I have no idea what I am going to say to them when they ask. I also have no idea if Alice and Evelyn are going to be speaking to the police either, but I can't even think about that right now because I've just lost my husband and my daughter has lost a man she loved like a father. That's why I make sure to stay with her as we are taken into a private room, and I want to ensure she is okay before I worry about the police.

'Come here,' I say, attempting to hug her, but she recoils when I get close.

'Get away from me!' Cecilia cries, looking angry. 'And you can stay away from me until you tell me the truth!'

'The truth?'

'Who are you?'

'What? It's me, your mother.'

'Why did they call you Fern? And why did Tiffany, or Evelyn, or whatever her name is, say you killed her dad?'

I guess I'm really having this conversation.

'I don't know. I...'

It's my natural tendency to lie my way out of trouble, and only when the lie doesn't work do I resort to violence, but this is different. This is my daughter, so it's harder to lie to her, especially now she's grown up, and as for violence, there's no way I'd ever do anything to hurt her, no matter if it's a matter of protecting my secret or not. That's why I stop the line of thought I was having, the one in which I was just going to play dumb, and change tack because now Pierre is dead, I don't see how this can get much worse, especially when Cecilia says what she does next.

'If you don't tell me the truth then you'll never see me again,' my daughter says, leaving me in no doubt as to what will happen if I even try and slip another lie past her. So I won't bother. Why would I? She already has my real name and what I've done to go off; it won't take her long to fill in the blanks on the internet. So here goes...

'I haven't been honest with you,' I begin with, feeling even more nervous now than I did before Drew died and I went from being an innocent member of the public to a criminal. 'I told you that we left England because I had an abusive partner. But that wasn't the truth. The truth is...'

This is so hard. Harder than taking another life, or at least it feels like it in this moment, in this quiet, private part of the hospital where so many other lives are being saved in the rooms around us.

'The truth is, we left England because I was on the run from the police,' I say, shaking as I speak. 'I still am on the run from them to this day.'

'You're on the run? What did you do?'

Where do I even begin?

'I made some mistakes. Handled things the wrong way. I—'

'What did you do?'

Cecilia isn't going to let me be vague.

'I found out my husband was having an affair. So I came up with a plot to have him killed and for his mistress to be framed for it.'

Cecilia looks mortified, but she barely even knows the half of it, though she starts to fill in some of the blanks herself.

'That was Evelyn's dad?' she asks and, when I nod, she figures that the woman she just met at dinner tonight must have been who my late husband cheated on me with.

She already knows far more than I ever wanted her to, but currently, she doesn't seem to have made the connection that I am the doctor's widow made infamous in the British newspapers.

'You killed your husband and framed his mistress,' she says, repeating the facts back to herself. 'That's why you ran? That's why I've had to go my whole life being told that England was this scary place that I could never go to?'

'I was trying to protect us.'

'You were trying to protect yourself!' Cecilia cries, tears in her eyes now as she learns who her mother really is. 'You selfish bitch! You've ruined people's lives and lied to me every single day, and now Pierre is dead because of you!'

'That wasn't my fault! I didn't chase him into traffic,' I try, but I know it's pointless because of course I'm to blame and Cecilia knows it. But before she can say anything else, and before I have to make the grim decision about whether or not I tell her anything more, including what really happened to her dad, we are interrupted by a police officer entering the room.

'I just need to ask you a few questions,' the pensive looking man says, probably because he's aware that we've just lost a loved one and now he has to bring more stress to our lives. But he has no idea just how much stress the two of us are really under.

Yes, we're mourning Pierre, but we're mourning something else too.

We're mourning the fact that we're no longer the loving mother and daughter duo that we thought we were. And things are only likely to get worse from here, starting with answering the police officer's first question.

'Why was the deceased running into traffic?'

TWENTY-NINE
CECILIA

I've seen a man I've loved for most of my life die in front of me, and then found out my mum is a pathological liar, who is not only capable of plotting somebody's murder but getting away with it.

So the question has to be; why am I helping her right now?

'We thought we heard somebody shout the word terrorist behind us,' I say in answer to the police officer's question as to why we ran into traffic.

'Terrorist?'

'Yeah, there was panic. I thought other people were running. But it all happened so fast. I don't know what was going on.'

I look to Mum so that she knows to take over the lie, and perhaps unsurprisingly, given how good she is at this, she doesn't skip a beat.

'We thought we were in danger,' she says. 'We tried to cross the street as quickly as we could, but Pierre got hit and...'

Her voice trails off now because we all know what happened next, but she's said all she needed to and, more importantly, left out what she needed to. Neither of us mention the fact we were being chased because my mum had just been unmasked as the criminal she is. But I'm only helping because I feel there is far more that I need to know about it all yet, and I'll only get the chance to talk to Mum and get those answers quicker if she isn't arrested by this officer. I might want her arrested in future if I deem her lies to be too much for me to bear, but for now, I want her free so she can tell me everything, and I can let her know exactly how it feels to have been lied to for all these years.

'None of the witnesses have mentioned anything about a panic or hearing the word terrorist,' the police officer says, and it's hard to tell if he is just stating a fact and nothing more, or coolly pouring doubt onto our version of events. But Mum and I both share a look before sticking to our story.

'Like I said, it all happened really fast. I didn't really know what was going on,' I repeat before rubbing a hand over my weary face in the hopes that this police officer will get the hint – I'm emotionally exhausted and he should leave us alone for a while. Thankfully, he does just that, offering us his condolences before mentioning that we have to make official statements at a more suitable time. Then we're left alone. But while Mum might be breathing a sigh of relief, I quickly make it clear that this is far from over yet.

'Pierre was a good man,' I say defiantly. 'And because you lied to him, he is dead. He never would have been with you if he knew what you had done.'

'Don't you think I know that?' Mum says, surprising me a little. 'I'm well aware that he would have hated me, just like everybody back in England hates me too. But I was trying to give us a good life. I wanted you to have as normal a childhood as I could give you. That meant I had to take you away to some-where new, somewhere safe, and build a life for us there. It also meant allowing myself to trust another man again so you could have a father figure in your life.'

'But you took away another person's father figure!' I cry. 'Somebody lost their dad because of you.'

Then I realise Mum must have been lying to me about my own dad. If he wasn't some fictitious abusive ex, who was he?

'Where is my father?' I ask nervously. 'What happened to him?'

'Cecilia, please—'

'Where is he?' I repeat, in no mood for Mum's stalling tactics.

'I don't know,' is her response.

'What do you mean you don't know?'

'Please, just believe me when I say that it is better if you don't make me talk about this.'

'Better for who? Me or you?'

'For both of us! I love you and I'm trying to keep this family intact!'

'What family?'

My loud question makes Mum shut up, but I don't try and sugarcoat what I just said.

'This isn't a proper family. I don't know my mum or my dad! At least my dad has an excuse to be a stranger to me. I've never met him before and I don't know if I ever will. But I've known you my whole life and you're still a stranger to me! You're a liar and you've not just ruined other people's lives, you've ruined mine too!'

I've had enough of Mum now and I need to get out of this room, especially because it's obvious she isn't willing to tell me anything more. It's also obvious that something terrible happened with Dad; but if she won't tell me the truth, I know a couple of people who surely will. But before I can get away, Mum comes after me and stops me in the doorway before I can escape out into the corridor.

'Cecilia, please. Just calm down and let's talk about this.'

'I'm trying to talk about it, but you're not telling me the

truth, and I told you what would happen if you did that. I'm gone!'

I try to pull away, but Mum holds firm.

When did she get so strong?

'I'm trying to protect you,' Mum says. 'Why won't you let me do that?'

'Protect me from what?'

'Everything!'

That's a cryptic answer and it doesn't tell me anything, so what's the point of me staying?

'Get off me!' I cry, and while Mum says no to that, she has little choice but to loosen her grip on me when a nurse walks past our room and turns her head to see what all the noise is about. No sooner has Mum let go of me than I am away, running down the corridor. I hear Mum calling for me to come back, as well as the nurse asking her if everything is okay, but I don't stop. I am running through the hospital, trying to find my way out of here through this maze of corridors. I eventually manage it and suck in mouthfuls of fresh air once I'm outside, where I see several ambulances parked up as well as a few patients sitting on benches or in wheelchairs, smoking or chatting or just having a break from the dreary environment inside. They might get out of here alive, but Pierre never will, and I feel sick at the thought of his body growing cold as it lies on a bed somewhere in the building behind me. That only makes me want to get even further away from this place as fast as I can, so I hail a taxi and, once I'm in it, it's a relief that I don't see Mum running outside to stop the driver taking us away.

I can't relax once we're on the road because this isn't over yet. It's not even close, and I don't know how it is going to end. All I know is that Mum is not who she says she is, and I want to learn more. But I can't trust her not to lie. I have to learn it from somebody who will tell me the truth, as bad as it may be, and that's why I have to find Tiffany, or Evelyn, which is apparently her real name. They could be anywhere in this city and may very well be planning to leave it quickly based on the fact they chased a man to his death on the city streets. But at some point, surely Evelyn will go back to the apartment to get her things. Her passport will be there, so she can't leave Paris, meaning there is a chance I could catch them at the apartment before they vanish, potentially forever.

If I get to them then I might finally know the truth, not just about Mum, but about my life.

If I miss them, I'll be left with questions that might haunt me until the end of my days.

I have no choice.

I have to find Evelyn before she leaves.

Or before Mum finds her first and shuts her up.

THIRTY

EVELYN

No matter how hard I try, I just can't get the image out of my head.

The image of that man flying through the air before landing hard on the concrete road.

He has to be dead, there's no way he could have survived that. The car was going too fast; he landed terribly; he didn't get up. He didn't even move at all.

I saw a man die right in front of me.

My body is cold, shaky and weak, and I guess this is what shock feels like. I don't know how long it's been since I saw that man get hit by the car, but everything that has happened since has been a blur.

'We have to go!' she urges me as she pulls on my hand, the one that doesn't have a knife in it. 'Evelyn, quick! We have to get out of here now!'

I understand the need for urgency, but it's impossible to tear myself away from the sight in front of me. I am staring at the body in the middle of the road and praying it shows a sign of life, any sign, so that I will at least know that I haven't just inadvertently chased this man to his death. He hasn't moved, so I haven't been able to get that reassurance I am so desperately seeking. All I have are the facts, which are that I chased this man into traffic while running after his wife with a knife, and because of that he is dead and, technically, I am guilty of causing this to happen.

But it isn't just me who knows it. Mum knows it too, which is why she is so keen for me to get away from the scene as quickly as possible.

'Evelyn! Listen to me! We need to go, or you'll be arrested! Do you want to go to prison?'

It's only now that I'm able to avert my eyes from the body and I look at Mum to see how worried she is for me. I know she is right. I have to run, or I'll be blamed for this. But it isn't really my fault. It's the fault of the woman who is now going to check on the body.

I get a glimpse of Fern rushing back into the congested road, seeing her weaving between the stationary vehicles as she tries to get to her husband as quickly as possible, and I see how upset she is at what just happened. I know she is the one to blame for this because I had been chasing her and for good reason. She's the notorious Fern Devlin and she killed my dad. She's been on the run ever since. But now I know what she feels like, because I just killed somebody.

Now I'm running too.

I follow Mum as she drags me away, away from the body and from Fern and Cecilia and any of the drivers and pedestrians and anybody else who might have seen what happened. Away too from the paramedics on their way and the police officers coming to arrest somebody for this incident. We keep running until we are a safe distance from the scene, and we only stop when I tell Mum that I physically can't run anymore. But it isn't fatigue that causes me to stop. It's the feeling of being overwhelmed by everything that has happened. I need a break. I need a minute. Unfortunately for me, Mum keeps saying we have to keep going.

'We have to get out of Paris as quickly as we can,' she says to me as I hear sirens in the distance. 'We have to go to the airport and get the first flight out of here. Or take the Eurostar. Whichever's going to be quickest. But we have to go, and we have to go now!'

Mum seems to think our next move is simple, but how can it be when there is still so much unresolved?

'What about Fern?' I ask.

'What about her?'

'She'll get away again!'

'I don't care! We have to get away or we'll be blamed for what just happened!'

'But it was her fault! I had to chase her! For Dad!'

It made so much sense for me at the time to go after Fern, even if it was dangerous and stupid to do so, because what else could I have done? Shrugged my shoulders and told Fern that all was forgiven? I'm not Mum. I can do better than that. Or at least I thought I could.

There are more sirens filling the night air and I imagine the first responders are already on the scene now, trying to revive the victim. But will they be successful? I need to know, but Mum doesn't seem to care.

'Don't you see? This is what I tried to tell you whenever you blamed me for letting Fern get away the last time. Death follows that woman everywhere! It's not worth trying to stop her because somebody always gets hurt and it's always somebody else, never her! Now that man might be dead, and we'll get blamed for it, and she'll vanish like she always does. This is just how it works with her. But I'm not going to let her send you to prison like she sent me there! We have to go *now!*'

Mum pulls on my hand again, but this time she grabs the one with the knife in it, and I drop it. It clatters loudly on the floor and attracts the attention of a pedestrian walking on the other side of the road. Mum picks it up quickly and tells me we need to get rid of it because it won't look good if the police find us with it. She then tosses it into a bin before urging me to move again.

I realise now she is right. I see why she left Fern. Bad things follow that woman around and this is bad, very bad. The sirens are proof of that. For so much of my life, I've been wanting revenge for my father, a man I never met and who has been dead for years. But now I see that I should have been more focused on my mother, a woman who has dedicated a large portion of her life to raising me. Now I need to make sure that the pair of us are safe – we're the only ones left alive for Fern to potentially hurt, which is nothing that Mum hasn't been trying to tell me herself for years.

'Okay,' I say, agreeing to Mum's plan that we should leave Paris as quickly as we can before things get any worse for us. But then I realise there is just one small problem with that plan.

'My passport!' I cry. 'It's at the apartment!'

Mum's face drops when she realises I don't have the one thing I need to get out of the country.

'We'll have to go and get it,' I say, and there really is nothing else we can do.

'Quickly!' Mum cries. 'Which way is it?'

I point the way and set off with Mum following behind me, the sirens growing louder by the second.

It only takes us five minutes to get to the apartment and I'm glad I still have Antoinette's key to get in, otherwise I really would be screwed. Gaining access, I rush inside and grab my bag before checking inside it that the passport is where it should be. I find it zipped inside the inner pocket, and once Mum sees it, she tells me it's time to go. So many of my things are strewn around the apartment, like my clothes and toiletries, so I start gathering them up too.

'What are you doing? Come on!'

Mum drags me away and now we're back at the door, which we're just about to leave through as soon as I pull it open when...

'Antoinette!'

I almost drop my bag in surprise when I see my friend standing outside. I haven't seen her since we left her behind at the restaurant and, only a second ago, I never thought I'd see her again.

'What the hell is going on?' Antoinette asks angrily. 'What was all that about at the restaurant?'

As crazy as it is, I realise Antoinette only knows half of what has happened tonight and has no idea about the accident after we left the restaurant. That's a good thing, but it's still bad that she's interrupted our escape, and I'm not sure what to tell her.

'It's a long story, but we have to go,' Mum says, answering for me, and she pulls me past Antoinette.

'A long story? What is going on?' Antoinette cries, but it looks like the plan is for us both to ignore her and keep going – it seems like it's working too.

Right up until the moment somebody else arrives outside the apartment.

THIRTY-ONE
CECILIA

I didn't know where to go when I left Mum at the hospital, so I came straight back to the apartment and it's a good job I did, because if I hadn't, it looks like I would have missed Evelyn and Alice trying to escape. They both look surprised to see me, but I can't say I'm surprised to see them wanting to get out of here as quickly as they can.

'Where are you going?' I ask them as they stand before me, their bags with them and Antoinette standing just behind them.

Neither Alice nor Evelyn says anything, so I ask them again, trying to keep calm.

'Where are you going?'

'Is he okay?' Evelyn asks me, which at least shows that she cares about the devastation she just helped cause.

'What do you think?' I reply coldly, and Evelyn gets the message, tears welling in her eyes as the full horror of the situation dawns on her. But just in case she still thinks there is hope, I make it clear.

'He's dead. I left Mum at the hospital with him. Well, Mum and the police.'

'Pierre's dead?' Antoinette asks in horror, and I nod my head sadly.

'The police?' Alice says, looking as upset as her daughter now.

'Yeah. They have lots of questions about what happened.'

'Oh God,' Evelyn cries.

'But not as many questions as I have,' I say before Evelyn can get any more upset.

'We're terribly sorry about what happened. We didn't mean for Pierre to get hurt,' Alice pleads. 'It was an accident. We were in shock. We never expected to see...'

'Just tell me the truth about my mother,' I snap back. 'That's all I want. If you do that, maybe I'll let you walk away before the police find you.'

Standing on the street outside an apartment might not be the best place to have a conversation like this, but I don't think there's going to be anywhere that will make it any easier, so I wait for Alice or Evelyn to give me the facts, however horrible they are.

'Your mother has done some terrible things,' Alice says, speaking first. 'She's hurt so many people, including myself. But I'm one of the lucky ones. I'm still alive. Many others aren't.'

'Like your father,' I say quietly to Evelyn, and she nods.

'I had an affair with Fern's husband,' Alice goes on. 'That was my fault and I take my share of the blame for that, but I could never have known what Fern would do if she found out about it. When she found out about it. I could never have known she would plot with Rory, my partner at the time, to kill Drew. And then she killed Rory afterwards. I was framed for Drew's death and went to prison, and it looked like I would be there forever. The only reason I got out is because somebody helped me.'

Alice stops talking, clearly on the verge of saying something even more difficult than what she has already said.

'It was your father,' she eventually tells me. 'He's who got me out of prison. But he lost his life in doing so. Fern killed him. She killed him when she realised he had tricked her into confessing to her previous crimes. That's when she went on the run.'

The true severity and horror of what my mother has been capable of hits me like an avalanche, and any thoughts I had about this being some kind of mistake or overreaction are wiped away in an instant. It's as bad as it could be. The last memory I have of my mother being a loving parent vanishes in that split second, as I realise how awful a person she really is.

'How did she get away with all that for so long?' I ask. 'How could the police not catch her?'

'She's so clever,' Alice says, almost respectfully. 'And lucky. It's a combination of things, but she's always gotten away with it.'

'She could have been stopped,' Evelyn says now, looking to her mother.

'I had the chance to have her arrested once,' Alice admits to me. 'When you were just a baby. But I let her go.'

'Why?' I ask, amazed this all could have ended back when I would have been too young to remember any of it.

'She saved my daughter's life,' Alice says, looking lovingly at Evelyn. 'I couldn't punish her after that, so I gave her a chance. I let her go and she vanished. I haven't seen her since. Until tonight.'

I process it all in the very limited time available, before asking the most obvious question I have.

'Are you still willing to let her get away with it?' I ask Alice, and she nods her head.

'Yes. I can't hate that woman, despite what she has done, because without her Evelyn wouldn't be here.'

I look to Evelyn, because I suspect she has a different opinion based on how she chased Fern out of that restaurant.

'What about you?' I ask. 'Are you going to let her go again?'

'She should pay for what she has done,' Evelyn replies, looking scared in the moment, but clearly still passionate about hurting my mother. 'She might have saved my life once, but she has ended others' and that's not right.'

Evelyn looks like she has more to say on this matter, but the sound of a siren in the distance seems to focus her mind.

'I don't want to get into trouble,' she says, fearing the police's arrival. 'I'm sorry about what happened tonight.'

I can see that both Alice and Evelyn are afraid of the repercussions of Pierre's death, and I can't blame them, because it must be very frightening to be in another country and fearing arrest. I can also see that none of this is their fault, not really. So much of what has happened in their lives has been a reaction to something my mum did. While it might have all started with Alice's regrettable affair, it has ended here, with several innocent people paying for my mother's mistakes.

I say nothing as I step aside, clearing the way for Alice and Evelyn to leave and carry on to where they were going before I interrupted them. I'm guessing it's the airport, or possibly the train station, but wherever it is, I don't wish to hold them up any longer, not now they have told me the truth.

Alice looks keen to leave and makes a move, but Evelyn doesn't want to go quite so fast.

'What about the police?' she asks me nervously.

'I'll deal with them,' I say, hoping that gives her a little comfort during her journey home.

'What about your mum?' she asks me, perhaps more anxiously.

'Leave her to me,' I say coolly before I walk into the apartment, leaving Alice and Evelyn to make their escape behind me.

I hear Antoinette following me into the apartment and I

know she's going to have a million questions, which she does, although the first one she asks me is rather sweet.

'Are you okay?' she wants to know, and while I could have fought back my tears if she'd asked me about Mum or Pierre or any of the horrible things I've learnt about tonight, it's that one question that cuts through my defences, and before I know it I'm crying on my best friend's shoulder. It takes a while for the tears to stop, but when they have, Antoinette starts again with the questions, though I am not in any mood to answer them. Perhaps her most pertinent question is what I plan to do next, but while I don't tell her, I already have something in mind. That's why I go into my bedroom, and when my friend isn't looking, I put my passport into a small rucksack along with a few items of clothing and my purse.

'I need to go for a walk and clear my head,' I say when I emerge from my bedroom. Antoinette offers to come with me, but I refuse. 'I just really need to be on my own right now,' I say before telling her that I'll be back, as the police will probably be here to ask some more questions soon.

'What shall I say to your mum if she comes back and asks where you are?' Antoinette wants to know as I open the door, and that's a good question.

'Tell her I don't want to see her yet,' I say with my rucksack on my shoulder. 'I'll let her know when I'm ready again.'

I leave and head down the street, my pace brisk and my mind focused, despite the chaos of the evening so far. I would have thought that at such a crazy time as this, my thoughts would be erratic, and I'd have no idea what to do next, but that hasn't been the case. What I need to do next has come to me loud and clear, and while it terrifies me to even consider going through with it, I feel like it is the right course of action. That doesn't mean it's the best course of action, but how this all plays out remains to be seen.

I keep walking until I reach the station, then I go inside and check the departure screens. Despite my grave misfortune tonight, I'm in luck now because I see there is a service due to depart here in thirty minutes, so I don't waste any time and go straight to the employee behind the desk and purchase a one-way ticket from him. Then I take my place in the queue and, when the time comes, I show my passport to the border official who wishes me a good trip. But I'm no tourist, despite the bag on my shoulder and the fact I'm now boarding a train that will take me into another country.

I'm not going to England to see the sights.

I'm going to England to end all of this, once and for all.

Mum will hate me for doing this.

But right now, I hate her too.

So I guess we'll be even.

THIRTY-TWO

FERN

'Answer the phone, you foolish girl,' I say out loud, infuriated at yet another one of my calls going straight to Cecilia's voicemail. I cannot get my daughter to pick up her phone and, as long as that is the case, I have no idea where she might be and what she might be doing, which is worrying for all sorts of reasons. I'm afraid for her mental wellbeing after Pierre's death, because that is a trauma that isn't easy to process quickly. I'm also afraid for her because she has found out some shocking things about me tonight, and I worry how she is coping with all of that. But I'm also being selfish and worrying about myself too, because what if my daughter has decided to go to a police station and tell them everything that has happened this evening? It sure would be a cruel twist of fate if, after avoiding the British police for so long, as well as several of the people I have wronged with my crimes, it ends up being my own flesh and blood who brings me down. But until I know what Cecilia's next move is, it's impossible to stop imagining a detective walking into this private hospital room and telling me that my time on the run is over.

And then I see an actual detective right in front of me.

'I'm Detective Mathieu. Can I have a word with you?' the

woman with the short black hair says, and I instantly start to panic that the worst has happened, and my daughter has given me up to the police. But there's no sign of any handcuffs yet and, after taking a seat, the detective offers me one opposite her. I've been pacing around this room for a while, ever since Cecilia left, and a nurse told me that I'd be able to see Pierre's body once the examinations had been completed. I could have run from here but I haven't been able to do that for two reasons. One, I want to properly say goodbye to Pierre and not have my last memory be of him dying in the back of an ambulance. And two, I am still hoping that my daughter will come back here and, when she does, I want to hear her say that she understands why I did everything that I did, and she forgives me for all of it. I might be being optimistic on that second part, but I can hope, and as I take a seat opposite the detective, I am hoping this conversation goes as well as it can.

'I'm sorry for your loss,' Detective Mathieu says as I think about how she seems far too young to be having a serious talk like this one. She looks to be in her thirties, and there must be a million other lines of work she could be in that aren't as dreary as sitting in a room like this talking to a doctor's widow. Maybe she enjoys it, and I get the sense that she does when I see a light in her eyes as she tells me what the plan is regarding the investigation into my husband's death.

'We are checking the CCTV cameras on the street where the accident took place as well as the surrounding ones, and I'm confident we will soon have a better idea of what really happened,' she says. 'I know you told my colleague you thought there was a bit of a panic, and you started running, so we are going to try and determine the start of that panic and if anybody else was running.'

'I thought it was just an accident,' I say quietly, looking down at the detective's shoes.

'It may be the case, but we need to look into everything,

which we will do, and we will inform you as soon as we have more information.'

That is probably supposed to be comforting for me at a time like this, but it only makes me feel worse, because I don't want the police looking at those cameras. If they do then they might see Alice and Evelyn running after us and know that they were the reason for Pierre running into traffic. Then all they will need to do is find the pair of them and ask them what it was all about, and if they tell them the truth, I'm screwed.

The detective offers me her condolences one more time before she leaves the room, but I have a feeling I shouldn't hang around in here too long myself, not if the police are already looking for Alice and Evelyn. Where are they now? Just like Cecilia, I have no clue, and it's terrifying to have my fate so precariously dangling out of my control. The only thing I can control now is whether I stay here or whether I leave. I stand up, making up my mind that going has to be better than staying and waiting for my arrest to be made. But just as I step outside the room, I see the nurse is back again and she has an update for me regarding my husband's body.

'If you're ready, you are able to see him now,' she says, a very caring look on her face, and it seems like her heart is breaking for me as I stand in front of her listlessly.

I probably should leave but I should also see my husband one last time, and I'll have to take the chance of being arrested in order to be a good wife.

'Okay,' I say quietly before the nurse starts leading the way, taking me along several corridors and only stopping once we are outside a door, behind which lies the body of my late husband.

'Take as long as you need,' the nurse says to me, gently touching my shoulder for a moment before leaving me to it, and I stare at the door handle for several seconds before taking a deep breath and going in.

The room is cold and metallic, stripped of all identity and

soul, which is probably what makes it a good place to store the dead. The only thing in the room is Pierre's body on a slab, though it's currently covered by a white sheet, allowing me a few moments to compose myself further before I remove it and face what's underneath.

With a shaking hand, I gently lift up the top half of the sheet and, when I do, I see Pierre's pale, stoic face before me. His eyes are closed and the blood on his hair has been cleaned away, making him look neat and tidy. He always was a smart man, and he looks smart now, even in death. I let go of the sheet when I'm at his upper chest, not needing to see any more of his body other than the head and shoulders, because I don't want to know what injuries were sustained lower down. Then, as I look at my poor husband's lifeless face, I start with the first thing that has to be said.

'I'm so sorry. This is all my fault.'

A solitary teardrop falls from my face onto the white sheet below me, and I wipe my cheeks so no more can fall and possibly land on the body.

'You were such a good man. Thank you for loving me and my daughter.'

I have to wipe my face again.

'I'm going to miss you so much. I don't know what is going to happen next, but wherever I end up, you will always be in my thoughts, I promise.'

I tentatively expose Pierre's hand under the sheet and take hold of it, giving it a gentle squeeze even though I know he won't be able to feel it. I keep hold of him for several minutes, but there's nothing more I can say other than, 'I love you.'

By the time I leave the room, there's no point in me trying to wipe my tears away because they are falling too fast, and I walk right past the nurse who tries to offer me a tissue as I go. I keep walking until I find myself at the exit, only pausing there to try and call Cecilia again. But there's still no answer, so I can only leave a voicemail.

'I'm so sorry. I really am. Please forgive me. I don't want to run again, and I won't if you say you still want to see me, but I just need to know. Please, give me a call.'

I end the voice message then and start walking, figuring I'll find a taxi somewhere and be on my way. As I look, I am praying my phone will ring and it will be my daughter telling me that she does want to see me again. Until then, I wonder where Alice and Evelyn are and whether the police have caught up with them yet, or if they have gone to see them of their own accord.

I hope not.

I hope they have some sense and get out of Paris as quickly as possible, avoiding any scrutiny from the police about what happened with Pierre.

Please just go back to England and leave me alone, I pray silently as I find a taxi to get into. Please just let me try and live what's left of my life in peace.

THIRTY-THREE

ALICE

There's been many times when Arberness has reminded me of dark moments in my life, but I can safely say that I'm glad to be here now. I was certainly glad when I got back here thirty-six hours ago after we had landed in Manchester and made the rest of the journey home. The time it took for Evelyn and me to board our flight from Paris had been a nerve-racking one, and I hadn't been sure we were going to make it out of the country safely until the plane backed away from the gate and the engines started to fire up. Even then, I had been worried the pilot was going to receive a call from the tower telling him to abort take-off because there were two passengers on board who the police wanted to speak to. Then I was imagining being marched off the plane in handcuffs alongside my daughter while the rest of the passengers watched on, peering out of the plane windows as we were taken across the runway and put into the back of a police car. From there, I was fearing we would be shown CCTV footage of the pair of us chasing Pierre to his death, and then we would be arrested for involuntary manslaughter or whatever the best charge was that the prosecutors felt could stick.

None of that happened. We were able to board easily enough, and the plane took off right on time. Once we were in the sky, the cabin crew moved through the aircraft offering refreshments, and Evelyn and I both had a glass of wine to calm our nerves as we soared up to 38,000 feet. We landed without issue either and we got back home to the safety blanket of this sleepy village where it can often feel like the rest of the world doesn't even know this place exists. That's just the way we like it at the moment, as Evelyn and I prepare for another day of wondering just what is going on in France with Fern, Cecilia and the police investigation into Pierre's death.

'There's a new article online!' my daughter says as she comes rushing into my bedroom just after seven a.m. with her laptop in hand.

'What does it say?' I ask, my stomach lurching as I sit up in bed, though I wasn't resting before. I've been wide awake for hours, tossing and turning after another restless night.

'I'm just translating it,' Evelyn tells me, so I have to be patient while she uses the internet to convert the French article she has found into English. 'Got it!' she cries a moment later before she sits down on the bed beside me so we can both read what's on the laptop screen.

MYSTERY STILL SURROUNDS DEATH OF MAN IN PARIS

That sounds promising, but I have to read more to find out for sure. Thankfully, when I do, I see that so far the police are still struggling to learn why Pierre ran out into the traffic. This article features an update from Detective Mathieu, a name I recognise from a few other articles recently, and she has spoken about the findings from the CCTV cameras in the area of Pierre's death. She says that due to how dark it was and how crowded the city streets were, investigating has been tough.

There's also the fact there was only one camera on the road where Pierre got killed but not on the streets leading up to it, and that one camera was not in a convenient location to show the entire area where the incident took place. Therefore, the police can't be sure if he was being chased or running away from some unknown threat.

'Thank God,' Evelyn says after she has finished reading the article, because she's come to the same conclusion as me. This is good news, not for Detective Mathieu but certainly for us, because it appears our involvement in Pierre's death has gone undetected. An article yesterday mentioned a few witnesses, but all of them had spoken of their confusion and said that, while they had noticed a few people running, they didn't really see all the faces or what they were running from. That is one less thing to worry about, but perhaps the biggest thing we were worried about hasn't happened either. Cecilia obviously hasn't given our names to the police, or we would have been contacted by now. She's allowed our presence that night in Paris to stay under the radar, and we are grateful for that. It all hinged on her, because we knew Fern wouldn't tell the police about us; she'd be mad to, because then we'd simply give her crimes up as well. As it is, the four of us seem to have gotten away with what's happened, although I can only really speak for me and my daughter. I don't have any idea what Fern and Cecilia might be doing now. They could still be in Paris, or they might have returned to the village where their home is. It's possible Cecilia has fled from her mum and maybe Fern has fled too, figuring she is better going back on the run rather than hanging around to see what happens next. I have no idea and I doubt I ever will know, not unless something happens to make it into the French news articles that Evelyn checks for several times a day.

'What are you doing?' I ask Evelyn as she takes back her laptop but continues to use it.

'Just looking for any more news,' she replies, which is

sensible but also makes me feel sad – it's a sign of how worried she is. I wish I could tell her that everything is going to be all right and there's nothing more to worry about, but I can't, at least not yet anyway. Hopefully, with enough time, it will become obvious to us both that the police in Paris aren't going to identify and question us; when that day comes, my daughter might get some peace.

'What would you like for breakfast?' I ask her as I get out of bed and put on my dressing gown. I will put some proper clothes on later, especially as I have barely got dressed since we got home from Paris, but for now, I just want to be comfortable. Neither of us have left the house since we got back, but I think today should be the day when we go outside and get some fresh air. I may even suggest the two of us get lunch at the village pub, but first things first; a cup of tea and a slice of toast.

Evelyn tells me she'd like some toast, so I go downstairs to make it, happy that I won't be eating alone again, though well aware that the circumstances for Evelyn's early return from travelling are not good ones. My daughter should still be in Europe somewhere, seeing the sights, but she's back here already and in a worse state than she was before she left. The only thing that is better than before she went is our relationship. The experience we shared in Paris has brought us closer together. While I wish it hadn't happened and a life hadn't been lost, at least my daughter now understands my reasons for letting Fern go when I did.

She understands just what happens if somebody thinks they can get the better of her.

Evelyn also saw exactly how much I love her and how far I am willing to go to keep her safe, based on how I reacted after Pierre had been hit by that car. While my daughter went into shock, I kept my composure long enough to ensure she made it away from that scene safely and evaded the law. If the police had spoken to her, she would have most likely been in such a bad way that she would have just told them the truth, and then they would have had no choice but to arrest her for causing Pierre's death. But I made sure that didn't happen and Evelyn knows that, which only makes her feel closer to me, despite the trying circumstances.

I'm not sure how long my daughter will be back home for, but I'll try to enjoy it for as long as it lasts. However, I will also be happy when the day does come that she leaves, because it must mean she is moving on again with her life. For now, we will have another quiet day in Arberness, checking the news and seeing if anything is happening many miles away from here that could impact us.

As the kettle boils and the toaster does its job, I glance out of the kitchen window to check on the weather for our potential walk later. But it doesn't look good – the sky is grey and it looks like it might rain.

I think I remember reading that a storm is on the way.

Hopefully it's only the weather type and not any other kind.

THIRTY-FOUR

CECILIA

Large raindrops start hitting the windscreen of the car I am travelling in, and it doesn't take long for the driver to turn on the wipers to get rid of them. But it's impossible to have totally clear vision, because the heavens really have opened above us and the rain is torrential now.

'Welcome to England,' my taxi driver says to me with a chuckle, hinting that the weather is like this here most of the time, and it's pretty much what I expected. I had heard it wasn't usually sunny in this part of the world. But I'm not here for a holiday, so I don't really care if the sun is obscured by clouds, which is a good thing because it really is getting stormy out there.

'How long until we get there?' I ask the driver as the windscreen wipers continue to work overtime.

'About ten minutes or so,' he replies. 'Unless the main road in is flooded when I get there. But let's hope not.'

He chuckles to himself again, but I'm not laughing. I don't want anything getting in the way of me reaching my destination, not now I'm so close, and certainly not after how far I've travelled just to get here.

I left Paris on the Eurostar and disembarked in London, my first time on English soil, and in getting there I'd broken the promise I'd made to my mum throughout my whole life. I was where she always told me I was not to go, but I wasn't going to stop. I had to spend a night in the capital while I waited for the next day's train services to begin, and then I boarded the first train I could get on to go north. I had boarded a train to Manchester and, once there, I spent some time doing a few things in the city that were important to me. Having spent the night in Manchester, I set off again at eight a.m. this morning and, after arriving in Carlisle, I found a taxi to bring me here on the final leg of my journey.

It's been a long trip and it's been made even longer whenever I've seen Mum trying to call me or leave me voice messages, but it's almost over now. She has no idea where I am because I haven't answered any of her calls or replied to any of her messages, so I guess she's getting her own message loud and clear that I don't want to speak to her.

Not yet, anyway.

'Almost there,' my driver says a few minutes later and, mercifully, the rain seems to have eased a little before I am due to get out of this car. I look ahead to see where we are approaching, but I don't see much of anything yet, which is weird because the driver said we were nearly there. But then I do start to make out a few houses on the hill in the distance before we round a bend and I see more buildings congregated together, all of them alongside a large body of water.

'You can usually see the southern tip of Scotland from here,' the driver tells me as if acting as my tourist guide now. 'But not today, not in this weather.'

It is very gloomy and a mist hangs above the water, giving this place a very ominous feel as we arrive. It's almost as if the universe is adding a sense of foreboding to mark my entrance here, and maybe that is right because things are certainly going to get dark here if everything goes to plan.

'Where would you like me to drop you off?' the driver asks me.

'Down by the beach, please.'

'The beach? In this weather? Are you sure?'

'Yes, thank you,' I say as I reach into my purse and take out my credit card. The driver thinks I'm crazy but I'm sure he'll still be more than happy to take my money and, of course, he is. He hands me the card machine after parking, and I tap my card on it to transfer the fare to him before thanking him again and getting out.

'Have fun!' he says a little sarcastically as the rain begins to fall again, and while he is quick to get out of here, I am stuck now, which is fine by me. I make my way onto the sand that is soaked by the raindrops. The grains stick to the bottom of my feet, but I'm not worried about ruining my shoes. I only want to find a particular place on this beach, and the news article I have on my phone is going to guide me.

It takes me about five minutes to roughly find the spot on the beach where Doctor Drew Devlin died. I stand and survey the scene quietly as the raindrops hit the sand all around me, trying to imagine the time when my mum was here. She lured Drew down here under false pretences and had her accomplice, Alice's partner, kill him. That was the start of it all, the start of my mum's life of crime, and she's been committing crimes ever since.

I feel sorry for Evelyn that her father lost his life here, in such a sombre place and in such a terrible way. I know what it's like to lose a dad in awful circumstances too, and it isn't just Drew's death scene that I have visited since I came to England. I was at the Pink-Tree Hotel in Manchester yesterday, which is where all the news articles told me was the scene of the death of the man I presume

was my father. Fern killed Greg in room number 6E; I asked the
hotel porter if I could see that room. It might seem morbid of me to
have wanted to stand in the place where my father was stabbed to
death by my mother, but I asked anyway, though I was told somebody was staying in the room and it wouldn't be possible.

I wonder if the guest knew what had happened in that
particular room before.

If so, they might have asked for a different one.

Even if I had been allowed into the room, I knew it wouldn't
be like being close to my late father, so that's why I made sure to
visit his grave too, his real final resting place. The rain-soaked
cemetery I found his headstone in resided in a quiet corner of
Manchester, and the bouquet of flowers I left for him added a
rare touch of colour to the gloomy setting. I had imagined saying
a few words when I got there, something to break the silence
even if he could no longer hear me, but I didn't in the end. It
was strange to know I was standing where the bones of my dad
lay. In terms of my life's journey, he was only involved in the
conception and literally lost his life mere minutes after it. But
that's not his fault; I'm sure he would have been a good father if
he had been given the chance.

He was denied that opportunity.

The wind is strong on this part of the beach and, along with
the rain and the swirling water only a few feet away, it makes
for a very grim setting when it's like this. I'm sure it looks lovely
on a summer's day, but it's still no place to die, yet this beach
was the last thing Drew ever saw.

Mum made sure of that.

I leave the desolate beach after ten minutes alone with my
thoughts and head for the village, figuring I should be able to
find my way around here easily enough. According to everything I have read about Arberness, since I realised what a big
part it plays in my mother's history, this place is tiny. I already
got a good sense of that in the taxi here, but I can see it even

more now I'm right amongst it. Not many people are on the streets given the weather, which means I don't have to have a conversation with any 'friendly local' who might ask me who I am and what I am doing here. They'd surely scurry away back to whichever house they live in if they knew those things. It also means I'm not going to bump into Alice or Evelyn yet, and while I will make sure to see them soon enough, I'll let them enjoy the peace a little longer too.

My next stop is the village pub and, as I walk in, the two old men who are drinking at a table in the corner look up from their pints to see who has just entered. When they see me, an unfamiliar eighteen-year-old female, they seem surprised, but I suppose it's not every day that a young woman walks into a venue like this. This pub is certainly dated, and the man who runs it looks dated too as I approach the bar and receive a warm welcome.

'Good afternoon. What can I get you?' the landlord asks me, stroking his grey beard with one hand while he uses the other to lean against one of the beer pumps. He looks too old to be on his feet all day, but maybe he just loves his job. I wonder if he was the owner here back when Mum lived in the village. If so, she would have drunk in here, and it feels weird to think he may have served two generations of our family.

'A vodka and lemonade, please,' I say, taking a seat at the bar.

'Can I see some ID, please,' I'm asked next, which is probably to be expected.

'Sure,' I reply, taking out a card from my purse, and when the landlord inspects it, he raises his eyebrows.

'You're from France?'

'Sure am.'

The man hands me back my ID before getting to work on my drink, but I expect he'll have another question for me shortly. The two men in the corner have also gone back to minding their own business, but I have a feeling they will be interested in me again very soon too.

'There you go,' the landlord says with a smile as he places my drink down in front of me. 'So, what brings you to Arberness? Are you travelling?'

'Not quite,' I reply before asking if he has a straw.

'Of course,' he says, handing me one, and I use it to stir my drink a little before taking a long, thirsty sip. When I'm done, I place my glass back down and prepare to instantly become the talk of this village.

'My mother used to live here,' I begin as the landlord picks up an empty glass and starts polishing it with a dishcloth.

'Oh really? I've lived in this village my whole life, so I'll definitely know her. What was her name?' the landlord asks.

'You'll definitely know her,' I say with a nod. 'Fern Devlin.'

The landlord drops the glass he was holding, and it shatters loudly on the hard floor behind the bar. But I don't flinch. I just turn to look at the two men in the corner and, unsurprisingly, they are looking right back at me.

'Did you say Fern Devlin?' one of them asks me nervously, and I nod my head.

'Do you know where she is now?' the other one asks, and I do the same again.

'I think I need to call the police,' the landlord says as he steps away from the broken glass by his feet, but just before he can get to the phone, I raise my hand, causing him to stop.

'Just be patient,' I say. 'There's no point in the police trying to find her because she's too good at hiding. I've got a better idea. Leave her to me.'

THIRTY-FIVE

FERN

I've decided to stay in Paris and wait for Pierre's body to officially be released for burial back in the village, but I've not just hung around for that, as important as it is. I've stayed because, so far, the police haven't shown any more interest in me, allowing me to think that I might be able to carry on with my life without fear of being arrested. My secret identity still seems to be a secret, at least from the authorities anyway, so no need to panic yet. I've also stayed in Paris because this is where Cecilia was living and I have to assume she is still here somewhere, lying low and possibly waiting for me to leave first. I've been to her apartment several times to try and catch her coming or going there, but the only person I have seen is Antoinette. I haven't had a very welcoming reception from my daughter's best friend whenever I have approached her to ask where Cecilia is; she's always looked terrified to see me before saying that she can't help me and then asking me to leave. I guess she knows exactly who I am now, and has read everything about me online, so is understandably nervous around me these days. I did worry she might have been a threat to me and could have gone to the police and told them who I was, but she doesn't seem to have done that. It could be fear or it could be out of loyalty to Cecilia, but whatever it is, Antoinette has kept quiet so far, thankfully. I don't pose a threat to her either, at least not unless she has been lying to me, but I have no reason to think that she has been.

Wherever my daughter is, not even her best friend knows.

It was awful to see Antoinette so wary of me when I saw her most recently. I've known her since she was a little girl, waving to her and her mother in the playground. Cecilia would tell me all about the new best friend she had made. I've seen her grow up alongside my child and, while we're not flesh and blood, I almost considered Antoinette another daughter of my own because of the amount of time she spent at our house in her youth. But any relationship we had is clearly over now Antoinette knows about my past, and I have all the news stories online to thank for that. I bet she's read every one of them, and if she has, no wonder she was nervous when I approached her. She might have even been trying to predict if I was going to make her my next victim, which is ludicrous, but that's the problem once you become known as a serial killer.

People are just waiting for you to kill again, which is a terrible reputation to have precede you.

But things are different this time. I'm not sure I have it in me anymore to take another life to protect my own. Or maybe I'm just hoping that with age has come a calmness that will prevent me from killing, but who really knows until I'm properly put to the test again? Maybe it's not really a calmness that has come over me anyway, maybe it's more of a malaise, or worse, a depression. There's the trauma of Pierre's death to deal with, losing the man I loved and the future we had together. But even worse than that is thinking I'll never see my daughter again. That in itself is enough to make me give up and no longer want to fight for anything, but what else can I think when she won't allow me to make contact with her?

I need a miracle.

And then I get it.

It's as I'm sitting on a bench by the River Seine, the sun reflecting off the water and numerous Parisian pedestrians scurrying across the bridges that overlap it, when I hear my phone ring. As I take it out of my handbag, I expect it will be somebody from the mortuary calling me to let me know Pierre's body is now ready to be moved. But it's not.

It's Cecilia.

'Hello!' I call out loud and clear so she can definitely hear that I have answered. I stand up from the bench and move a little closer to the river's edge. Why is it that people like to stand up and pace around whenever they take an important phone call, as if the other person won't be able to hear them if they stay sitting? I don't know, but I'm certainly pacing now.

'Hi, Mum,' comes the quiet voice from the other end of the line.

'Where are you? Are you okay?'

'I'm fine.'

'Why haven't you been answering my calls?'

'I just needed some time.'

'I wish you'd let me know you were okay. I've been so worried. I didn't know what to think.'

'Worried for me or worried for yourself?'

That's a harsh question but, sadly, I can see why Cecilia has asked it.

'Worried about you, of course,' I try to assure her, but it probably comes off as a little false – it would be unusual, if not downright weird, for me not to be concerned about how Cecilia has reacted to my secret.

'I suppose you want to know if I've spoken to the police,' Cecilia says.

'No, I just wanted to make sure you were safe.'

'So you don't care if I have or not?'

'No. Well, I mean, I hope you haven't, but only so I might get the chance to explain things to you properly, before whatever has to happen next.'

I don't know what my daughter wants me to say, so I'm just trying my best to let her know that she is my priority.

'I haven't said a word to them,' Cecilia says, which is a huge relief, before she adds one crucial word. 'Yet.'

'Just come and meet me and let me explain this all to you, face to face,' I beg. 'I know the things you will have heard or read about me will sound awful, but I had a reason to do all of them and I just need the chance to explain myself to you. Please, will you give me that?'

'Yes,' Cecilia replies calmly, which is more positive news.

'Great! Where are you? I can come and meet you right now. Are you still in Paris?'

'No, I'm not.'

'Are you back in the village?'

'No.'

'Where are you then?'

There's a pause before my daughter answers me.

'I'm in Arberness.'

I can't have heard her right. There had to be a bit of interference down the phone line. She can't have just said what I think she did.

'Sorry, what?'

'I'm in Arberness, Mum. You know it well, don't you?'

Of course I know it, and Cecilia is well aware of that, but I'm not confused about where it is. I'm confused as to why the hell my daughter has decided to go there, of all places.

'What are you doing there?' I ask, the tension I've carried in my body for the last few days only strengthening now.

'I've come to visit a few people.'

I can guess who she's talking about, but don't want to say their names.

'I haven't seen Alice and Evelyn yet,' Cecilia says, mentioning them for me. 'But I will.'

'Why? What are you doing?'

'I'm trying to get to know my mother better. I've already spoken to a few of the locals here about you. They all have lots of stories to tell.'

I bet they do.

'Cecilia, whatever you think you have to do, you don't. The only person you need to talk to about all of this is me, so please, just leave there and come back to France and we can talk properly.'

'How about you come to me?' she asks. I have to think carefully about my answer to that one.

'You know I can't do that,' I say honestly. 'I'll be arrested if anyone finds out that I'm back in England. Then we'll never get to talk, at least not outside of a prison visitor room.'

'That's not my fault.'

'I know it's not your fault. It's just how it is. Please come back to France. Please let us talk here.'

'No, I think I'm going to stay here,' Cecilia says, and I hear the wind blowing, but it's not at my side of the call. It's from the other end of the line. It must be that notorious Arberness wind blowing down from Scotland. I wonder if my daughter is near the beach while she makes this phone call. If she is, she is right near the spot where I watched Evelyn's father die.

'Cecilia, please. I don't know what you want me to do,' I admit.

'I want you to come and see me here in Arberness.'

'What?'

'You heard me. I want you to come here. If you do that then we will have a relationship going forward, whatever happens after that.'

'What if I don't come?'

'Then you will never see me again.'

'Cecilia, I can't. You know the police will be looking for me.'

'You can get here if you really want to,' she tells me calmly. 'It just depends on how desperate you are to do that. How desperate you are to see me again. If you don't come then I'll know how you feel about me.'

'Cecilia.'

'Goodbye, Mum.'

The call ends and, despite trying to get my daughter back on the line, she refuses to pick up. I guess she has said all she needed to say. She's told me the situation, and now she really has put my loyalty to the test.

Either I put myself first and never see my child again.

Or I put her first and face the wrath of Arberness, and every police officer who has ever tried to get me to face justice.

As I stare out across the Seine, I have no idea what I'm going to do.

THIRTY-SIX

EVELYN

Nobody likes to wait and see what happens. People prefer to make predictions. At least that way it feels like they have some control over the future, even if they end up being wrong. That's why I've made a very confident prediction recently, and it's one I've been doubling down on ever since as more time has passed. I've felt like the odds of me being correct have only increased.

I have predicted that the woman I hate most in the world, Fern, will not return to Arberness.

And so far, I have been right.

I'm currently at home with Mum, the two of us sitting on the sofa with a drink in our hands and the television on. She has a cup of tea, I have something a little stronger, but neither of us are particularly relaxed, nor are we paying attention to what we're supposedly watching. The TV is on more for background noise than anything else, and we desperately do need something to break through the silence. It's tense in here, as well as a little awkward, and that's for a few reasons, but mainly because we're not the only two people in the house. We've been joined by a third person who has been visiting us occasionally over the last three days. It's a person who I was very shocked to see in Arberness because I never thought I'd lay eyes on her again. I was even more shocked when she told me why she was here and what her plan was.

It's Cecilia and, despite the fact that we are on the opposite side of this situation with Fern, she made one thing very clear when she first showed up on our doorstep the other day.

She's on our side now.

It was scary to see her and just as scary to imagine what it might mean for me and Mum going forward, but Cecilia quickly put our minds at ease, and since she has been here we have bonded over our shared experiences and heartache. That doesn't mean her stay has been an entirely enjoyable one, though.

At the moment, Cecilia is also pretending to watch the TV with a drink in her hand, but I know it's only a matter of seconds before she checks her phone and then goes to the window to have a look outside. I know that because it's what she does every five minutes – and here she goes again.

Checking her phone. But there are no messages or missed calls.

Now going over to the window. But nobody is coming to the door.

'Can we just stop this and accept that she's not coming?' I say when I've grown tired of all our lives being left in limbo. 'She's a coward and she isn't going to come back, no matter what.'

I know that must be a hard thing for Cecilia to hear but, as usual, she gives very little away, simply checking her phone again. I look to Mum, but she doesn't say anything either, probably because we've already said everything we've needed to and saying any more is only repeating ourselves. I know I'm certainly repeating myself in what I just said, but one of us has to talk some sense. One of us has to stop all three of us sitting here for the rest of our lives – waiting for somebody, who clearly has no intention of coming, to turn up at the door and end this once and for all.

'I have a plan to get Fern to come back to the village.'

That's what Cecilia had said to my mum after she had answered the door to her the other day, and what she repeated to me after I'd come downstairs to see what had got Mum so surprised. I heard Mum keep asking somebody what they were doing here, so I left my bedroom and went to investigate and, when I did, I found Cecilia in our house.

'I want to help you both,' she had said then. 'It's not fair what my mum has done to you and to everybody else in this village. I want her to hand herself in so everybody can have some closure, me included, and I think that might happen soon.'

Through it all, I had thought that if anybody would bring Fern Devlin to justice then it would have been me. But after what had happened in Paris, I had been prepared to let that go. I certainly hadn't been expecting a development like the one that landed on our doorstep.

Fern's daughter wanted to be the one who got revenge?

'What the hell are you talking about?' I'd asked, not daring to dream that anything Cecilia had said was actually going to come true.

'I've phoned my mother and told her where I am. I then said that if she ever wanted to see me again then she had to come back here. So she has no choice. She has to return to Arberness or lose me as a daughter forever.'

I'd looked at Mum and frowned then because, to me, that sounded like Fern still had a choice.

'She could just decide not to come!' I said, shocked that I seemed to be the only one who saw a major flaw in this plan. 'You really think she'd give up her freedom for you or anybody else? She's selfish, that's why she's done all the things she has. Because she only cares about herself, no one else.'

'She'll come,' Cecilia had said, trying to appear confident, though I definitely detected a hint of uncertainty in her voice and her expression, like she was trying to convince herself as much as us. That's when I felt a little sorry for her, because she had clearly told herself that, no matter what her mother had done, she wasn't going to risk her daughter's love to get away with it. Sadly, that's where I felt she was wrong.

'My mum was right all those years ago when she let Fern walk away,' I had said, looking at Cecilia and Mum standing beside her. 'She knew it was better to do that than risk any more harm coming to anybody. I never listened and hated her for that, but now I know she was right. Look at what happened when I tried to catch Fern. An innocent man died and, if we hadn't been lucky, I could have gone to prison for that. We need to just leave Fern alone, before anybody else gets hurt.'

I was aware that I was talking as much to my mother as I was to Cecilia, acknowledging that all the years of lamenting how Mum let Fern get away were a mistake on my part. I know Mum appreciated that acknowledgement too, though she didn't say anything at the time. She stayed very quiet as Cecilia and I went back and forth debating what Fern's next move would be, so much so that it got to the point when the pair of us were desperate to hear her thoughts on it. That's when Mum finally spoke up and let us know what she predicted Fern would do after being backed into a corner like this one.

'She'll come,' Mum had said then, surprising me.

'What? Why do you think that?' I'd asked.

'Because she won't want to lose her daughter. She'll do anything to keep you in her life, Cecilia, even if it means going to prison. As long as she knows you'll visit her, that will be okay. As a mother, that will be better than being on the run and having no daughter at all. I believe Cecilia is the only person Fern would potentially give up her freedom for.'

Cecilia had nodded, clearly on the same wavelength, but I'd still been unsure.

'Why are you talking as if Fern is going to make a rational decision and put love before herself?' I'd asked. 'Why are you assuming she cares about anyone more than she does her own wellbeing? She's killed people in cold blood. She's told a thousand lies. She's not just capable of committing serious crimes, but she's very good at getting away with them too. So why do you think she'll just throw away whatever life she has left and make it easy for the police after all this time? So her daughter might come and visit her once a month in prison? Please, it's just not going to happen.'

'We'll see,' was all Mum had said then, before she had asked Cecilia where she planned to stay in Arberness while we all waited for Fern to get here. I'd had to return to my bedroom because I couldn't exist in whatever fairy-tale land those two were clearly trying to live in, but when I'd re-emerged a few hours later, I learnt that Mum had invited Cecilia to stay with us and Cecilia had accepted that invite.

'You're both deluded,' was all I had been able to say to them, and my opinion on them both hasn't changed in the time since. That's because absolutely nothing at all has happened to prove me wrong. There's been no sign of Fern and I doubt there ever will be. That's why I'm just about to get up from this sofa, turn the television off, tell Mum that we need to get on with our lives and then I'll politely ask Cecilia to leave. But just before I can do that, something unexpected happens.

The phone Cecilia has been checking for the last three days finally comes to life.

'It's Mum!' Cecilia says as she leaps off the sofa, her ringing phone in her hand.

'Answer it!' Alice cries, also getting up off the sofa, leaving me sitting, though I am just as keen to hear what the reason for the call is. But, as the voice of reason here, I try to dampen the sudden enthusiasm that has swept through the room.

'She's probably just going to tell you that she can't do it,' I say with a sigh, but Cecilia ignores me and answers the call anyway.

'Hello?' she says nervously.

Neither me nor Mum can hear what is being said from the other end of the line, but we do notice Cecilia's eyebrows rise before she goes over to the window and looks out again.

'I understand,' is all she says next before ending the call.

'What's going on?' I ask, expecting this to be the moment when Cecilia tells me Fern isn't coming after all, and then all that will be left for me to do is say I told you so, although I'm not mean enough to do that – Cecilia's heart will be breaking about her mum giving up on her.

But that's not what is happening at all.

'She's here,' Cecilia says, turning away from the window to face us both. 'She's back in Arberness.'

THIRTY-SEVEN

FERN

Why is it that life often comes full circle? No matter what we do and what we intend to do in the future, it seems like we always end up back where we started. That's what's happened to me. Despite all the years, all the running and all the lies, I've ended up back in the place where it all began.

This is where I decided that the doctor had to die.

And this is the exact spot on the beach where I watched that happen.

The chill in the wind is as familiar as the landscape that surrounds me as I stand on the sand and try to embrace my surroundings. I never wanted to come back here, nor thought I'd ever be tempted. Only an idiot would return to the scene of a crime.

I guess this makes me an idiot then.

But does it really? Or does being back in Arberness make me something else, something far better? I like to think so. That's because I haven't come back here due to a stupid mistake or for some selfish egotistical reason. I'm back here for the only thing that really matters in life for a parent.

I'm here for my child.

I'm potentially giving up my freedom for Cecilia, although there may still be a way for me to avoid prison if I can convince my daughter that is not the best thing to happen. I don't want to be behind bars, but more than that, I don't want to live if my daughter hates me, so something has to give.

I'm risking everything right now just for a chance to see my child.

So where is she?

I look around the desolate beach but see no signs of my daughter, despite calling her ten minutes ago and telling her that I was here. I've granted her the wish she made when she phoned me in Paris. I've returned to this village so that whatever happens next, I will still be able to see her in the future, even if I will be wearing a prison uniform during those times and have to return to a small cell afterwards. The thought of being put into handcuffs by a smug police officer makes me feel sick, just as sick as spending the rest of my days eating dreary food in dull clothes surrounded by depressing individuals who, unlike me, weren't smart enough to get away with their crimes and got caught rather than gave themselves up.

It was a long time ago when a dogwalker made an anxious phone call to say that they had discovered a body on the beach here, a discovery that sparked a huge investigation and saw this village overwhelmed with journalists from far and wide. Imagine if I hadn't had Drew killed. What would have happened instead? Would the pair of us still be living here, sharing that house we bought on the beachfront, the one I can see in the distance? Would Drew still be going to work as the village doctor every day, pretending to be the smartest and most compassionate man in Arberness, while secretly being nothing like that? Would his affair with Alice still be ongoing, or would he have got bored of her and moved on to somebody else? Perhaps a new addition to the village, another woman to catch his eye, some pretty blonde or brunette who flicked her hair in the pub and captured his attention? What would've become of me, the dutiful wife, sitting at home, trying to come up with ways to make my philandering husband happy, but knowing that no matter what I did I could never trust him again and, worse than that, I'd never be enough for him either.

I could have chosen not to be a killer. I could have been so much more. Or am I just lying to myself? Did I really only ever have a straight choice?

Be the betrayed wife whose best outcome was a bitter divorcee? Or take back the power and make my husband pay for what he had done to me?

It felt like there was only one real option at the time, so I made my choice.

Now I have to stick with it.

I see movement on the beach in the distance and feel butter-flies fluttering in my stomach, as I expect it is Cecilia on her way to see me. As I watch the figure get closer, I realise it is not her. The movements don't match my daughter's. This person moves slower, a little stiffer, suggesting they are older than my eigh-teen-year-old child and, sure enough, as they get nearer, I see it is not her at all. But I still recognise who it is.

It's Audrey, my old next-door neighbour here.

If I ever thought I was getting old as sixty approaches, I'm not sure how Audrey feels herself, because she must be in her mid-nineties by now. It's lovely to see that she is still active and enjoying a walk on the beach, albeit with the help of a walking aid, although I'm not sure how much she will be enjoying it when she looks up from the sand and sees who she is sharing it with this morning.

As Audrey slowly approaches, her head bowed and still seemingly oblivious to the fact that I am here, I think about the time she visited me and Drew as we first moved into our new house here in Arberness. She kindly called by to welcome us to the village and brought us a lasagne she had cooked, which we gladly ate because our fridge was empty and all our pots and pans were still in boxes. I remember how friendly she was and how her eyes lit up when she first saw Drew, my handsome husband who breezed past her and probably made her feel thirty years younger when he flashed her that devilish smile of his. But most of all, I remember what she said just after I had welcomed her into my new house and, out of habit, had locked the front door behind her.

'Oh, you don't need to worry about locking your doors here, dear. There is no crime in Arberness.'

Oh, Audrey. How innocent you and everybody else in this village once was.

I bet everybody here locks their doors at night now.

Audrey is almost upon me, yet she still hasn't seen me with her head and shoulders so stooped, so I decide to make my presence known to her so that she doesn't get the biggest shock of her life in a few seconds' time.

'Hello, Audrey,' I say, just loudly enough to be heard over the wind.

Audrey looks up before her face drops in horror and she loses her grip on her walking aid. As I watch it fall to the sand, I realise I have failed in not wanting to shock her, because she's clearly stunned at my appearance here and looks as if she has just seen the bogeyman.

'Let me get that for you,' I say as I lean down and pick up her walking aid before I attempt to hand it back to her. She just stares at me open-mouthed, that is until I tell her that I am not here to cause trouble and don't mean her or anybody else in this village any harm.

Audrey reluctantly takes back her walking aid, eyeing me suspiciously before she sets off past me, moving in a far faster fashion than she did to get here. I guess she can still move quickly when she really has to, and she must feel she has to right now because she is really moving across the sand, attempting to put as much distance between herself and me as possible. But I don't have the time to think about how this once receptive woman is clearly terrified of me these days, because I see more movement on the beach and, this time, it is my daughter who is on her way. She has company and, as the three figures get closer, I see that Alice and Evelyn are with her too. That's to be expected though, because when I called Cecilia and told her that I was here, I asked her to meet me at the beach and for her to bring the other two with her.

I walk towards them to meet them in the middle, at the same time respectfully moving away from the spot where Drew lost his life – it would be harsh of me to expect Evelyn to stand for any length of time in the spot where her dad died. Even more so when I consider what I have to say to her when she joins me.

'Thank you for coming,' my daughter says to me as we meet, though she stays back enough to suggest she is unsure about a hug.

'Of course I came,' I reply, gazing into my beautiful daughter's eyes. 'So, what do you think of Arberness?'

'It's quiet,' Cecilia replies, giving the understatement of the year.

'Yeah,' I say with a sad laugh.

'But not for much longer,' Cecilia adds ominously, and I suspect she means because the police will be here soon.

'Is this what you really want?' I ask her, but she just shakes her head.

'Talk to them first,' my daughter says. 'Don't you think you owe them an apology?'

I look to Alice and Evelyn standing a little behind Cecilia, and I know my daughter is right.

'I'm sorry,' I say to them both before addressing each of them more directly. 'I'm so sorry, Evelyn, for what I robbed you of. You never got to meet your father because of me, and I deeply regret that.'

Evelyn says nothing as she hears my apology, then looks distantly past me, possibly at the point of the beach where Drew passed away. As she does that, I look to Alice.

'I'm sorry for what I put you through,' I say, even though I've already apologised to her once before, back in Cornwall, though I'm sure I'm overdue saying it again. 'The fact you forgave me once shows you are a far better and stronger person than I could ever be.'

Alice seems slightly moved by that statement and, while she stays silent like her daughter, she does at least give me a nod to show she appreciates what I have just said. That just leaves me with Cecilia.

'I know saying sorry doesn't even come close to making up for the things I've done to you,' I begin with. 'Hurting your father. Lying to you your entire life. Keeping you from discovering who you really were and where you really came from. I'll never be able to forgive myself for many things, but those things are the worst.'

Cecilia maintains eye contact with me as I speak, which I hope means she is understanding just how much I mean what I am saying.

'When you phoned me to tell me I had to come back here or risk never seeing you again, I knew I had no choice. Not really. You're the only thing I have to show for what is left of my life, and the only person who can prove that I'm not the monster the media make me out to be. I hope that one day, in time, you will be able to let others know that despite what I've done and the people I have hurt, I did have a good side. A caring side. A fun side. A normal side.'

Cecilia has tears in her eyes now and so do I, as the last eighteen years flash through our minds – the late nights when my baby needed me to hold her to help her sleep, the early mornings when I would get her ready for school, the weekends filled with activities and the Christmas holidays that I always tried to make so special. The conversations, the hugs, the laughter, the love. It's not all been bad. Has it?

'It's okay, Mum,' Cecilia says now, letting me know that it hasn't, and she steps forward before hugging me tightly.

I squeeze her as if it's the last time I will ever get to feel her, which I'm hoping it won't be, but who knows what happens next? Certainly not the three people I am with on this beach, because I haven't told them what the next part of this is.

As my daughter and I separate, I wipe away a couple of tears from my daughter's cheeks before speaking again.

'I made another phone call after I rang you,' I say to Cecilia. 'I called the police in Carlisle and told them where I would be and at what time.'

I check my watch and see that it is almost eleven o'clock, which means we should have more company any minute now.

Cecilia, Alice and Evelyn look shocked that I would be the one to call the police rather than any of them, but they should know me better than this by now. As the one who started it all, I had to be the one who ended it. As I hear sirens in the distance, I know it will be over very soon. I can hear the whirring of rotor blades and look up to see a helicopter cutting through the grey sky above, on its way over this beach to give the officers on the ground an update on my position from up high.

Several police cars quickly line the road at the top of the beach. The officers inside them disembark and run down onto the sand, all of them spreading out and ensuring there is no escape for me, unless I choose to go into the water, not that I will.

As Arberness feels like it is closing in on me rapidly, and not for the first time, I smile at my daughter.

'You'll come and visit me?' I ask nervously, seeking confirmation that my daughter will stand by me now that I've kept my end of the bargain and returned to face the music.

'Yes,' Cecilia says, more tears running down her cheeks than I could possibly hope to wipe away before I'm arrested. I try my best but, seconds before the first police officers reach me, I make sure it's clear that I'm not going to give them any resistance now the time has come. I demonstrate that by slowly sinking to my knees and putting my hands out in preparation for the handcuffs, and when the feeling of that cold, hard steel hits, it's almost a relief.

I make sure to smile at Cecilia before I am taken away, just so she knows that I am going to be okay, although that remains to be seen.

Will I really?

Or just like that night on this beach with Drew, have I made yet another grave mistake?

THIRTY-EIGHT

ALICE

Arberness beach. So much has happened there that it's impossible for it not to be on my mind today. I guess that's why I'm currently designing a whole new batch of greetings cards and all of them have a beach theme, modelled loosely on that beach not far from my home in this village. That stretch of sand, that swirling water and the people who visit it. I'm drawing it all now, creating new cards that I can sell and help grow my business. Things certainly seem to be going well these days, and I'm feeling as positive about things as I can ever remember.

I suppose the reason for that is an obvious one.

The doctor's wife is no longer casting a shadow over my life.

It's been three months since that day on the beach when Fern, having made a shocking return to Arberness, willingly allowed herself to be taken into custody for all the crimes she had gotten away with for so long. That's just over ninety days that she has been without freedom now, although that's a mere drop in the ocean compared to what she is facing in the future. Having confessed to everything, there was no need for a trial, and Fern Devlin was finally sentenced on a blustery Friday morning last week. The hearing had been held at Manchester

Crown Court after the court in Carlisle had been deemed too small to hold such important proceedings. Such was the media attention in Fern's case, a bigger court was necessary so that journalists from all over the UK could crowd into the courtroom and witness the sentencing of the woman they had written so many articles about. There was room too for reporters from Paris, several intrepid French journos crossing the Channel because they had a vested interest in the case too, considering Fern's actions had infiltrated their city and kept their news-hungry readers clicking on all the online articles that were written about them.

I was present in court, alongside my daughter – the pair of us dressed modestly, as if to avoid drawing attention to ourselves, which was futile because we must have had our photos taken at least a thousand times before we made it up the steps outside the courthouse. It was tough to be under the glare of the media spotlight again, as well as have renewed interest from the police who had to corroborate several things with us in relation to Fern's confessions. But it had to be done, we had to be there and, because we were, we got to witness the moment the doctor's widow was finally punished.

———

'Will the accused please rise for sentencing?' asks Judge Clary, the sixty-year-old man with a permanently furrowed brow who has overseen the proceedings so far. Those proceedings have consisted of a very long and brutal account of everything that Fern Devlin is guilty of, which is why the judge is not the only person in the courtroom who looks tired. But no one looks more tired than the woman getting to her feet at this second.

As I watch Fern stand up, I don't see a cold, calculating killer with a talent for murder, fraud and telling more lies than most humans could ever even dream of. I simply see someone who is ready for all of this to be over so she can see what is waiting for her on the other side of it. Mercifully, the judge is just about to tell her exactly what that is.

'Fern Devlin, while the charges against you are severe and abhorrent, the court must thank you for the way you have conducted yourself during these proceedings. You have been open and communicative, enabling the legal team that surrounds you to work efficiently and speeding this process up significantly. In doing so you have also spared your victims, some of whom are in this court today, any added distress on top of that which you have already caused them, and I know they are grateful for that. I have spoken to them myself during these proceedings. However, that is not to forget that you purposely and strategically prolonged the suffering of all involved by going on the run and living under a false identity to evade capture. Many people have been affected by your selfish choices, and I made sure to get accurate accounts of just how far and wide and damaging those impacts were.'

I saw the judge glance at me then and recalled the short conversation we had, in which he simply asked me what the biggest impact of Fern's actions had been on my life. I had answered just as simply, telling him that the worst thing that had happened was that I had lost so many years of my daughter's childhood to countless worries – that she would one day grow up and be traumatised by the news of what had happened to her father. Judge Clary obviously wanted to take into consideration the emotional impact on everyone involved in Fern's actions, so he could take those into account when deciding the punishment. I know he spoke to Evelyn too and asked her the same thing, and while she didn't tell me what her answer was, I can guess.

Because of Fern, she will never know what it's like to have a dad, and I don't think there's a person in the world, never mind a judge, who wouldn't have been moved by a fact like that.

'With all that said, there can be no getting away from the grievous nature of your crimes,' Judge Clary goes on. 'So even with your cooperation taken into account, I must still look to punish you with the full severity that the law allows me.'

That sounds ominous but Fern remains composed, standing perfectly still with her hands together in front of her, resting lightly on the grey prison uniform she has been wearing ever since she was taken away in handcuffs on that blustery beach.

'For the premeditated plotting of Drew Devlin's murder with Rory Richardson, I sentence you to twenty years.'

The mention of Rory, my late husband, stirs up feelings of regret and shame inside me, as it always does, so I can only imagine what it's doing to Fern as she stands there and hears that she has two decades to spend behind bars now. But that's only the beginning.

'For the murder of Rory Richardson, your initial co-conspirator whom you turned against, I sentence you to fifteen years.'

Fern remains stoic as another heavy sentence is handed down.

'For perverting the course of justice by framing Alice Richardson for Drew Devlin's murder, and taking into account the time Alice mistakenly spent in custody for this, I sentence you to twelve years.'

I try to keep calm as my name is mentioned, not thinking back on the prison time I served for that crime, but focusing instead on how I am free now and Fern is not.

'For the murder of Greg, a man you previously knew as Roger, as this particular crime was so brutal and selfish in nature, I sentence you to twenty years.'

There are sobs in the gallery now from some relatives of Greg's, the poor man who was stabbed to death with a broken beer bottle in a hotel room not too far away from this court, shortly before Fern went on the run. They've also had to come to terms with the knowledge that their lost loved one fathered a child in Cecilia, just before his untimely demise, though for now, their priority has been justice over forming new relationships. Funnily enough, that's the next crime on the judge's list.

'For the further perversion of justice caused by misleading investigators into Greg's death, as well as opting to go on the run when the true nature of your guilt was brought to light, this warrants some pause before sentencing.'

The courtroom is silent as the judge considers his next words.

'Fern Devlin, for all the crimes previously mentioned, through various means, you were able to avoid punishment for over eighteen years. That's eighteen years in which not only the surviving victims suffered, but countless hours of police time were spent on trying to locate you. That's manpower that could have been put into other cases, and who is to say how many other crimes could have been solved if so many resources weren't being spent on the search for you? It's fair to say that the true extent of your actions may never be fully known, and for that, because you chose to run rather than end this much sooner, I sentence you to nine years for evading justice.'

I'm starting to lose track of all the sentences, and I wonder if Fern is too, but I'm also wondering exactly how much time she is going to spend behind bars. I assume all these sentences are going to run concurrently. I think the longest one she received was for twenty years, so I guess that's the total time she'll be in prison, with a few years probably removed for good behaviour at the end. But then the judge speaks again.

'The crimes you are guilty of occurred consecutively, separate crimes on separate dates over a long period of time. That is why I considered having you serve these sentences in the same fashion, meaning consecutively. That would total seventy-six years, but given your age, I have decided to keep this simple and categorise all your punishments into one. Fern Devlin, I hereby sentence you to a whole life order.'

As those words ring around the courtroom, I study Fern and how she takes the news, now that it is official, that she will never be released from prison before her death. I can't be sure, but there might have been a small part of her hoping that one day, maybe twenty years from now, and if she was still alive and well, she could be released to enjoy a little time before she passed. But the judge has just removed that as a possibility and, once Fern is taken from here, this is the last time she will ever breathe air that is not surrounded by prison walls.

As Fern is led away by two police officers, a couple of people in the gallery shout insults at her, aware this is the last chance they will ever get to make their feelings known directly to this woman. But most people in the court are silent, including myself, Evelyn and Cecilia, who I can see staring at her mother as she is led away. As I watch Fern go, I see her mouth the words 'I love you' to her daughter, before it looks like she will disappear down the stairs and be out of my sight forever. But just before she does that, Fern stops and looks back. I realise that she is staring right at me.

We hold each other's gaze for a few seconds before Fern is nudged on her way again by the officer on her right and, seconds later, she is gone.

'What was all that about?' Evelyn asks me as we leave the courtroom ourselves, referring to the look the condemned woman gave me.

'I'm not sure,' I admit before wondering if it actually might be obvious. 'Maybe because she still thinks deep down that I started it.'

———

I look down at the greetings card I was designing and realise that, in my daydream, I have made a bit of a mess of it. Screwing it up and preparing to start again, I tell myself to concentrate, but before I can get back to work, Evelyn enters the room.

'I thought you should see this,' she says before handing me her phone and adding, 'I'm sorry.'

'What is it?' I ask as I look at the phone and see a news article on screen, but the headline accompanying the article tells me before my daughter can.

DETECTIVE WHO BOTCHED DOCTOR DEATH DIES

I realise what has happened, sorry to get the news from this source rather than a simple phone call from the hospital, but read on to learn more about poor Detective Tomlin's passing, feeling sad at the loss of the man I was once close with and a man who played a part in Evelyn's very early life. It's such a shame that the journalist who wrote this article has decided to go with the angle that Tomlin messed up Doctor Devlin's murder investigation, because what really happened is that he was tricked by Fern and he's far from the only one who that happened to. Hopefully, some of the other articles that might be written about him will be more positive and, if not, I will have to make it known what a good man he was. I guess I can do that by attending his funeral, alongside my daughter, if she wishes to accompany me, and I will speak to any loved ones who are there to pay their respects to Tomlin too, not that I ever met many of them in the time I knew him.

'At least he's at peace now,' Evelyn says as I hand her phone back to her. 'You said he was in a lot of pain the last time you saw him.'

I nod because my daughter is right. Tomlin was in pain the last time I saw him, which was only a day after Fern had been sentenced to life in prison. I went to the hospital to tell him the news, though he already knew it. The nurses told me he had been avidly watching the TV in his room as updates from the court filtered out for the public. But I wanted to give him confirmation from somebody who had been right there in the same room as Fern and, after I told him how Fern was as she heard her fate, he only had one thing to say about it all.

'Good,' Tomlin had said, forcing a smile onto his face for a brief moment before the pain that was gripping his weak body overpowered him again and he closed his eyes. I'd held his hand for a moment then before saying goodbye, and I guess it really was goodbye. Now he's gone.

As Evelyn leaves the room again and I shed a small tear for Tomlin, I can't help but think about the timing of his death, coming so soon after Fern's sentencing. It's almost as if he hung on until he knew what was happening with her. Maybe he did, or maybe it's just a coincidence. But knowing that stubborn detective like I did, I have a pretty good idea of which one it was.

I guess that's another character in this whole sorry story taken care of. I should just be glad myself and Evelyn came out of it all okay.

But what of the protagonist?

What has become of the doctor's wife?

EPILOGUE

FERN

I've spent a large portion of my existence avoiding being locked away. Now I'm here, in prison, trapped with other criminals and with no way of ever experiencing the type of life I was once accustomed to.

What's it really like?

I guess I should say that it's terrible, especially if anybody connected to the justice system is listening, because I'd want all of them to think how much I am suffering so that one day, maybe, they might be kind enough to give me a reprieve and let me out when I'm in my nineties, perhaps. I would certainly say that it's bad in here if my daughter was within earshot, because I want to make sure she is never tempted to commit a crime and end up following in her mother's footsteps straight into a prison cell.

But what's the truth?

Those who know of me and my story would assume that the truth is hard to come by.

But here it is.

Prison hasn't been so bad.

Sure, the first night was awful and it took me a little while to get used to my new surroundings, but once I did I made sure to do what I always do when put into a new environment.

I made the most of it.

Whether I am swanning around a city wearing designer clothes, or going on the run as a poverty-stricken single mother, or living a quiet life in a small French village, or living as a prisoner in a high-security facility, I always adapt to my circumstances. I might not have the bank balance I once had as a doctor's wife, or the freedom to move in several social circles and entertain guests in my large house, but I still have something that other people gravitate towards.

I have my charm.

That's certainly served me well in here.

After accepting this was my new life, I quickly went about making the best of the situation and that meant making friends. From fellow prisoners to the wardens who watch over us all, I worked on charming each and every one of them, building a new network for myself rather than dwelling in my cell and hiding away like some people on the outside might like to think I was doing. It didn't hurt me to quickly realise that I was the most famous prisoner within these walls, and I used that to my advantage, capitalising on the respect, fear and recognition that the news reports had garnered for me. Some new prisoners might get tested early on in their stay by being threatened and forced into proving their toughness, but I never had to do such a thing. Everyone knew I was tough because the media had already told them I was, so nobody dared try and take me on in a fight. Then there's the fact that in an all-female prison surrounded by many women who end up hating men, the fact I have killed three members of the opposite sex in my time has gone some way to ingratiating me further.

'You're the Black Widow! Cool to meet you!'

'Well done for killing your cheating husband! I'd have done the same!'

'You're one crazy bitch. But I love it!'

Those are just some of the things fellow prisoners have said to me since I've been in here; it quickly became apparent to me that I could utilise my fame in prison to gain some advantages. I'm basically running this prison wing now, from having my pick of all the best jobs in here to knowing the right people when it comes to having certain 'luxuries' smuggled inside. The latter might technically be against the rules, but considering I've already been told I'm in here until I die, I can afford to take a few chances. But one thing I am not tempted to do is try and stage a prison break.

For the first time in a long time, I am not looking over my shoulder every day and waiting to be caught. That relief means I am sleeping easier, even with a cellmate who occasionally snores, and if I'm honest, I quite like the routine in here. Every part of my day is mapped out, from sunrise to sunset, and it is quite freeing not to have to waste mental energy deciding what to do with every hour that comes. It's certainly freeing being able to be my more authentic self rather than the heavily disguised version I spent so long projecting. I also don't have to think about money here, which would have been a dream back when I was a single mum on the run and constantly living in fear of starving either myself or my baby. Sure, it's not exactly a hotel, and I can't take part in wine and cheese nights with my old friends like I did when I was married to Drew, but it's okay. However, the main reason I am not tempted to try and escape from here, even if I could, is that it would not be fair on my daughter.

Cecilia is able to move on with her life now my fate has been confirmed, and I don't want to throw all that into disarray again by trying to go back to my life on the run. I've had my chance at living, and while some would say I wasted it, a few in here might argue I maximised it. The point is that it's not about me anymore. It's about my child, who has made me a better person in all sorts of ways, but perhaps the biggest is that she has made me face up to the consequences of my actions – and what a lesson that is for her to carry on as she goes through her own life. My daughter is still young and can do anything she chooses to, and I know I'll take far more pleasure from hearing about her journey than I will trying to prolong mine outside of these four walls. And hear about it I will, because it's time for my daughter's next visit now.

Despite being the queen bee in this prison, my favourite time is always when Cecilia is here to see me. I'm excited as I walk into the visitor room and see my daughter at one of the tables. She looks pretty, far prettier than her mother is these days, but then she is wearing her own clothes and has access to make-up. I've pretty much given up on beautifying myself ever again, because spa days aren't really an option in here, even for prisoners as well connected as me.

'Hi, darling,' I say as I take my seat and smile, not to pretend I'm okay here, but to show that I actually am. But my daughter already knows that because I've made it clear that while this is no holiday, I'm not in danger. I'll be able to serve out my sentence safely as time goes by with minimal issues, thanks to all the respect I command from the other inmates in here.

I'm not proud of being a notorious killer, but there is one perk.

No one will mess with me in here.

'Hi, Mum,' Cecilia says, looking around awkwardly at our surroundings. I suppose this isn't the usual place a mother and daughter would get together for a catch-up.

'What have you been up to since your last visit?' I ask, trying to keep things light.

'I've just got back from a week in London. I made some new friends down there so I might end up going back to the city to look for work,' she replies, which sounds both exciting and worrying.

'You'll still come and visit me even if you're in London?' I ask nervously, aware that it's at least two hours from Manchester on the train, which my daughter might deem too far to come and see her criminal mother on a regular basis.

'Yes, I'll still come, don't worry.'

'Thank you,' I say, relaxing now I've been reassured.

Cecilia tells me how she has been seeing a careers adviser and has a few ideas for her next steps in the working world, which might even involve applying to a few university places. After learning her whole life in France had been based on a lie, she decided that she was going to rethink things and that included her fashion job in Paris. I was sad to hear that, she had seemed so happy, but she said she might go back to it one day, though not before taking the time to try and connect to who she really is. That means a lot of time spent in England, her real home country, where she has been travelling, making friends and exploring as many options as possible as to what to do next. Some might say she is trying to run from the fact she is my daughter by looking to reinvent herself, but I believe it is simply the way she says it is.

She just needs to find her own path, completely separate from the one she was on in France, because that one was based on a lie.

I suppose I should just be grateful that the revelation that she is the daughter of an infamous serial killer hasn't totally wrecked her life and led her down a path of misery, shame and regret. Instead, she's showing great strength, focusing on the future rather than the past, keenly aware that her mental health depends on it. The only time she does delve into the past is when she comes here, or when she messages Evelyn, who she has kept in touch with because they were once friends and they will always be bonded by me.

'Have you had any thoughts as to what you might study if

you do go to university?' I ask, interested to find out what her options might be.

'I'm not sure yet. Maybe medicine. I was thinking about becoming a doctor.'

My face drops and I am just about to ask Cecilia if she thinks that is a good idea given our family history when she laughs.

'I'm joking, Mother. Don't worry, there will not be any more doctors in either of our lives,' she says, and it's a relief that we can have a moment of light-heartedness despite our troubled past.

'Well, whatever it is that you decide to do, I know that you'll be brilliant at it,' I say with a smile, but also a pain in my heart. If my daughter does graduate one day, I won't be there to see it. Nor will I be there to witness her build her career, but that's no different to me missing out on her future wedding or visiting her home one day or playing with the grandchildren she might eventually have. I'll miss it all, resigned to just hearing stories about her life while I sit in this room, and that's easily the worst part of my punishment. I can take the rubbish meals and the lack of direct sunlight for most of the day, but not seeing my daughter live her life is tough and will only get tougher the more things she adds to it. But at least I can still see her, albeit in these very unusual and restricted conditions, and that's because I granted her the wish she had when she asked me to return to Arberness.

I kept my promise to my daughter and, because of that, I still have something to live for.

The rest of our visit goes far too quickly for my liking, despite me trying to savour every single second of it like I always do. By the time I am told it's over, I have to face the fact that I won't see Cecilia for a while again now.

'Have fun out there,' I say, before almost telling her not to do anything that I wouldn't do, but I bite my tongue and realise that's probably not the most sensible thing I could say, given the circumstances. I hope there are as few similarities between me and my child as possible, but one of them is clear. We are both survivors. Cecilia has survived what I have put her through. Almost just as amazingly – I have survived it all too.

Despite the things I have done, things that were a very long time ago but no less damaging with the passage of time, I am still here. Still standing. Still going. That's how I like to see myself – as a survivor more than a victim. The only time I ever was a victim was when I first found out about Drew's affair, an affair no happily married wife ever asks for. Back then, for a short while, I was nothing more than the poor doctor's wife. But, due to what he did to me, and the fact I had to take so many actions in self-defence in the aftermath of my revenge, I transformed into something more powerful. Ultimately, what happened in the end means that, whatever anyone might call me now, no one will ever say that I was simply a victim.

It's harsh, but then maybe I like it that way. It will mean I'll always be remembered for taking action as opposed to being passive, and I will be remembered as cunning rather than naïve. Do I ever miss my old self? No, that woman is long gone. What I miss now are far less selfish things. Like my daughter, obviously, because I don't see her enough. I miss Pierre too, and regret that our love ended so tragically and untimely. I miss my parents, though it was a huge relief to know that they are still alive and still in good health. Hopefully, I can reconcile with them one day, but I accept they are still processing everything that their daughter has done in her life. And I did a lot. I also miss my old friends, friends whom I never expect to hear from again, but friends I have great memories with that I will cherish forever. Perhaps most of all, I miss being like everybody else – a normal, functioning member of society. That'll never be me again. I'm too famous and too feared for that.

But I survived it all.

I guess that's the most important thing.

As my daughter leaves the prison, I am led straight into the canteen where I join all the other prisoners for lunch. This is one of the highlights of the day, which isn't saying much in here, and as I take my place in the queue to get food, I am wondering what is on the menu. I'm guessing it's nothing particularly appetising, and I'm right when I see the sloppy offerings being scooped into the bowls of my fellow inmates ahead of me. Fortunately, there is a fruit bowl too, so I decide I'll stock up there rather than risk food poisoning by eating whatever the prison chef has cooked up in the kitchen today.

Reaching the fruit bowl, I take a banana and an orange, but it's the sight of the juicy green apples on top that get my attention, and the famous old saying plays in my head, causing me to smile wryly as it does.

An apple a day keeps the doctor away.

Given my history, I guess I better play it safe then.

I'll take two.

A LETTER FROM DANIEL

Dear reader,

I want to say a huge thank you for choosing to read *The Doctor's Child*. I hope you enjoyed following the misadventures of Fern Devlin for a fourth time! If you did enjoy it and would like to keep up to date with all my latest Bookouture releases, please sign up to my Bookouture newsletter at the following link. Your email address will never be shared, and you can unsubscribe at any time.

www.bookouture.com/daniel-hurst

I hope you loved this fourth book in *The Doctor's Wife* series and, if you did, I would be very grateful if you could write an honest review. I'd like to hear what you think! You can read my free short story, 'The Killer Wife', by signing up to my Bookouture mailing list here.

You can also visit my website where you can download a free psychological thriller called *Just One Second* and join my personal weekly newsletter, where you can hear all about my future writing as well as my adventures with my wife, Harriet, and daughter, Penny!

Thank you,

Daniel

KEEP IN TOUCH WITH DANIEL

Get in touch with me directly at my email address daniel@danielhurstbooks.com. I reply to every message!

www.danielhurstbooks.com

 facebook.com/danielhurstbooks
instagram.com/danielhurstbooks

PUBLISHING TEAM

Turning a manuscript into a book requires the efforts of many people. The publishing team at Bookouture would like to acknowledge everyone who contributed to this publication.

Audio
Alba Proko
Sinead O'Connor
Melissa Tran

Commercial
Lauren Morrissette
Hannah Richmond
Imogen Allport

Data and analysis
Mark Alder
Mohamed Bussuri

Editorial
Natasha Harding
Lizzie Brien

Copyeditor
Janette Currie

PRAISE FOR USA TODAY BESTSELLING AUTHOR JAN MORAN

Seabreeze Inn and *Coral Cottage* series

"A wonderful story... Will make you feel like the sea breeze is streaming through your hair." – Laura Bradbury, Bestselling Author

"A novel that gives fans of romantic sagas a compelling voice to follow." – *Booklist*

"An entertaining beach read with multi-generational context and humor." – *InD'Tale* Magazine

"Wonderful characters and a sweet story." – Kellie Coates Gilbert, Bestselling Author

"A fun read that grabs you at the start." – Tina Sloan, Author and Award-Winning Actress

"Jan Moran is the queen of the epic romance." —Rebecca Forster, *USA Today* Bestselling Author

"The women are intelligent and strong. At the core is a strong, close-knit family." — Betty's Reviews

The Chocolatier

"A delicious novel, makes you long for chocolate." – *Ciao Tutti*

"Smoothly written...full of intrigue, love, secrets, and romance." – *Lekker Lezen*

The Winemakers

"Readers will devour this page-turner as the mystery and passions spin out." – *Library Journal*

"As she did in *Scent of Triumph*, Moran weaves knowledge of wine and winemaking into this intense family drama." – *Booklist*

The Perfumer: Scent of Triumph

"Heartbreaking, evocative, and inspiring, this book is a powerful journey." – Allison Pataki, *New York Times* Bestselling Author of *The Accidental Empress*

"A sweeping saga of one woman's journey through World War II and her unwillingness to give up even when faced with the toughest challenges." — Anita Abriel, Author of *The Light After the War*

"A captivating tale of love, determination and reinvention." — Karen Marin, Givenchy Paris

"A stylish, compelling story of a family. What sets this apart is the backdrop of perfumery that suffuses the story with the delicious aromas – a remarkable feat!" — Liz Trenow, *New York Times* Bestselling Author of *The Forgotten Seamstress*

"Courageous heroine, star-crossed lovers, splendid sense of time and place capturing the unease and turmoil of the 1940s; HEA." — *Heroes and Heartbreakers*

BOOKS BY JAN MORAN

Summer Beach Series

Seabreeze Inn

Seabreeze Summer

Seabreeze Sunset

Seabreeze Christmas

Seabreeze Wedding

Seabreeze Book Club

Seabreeze Shores

Coral Cottage

Coral Cafe

Coral Holiday

The Love, California Series

Flawless

Beauty Mark

Runway

Essence

Style

Sparkle

20th-Century Historical

Hepburn's Necklace

The Chocolatier

The Winemakers: A Novel of Wine and Secrets

The Perfumer: Scent of Triumph

Seabreeze
Book Club

USA TODAY BESTSELLING AUTHOR
JAN MORAN

SEABREEZE BOOK CLUB

SUMMER BEACH, BOOK 6

JAN MORAN

SUNNY PALMS

PRESS

Library of Congress Cataloging-in-Publication Data

Moran, Jan.

/ by Jan Moran

ISBN 978-1-64778-045-6 (epub ebook)

ISBN 978-1-64778-047-0 (hardcover)

ISBN 978-1-64778-046-3 (paperback)

ISBN 978-1-64778-049-4 (audiobook)

ISBN 978-1-64778-048-7 (large print)

Published by Sunny Palms Press. Cover design by Sleepy Fox Studios. Cover images copyright Deposit Photos.

Sunny Palms Press

9663 Santa Monica Blvd STE 1158

Beverly Hills, CA 90210 USA

www.sunnypalmspress.com

www.JanMoran.com

1

"It's a wonderful home for you," Ivy said, surveying Mitch's casual beach cottage where Shelly's suitcases and a few moving boxes were stacked in the corner. Sea breezes wafted through the open windows facing the ocean. Ivy breathed in the fresh, natural scent of warm sand, sunshine, and saltwater that filled the simple cottage. "Such a cozy space. It feels light and happy."

"One bedroom is all we need right now." Shelly tucked the sunflowers Ivy had bought at Blossoms into a chipped, blue ceramic pitcher. She placed the arrangement on a wooden picnic table in the dining alcove. "This is more room than I ever had in New York. And just look at that view."

Her sister was moving into her new husband's home in Summer Beach, not far from the Seabreeze Inn she and Shelly had been operating for a little more than a year. Shelly was close enough to walk to work at the inn, and Ivy couldn't be happier for her.

Still, she felt a twinge of sadness. Ivy would miss sharing coffee in the morning or a glass of wine on the terrace and discussing the day's events with her.

"I'm glad you're happy," Ivy said. Before her sister's

wedding, Ivy had been concerned about the relationship. Still, since Shelly and Mitch had returned from their brief honeymoon in Baja California—basking at a friend's beach house—their relationship seemed solid.

Maybe that's what she and Bennett should do. They needed something; she knew that.

"Mitch says this is one of the original beach cottages." As Shelly glanced around, she brushed back wayward strands of hair that had escaped her casual topknot. She wore a turquoise sundress that had belonged to their mother, so it was a little short for her. Around her neck were layers of silver and turquoise that she'd brought back from her trip.

Shelly went on. "I know this place looks a little shabby, but Mitch swears it's sturdy."

"Shabby chic is a style," Ivy said, gesturing toward the chipped pitcher. "It fits here."

"This place might be small, but it's paid for," Shelly said. "Mitch bought it when he first started making money at Java Beach. Bennett told him beach property would be a good investment. Later, one of his regulars gave him a stock tip about a hot new technology company over coffee, so Mitch put some money into the company. When the stock shot up, he sold it and paid off the house."

"I'm impressed," Ivy said, checking out the whitewashed overhead beams. They seemed solid enough, much like Mitch. Despite a tough childhood and a grave misstep as a teen that had landed him in prison for a year paying off the theft he'd committed, he had made something of himself. But most of all, he loved her sister. "When did he tell you that?"

"While we were lounging on the beach in Baja." Shelly smiled. The sun had brought out the freckles on her nose and cheeks.

"That was a nice surprise," Ivy said. "And there's plenty of room on the lot to add on another bedroom or two when you need it."

Ivy wondered how soon Shelly and Mitch would start a family. Her sister had been eager to have a child for years, and at her age, she didn't have much more time. Mitch was nearly a decade younger than Shelly and still in his late twenties. Ivy wasn't sure if he felt the same urgency as Shelly.

Shelly heaved a sigh. "That's the last thing I want to think about now. First, I need to kick this stomach bug I picked up in Mexico. Mitch warned me against drinking unfiltered water." A shadow crossed Shelly's face, and she glanced away. "Besides, I have to spruce up the place." She tapped on the weathered wooden table. "I'll sand this and give it a coat of white paint. The old bookshelf there, too. I need a place for my books."

"We can do a lot with paint." Though Shelly had swiftly changed the subject, Ivy had caught it, along with the flimsy excuse she gave. Ivy wondered about that. As a child, when-ever Shelly didn't want to do something or was hiding some-thing—such as forgotten homework—she'd feigned illness.

Ivy hoped Mitch hadn't changed his mind about starting a family. Earlier, he'd been reticent about having children because he'd grown up with an abusive father and feared he might have inherited the psychological tendency. But she thought he'd worked that out in therapy before the wedding.

Ivy had to ask. "Are things okay with you and Mitch?"

"It's just that everyone is asking about us starting a family, even if they are joking about it." Shelly threw up her hands. "I've waited forever, okay? And it's getting kind of personal. It will happen when it happens. Or not."

"I completely understand, and it's your right not to talk about it." Rather than press the issue, Ivy put her arm around Shelly's shoulders and nodded toward a battered surfboard propped on glass blocks that served as a coffee table. "What about this surfer dude theme?"

"It's going to be history in about a week." Shelly twisted her lips to one side. "I feel like I'm living in Java Beach. Fortu-

nately, Mitch says he's ready for a change, so he can move that
to the coffee shop."

In the small, airy cottage, vintage surf posters lined the
walls, the windows were bare, and a denim-covered futon
served as a couch. The hearth of a stone fireplace held a mix
of seashells and driftwood probably collected from the beach.

It was clear that Mitch had taken little interest in his
home, but he spent most of his time at Java Beach serving the
best breakfast in town or taking tourists on charter tours on his
boat. He worked hard, though he still fit in surfing almost
every day to unwind.

"What are you planning to do with the place?" Ivy asked.

"I want to put in a garden right away—I have vegetables
and herbs that I started in the greenhouse at the inn. Mitch
and I have talked about transforming the rear yard with stone
pavers, a covering, and a fire pit. Once that's underway, I'll
begin on the interior. Mitch liked my idea of blue and white
with cheerful pops of color. I'll video the entire process for my
channel."

Shelly had been running a lifestyle video blog that over the
past year she'd expanded from her New York City floral
arrangements and thrift shop finds to include the work she'd
done on the old beach house that Ivy's husband had unexpectedly left her after he died.

As Ivy looked around, she bit her lip. "Do you have time
for all that right away?"

"Why wouldn't I?"

"It's summer, the inn is at full capacity, and the house
needs work."

The Seabreeze Inn had been the summer home of Amelia
and Gustav Erickson, wealthy art collectors from Germany via
San Francisco. The palatial old home the couple had once
called Las Brisas del Mar had become dated and worn over
the decades.

"My landscaping is still in great shape, isn't it?"

"I really need help with more than that." Although Shelly and Mitch had been back only a few days from their honeymoon, Ivy was already a little miffed at Shelly's attitude.

Last year, Shelly had helped transform the overgrown grounds and redecorate the shabby interior. Since they'd arrived, the old house had become a new center of activity in the village. And it had given Ivy and Shelly a chance for new beginnings. They had agreed to split the earnings.

Shelly rolled her eyes. "Okay. You don't have to keep asking."

Ivy bit back a comment. Moving into Mitch's house was supposed to be a happy time for Shelly, and Ivy didn't want to ruin it with an argument. After all, her sister was thrilled to be living her dream at long last.

Ivy turned toward the boxes of Shelly's belongings that Mitch had brought from the inn. Seeing her sister's belongings in the cottage brought home the reality that Shelly was gone. Ivy felt a strange tightness in her chest. She rubbed a spot just beneath her collarbone.

Maybe it was separation sadness. Ivy and Shelly had been through so much together in the last year. Little more than a year ago, with their lives at the lowest points they'd ever known, they had decided to start fresh in Summer Beach. And now, this was supposed to be the happiest time in Shelly's life.

Mine, too, right? Ivy thought about Bennett and how understanding he had been with her.

She bit a corner of her mouth. "It's going to be quiet at the inn without you."

"Hey, I'm still working there," Shelly said, slinging an arm around Ivy. "I'll be back soon. I just need a couple of good nights' sleep after our trip." She grinned. "I won't bore you with the details—just beware of cloudy water."

"I hope you get over what that is." Hearing Shelly say she would return calmed Ivy a little. "Still, it won't be the same without you around all the time. Whose room will I run to when the storms hit?"

"Won't Bennett be right there beside you?"

Ivy shrugged. "I don't know what people would think about that."

Shelly's mouth dropped open. "You're kidding, right?"

"That was a commitment ceremony. It's not really legal without a marriage license." It was Ivy's fault for not updating her driver's license and passport. Every proof of identity she had was expired, and she had no idea where her birth certificate was.

Rolling her eyes, Shelly said, "Who cares? Brother Rip, a *bona fide* man of the cloth, performed the ceremony. Besides, you're adults. And everyone knows you're a couple in Summer Beach. Geez, don't be so old-fashioned, Ives."

But I am, Ivy wanted to say. It had only been two years since her husband had died, and she was just getting back on her feet financially—and emotionally. While her adult daughters seemed okay with Bennett's new place in their lives, Ivy wanted to make sure they hadn't been caught up in the excitement of the crazy wedding weekend that had turned out far different than planned. What had started as a guest wedding had turned into a hasty, though beautiful, ceremony for Shelly and Mitch.

"Bennett understands," Ivy said.

Shelly arched an eyebrow. "Does he?"

"He's patient. And this is all so new to me." Ivy fidgeted with a frayed seam on her yellow cotton sundress. Bennett had been her surfing crush when they were teenagers, and now he was the mayor of Summer Beach. She might have dreamed of being with him as a kid, but she had never imagined her life might turn out this way.

"New is good," Shelly said.

Ivy shifted and leaned against the edge of the table. "It's just that sometimes I still wake up expecting to see Jeremy next to me. And I'm so relieved when I realize I'm free, even though I have a lot of responsibilities."

"And Bennett."

"I do love him," Ivy said. She'd been a stay-at-home-mother in Boston when her husband had died from a sudden aneurysm. Becoming a beach-front innkeeper had been the farthest thing from her mind. So was remarrying, although she truly loved Bennett. "We agreed that our ceremony was simply to announce our intention."

"You're not kids," Shelly said pointedly. "It's okay to do whatever you want."

"We'll get there," Ivy said, feeling a little foolish, but she couldn't help how she felt. The past year had been incredible, not only because she'd fallen in love again, but also because she'd risen to the challenge of running the inn. On her own, she'd pushed herself far beyond her comfort zone. And prevailed. That felt good, but would she lose that again in marriage?

Shelly quirked her mouth to one side. "I agree with Mom. Bennett's a hot commodity. Be careful you don't let him slip away."

"He's the one who should be worried I don't get away," Ivy shot back, mustering more confidence than she felt.

She wished she could talk to her mother. When Carlotta and Sterling Bay had pulled into the first port they'd planned in Mexico, they'd called each of their children to tell them what a wonderful time they were having. But they decided that it took too long with poor connections. They promised to rotate calls among their children in California.

Ivy figured her parents were somewhere off the coast of Mexico or another Central American country now, soaking up the sun on the first leg of their voyage around the world—which was partly the reason Shelly had eagerly jumped at the opportunity to get married before they left. Had she and

Bennett succumbed to the moment, or was this a real marriage?

Shelly laughed. "At least he can't call you easy."

Ivy felt her face flush. The last two years had been a roller-coaster of life changes and emotional upheaval. After all Jeremy had put her through—especially the revelations that surfaced about his mistress Paisley—after he died, why did she sometimes reach for Jeremy in pre-dawn slumber? As much as she loved Bennett, she worried that her subconscious self wasn't entirely ready for such a shift.

She owed it to Bennett to be all in.

Yet, Ivy was enjoying her new life now. With each day, she was discovering more of who she was and what she wanted. Ivy figured it sounded silly to say that at her age. Shelly prob-ably wouldn't understand, and she wondered how Bennett would take that.

Ivy shrugged away from Shelly. "Give me a break, Shells. It's been a crazy, tumultuous, stressful year." She'd barely managed to avoid a looming tax sale, and filling the inn with guests was still a challenge in the off-season.

In fact, she wondered if what she felt for Bennett was true love or an emotional grasp? She'd been so lonely the year after Jeremy's death. Maybe she was still protecting her heart.

On the other hand, who was Ivy Bay now? She was not the college freshman she'd been when she'd met Jeremy. She wanted her turn to flourish.

She and Bennett were still trying to decide what to do about their living situation. After their commitment ceremony, they'd spent a romantic evening in his apartment, the old chauffeur's quarters above the garages, and he'd strummed his guitar for her just as he had once done. Her room in the main house was awfully close to the guestrooms, but she still felt out of place in his apartment.

Admittedly, she enjoyed the freedom of having her own

room. But it was more than that. She wanted to be absolutely certain this time around.

Shelly folded her arms, scrutinizing Ivy. "I know what you need. A proper honeymoon. Being on the beach in Baja without any distractions was incredible. No Java Beach, no Seabreeze Inn—as much as we love all that. Mitch and I needed that alone time for the right start to our marriage."

"I have no time for that with the summer crowd here," Ivy said, surprised that Shelly would think she did. Summer was their biggest season, and Ivy couldn't risk that income. It had been hard enough without Shelly, but Ivy had been happy to cover for her while she and Mitch were away. She wanted her sister to have an excellent start to the married life she'd dreamed of for so long. "We have to make our numbers for the year."

"That's a shame," Shelly said. "I think you and Bennett need to bond more."

"I think I know more about bonding with a husband than you do," Ivy said, bristling at Shelly's comment. As if that would be the simple solution. "Suddenly, you're an expert?"

Shelly pressed a palm forward. "Geez, chill. I meant this marriage with Bennett will be a lot different for you. Jeremy could be a real jerk. Honestly, I don't know how you put up with him all those years."

"I loved him, and he was a good provider and a great father to the girls." At least, that's what Ivy had told herself for years. With his French accent and passion for living, Jeremy had easily swept her into his world, although he had lived a double life without her knowledge. Now, even she had to admit his serious flaws.

Shelly rolled her eyes. "Was he your best friend?"

Ivy couldn't answer that. "I am not taking marriage advice from you when you've been married for what, ten minutes?"

"Two weeks. And you're in denial."

"I am not."

"See? You're even in denial about being in denial."

Ivy shook her head.

"Seriously, you've got the man you've always really wanted right in front of you. Don't blow this, Ives."

"Says the one who always leapt first and regretted it later. I like to organize my life."

"I did not jump into anything with Mitch. I'm sure of my feelings for him." Shelly eyed her with some suspicion. "Besides, you already took the leap. Why are you back-pedaling now?"

Ivy couldn't explain it, and Shelly would never understand. She'd given so much to her husband and daughters—sometimes, they sucked the oxygen out of her. She needed time to breathe on her own.

Maybe that's silly. But there it was.

"Can I help you unpack?" Ivy asked, shifting the conversation.

"It won't take long," Shelly replied with a flick of her shoulder. "But you can help me squeeze my clothes into the closet." She picked up some hanging garments from the stack. "I'm looking for an old armoire; I need more hanging space."

"Antique Times might have something," Ivy said, relieved that Shelly let go of the marriage topic. "Nan and Arthur are always getting in new pieces."

Shelly grinned back at her. "New old pieces, you mean."

Ivy folded a stack of hanging clothes over her arm and followed Shelly into the bedroom. They managed to stuff what Shelly had brought into the narrow closet, although she still had a lot left at the inn. Ivy had given her a new set of sheets and a duvet that Shelly had admired at a local home goods shop, along with fluffy white towels. Together they changed the linens, and Shelly arranged pillows Ivy had made on the bed.

"Wow, what a difference already," Shelly said, her eyes sparkling with delight. "I love your artistic pillows."

Ivy had painted palm trees and beach scenes on pillows for the new gift shop they'd set up in a corner of the inn's parlor. "They're selling well. I'm even taking special orders."

"Look at you go," Shelly said. "Poppy told me you got a commission for a beach painting, too."

She had, and she'd been thrilled about it, even though she was a little nervous about making sure the client liked it. "Maybe I have a future as an artist after all."

Her parents had sold several of her paintings at the art show they'd hosted on the grounds of the Seabreeze Inn. The extra income was welcome, though she barely had time to paint between running the inn and giving art lessons to guests. The pillows were quick and easy for her, yet she missed having the time to contemplate and finish more serious pieces.

The summer tourist season was underway, and filling guestrooms was the highest priority. Businesses in Summer Beach that catered to visitors earned most of their income in the summer. Fortunately, reservations at the inn were steady, and Poppy's online ads were filling rooms during the week, too.

"I've got to rush back," Ivy said. "We're expecting a lot of new guests for the weekend."

"I'll come in after I take a nap," Shelly said, stifling a yawn. "I've been so tired ever since we got back. But I promise I'll get back in my groove."

"We've got this now." Ivy tilted her chin, still smarting from Shelly's earlier comments. "Poppy is there, and after her classes, Sunny shows guests to their rooms."

Shelly heaved a sigh. "Don't be a child. I'm not abandoning you."

"Says the younger sister."

"Can we stop this?" Shelly flung her arms around Ivy. "Now you know what all that sisterly advice you dish out feels like."

"Okay," Ivy said begrudgingly. Shelly was probably right;

Ivy had a lot on her mind. "Relax and get unpacked. And I could use your help this weekend."

"You got it." Shelly slapped her hands against her cheeks. "Maybe I just need another cup of coffee. I can't let you have all the fun."

Ivy managed a grin. "See, I knew you were missing the inn already. Just remember what you said when I ask you to work on the lower level with me."

"Oh, no," Shelly said, wagging a finger. "You're the one who knocked the hole in the kitchen wall and opened up that mess."

"With your help," Ivy said, her mood lifting. She poked her sister. "Seriously, we have to put that space to good use."

"Any ideas?"

"We could create meeting space down there," Ivy said. "Maybe we could attract small corporate getaways in the off-season. They could hold strategy sessions or host private gatherings."

Shelly grinned. "Sure, like an old speakeasy. Or a casino night fundraiser. That would be cool. Maybe the Ericksons used that level for secret parties during Prohibition."

They talked a little more, and Shelly promised she'd see her soon.

As Ivy strolled back to the inn, she thought about options for the space that had been sealed for decades. Ivy turned a corner in the beachside neighborhood, and the Seabreeze Inn loomed ahead past the village. The grand Spanish Revival-style house had revealed the former owner's passion for secrecy. Now, Ivy was fairly certain they'd discovered all they were going to find—from priceless paintings to important jewels of historical significance.

She had turned all those beautiful items over to the FBI to be returned to former owners. All she had gained was publicity for the inn, which had helped, but it wasn't the millions some visitors imagined she'd profited.

If only Amelia Erickson had tucked away a little cash, too.

Peering at the roofline, Ivy thought how she could use a smidgen of that now. The high winds last week had dislodged a few more tiles on the roof. Her brother Forrest, who was a contractor, had patched the roof. Eventually she'd have to replace it. On a house of this size, a new roof would be quite expensive. She had to find another way to increase the income to provide maintenance to the property.

Or this summer might be their last.

Ivy was eager to use the inn's lower level, which had been concealed for decades. This is where she and Shelly had discovered the furniture and artwork Amelia Erickson had stashed when she had feared a West Coast invasion during the Second World War. In the 1940s, an enemy submarine had run aground on the coastline, so it wasn't such a far-fetched concern.

After a brisk walk from Shelly's bungalow, Ivy turned into the property and hurried past stately palm trees that stood like sentinels on guard. She strode along the stone path where Shelly had planted purple and pink petunias along a border of white alyssum. On this sunny day, butterflies flitted among pink hibiscus and lavender bushes.

Her sister had put her horticulture degree to good use in bringing the neglected grounds back to life. This year, Shelly had added rambling white roses and pink bougainvillea.

Ivy hoped Shelly would continue to keep it up now that she was married and planning to start a family. Her sister meant well, but Ivy knew how much time it took to be a wife and mother.

She hoped Mitch hadn't changed his mind about starting a family. It wasn't anything Shelly had said, but Ivy sensed that something wasn't quite right—beyond her sister not feeling well.

· · ·

When Ivy walked into the inn, Poppy met her at the front door.

"Aunt Ivy, I have a confession to make," Poppy said, looking remorseful. "I've done something awful."

"I'm sure it isn't that bad." Her niece was so thoughtful and efficient, Ivy couldn't imagine Poppy purposefully doing anything even remotely worth confessing.

"You know that antique glass platter of Amelia's that you like so much?"

Immediately, Ivy knew where this was going. "The one that was chipped? I saw a crack in that just the other day. I probably did it while I was doing the dishes."

Poppy's shoulders relaxed. "You did not, but that's nice of you to say."

"No, I'm quite sure I did. We probably ought to throw it away."

"Well, it doesn't matter because I finished it off while you were gone."

"I hope no one was hurt."

"Just my pride."

"That can be mended," Ivy said. "You can help me find another one in the butler's pantry." She led the way toward the storage and serving area off the kitchen. "I wonder why we still call this a butler's pantry?" Ivy mused as she entered the long, narrow room. "I doubt if any actual butlers will ever darken this door again."

Poppy smiled. "Thanks for not being upset, Aunt Ivy. I know it was your favorite."

"You're more favorite than that," Ivy said, dismissing the thought with a wave of her hand. "Now, let's explore these cupboards and see what we have to choose from for the morning muffins."

Ivy opened the tall cupboard doors that reached to the ceiling. Vintage crystal, china, and flatware had never been removed. The house had been used for charity events for years. Some pieces showed the wear while others looked as if they hadn't been touched since Amelia left.

Poppy opened a cupboard. "This looks like the serving platter department. What about those dark pieces up at the top? I can't tell what they're made of."

Ivy squinted at the top shelf. "Those are probably silver." She grinned at Poppy. "Unbreakable, so let's have a look. Could you bring the step ladder here and hold it for me?"

"On it," Poppy said as she fetched the small ladder.

Ivy gathered the folds of her yellow sundress in one hand and climbed the ladder. "These are beautiful. Sterling silver, I would guess. Amelia only bought the best." She reached for a rectangular piece that was rimmed with intricate scrollwork. Handles were fashioned from the same pattern.

"If Shelly were here, she'd probably be wondering how much we could get for them," Poppy said.

"I know, but I like to keep as much intact in this old house as I can." Standing on her tiptoes, Ivy grabbed the handle. "This is heavy. Can you grab it? I'll pass it down to you."

"I'm ready," Poppy said.

Ivy slid out the tray and handed it to her niece. As she did, a small book that had been propped behind the platter fell face forward with a puff of dust. Ivy sneezed. "Hold on, I see something else. Nothing has been cleaned in years up here."

Below her, Poppy put the silver platter on the counter. "Need a cleaning rag?"

Ivy reached for the book and slid it out. She blew dust from the top of the leather-bound book. "Definitely." She tucked it under her arm and started down the ladder.

Poppy peered up at the shelves. "I can get up there and wipe it all down for you."

"Only if you have some free time. And get Sunny to help you." Ivy turned over the small volume. "This looks interesting." She looked up at the top shelf. "Might want to check to see if anything else is hidden up there. You know how Amelia was."

The old house had protected the former owner's treasures well. From paintings stashed behind a brick wall that led to the lower level to crown jewels stitched inside of a doll in the trunk of the vintage Chevy, Amelia Erickson had been a master of concealment.

Carefully, Ivy thumbed through the yellowed pages of the slim volume. "It looks like a guest registry of some sort."

Poppy peered over her shoulder. "Since it's in the butler's pantry, would it be a record of dinner guests? Although it seems weird that they would sign in."

"People did things differently back then, especially among the upper classes. And having come from Europe, the Ericksons had more formal ways than in the States, even in their beach house. They had their standards to uphold."

Poppy nodded. "It seems fussy in a way, but on the other hand, it would make regular dinners more special. Sort of like dressing for dinner. I've been reading a historical novel with characters changing clothes more times in a day than some people at the beach change in a week. I keep thinking about the laundry they had to do."

"Wealthy people had staff for that," Ivy said. She turned to the front page of the book and began to read. *"The Literary Society of Summer Beach, Presided Over by Amelia Erickson."*

"I wonder what kind of books they were reading?"

"Let's see." Ivy turned the page. "Wow, look at this. The first one was *Pride and Prejudice.*"

"Oh, my gosh, they were reading Jane Austen?" Poppy squealed with delight. "I read that book in college. And did you see the movie? We were all in love with Mr. Darcy."

"Tall, dark, and moody never goes out of style." As Ivy said that, a funny thought struck her. In a similar fashion, Bennett had been her Mr. Darcy. "I saw the film, but I've never read the book."

"You have to, Aunt Ivy. You'd love it. I read it in my English classics literature course. I think that book was written in the late 1700s."

Ivy ran her hand over the faded ink with reverence. "That sounds about right."

"So Amelia and her friends were reading the classics, too."

"It's interesting to think of it that way, isn't it?" Ivy read through the list of signatures neatly entered on the thick ivory paper. "Josefina Osuna. Vana Spencer. Allison Margolese. Karin Becker. Marta Mueller." She paused and looked up. "What a treasure this is."

"I wonder why she hid it in the cabinet?" Poppy asked.

"It might have been to protect some of the attendants, or maybe it was due to her advancing Alzheimer's disease. We'll never know."

Poppy's eyes flashed with excitement. "Now I can't wait to clean all the cupboards. Maybe we'll find more of Amelia's hidden treasures."

Ivy laughed at that. "Shelly is always looking for a hidden pot of gold. Maybe this time you'll find it, although I doubt it. But if you do, we still need that roof repaired." She shook her head. There would be time for that later. "Come on, let's clean up these items before today's guests arrive."

"How do we clean this silver?" Poppy held up the tarnished platter.

Ivy inspected the old piece. It was heavily oxidized and discolored, and her first thought was to call her mother. But of course, Carlotta was a thousand miles away on board the boat with their father. And no doubt having a wonderful time. Ivy wouldn't disturb her for this.

"I don't know if we can restore it to its former magnificence," Ivy said. "However, I seem to recall that your grandmother once used a solution of vinegar and baking soda in a sink full of water. I'm not sure if that's entirely correct, but it's worth a try."

"We could ask Auntie Google," Poppy offered.

"I suppose we could, but I'm pretty sure of the vinegar. Mom uses that a lot."

"Like we do for the windows in this place."

"It sure saves on cleaning supplies," Ivy said, smiling. Back then, with a young, growing family, Carlotta had learned to cut corners. Even today, Ivy preferred many of her mother's old methods honed long before store-bought versions arrived on grocery shelves. Carlotta had saved money so that she and Sterling could start their import business.

Ivy walked toward the cleaning supply cupboard. "Would you research online while I get supplies?"

Poppy pulled her phone from the back pocket of her white jeans. She tapped the screen a few times. "Here it is, Aunt Ivy. Actually, there seem to be several methods. One woman says to pour white vinegar and baking soda into hot water in a foil-lined pan or sink, but don't use straight vinegar. This guy swears by lime juice and salt. And another woman says that toothpaste or detergent is good to use."

"Whatever we choose, let's be careful not to scratch the surface," Ivy said. "I have an idea. Why don't we call Arthur and Nan at Antique Times? I bet they'll know."

While Poppy called and spoke to Arthur, Ivy brought out a feather duster from the supply closet. Working carefully, she whisked away decades of dust from the cover of the guest book. "A literary salon," she mused to herself. She could hardly wait to read through the guest ledger.

Ivy glanced at the kitchen clock. She didn't have much time before guests began to arrive. Motioning to Poppy, Ivy left the small volume with reluctance and made her way into the foyer to welcome new guests. She could trust the silver cleaning to Poppy.

As Ivy approached the entryway, through the window she saw a car slow in front of the house. Just in time, she thought.

Many visitors drove by the old house, but this might also be a guest.

Shifting her attention to work, Ivy sat at the front desk and checked the list of expected guests. She was grateful that summer bookings were going well, but she still needed more to pay for years of neglected maintenance.

Behind her, she heard sharp taps on the wooden stairs. Moments later, a tiny Chihuahua shot past her.

"Pixie," Ivy called out. "Stop right there."

Pixie's toenails clattered across the parquet floor as she made her escape—no doubt looking for something to snatch and carry back to her lair. Pixie belonged to one of their long-term guests, Gilda, who had lost her home in the Ridgetop Fire last year.

"Oh, no, you don't, you little thief," Ivy said, starting after her. Just then, she spotted a new guest coming up the walkway.

"Poppy," she cried out, cupping her hands like a megaphone. "Pixie alert. Heading toward the dining room. I have to check in a guest."

"I'll corner her," Poppy called back. Her niece raced from the kitchen and rushed after the little dog, who was making a mad escape toward an open door to the veranda. "Where's Gilda?"

"Upstairs. She probably doesn't realize Pixie slipped out."

Gilda often worked with her headphones on, and if the door hadn't shut properly, Pixie could push it open. Yesterday, she'd made off with a guest's silk scarf, and Ivy had spied her dragging it up the stairs like a prize. Fortunately, the woman hadn't noticed it missing, though Ivy insisted on having it dry cleaned. Louise at the Laundry Basket had tended to it right away.

The front door opened, and a young woman stepped inside. She was an attractive thirty-something in jeans and boots, though her hair was a little disheveled as if she'd been traveling all day. She dropped a bag beside the desk with a thud and heaved a sigh.

"Welcome to the Seabreeze Inn," Ivy said brightly, striding back to the desk. "Checking in?"

The woman ran a hand over her hair and assumed an attitude. "Isn't that obvious?"

"Well, yes," Ivy replied, reining in a comment. Traveling was tiring, and this wasn't the only weary guest who'd ever arrived suffering jet lag or travel challenges with an attitude to match. "Your name, please?"

The woman hesitated, glancing around. She seemed taken in by the grand architecture before regaining her attitude. "Geena Bellamy. And I need a porter."

"I'll be happy to help you with your bags," Ivy said. "We don't have porters at our little inn—despite the grand entryway. You'll find Summer Beach is pretty relaxed."

Geena frowned. "I'm not here to relax."

Ivy quickly shifted course. "If you're here on business and need to print anything, we have a printer in the library."

"Got her," Poppy called out as she swooped past them with Pixie in her arms.

With a degree of horror, Geena watched Poppy climb the stairs. "You allow dogs here?"

"We do," Ivy replied.

"I'm allergic to dogs," Geena said pointedly.

"Not to worry. Your room is at the other end of the hall. I hope you'll have a productive stay." Ivy understood how severe pet dander allergies could be. She hoped the woman wouldn't have issues.

"I do, too."

Ivy detected more than a trace of animosity in the woman's voice.

"Am I checked in yet?" She rubbed her eyes. "My allergies must be starting already."

"The fresh ocean air might help that." Ivy handed her the key. "Shall I show you to your room now?"

"I can find it by myself. And carry my own baggage. I mean, what else is new?" She picked up her bag. "I've heard about this old house. Mind if I have a look around?"

"Not at all," Ivy said as Geena started for the stairs. That wasn't an unusual request; many architecture aficionados came to appreciate Julia Morgan's design. Others had read about the treasures discovered here.

"Excuse me," Ivy called out before Geena reached the stairway. Although she was unpleasant, she was still a guest. "We have a wine and tea gathering with appetizers this after-noon in the library. Maybe you'd like to stop by to unwind."

"I don't need to unwind, and I don't like crowds." Geena continued up the stairs.

"It's usually a small group..."

Geena ignored her, and Ivy turned back to her desk. At least she'd tried.

Poppy stepped around the corner. "Some people just want to be miserable."

"You heard all that?"

"Enough." Poppy swung her silky blond hair over a shoul-der. "Don't let her rain on your day, Aunt Ivy. She'll be gone soon enough. That's what you always say."

Ivy didn't have much time to worry, though. Another group of guests was arriving. Sometime later, after Ivy had finished checking in all the guests for the evening, Shelly breezed in.

"Better late than never," Shelly said brightly.

Ivy looked up from her paperwork at the guest desk. "Glad you could make it, seeing how it's almost time for our after-noon gathering."

Shelly smirked. "Lighten up, Ives. I'm here. What do you need help with?"

Ivy hadn't been able to get the literary guest registry out of her mind. Quickly, she told Shelly about what she and Poppy had found.

Ivy led her to the kitchen and showed her the guest book. She swiped the feather duster over it again and opened the book. "Look at all these names. And the books they were reading." Ivy was entranced. "Doesn't that speak to you?"

Shelly shrugged. "I don't see what's so exciting about that. I'm still waiting to find the stash of gold."

Ivy smiled at that. "What do you think about continuing Amelia's literary society? We could start a book club."

Shelly put her hands on her hips. "And just how does that make us money?"

Ivy wasn't quite sure yet. "It's good business to give back to the community." She paused, recalling something her mother had once told her. "Often, you have to give before you get."

"Oh, all right. Just stop quoting Mom. I would've done it anyway." Shelly grinned. "It could be kind of cool. I went to a couple of book clubs in New York. For most of the members, it was an excuse to leave the kids at home and drink wine."

"With that kind of experience, I could really use your input," Ivy said, grinning. "We have to do something with the downstairs."

"In that case, I have another great idea." Shelly twisted her lips to one side. "We could create a haunted house for Halloween. Your book club could read one of Stephen King's horror novels—how about *The Shining?*"

"About a haunted inn? You've got to be kidding. That's way too close to home. Pun totally intended."

"Oh, come on. We wouldn't even have to clean up the place." Shelly laughed, clearly enjoying this. "Now, that would be authentic, especially since Amelia is still in residence."

A chill coursed along Ivy's spine. "There's no proof of that."

"You believe what you want, and I'll believe what I know."

"Come on, Shells. We can't afford to scare the guests."

Shelly laughed and poked her back. "People love to be scared, Ives. You know you'd secretly like to see Amelia again. Think of all the questions you could ask her. Such as why she shoved a guest book behind a platter. Or where she hid the gold."

Ivy shook her head. Still, Shelly had a point. She wished she would have had the opportunity to speak to Amelia Erickson. What a life the woman had lived. And what a difference she had made in the lives of others during her life—and after. Her life had truly mattered.

Shaking an unsettling feeling from her shoulders, Ivy turned to her sister. "Maybe we'll stumble upon your gold yet, Shelly. Or something just as valuable." She tapped her fingers. "In fact, I think the new Summer Beach Book Club might open new doors for us."

"Oh, all right," Shelly said. "What can it hurt?"

*S*ince she and Shelly had talked about the book club, Ivy hadn't been able to get that—or the vintage guest book—out of her mind. Still, she had to visit Nailed It in the village to buy some supplies for the old house. Like an aging grand dame, Ivy had to keep the house in cosmetic fixes —wood glue and hinges for one of the guest bathrooms, weather stripping for a door, and a silicone lubricant for sticky windows. She tucked a canvas bag under her shoulder and stepped outside on the front path.

After turning toward the village, Ivy spied her retired neighbor ahead. Darla's royal blue hair shone like peacock feathers in the sunshine. "Hi, Darla," she called. "Wait up, and I'll walk with you."

Darla turned around, her glittery visor flashing. "What's up?"

"I know you love to read," Ivy replied. "Shelly and I have decided to start a Summer Beach book club. Would you like to join us?"

Darla grunted. "Who else is in it?"

"You're the first," Ivy said. Darla could be abrasive, but

Ivy knew there was a reason for that, and she tried to excuse it. Shelly might not like having Darla in the book club, but if their neighbor found out about it and she hadn't been included, Ivy would never hear the end of it. "We thought it would be fun to gather some people who love books."

"Could be."

Darla always sounded cranky with her gruff voice, but Ivy knew that a warm heart lurked under her rough façade. Her relationship with Mitch as a sort of surrogate mother was proof of that. "Does that mean you're interested in joining us?"

Darla threw her a look of exasperation. "Okay. Put me down for it. What are you reading first?"

"We haven't gotten that far yet. Maybe you have some suggestions."

"You bet I do. But I need to know which genre." She lowered her voice as a chatty group of local women jostled past them on the sidewalk. "You don't want your romance readers mixing with your sci-fi or horror readers. Although I read everything. Not many people do." She jerked her head back at the ladies they'd passed.

"Oh, right," Ivy said, taking note. "Good point."

"We could have different clubs," Darla said. "Could be a lot of work, though. I don't know if I'd have the time."

"I wouldn't want to put too much pressure on you." Ivy hadn't planned on Darla taking over. "I thought we could support Pages by ordering books through the shop." Ivy knew Paige was a regular at Java Beach with Darla's cadre of friends. Everyone in town was fond of her. "Maybe we'll get the whole village reading this year."

"She'd like that," Darla said. "There used to be a group of women who met at her shop to talk about books, but that was years ago. They're all gone now." She paused, shading her face from the sun. "Paige is more than a bookseller; she's a book whisperer," Darla added in a reverent tone. "The best I've ever known."

"What does that mean?" Ivy asked.

Darla shifted from one foot to another. "Paige has an uncanny way of knowing which book a person needs to read, even before they tell her what they're looking for. Books that really touch your soul. It's almost spooky."

Ivy considered that. "Sort of like a book therapist?"

"That's it." Suddenly self-conscious, Darla waved a hand as if to dismiss what she'd just said. "But don't tell anyone I said that. It's not like I believe in that kind of stuff."

"Of course not," Ivy said, wondering why Darla would want to keep that a secret. Nothing seemed to be a secret in Summer Beach, where Java Beach was gossip central. "But I don't think that sounds unusual."

"Well, to some, it is."

Ivy seemed to have touched on a sensitive nerve with Darla. Thinking that it might have to do with her late son, she avoided the topic. "Maybe you could put together a list of book suggestions."

She wasn't just trying to humor Darla; she was genuinely interested in what her neighbor was reading. Her mother had once said that you could tell a lot about a person by what they read. Sometimes it was surprising.

"I'd like that," Darla said, visibly relieved. "Paige will be happy to hear about this, too."

"I'll go by her shop after the hardware store," Ivy said. Paige could give her insights into running a book club, too. She'd once been a member of a club in Boston, but that had been years ago.

After leaving Darla at the door to Java Beach, Ivy went next door to Nailed It to buy her supplies.

Once she'd filled her bag and chatted with the owners, Jen and George, Ivy continued on to Pages in the village.

At the entrance to the bookshop, the chime of small,

silver-toned books suspended from a chain on the door rang like fine crystal in the quiet atmosphere. The fragrant air was redolent of home-cut roses, a salty ocean breeze, and that beloved old book aroma. Although the shop looked like it needed a few repairs—peeling paint, stained ceiling, thread-bare carpet—it was a haven for magical escapes with comfy reading areas and whimsical, hand-painted signage and airy design.

Ivy was immediately spellbound. A small plaque by the door identified the building as a 1928 Lilian J. Rice design, noted for her Spanish Colonial Revival design of the Inn at Rancho Santa Fe. Ivy wondered if she had known Julia Morgan, the architect who designed the Seabreeze Inn, originally named Las Brisas del Mar.

"Welcome," called out a spry older woman who was teetering on a wooden ladder to reach a book on a high shelf.

"Would you like me to get that for you?" Ivy asked, concerned.

"Thank you, but I'm quite sure-footed," the woman replied. "I'm Paige with an *i*." Her bright blue eyes twinkled behind lapis-blue glasses. She snagged the book and delivered it into the arms of a waiting child. "Here you are. Everything you need to know about Mars."

The little girl's eyes lit with excitement. "I have to read everything on it because I'm going to be an astronaut someday."

"I believe you will be," Paige said with sincere assurance. As she nodded, her stylish, wavy silver hair skimmed her shoulders.

Delighted, the little girl raced to a corner of the shop where a rag rug and a jumble of embroidered pillows made for a soft landing when she plopped down.

"Her parents were great readers at that age, too," Paige said before her attention was pulled away by another patron.

Ivy glanced around. The store was like a magical cottage,

with antique shelves holding a variety of books, from best-loved classics to new titles. An old surfboard fashioned into a bookshelf displayed beach books while well-worn armchairs and benches provided spots for people to perch while they browsed. And at the center of the shop was a grand, sweeping staircase that had books stacked along one side of each step.

"Excuse me, ma'am," a young boy said. Clutching a book, he climbed the staircase. Each wooden step creaked under his slight weight.

Ivy looked closer at the staircase. Its uneven steps were in need of repair. However, every riser had a quote painted on it in fine, bold strokes and bright colors. Drawn to the artistry, she bent to read the first one, brushed in marine blue.

"There are some things you learn best in calm, and some in storm."
— Willa Cather, *The Song of the Lark*

Ivy thought about the past two years, which had certainly been tumultuous, yet she valued the experience. She'd learned that it was never too late to recreate your life—even if the path was uncertain. Stepping closer, she peered at turquoise lettering on the next one.

"I am not afraid of storms, for I am learning how to sail my ship."
— Louisa May Alcott, *Little Women*

There was a theme, Ivy realized. And yes, she might not have known much when she'd embarked on this entrepreneurial journey, but she was learning every day. She raised her gaze to the crimson words on the next riser.

"Beware; for I am fearless, and therefore powerful."
— Mary Shelley, *Frankenstein*

Ivy chuckled to herself. She hadn't quite attained a level of fearlessness—but she was working toward it. Straightening her shoulders, she realized that over the past year, she had become less likely to stay awake with worry—and more confident that she could handle whatever arose. That felt powerful, indeed.

Letting her gaze travel up the wondrous staircase, Ivy saw that some risers had been painted over—as if the artist had discovered a new truth in the pages of a book. *What magic awaits all whose footsteps fall here*, she thought.

When Paige turned back to her, Ivy introduced herself.

"I've heard all about you," Paige said, her eyes lighting with pleasure. "How fortunate that you've found happiness with our Bennett. You're looking for a book today?"

"Quite a few, actually. My sister and I are starting a book club at the Seabreeze Inn, and we hope you can supply the readers." Ivy went on to tell her about what she had in mind.

"Why, I'd be honored to help you revive the literary tradition at Las Brisas del Mar," Paige said, using the original name of the old beach house.

"Was it well known for that?"

"Indeed. For all the arts, of course."

Ivy smiled at the thought. "I just found a guest book for Amelia Erickson's literary society."

"That's definitely a sign that you must forge ahead with this idea," Paige said with a vigorous shake of her head. "Amelia's literary salons were quite famous. She brought in noted authors to speak—which you could do as well. Her library must have been magnificent." She placed a hand over her heart and sighed at the thought.

Paige's love for books touched Ivy. "There's not much left in the way of books, I'm afraid. But perhaps we'll rebuild." Ivy gestured to the staircase. "I love your selection of quotes. Who is the artist?"

"My daughter," Paige said. "She grew up here, and her first attempts were in crayons. Over the years, she became more discerning, both in her art and her philosophy. She teaches at a university in Los Angeles."

"How nice that she's still close." That explained the changing of quotes, Ivy thought. She glanced around. "Your store is so welcoming and charming. I love your use of color. "

With a wistful expression, Paige took in the shopworn space. "Sometimes I think love and old paint are all that's holding this place together, but I like to honor the past. We're kindred spirits like that, I think." Paige paused and put a finger to her chin. "You haven't read Jane Austen, have you?"

"I was just discussing her with my niece," Ivy said. "Actually, I've only seen the film."

Paige nodded knowingly and adjusted her glasses. "I'll bring a copy of *Pride and Prejudice* for you. No time like the present to see what you've been missing."

"I don't know if I have the time to read such a long book."

Paige's eyes sparkled. "Perhaps you haven't been reading books with the right message for you. And, 'if a book is well written, I always find it too short.' That's not mine, that's Jane Austen, but the sentiment still rings true."

"Maybe so," Ivy allowed. "Some in town say you're a book whisperer. They say you always know the book a person should read."

A demure smile played on Paige's bright, lightly lined face. "I've simply read a lot of books in my time."

"But how do you know what kind of book a person needs versus what they think they want?"

"It's in the eyes, which are the window to their soul, to paraphrase Shakespeare." Paige's eyes sparkled—as if she held a secret known only to her. "Let me know when the first book club meeting will be."

Another customer drew Paige's attention. Ivy was happy to host the book club, but between guests and family, she hardly had time to read, especially an old book that probably went on and on. She sighed, resolving to skim it, at least.

Why Paige thought she might like *Pride and Prejudice* was beyond her. After all, she'd seen the movie years ago, though she could hardly remember much of it except for the handsome Mr. Darcy.

*O*n the way back to the inn, Ivy decided to take the beach route because she'd missed her morning walk. Poppy was looking after the inn, and Shelly should be there soon, so she wouldn't be missed. Drinking in the ocean air, she slung the canvas shopper over her shoulder and slipped off her sandals.

With determined steps, she stumbled over the dunes until she reached the damp, sea-smoothed sand near the water's edge. As she did, Shelly's words about Bennett rushed through her mind.

Seeking to understand her hesitance with Bennett—though she did not question her love for him—Ivy thought about how she'd come to this point in her life.

Over the last couple of years, she'd traded her life as an anticipatory problem-solver—perfectly laundered shirts for Jeremy, new clothes for Sunny, drama lessons for Misty, nutritious meals for all—for a life where she was responsible for only her well-being.

Not counting guests of the inn. Or Sunny. Or running a business.

On the other hand, maybe she was too busy.

She put the roof over her head—although technically, it had been Jeremy's earned income. But hadn't her daily toil been worth something?

Of course, she told herself.

Now, her labor was measured in what a guest would pay for a clean, well-decorated room, a morning meal, and pleasant conversation. She was trading her skills on the open market. And that had bought independence.

She rather liked that feeling.

It was like that first sip of Coca-Cola—all fizzy and sweet and caffeinated. A lot like lust, and even a little like love, except that real love, she thought, deepened into a smooth liqueur of the richest flavor—perhaps the color of Bennett's golden hazel eyes.

When it wasn't right, love settled into a feeling akin to tolerance, excuses for the other, and resignation that this was all there was and would ever be. She knew that feeling—and never wanted it again. But with Bennett, the feeling was different from what she had known before.

Was it really?

With each step, she dug her toes deeper into the sand. Water swirled around her ankles as the sea spilled in and swept out again.

Blinking against the bright sunlight that blazed against the glittering sand, she felt a stark realization hit her like a chilly Pacific wave.

While she had loved Jeremy, they had not been *in* love. The *I've-got-your-back*, *in-sickness-and-in-health*, *first-signs-of-gray*, and *post-baby-belly* kind of love that loves regardless. With Jeremy, she had to maintain her Standards with a capital S. To him, a slight muffin top and gray roots meant she had let herself go in the most egregious manner.

It wasn't her imagination; he'd told her so.

Now she knew that had been a warning before he settled on a younger model.

So now, the love of a good man who accepted her for who she was—with a frown too deep, a sprinkle of gray, a soft muffin-top around the middle—was heady stuff.

However, that didn't mean she had to give up her hard-won accomplishments, did it? She loved making her own money and spending it any way she pleased, even though it was usually on paint or repairs for the house. Her budget might not be as large as when she'd been with Jeremy, but it was all hers. She didn't have to think twice about buying a new pair of sandals, even if she really didn't need them in orange.

For the first time in her life, she was truly in charge of her life and her decisions. As a young woman, she'd gone from being dependent on her family to being dependent on Jeremy. Now, there was no one to report to, no one to ask for permission. Except for taxes and guests, she had her freedom.

Oh, yes. Heady stuff, indeed.

Her forceful footsteps scared a lone shorebird, who skittered back to the safety of its flock.

Silly bird.

On the other hand, she'd encountered loneliness in Boston after Jeremy's death. Living in a rented room, her daughters busy with their lives, her friends juggling commitments with family and other married couples as she once had. The best decision she'd ever made, crazy though it seemed to her friends back east, had been to take on the dilapidated old house that Jeremy had never meant for her to have and create a livelihood for herself.

Slowing her step, she wondered if welcoming Bennett fully into her life would mean giving up the personal agency she'd just discovered? Sure, it was all professions of love and moonlight kisses now, but would she end up taking on the responsibility of the care and tending of a full-grown man? Would she be the one in charge of shopping, groceries, laundry, medical appointments, relatives' birthdays, and so on *ad infinitum*?

Would his needs eclipse hers?

Bennett didn't seem like that type now, but she was wary— not of him, necessarily, but of her actions.

It would be too easy to fall into the role of full-on help-mate again—not that that was entirely a bad thing, mind you —but at her age and station in life, she yearned to do more— to live for herself, too. She wanted to paint, tuck money aside for her eventual retirement, take a few pleasure trips, and buy purple shoes if she felt like it. Not that she couldn't do those things with Bennett.

So why hadn't she done those things with Jeremy?

Because his needs and those of their children had always come first.

She stooped to pick up an interesting pink shell, broken but still beautiful. That's how she felt now.

Turning this dilemma and new thoughts over in her mind, she walked on until she finally reached the inn. With a renewed sense of purpose, she kicked sand from her feet and entered the nest of her own making.

Ivy PLACED the broken shell on the kitchen counter. Cut flowers were in the sink, and Poppy emerged from the butler's pantry with several small vases.

"I found these for the guest rooms," Poppy said. "Amelia had so much here. I can't imagine what their place in San Francisco was like." As she trimmed the flowers, she asked about the book club.

Ivy eased onto a stool. "There's a lot of interest. I just spoke to Paige about it, and I told Jen, Darla, and a couple of others about it. Everyone seems interested."

"Here, too," Poppy said.

"Who?"

"Gilda and Imani for sure," Poppy said. "We talked about it over breakfast. Gilda writes book reviews for magazines, so she volunteered to compile a potential reading list. Imani listens to audiobooks at Blossoms when business is slow, so she keeps up on books, too."

"New or classics?" Ivy asked.

Poppy snipped a rose. "Something beachy would be fun."

Ivy lifted a corner of her mouth in thought. "Let's make a list. We can compare notes at the first meeting."

"Everyone knows lists are your department," Poppy said. "Besides, I have to babysit the vegetables out there for Shelly." She nodded toward the rear garden where lettuce, tomatoes, sugar snap peas, and peppers grew.

Ivy shook her head. They all missed Shelly's help at the inn.

Poppy stuffed flowers in the vases.

Ivy slid from the stool. "I'll put those in the rooms."

"Thanks," Poppy said. "By the way, do we have any more ink for the printer, or should I pick up more in town?"

"I've already done that," Ivy said. "You'll find an extra cartridge in my shopping bag over there. You must be doing a lot of printing."

"Not me," Poppy replied. "It's for one of our guests, Geena Bellamy. She's printing a load of legal-looking documents. If she keeps this up, we should charge her. Though I wouldn't mind if she were at least nice about it."

Ivy narrowed her eyes. "We're not a copy center—that's merely a limited service for guests. I'll speak to her when I see her."

AFTER CHECKING in the day's guests, Ivy and Poppy set up for the late afternoon event in the music room. Celia, a friend who underwrote the music program at the school, brought in a talented young pianist to play, and everyone gathered for a glass of wine or a cup of tea before going out for the evening.

Yet, there was still no sign of Shelly.

Resigned to do without her sister, Ivy plugged in the electric tea kettle while Poppy arranged wine glasses. It was a casual, self-serve affair that guests enjoyed. After setting up, Ivy and Poppy went to the kitchen to make a grocery list for the coming week.

A voice rang out.

"The cookie man has arrived," Mitch said as he strolled into the kitchen holding a pastry carton that smelled of sweet spices. He looked like he'd just returned from the beach. His spiky blond hair stuck out at all angles, framing a sun-reddened face, and he wore an old T-shirt and flip-flops.

"What are we serving today?" Ivy asked.

He flipped open the lid of the carton. "Oatmeal raisin and s'mores cookies with chocolate and marshmallows and graham crackers—all fresh from the oven. Who wants one?"

"Yes, please," Poppy said. She reached inside for a s'mores cookie.

"I won't say no to the oatmeal raisin," Ivy said. "Although I should."

"You've got to live a little every day," Mitch said with a quirky grin. "Did my team at Java Beach take good care of you while Shells and I were away?"

"They did," Ivy replied, selecting a cookie. "I heard you had a good trip."

"The absolute best." Youthful exuberance lit his face. "Shelly is amazing, and it's so cool to have a real family now. Hey, I'm actually related to you and Poppy now."

Ivy laughed. "By marriage."

"I'm one lucky guy." He glanced around. "Where's Shelly?"

"She's not here yet," Ivy said. "I saw her earlier, and I'm a little worried about her. She said she hasn't been feeling very well."

"It's probably a case of Montezuma's Revenge," Mitch

said, making a face. "Guess I've got a stomach of steel. Poor Shells."

"You'll let me know if I can do anything for her?"

"Sure. I think she'll be okay, though."

Ivy pressed her lips together, refraining from comment. Shelly and Mitch were a couple now, and it was clear they didn't need Ivy hovering around playing concerned older sister. They were certainly adults and had a new life to embrace.

Or was Shelly taking advantage of that? It wouldn't be the first time.

Ivy took a bite of the cookie. "These are delicious," she said, savoring the warm oatmeal and raisins with a hint of cinnamon.

Just then, the back door banged open.

Shelly rushed in with a self-conscious grin on her face. "Late again, right?" She paused to kiss Mitch. "Hi, babes."

Shelly didn't look like she was feeling bad. In fact, Ivy thought she looked bright and well rested. "Did you have your nap?"

"I really needed it," Shelly said. "Except I'll probably be up half the night again."

"That's cool," Mitch said. "We can meet my friends in the village. They're playing at Spirits & Vine tonight. It's hot jazz night."

"Cool," Shelly said, darting a glance toward Ivy.

"I'm glad you're feeling better," Ivy said evenly. Maybe Shelly had made a miraculous recovery. Still, she resolved to have another talk with Shelly. In private.

Footsteps sounded on the stairway, and Ivy put the grocery list aside. Guests were gathering in the music room, and Bennett would return from City Hall soon. They had a routine, and Shelly knew it as well as anyone.

"I'll go see to the guests," Poppy said, glancing between them and quickly making herself scarce.

"Thanks," Ivy said. "Time to be a host," she added, casting a look at Shelly as she pushed through the kitchen door.

"Be right there," Shelly called after her.

Guests might have arrived as strangers in the music room, but Ivy made sure that people met and left as friends. They'd even had one couple who met and began dating at the inn over the holidays. After the gathering, guests filtered out to restaurants in Summer Beach.

Ivy collected the dirty dishes and glassware left behind. Although Shelly had arrived, she'd also disappeared too shortly after the event began. Ivy didn't know whether her sister was sick or simply disinterested, but she was trying her patience.

If Shelly no longer wanted to work at the inn, they would have to have that conversation. Ivy didn't want to feel like she had to monitor her—they had been partners before. *All in together toward a goal.* She missed that.

In the kitchen, Bennett had stationed himself at the sink. "Since you're short-handed, I'll whip those dishes out in no time," he said, filling the sink with sudsy water.

"You've noticed, too," Ivy said.

"Hard not to. But I'm sure Shelly will come around soon."

Ivy stacked up the dishes. "Wish we had a dishwasher," she said. The house had never had one. Unfortunately, that was nowhere near the top of Ivy's lengthy to-do list.

"You've got me," Bennett said, grinning.

"Thanks, sweetheart." Having a partner made all the difference. She picked up a dish towel. "I'll dry. And I don't expect you to step into Shelly's position." Ivy didn't like feeling this way about Shelly, but she needed help.

Bennett grabbed one end of the towel and drew her toward him, his eyes twinkling with mischief. "Have I told you how much I love you today?"

As he tucked his arms around her, Ivy looped the towel

around his neck. "Not since breakfast." Gazing into his warm hazel eyes almost made her forget about Shelly—and her hesitation about their relationship.

In his embrace, she felt safe and loved—and a little guilty for thinking that might not be enough. Bennett was everything she could want in a man.

But what she wanted was to be certain. No mistakes. Not at her age. Besides, their marriage wasn't legal yet. Blessed, but not legal. Left hanging—that's how she felt.

"I'm all yours, sweetheart," Bennett said, his voice husky with emotion. He covered her hand with his and swept it over his heart. "You have all my love."

Under her palm, his heart beat with surprising intensity. Ivy splayed her hands against his firm chest. She noticed the way other women looked at him. Single women, guests, tourists—even the new guest, Geena Bellamy—a surly, unpleasant young woman even this evening—had eyed him from across the music room. For the most part, he seemed unaware of the attention. Or maybe he was used to it.

She met his lips with hers. "You're forever in my heart." That much was true. She'd never forgotten the young surfer with the guitar on the beach, even two decades later.

Laughter filtered in from the veranda. Moments later, Shelly burst into the kitchen with Mitch right behind her. "Well, if this isn't the picture of domestic bliss." She winked at Ivy.

"I love a man who washes dishes," Ivy said.

Shelly had put on makeup and changed into a flowing white top and jeans with kitten heels. She still looked healthy and happy, and she seemed oblivious to Bennett doing her usual duty.

"And I love a man who cooks," Shelly said, giving Mitch a playful kiss.

Just then, the door to the lower level creaked open, and a gust of wind blew through the kitchen.

Ivy brushed a strand of hair from her face. "Must be a window open. I wonder who was down there last?"

"Not me," Shelly said. "I haven't been down there in forever."

"Well, it wasn't me." Ivy crossed the kitchen to shut it. "Maybe it was Poppy, although I can't imagine why." She tried to shut the door, but it seemed out of alignment with the doorjamb. "That's odd. It was shut just a few seconds ago."

Poppy swung through the kitchen door. "Did I just hear my name?"

"Were you downstairs?" Ivy asked.

"No, but I saw that new guest, Geena Bellamy, down there. She said you told her it was okay to look around."

Ivy rolled her eyes. "I didn't mean down there."

"I'll look at that door," Mitch said, tossing his towel to Shelly. He knelt before the old wooden door and swung it back and forth. "Bennett and I can fix this."

Shelly laughed. "I bet Amelia is up to her old tricks again."

"Don't you dare start on that," Ivy said, frowning at her sister. "It was probably an ocean gust. I should check the windows down there."

"I'll go with you," Shelly said, tossing the towel back to Mitch. "I know how you feel about ghosts."

"There is nothing of the sort," Ivy said, wishing Shelly would stop with such nonsense. She'd been irritated with her sister since she'd returned from her honeymoon. Still, priorities shifted in life, Ivy supposed. She'd have to accept that and work out something with Shelly.

Behind her, Bennett chuckled. "The kids in Summer Beach always thought they saw something. You probably remember that from the campfires we used to have on the beach."

"We were teenagers then." A strange feeling bristled along

Ivy's spine. Exasperated, she jabbed her hands onto her hips. "Not you, too."

"Just passing along information," Bennett said, turning off the faucet and stepping away from the sink as he dried his hands. "I'm through here, so I'll go have a look. Mitch, why don't you come with me?"

A thin white curtain at the window above the kitchen sink fluttered.

"Oh, no," Shelly said, pointing toward the curtain. "You're not leaving us up here with a ghost. Even if Amelia is a friendly one."

Ivy sliced her hands through the air. "That's it. We're all going. We need to figure out what to do with that lower level anyway." Not that she believed in ghosts, yet she couldn't help shivering.

*W*rinkling her nose against the stale odor, Ivy peered tentatively down the stairs to the lower level. "It smells musty."

After the FBI had collected the precious loot of artwork, and she and Shelly and Poppy had moved furniture they could use upstairs, they hadn't returned here often—except for the art show tours they'd held last year. Ivy planned to host another show later this summer.

"Could be mildew or mold," Bennett replied as he flicked on the light. "You can have it checked for leaks. Who's going first?"

"I will," Ivy said, steeling herself against the odor. "No spirits here."

Beside her, Poppy hesitated. "On second thought, I forgot that I need to check on a guest." She skittered away.

Ivy hardly blamed her. Gingerly, she made her way down the stairs, lifting the hem of her floral sundress to avoid the accumulation of dust. Once they were gathered at the base of the stairs, she swung around to Bennett. "Could you check the windows? One of them must have been left open."

Her voice echoed through the mostly empty space. Only a

few boxes and assorted pieces of antique furniture—Victorian sofas, wingback chairs, wool rugs, bar stools, a carved bar— remained in a storage area where Amelia Erickson had concealed her treasures during the Second World War.

Bennett nodded toward Mitch. "We'll check them."

While the men started off, Ivy glanced across the cavernous room. "This is a lot of space. We'll have to take this in phases."

"It's a pretty big job," Shelly agreed, shivering. "It's a lot cooler down here, even in the summer."

"It might have been built for storage." Ivy ran her hands over a brick wall. "Back then, people did a lot of canning. They could have stored winter and root vegetables here from neighboring farms. This entire area was once farmland and fishing." She gazed up at the windows that lined the top of the space.

"I've also heard the Ericksons had bowling lanes," Bennett said, joining them again. "Since they lived here during the Roaring Twenties and Prohibition, they might have had a secret bar, too."

"That could also explain why they built up the exterior grounds to hide this level," Shelly said. "Maybe it wasn't to hide from submarines after all."

The lower level was a half-basement with windows that looked out over the grounds and had been concealed from the outside with landscaping for years. Once uncovered, that section had required exterior repair and painting. Due to the cost, Ivy had left the interior in its original condition.

Ivy nodded toward an area that had rows of empty racks and individual wooden cabinets. "They must have kept bottles over there."

Mitch walked over, brushing dust from his hands.

"Sure wish they'd left some wine," Shelly said. "Could you imagine what that would be worth?" She heaved a sigh. "How about a lounge? We could sell wine and appetizers. Live jazz on the weekends would be great."

"I like it, but we'd have to have all kinds of permits for that, and we don't have the zoning to sell alcohol."

Shelly furrowed her brow. "Couldn't you get the zoning changed like you did on this place before?"

"That was a special situation," Bennett interjected. "An exception was made because the city needed the rooms to lodge local residents after the Ridgetop Fire. But selling alcohol here would be a real departure for the neighborhood. I don't think Darla and your other neighbors would like that. Zoning is there to protect neighborhoods. That's why you can give wine away, but you can't charge for it."

"Bet they had big parties here," Mitch said, grinning. "Maybe they were rum runners. You don't think they stored only wine down here, do you?" He pointed to a lighter space on the wooden floor in front of the wine racks and other shelves. "That's probably where the bar was."

"We can put it back," Ivy said, thinking of the one she'd seen. "Did you find the window that had been left open?"

Mitch shook his head. "*Nada.*"

"None of them were." Bennett brushed a hand over his short, cropped hair. "Found a few cobwebs, but that was all."

"We opened some to air out the place," Mitch added.

Everywhere Ivy looked was dirty, dingy, and dank. Shaking her head, she said, "I don't know how we're going to manage all this work."

Bennett put his arm around her shoulders. "You've got a good team here. You'll be surprised at what we can do."

"We could throw a barbecue and invite all the young, strong cousins for another cleaning and painting party," Shelly said. "Poppy could help us rally them. I'll bet Forrest would pitch in with some expert help in electrical and plumbing repair if we need it. And Reed is working full time with his construction company now."

"We can't keep calling on family to help us," Ivy said, recalling how much they'd helped them get the house ready for rentals last year. Their nephew Reed had seemed eager to show off his new skills in construction management.

Shelly folded her arms and stared at her. "Why not? You know we'll host the holidays here for everyone again this year —maybe forever at the rate the family is growing. Just wait until all the cousins get married and start having babies. No one except you has a house large enough for the entire Bay family."

"Good point," Ivy said. "I'll see if they can do it this weekend." Their twin brothers Flint and Forrest had nine children between them. *Too many Bays on this coast* was a frequent family joke.

"I'll manage the barbecue," Mitch said. "It will be fun. Like one of those old-fashioned barn raisings."

Shelly raised her eyebrows and poked him. "What would you know about that, surfer dude?"

"Hey, I read," Mitch protested.

Ivy tapped a finger on her chin. "When we were going through the things Amelia had stored last year, didn't we see some crates of old books?"

"We did," Shelly replied. "After the shelves are cleaned, we could bring them out."

"Paige said Amelia was known for her literary salon. There might be quite a collection here." They hadn't had time to sort through all the crates. But now, in her mind's eye, she could see the area taking shape.

"We could fill the bookshelves and spread some of the vintage rugs that are still rolled up over these wooden floors," Ivy said, growing excited. "We could have lively conversations late into the night without bothering any of the guests upstairs."

"So, what's the difference between that and a wine club?"

Shelly asked. "I thought books and wine went together like peas and carrots."

"Peanut butter and jelly," Bennett added.

"You and me," Shelly said, flinging an arm around Mitch.

Ivy ran a hand across her forehead. "Come on, you guys. Be serious."

Shelly laughed as Mitch swung her around. "Why start now, Ives? Our fun *chi* brings the right people here. Trust the process."

"Maybe I've been too serious," Ivy said. She was happy for Shelly; she just had a lot on her mind.

"That's right," Shelly said, giggling. "Rip up those lists."

"Never hurts to lighten up," Bennett said, giving her shoulder a little squeeze. Lowering his voice, he added, "You've been pretty wound up lately." A question seemed to linger behind his words, though he didn't voice it. Instead, he kneaded her neck with strong, gentle hands.

That much is true, Ivy thought, rotating her neck.

Without Shelly a hundred percent on board, Ivy had been working a lot of late hours. Tending to the landscape as well as the interior and guests was a lot for her to handle. Although Sunny was here, she was also taking summer school along with Jamir. She had miscalculated her credits and was still short for graduation.

Bennett kissed her cheek. "We're all here to help get it done—right guys? As Shelly said, let's make it fun."

Ivy appreciated his understanding and reassurance. This was another reason she loved Bennett. He never hesitated to pitch in.

Ivy paced the area. "Besides a book club, we could hold other events or rent this space out." As ideas came to her, the excitement of possibilities surged through her. "Wine tastings, lectures, and maybe even that jazz idea."

"Now you're thinking," Shelly said. "I could film events and post them online."

Shelly was growing more interested now. Maybe she had grown bored. "As people visit, more word gets around about the inn for weddings and other special events," Ivy said. "It would be a win-win for everyone."

Shelly's eyes flashed with excitement. "We could have book sales, offer merchandise, maybe get patron support. Plus, we could derive a little advertising income from my video views. I know there's a lot we could do."

"As long as you have time." Ivy glanced at Bennett, who was smiling at the exchange between her and Shelly. At least she knew she could count on him, and that was reassuring.

"I'd love to do this," Shelly said with an earnest expression. "I've got this, Ives."

"So why meet down here instead of upstairs?" Mitch asked.

"Good question," Ivy said, nodding. "This will be a dedicated space, so we don't have to worry about double booking. Like the wedding party we have later this month. They're taking over most of the downstairs."

Shelly groaned. "Please don't tell me we won't have another momzilla or bridezilla."

"Not at all. I booked this while you and Mitch were on your honeymoon," Ivy said. "They're a sweet, older couple, so the whole wedding affair should be fairly sedate. They're orchestra members, and the music they have planned will be beautiful."

"We had great music, too," Mitch said, nuzzling Shelly's neck. "Everyone rocked out all night."

"We'll never forget that weekend," Ivy said, smiling at Bennett. It was a time to remember for all of them. Now, as she watched Shelly and Mitch, she was so happy for them, even if Shelly had slacked off a little. Maybe that was inevitable.

The four of them walked around the downstairs area while Ivy made mental notes about cleaning and painting.

Bennett and Mitch inspected the structural elements while Ivy and Shelly talked about uses for the space.

"We could make separate areas," Ivy said, sketching out rough ideas on a pad she'd just retrieved from the kitchen.

"Eventually, we could have spa rooms on that side for massages and facials," Shelly added. "A lot of guests ask for treatments, and the spa in the village gets booked up in the summer. Old hotels often had salons and barbershops on the ground floors or in the basement, sort of like the old hotel on Coronado Island."

"These are all good ideas." Ivy made a note of that. Last winter, Bennett had taken her ice skating at the Hotel del Coronado, and she'd been intrigued with its history. "We'll have to be selective. That could be expensive to build."

"Then let's focus on what we can do now."

"The book club is easy enough to start, and people will see the space." Ivy held up her hands to frame the area for a visual. "Private wine storage on that side and a grouping by the bookshelves over there. The guys can help bring out rugs and furnishings. We could have this up and running soon."

"Except for the bowling lanes." Shelly laughed, glancing around.

"That would be a huge undertaking," Ivy said.

Shelly shivered. "It's still a little spooky. Are you sure you don't want to have a haunted house down here first?"

Ivy shook her head. However, she was starting to enjoy having a new project. As much as the old house was hers, it also belonged to the residents of Summer Beach. They had invited the community for events ranging from an art festival and holiday celebrations to egg hunts on the lawn. The Seabreeze Inn had reclaimed its place as a center of Summer Beach activity for local residents and guests alike.

A wisp of a breeze swept past her. Ivy shivered. Maybe it was a window Bennett and Mitch had opened, or maybe it was Amelia, pleased with her decision.

That is, if she believed in ghosts, which she certainly did not.

As Ivy looked around, she caught a glimpse of something on a lower bookshelf. Kneeling, she noticed a small book that had been shoved to the back and long forgotten. Reaching in, she slid it out.

"What's that?" Shelly asked, noticing what Ivy was doing.

"A little book of some sort." Ivy brushed dust from the leather cover. "*Songs from the Golden Gate*," she read. "By Ina Coolbrith." As she turned the brittle pages with care, she noted the date. "Published in 1895. It's a book of poetry."

"How cool." Shelly glanced over her shoulder.

Ivy continued turning pages. "A lot of these poems have a California theme."

"Imagine what it must have been like here in 1895," Shelly said. "Open land, no highways, no traffic. Not that Summer Beach has much now."

Ivy looked through the book and paused at a page. "Here's one entitled 'Sea-Shell.'" She began to read aloud.

"And love will stay, a summer's day!
A long wave rippled up the strand…"

Ivy paused and scanned the poem. Blinking against taut emotions, she hesitated before reading more.

Bennett looked up. "That's beautiful. I could set that to music with the guitar."

"That's not all of it," Shelly said, skipping ahead and picking up a few more lines.

"And plucked a sea-shell from the sand;
And laughed—O doubting heart, have peace!
When faith of mine shall fail to thee
This fond, remembering shell will cease
To sing its love, the sea."

Shelly paused and smiled. "Meaning that person will love the other forever." She drew her finger down the page. "Uh-oh, I don't think it ended well for our lovers, though. I wonder who Ina Coolbrith was and who hurt her?"

A yellowed card fluttered from the book. Ivy picked it up and read it. "Ina Donna Coolbrith. California's first Poet Laureate."

Mitch let out a whistle. "That's a big deal, isn't it?"

"Sure is," Shelly said. "And how cool is it that honor was given to a woman, right?"

Ivy reinserted the card into the slim volume and gazed up at the tall, empty wooden shelves. "Shelly, how many crates of books did you say we found?"

"Two, maybe three."

Ivy recalled what Paige had said at the bookshop. *A literary salon.* "That wouldn't fill these shelves. There must have been more."

"Why do you say that?" Shelly asked.

"Because Amelia Erickson never did anything halfway."

*B*ennett was seated at his desk in his office at City Hall, where expansive windows looked out over the village and the beach, all the way to the marina. With his windows open to the cool breeze, he could hear the distant roar of the ocean. While the view was inspiring, he was trying to keep his mind focused on the quarterly budget.

His desk phone lit up, and Nan's cheerful voice chirped through it from the front desk. "Call for you, Mr. Mayor. Shall I pass it through?"

He'd been working all morning and hated to lose his train of thought. "Did they say who's calling?"

"Just a minute," Nan said. Moments later, she came back on the line. "Her name is Diana Corbin, and she says it's quite important. She refuses to tell me what it's about, and believe me, I tried to wheedle it out of her."

The name seemed vaguely familiar, but he met a lot of people. Now that his concentration had been derailed, Bennett put down his pencil. "I'm sure you did your best, Nan. Might as well put the call through now."

He punched a blinking line. "Mayor Dylan here."

The caller introduced herself. "I don't know if you

remember me, but we met a couple of years ago at a fundraiser. How have you been?"

"Fine. Busy." He rubbed the bridge of his nose. "What can I help you with?" he asked cordially.

"It's what I can do for you. I started my own company, Corbin Executive Search. I have a high-paying position that you might want to consider. I was so impressed with the work you've done for Summer Beach."

"I'm flattered you thought of me, but I'm pretty happy here."

"This isn't too far away. Only a few hours. And it's a prestigious position."

Bennett chuckled. He didn't really care about that. "So is being the mayor of Summer Beach."

"I know you're joking, but the pay is incredible. Don't you want to know what you're worth?"

Bennett leaned back in his chair. That was an intriguing question, not that he'd consider taking another position. Still, he was interested in hearing what she thought his skills might bring in the market. "I'm listening."

Diana spoke quickly—as if he might escape any moment. "I'll send details. What's your email address?"

Still cautiously interested, he gave her his personal email address. It couldn't hurt to see what was out there, he told himself before hanging up.

Nan appeared at the door to his office, her short red curls practically sizzling with curiosity. "What was that about? In case she calls again," she quickly added.

"I met her at a community fundraiser," he said, offering a brief explanation. Still, that wasn't good enough for Nan.

"So, should I put her calls through again?"

Bennett hesitated. Not that he was interested, but it never hurt to listen. "I'd appreciate that."

After wrapping up the morning's business, Bennett left City Hall at lunch. In the village, he ducked into Get Away, a small shop plastered with travel posters. The store was next to Pages. The owner, Teresa, was a travel agent who'd lived in Summer Beach for years. She was busy with a gray-haired couple who were planning a tour of South America. Bennett recognized them from around town.

"Nice to see you here, Mr. Mayor," Teresa said. "I'll be with you shortly."

"No worries," Bennett said, grinning. "I thought I'd stop by to dream a little."

The older couple chuckled. "It's time you acted on those dreams," the husband said. "You're still a young man." He winked at his wife. "I heard congratulations are in order for you, Mayor. Are you here to plan a honeymoon?"

"I'm not sure I'd call it that," Bennett said, feeling his neck warm. His relationship with Ivy had become complicated, and he didn't know how to explain it—or what to do to get it back on track. He picked up a travel brochure. *The Amalfi Coastline.*

"Well, I'll bet Ivy would," the woman said. "Every woman should have a honeymoon, even if it is ten years late." She gave her husband a playful poke in the ribs.

"Don't make the same mistake I did," the man said, taking his wife's hand. "Fortunately, I managed to make up for it."

"Mostly," she said, her eyes gleaming with laughter. "This next trip just might do it."

As they turned their attention back to their business at hand, Bennett collected a few more brochures. *Paris, Hawaiian Islands, Nordic Tour, African Safari.*

He cast about for ideas, unsure of what Ivy might like. He needed to do something.

Bennett had seen a change in Mitch and Shelly after they returned from their honeymoon. Or maybe it was because Shelly moved into Mitch's beach cottage. Whatever the reason, they seemed more in tune with each other.

That's what was missing with Ivy, he thought, furrowing his brow. A couple of days after their commitment ceremony, they'd drifted back into their separate worlds. He understood that Ivy had responsibilities. Running the inn took a lot of effort and energy, and tending to her daughters was a priority.

He wasn't placing all the blame on her, though. As mayor, he had many duties during the day and after hours. Still, he wondered when they'd have the chance to spend more time together.

Or was this the new normal in relationships? A lot seemed to have changed in the last ten years since he'd been widowed.

This isn't really a marriage yet, Ivy had told him afterward. Bennett hoped she would change her mind. He realized the ceremony had been a last-minute decision, but he'd been thinking about it for months. It had seemed so right at the time, and Bennett loved her more than he'd ever thought possible again.

Still, they had yet to make a lot of decisions that couples usually did. He wanted them to come together as a couple, but she didn't seem ready.

Bennett passed a hand over his forehead. *The elusive Ivy Bay.* However, he knew she couldn't be pushed. Although he was trying to understand her reticence, he wasn't as patient as he made out.

As he thumbed through the travel brochures, he wondered what he could do to show Ivy how much she meant to him.

The travel agent called out again, "Are you sure you don't have any questions, Mr. Mayor?"

"Not yet," Bennett replied. At least, none that the travel agent could answer. He stuffed a few brochures into his pocket and left.

AFTER LEAVING WORK, Bennett swung by the marina to drop off supplies at his boat. As he walked toward the vintage vessel he'd restored, he saw his neighbor from the ridgetop sitting on his yacht with his buddies, having martinis and swapping stories. Tyler waved him down and introduced his friends, who were fraternity brothers visiting from Silicon Valley.

They talked a few minutes before Bennett thought about a men's book club he planned to organize. Given his high-tech entrepreneurial experience, Tyler would bring interesting views. Bennett told him about the new book club and invited him to a meeting at the inn.

"We'd like to hear your perspective on topics," Bennett said to Tyler. "You're a big deal for Summer Beach."

"Celia was talking about joining a book club at the inn," Tyler said, sipping his cocktail. "Is this the same one?"

"This one is for men only." Bennett's comment drew a variety of crass comments from Tyler's friends.

Tyler looked embarrassed. "Hey, you guys. This is the mayor of Summer Beach. Come on; show some class."

Bennett ignored the comments. "It's for thoughtful conversation and camaraderie. I thought we'd start with books on leadership or history."

Tyler lifted his glass in acknowledgment. "Count me in. I could use a break while Celia's busy with the music program."

"You're on." Bennett gave him a thumbs-up sign and started toward his much smaller boat. He was proud of it, though. He'd refinished the teakwood, polished the brass, and refurbished the interior.

He stepped onto his boat and stashed the supplies he'd brought before tending to minor repairs and cleaning. As he was working on the deck, his thoughts turned to Ivy.

Bennett understood her reluctance, or he thought he did. Jackie had been gone several years before he had even thought of dating again, and when he did, he hadn't clicked with anyone. He'd dated a few attractive, accomplished women, but the spark hadn't been there. Not until Ivy crashed back into his life.

He had been patient with Ivy, but he wanted to see their relationship progress. Something seemed to be holding her back, and he wasn't sure if it might have been something he'd said or done.

Or it might be that their work didn't leave time for much togetherness. He continued to address city business during the week, as well as a few real estate clients on the weekend.

As for Ivy, with the inn's steady flow of guests and ongoing repairs, she had a great deal of responsibility. Summer was the high season for tourists, and he understood that her time was at a premium. Not that he expected supper on the table every evening—in fact, he enjoyed preparing dinner with her—or for her and Sunny. Misty also visited from Los Angeles when she had a break. He got along with Ivy's daughters, and he was grateful that they accepted him into their lives, although it hadn't been easy with Sunny at first.

Could that be holding Ivy back? Bennett didn't mean to replace the girls' father. Still, he wanted to offer positive support because he knew just how messy life could be at their ages.

Maybe she just didn't have time to ease into marriage right now. Bennett and Ivy had enjoyed the short trips they had taken to Catalina, Coronado Island, and a nearby vineyard. Until they could get away on a longer trip, he wanted to do more for just the two of them.

The idea of a honeymoon was appealing.

Bennett let his mind wander as he worked on the boat. They could stay in a hotel in San Diego's Little Italy—Ivy loved Italian food, and they could explore the seaport. Or they might visit the nearby observatory and have a meal under the stars somewhere. Then again, a cabin near the artist colony of Idlewild could be quiet and intimate.

Short day trips might help, but the problem was that their schedules weren't very conducive to that right now. If he had a free weekend, the inn was at its busiest then.

After he finished his work on the boat, he headed back to

the inn, considering these ideas and options. Somehow, he wanted to do something magical for Ivy.

Maybe his buddies Flint and Forrest, Ivy's brothers, might have some suggestions. Ivy said they would be joining them this weekend to clean and paint the downstairs level, and he was looking forward to that.

He chuckled to himself as he thought of Shelly's talk of ghosts. Maybe they'd finally meet Amelia in the lower level, although he wouldn't suggest that to Ivy.

On Saturday morning, Ivy rose early. Her brothers Forrest and Flint would arrive soon with their kids to tackle the lower level cleaning and painting, and she still had to tend to breakfast and morning guest requests. Imani had volunteered to lead the beach walk and clip flowers for the entryway, and Poppy was filling in to teach Shelly's morning yoga class. Ivy was confident that everything would get done, but just barely.

As the scent of roasted coffee filled the air, Ivy dashed around the kitchen preparing the breakfast trays with the muffins Mitch had dropped off, hoping Shelly would arrive as early as she'd promised.

Sunny sauntered into the kitchen, her hair in disarray. She had pulled on cut-off jean shorts and a T-shirt emblazoned with the slogan, *Life is Better in Summer Beach*.

"Good morning, sweetie," Ivy said, giving her daughter a quick hug. "The coffee is on. Help yourself."

Yawning, Sunny took a mug from the cupboard. "I'll pitch in once I get a few sips of java juice down."

"You know where I'll be." Ivy began to set up the dining area, and Sunny joined her a few minutes later. They worked quickly, yet before they finished, guests began arriving for breakfast. Sunny looked down at her outfit. "I'll go change, Mom. Be back in a couple of minutes."

Ivy was glad she didn't have to ask this time. Even though this was their home, she liked everyone to look nice for their guests. Before long, the dining room was full of summer vacationers.

"It's good to have a full house again," Ivy said a little while later to Sunny after her daughter had changed and returned, looking brighter in a short, pink polka-dot sundress. Ivy looked across the dining room where guests were milling about, helping themselves to muffins, toaster waffles, soft-boiled eggs, yogurt, and a large fruit bowl. "Sunny, help me clear this table for the next guests, please."

"Sure, Mom." Sunny collected plates from a table where one set of guests had just departed, and another family was looking for a place to sit. She placed the dishes on a tray.

Ivy directed the guests to the table while Sunny swiped a damp cloth over it, brushing away crumbs. Although her spoiled younger daughter still had her moments, she was taking on more responsibility without excessive prodding, much to Ivy's relief.

This past week, Ivy and Poppy had called the family and invited them to a barbecue—with a hefty side of cleaning and painting downstairs. Only a couple of them had other plans, such as Elena, who was tending her jewelry shop in Los Angeles. Poppy rallied her cousins while Ivy made a list and ordered paint and supplies from Jen at Nailed It.

Ivy glanced at her watch, feeling a little perturbed. The family would begin arriving any minute, and Shelly had promised to arrive early to help set up downstairs. Sighing, Ivy realized she needed to let go. Her sister had a more exciting life with Mitch now, and the inn was no longer her most urgent priority.

As it should be, Ivy thought, checking her annoyance. Shelly had been so eager to sail into her sunrise, as she put it, and now she was.

"Good morning, Bettina and John, " Ivy said to the thirty-something couple who sat down. They had checked in the day before for a vacation stay. The woman wore a pink-and-green, seashell-printed bathing suit coverup. "What a cute outfit. You both look like you're ready for the beach."

"Thanks," Bettina said. "Do you think these clouds will clear up? We were hoping for a sunny day. I'm a nurse, so I spend most of my time indoors. I've been aching for sunshine."

"This is normal this time of year," Ivy said. "The marine layer will burn off in an hour or two, and then you'll have plenty of sunshine. But don't let that fool you into not putting on sunscreen when you go out."

Sunny piped up. "We have fresh muffins today. Apple-cinnamon and blueberry. I can bring some if you want."

Ivy put an arm around her daughter and smiled, proud of how she was beginning to pitch in and communicate with guests. "This is my daughter, Sunny. You're welcome to help yourself, too."

"Which shops in the village would you recommend?" Bettina asked.

"That depends on what you want. If you like vintage pieces, Antique Times is always fun to explore. The Hidden Garden has wonderful plants and garden decorations." Ivy named a few other boutiques in town. "Java Beach is great for coffee and lunch, and the Coral Cafe has a delicious menu for supper, along with a beautiful view of the ocean. Spirits & Vine is a lively wine bar with live jazz on the weekend."

"We'll check those out," John said, resting a hand on his wife's. "Bettina loves to read. Any place where we can find beach books?"

"Pages bookshop in the village has a good assortment." Ivy smiled, recalling Darla's comment. "The proprietor is so good at making book recommendations that some call her a book whisperer."

"Then we'll be sure to visit," Bettina said, her face brightening.

Ivy and Sunny moved through the room, chatting with guests while Poppy finished yoga and moved to the front desk. Mornings were usually busy with guest requests and questions.

Checking in with Poppy, Ivy asked if she'd heard from Shelly.

"She'll probably be here soon," Poppy said, sounding more hopeful than she looked.

Ivy touched Poppy's shoulder. "Thank you for filling in for her. It's going to be a busy day."

After the breakfast rush, guests were generally eager to go to the beach or shop in the village. A few often lingered by the pool, but not today. Sunny slipped away to her room to change into her painting clothes while Ivy quickly replenished the breakfast fare in the kitchen for family members who were coming to help. By the time she finished the first lot of dishwashing, she could hear laughter from the front hallway.

Her cleanup crew had arrived.

A voice bellowed down the hallway. "Where's Ivy Bay?"

"Coming," she called back to her brother, Forrest. After drying her hands, she picked up the sketch she'd made and met him in the dining room, giving him a hug when she saw him.

After asking about him and his family, Ivy said, "Have you heard from Mom and Dad yet?"

"This morning," Forrest replied, pushing a Padres baseball cap back on his head. "They'd just pulled into port at Panama where they met friends sailing from Florida." Forrest was muscular and solid, and he'd always been her protector. His twin, Flint, was a leaner version—a mammalogist who loved studying marine life and being out on the ocean.

Ivy wished their parents would call her, but she knew her turn was coming. "So they must be crossing the Pacific soon."

"Not quite yet," Forrest said, shaking his head. "They're talking about changing course and cruising to Bahia de Caraquez in Ecuador. Dad said the passage to the Galápagos from Salinas will provide steadier winds. From there, they would follow what they call the milk route—I didn't ask why it's called that—but it would take them to the Galápagos Islands, the Marquesas, the Tuamotus, and the Society Islands. That includes Bora Bora and Tahiti."

"What an amazing voyage," Ivy said, trying to imagine the fascinating trip they were on. "I almost wish I'd stowed away with them, but I have too much to do here."

"They said any of us can fly out to meet them. If you and Bennett are planning a honeymoon, that could be a sweet place."

"A honeymoon with Mom and Dad?" Ivy grinned at the thought. "I'm not so sure that's what Bennett would have in mind."

Forrest laughed and shook his head. "I guess I've been married too long to remember what young love was like. Not that you're that young." His face reddened, and he smacked his forehead. "What I meant was—"

"I need to cut you off right there for your own good," Ivy said, chuckling. "Do you need another cup of coffee or something to eat?" Even as a child, Forrest had stumbled over his words. But he'd do anything for her, and Ivy felt the same way about him.

"How'd you guess?" Forrest said. "I haven't been sleeping well. I've been worried about Mom and Dad, so when they called early this morning, I was relieved."

"We're all worried about them," Ivy said, leading him toward the coffee machine. "But they're more experienced sailors than any of us. And this is their dream." She poured a steaming cup for him.

As he sipped his coffee, Ivy showed him the sketch of the downstairs she'd made. "Think we can do something like this? I would like some flex space for events. Book club meetings, wine tastings, corporate retreats."

Forrest studied the paper. "This looks feasible. I'll inspect the area and let you know what we can do."

"I sure appreciate that."

"Now, where's Shelly?" Forrest asked. "I want to hear all about her trip to Baja."

"I haven't seen her yet, but when I do, I'll tell her you're looking for her."

Poppy gathered everyone in the kitchen, where the remaining breakfast muffins were quickly disappeared among the young cousins. Poppy's siblings—Rocky, Reed, Summer, and Coral—were there. Flint's children—Skyler, Blue, Jewell, and Sierra—were there with his wife, Tabitha. Everyone was ready to work.

Through the kitchen window, Ivy was relieved to see Mitch setting up the grill for the noon break. Shelly must be around somewhere.

Ivy could hardly wait to begin. She whistled for attention, and everyone turned to look at her.

"Thank you all for coming to lend a hand today," Ivy began, stepping up her energy level. "You have no idea how grateful I am to you. We're celebrating our first year in business, and I'm so thankful that we've made it this far. I know this old house still has a lot of good times left in it, but it needs a little more love and care right now. And I know this is just the team to do it."

"Whoop, whoop," Reed and Rocky called out. Now in their twenties, Forrest's sons were built like their father—tall, athletic, and muscular. "Let's do this."

Ivy pointed to a corner where she'd deposited cleaning supplies. "Team Poppy is in that corner with cleaning, Team Forrest is over there with repairs, and Team Shelly is right here with painting. We need volunteers for each one, so find a group and huddle."

"Where's Shelly?" Poppy asked.

Biting her lip, Ivy glanced around. "Mitch is here, so she must be here, too. I'll take over until then. Would someone go out and ask Mitch where Shelly might be? I saw him outside getting the grill ready for later."

Once again, Ivy was irked that Shelly wasn't here. She was trying to remain happy for her sister, but she'd had enough of Shelly shirking her duties. While Shelly was decorating the beach cottage and planting a new garden, it was also high season at the inn, and Ivy was paying her.

She would have it out with Shelly today.

After grabbing breakfast, everyone picked up cleaning supplies and rags, brooms and mops, and tools for repairs and trooped downstairs. Sunny took charge of the music, setting up a pair of speakers to broadcast an upbeat mix of tunes. She had also set up a buzzer at the front desk that had a remote ringer they could carry around with them in case a guest needed them upstairs—not that many were still in the house.

Downstairs, with the windows flung open, sunshine streaming in, and ocean breezes cooling the space, Ivy began to see the possibilities she'd had in mind emerge.

"Let's start in these sections," Ivy said, motioning to an area by the bookcases and the wine racks and cubbies. "Everything here needs to be wiped down. We've got at least fifty years of dust here, so put on a dust mask. And we need a window cleaning team that can prep window frames for painting." At some point, she would replace the old windows, but not this year.

"You got it, Aunt Ivy," Reed said. "Who's on windows with me?"

Rocky and Skyler stepped up beside him.

Ivy glanced around. All the cousins were pitching in, and

Forrest was inspecting the electrical system. She made her way toward him.

"How does it look?" Ivy asked.

"Your electrical system needs a professional. I'll send my guy next week."

When Ivy started to protest, her brother shook his head. "My cost. Have to make sure you're safe here." Forrest slapped his hand on the concrete wall. "I wouldn't worry. This place is built like a fortress. Made it through more than one earthquake, I imagine."

Ivy shuddered. "Don't even say that word." People often joked about the big one, but she couldn't imagine what she'd do if this house was damaged.

"It's our reality," Forrest said, raising his brow. "I hope you have earthquake supplies."

"We're prepared," Ivy said, acknowledging the fact. "We put flashlights in every guest room, and Poppy drew up an exit map."

Forrest grinned and shook his head. "I'll bring some more survival stuff over for you."

Eager to change the subject, Ivy shifted on her feet. She also needed to pick up the paint Jen had mixed for her. "Has anyone seen Shelly yet?"

"Oh, yeah," Reed said as he passed by. "I forgot to tell you, but Mitch said Shelly is coming in later. Guess she had some food poisoning or something."

Ivy pressed her lips together. It was one more excuse. Not that she didn't feel bad for Shelly—if she was actually sick. Every day, her sister had a reason for being late or not coming in at all.

"I need to pick up more paint and supplies," Ivy said to Forrest. "Can you oversee everything while I'm gone?"

Forrest grinned. "You know that's what I do for a living, right?"

Ivy made a face. "I'm a little flustered right now. Is there anything else I can pick up at Nailed It for you?"

Forrest squeezed her shoulder. "I'll let you know if there is. Ivy, try to relax. We've got this."

She patted his hand. "I will." Glancing around, she saw all the young cousins were pitching in and getting the job done. "Running this place can be overwhelming at times, especially during the high summer season."

"You've done an incredible job so far. I have to admit, last year when Angela and I heard you were taking on this old house and turning it into an inn—without any prior experience—we had our doubts. We didn't want to see you hurt again after all you went through with Jeremy. But I also knew that if anyone could do it, it would be you. My dedicated sister with reams of to-do lists and a huge heart. You're going to be okay, Sis."

Ivy threw her arms around Forrest. "You're the best brother ever," she said. "Well, you and Flint."

"Can't you leave out my other half for once?" Forrest chuckled.

"Hey, what's going on over there?" Flint called out from across the room.

"Aw, get back to work," Forrest said, waving to his brother.

"Just as soon as you do."

Laughing at their antics, Ivy hurried upstairs and grabbed the keys to the vintage Chevrolet convertible Bennett had renovated for her.

With the sun on her shoulders, she drove the short distance to the hardware store. While George loaded the paint she'd ordered into the truck, Ivy told Jen about the book club.

"Would you like to join us?" Ivy asked. "Paige is going to lead it."

Jen leaned against the hardware counter. "Sounds like fun. Count me in. If my sister can find a babysitter, could she come? Or maybe we'll trade off. She just moved here and needs a break from the kids from time to time."

"I'd love to meet her," Ivy said. She was fond of Jen, and they'd become friends after Ivy spent so much time and money in their store.

After saying goodbye to Jen, Ivy left. But instead of turning toward the inn, she decided to check on Shelly.

A few minutes later, Ivy parked in front of the beach cottage and knocked on the screen door. "Shelly, are you decent?"

Shelly's voice floated faintly through the house. "It's open."

Irritated, Ivy stepped inside. "Where are you?"

"In the bathroom. You can come in."

Preparing to have it out with Shelly, who was probably languishing in a bubble bath, Ivy opened the bathroom door. Instead, she was immediately alarmed.

Wearing a thin cotton nightgown, Shelly was curled on the white tile floor near the toilet, pressing a damp washcloth to her forehead.

"I can't get too far away from the toilet," she said in a thin voice. "Not much stays down, if you know what I mean."

Instantly, guilt coursed through Ivy for having thought Shelly was neglecting her duties. Kneeling beside her, she smoothed her hand over her sister's damp, tangled hair. "Mitch said something you ate didn't agree with you."

Shelly struggled to lift herself onto one elbow. Wrinkling her brow, she shook her head. "I don't think it's anything I ate."

"Then it could be a virus or a parasite. Didn't Mitch call it Montezuma's Revenge?"

"Montezuma had nothing to do with this. It's all Mitch's fault."

"You thought Mexico was a good idea when he suggested it." Ivy looked at Shelly and frowned.

Her sister's face was flushed, and her skin felt feverish. Ivy took the washcloth and rinsed it under cool water. She hadn't seen Shelly this ill in a long time, and she seemed to have lost some weight. As she wiped Shelly's forehead, she asked, "Have you taken your temperature?"

"I don't need to."

"Shelly, be sensible. I can take you to the clinic. Mitch shouldn't have left you here alone. Bennett could have easily managed the barbecue."

Ivy flexed her jaw with irritation. Mitch's youth was showing—he'd never had to be responsible for anyone else in his life. But that was beside the point. Shelly needed help now.

"I made him leave. Besides, I knew you'd be looking for him."

"And you, of course. I was worried about you."

Shelly leveled a gaze at her. "You've been angry, and you think I've been making excuses about work."

Ivy waved off the comment, but it was true. And she felt terrible about that. "I didn't realize you were so sick. I think you should come back to the inn where I can look after you. Take my room, and I'll stay with Bennett."

"You should be doing that anyway," Shelly said, attempting a smile. "But I'm okay here."

"Shelly, you look awful. You need to see a doctor."

"I have an appointment next week."

"Next week? If you can't keep anything down, you need to be checked out right away. You can get dehydrated very quickly. This could be serious."

"Oh, it's serious, all right." As haggard as Shelly was, her eyes gleamed. She pointed toward a blotter strip by the sink. "Mitch is a little freaked out."

Following Shelly's gaze, Ivy parted her lips in surprise. "Wait a minute, are you...?" She gripped Shelly's hand. "*Are* you?"

*T*he joy that bloomed on Shelly's pale face flooded Ivy with happiness, and she recalled how ecstatic she had been in discovering her first pregnancy.

"Just a few weeks, I think," Shelly said. "My body must be making up for lost time with this queasiness. I thought it might have happened in Mexico, and maybe it did, but the internet tells me it takes a few weeks—not that the web is always right. Anyway, we had no idea, so at least Mitch didn't feel like he had to marry me."

All the disappointment and animosity Ivy had felt earlier toward Shelly vanished. With an immediate outpouring of love, Ivy slid her arm under Shelly's limp frame and hugged her. "I'm so happy for you. This is just what you wanted."

Despite her weakness, Shelly managed a thin laugh, and her face lit with happiness. "We didn't think it could happen so fast."

"See, it's meant to be," Ivy said, stroking Shelly's hair. She knew how much this meant to her. "You've waited so long for this." Sitting beside her sister, she took her hand. "Have you told Mom yet?"

"You're the first. Besides Mitch, that is. I've been feeling so tired lately, and when I started getting sick and missed my monthly cycle this week, I suspected I might be pregnant." She chuckled. "You should have seen the look on Mitch's face when I showed him the test strip. But he was cool with it— thrilled, actually. Except that he was hovering all over me, making me nervous, so I finally tossed him out of the house. I told him to go make himself useful at the inn today."

"Do you want to call Mom now?" Ivy thought she would burst with this news.

"I'd really like that," Shelly replied, leaning against Ivy. "But I might need a few minutes."

"Take all the time you need."

"Is everyone at the house?"

Ivy nodded. "I left Forrest in charge. I think I insulted him when I asked if he could manage without me."

"You didn't." Shelly smiled at that.

"I had a lot on my mind. Like what was going on with you."

"Sorry if I haven't been around much. I know I've been slacking."

"You have a pretty good excuse now." Ivy ran water into a cup and gave it to Shelly to drink.

"I've never been this tired," Shelly said between tiny sips. "I haven't even felt like putting in the garden here."

"Don't worry, we've been looking after your garden at the inn. Your tomatoes are producing like mad. There are so many that I've been giving them to guests. The basil plants are going crazy, too. I've been making pesto."

"I'm glad." Shelly raised her head a little. "That actually sounds good. I might be a little hungry now."

"Do you have any saltine crackers or broth?"

"Oh, yum. Is that what I'm going to have to eat?"

Ivy grinned. "Maybe for a little while. Stay away from the spicy stuff."

With some resignation, Shelly nodded. "Mitch has matzo

crackers in the kitchen. He makes the best matzo and eggs dish for weekend brunch."

"That will work. How about some ginger tea or ginger ale? Lemon, peppermint, and ginger can help settle your stomach."

Shelly nodded. "An egg sounds good, too."

"Do you think you could manage to eat a little now?"

"I think so. But don't you need to get back to the house?"

Ivy waved off her comment. "They're fine without me. Forrest is in charge, and they won't be ready to paint until after lunch. Everyone has been cleaning, and when I left, they still had to tape and prep. I've got time to scramble an egg and call Mom with you."

A broad smile wreathed Shelly's face, and she hugged her knees to her chest. "I can hardly believe it. I'm finally going to be a mother."

"And you'll be a great, fun, wacky mom," Ivy said. "Just like ours was."

"She was, wasn't she?" Shelly managed a small laugh. "Last year, when we moved out here, I was so depressed. After my relationship with Ezzra fizzled, I thought motherhood would never happen for me. I tried to talk myself into thinking that wouldn't be so bad. I'd accepted that; it would have been okay." Her eyes sparkled. "But I'm really excited now."

Ivy looped her arms around Shelly, acutely aware that it was still early in her pregnancy. She prayed that it would progress well for her sister. But this was a moment to celebrate and look forward to the best. "Women have all sorts of options these days."

Shelly blinked a few times. "A couple of my friends in New York are childless by choice, and I have another friend who is seeing a fertilization specialist. I was even thinking about adoption."

"Those are all good choices."

"But I really wanted to have a child of my own. With

Mitch." A smile swept across her face again. "He's going to be such a great dad—once he settles down and stops treating me like a strange alien being."

Ivy laughed. "I'm glad to see your sense of humor is coming back. Now, how about that egg?"

"I think I can manage one."

After helping Shelly to her feet, Ivy led her sister into the cottage kitchen. Although it was small, Mitch kept the walk-pantry he'd built well stocked. An array of professional skillets and pans hung from a rack, and a block of expert knives sat on the counter. The rest of the house might look like a bachelor pad, but the kitchen was that of an accomplished cook.

In the refrigerator, Ivy found a bottle of ginger ale and poured it for Shelly. "Sip this first and see how you feel."

Shelly eased onto an old farmhouse-style pine chair at a small table and took a few sips.

As Ivy watched Shelly for adverse reactions, she told her about their parents' call to Forrest and their plans.

"Maybe someday Mitch and I could do that," Shelly said, resting her chin on her hand. "People sail with children all the time. We talked about taking our children everywhere with us. This one is going to learn to do yoga, sail, and cook." She smiled and pointed toward a basket on the counter. "You'll find the eggs there. Mitch buys them at the farmers market."

Ivy was glad that Shelly was in better spirits now. She lifted a red-checked napkin and picked out a speckled brown egg. After whisking and cooking it, she turned out the paltry offering on a white restaurant plate like Mitch used at Java Beach. She broke off a small piece of a matzo flatbread cracker and added it to the meager fare, hoping this would sit well on Shelly's tender stomach.

Ivy placed the plate on the table. "Don't eat it all at once."

"That smells good," Shelly said, lifting a tiny bite to her mouth.

"Just nibble slowly. Sort of sneak up on it. Your stomach won't like a lot at one time for a while."

Shelly nodded. "Small meals, I read. And who knew morning sickness could happen any time of day?"

"Afraid so."

While Shelly ate, they talked about the book club. "Darla is excited about it," Ivy said. "She's making a book list and inviting people for us."

Shelly sipped her ginger ale and nodded. "She needs something to keep her busy."

"How's Darla working out as a *de facto* mother-in-law for you?"

"Oh, she's all right," Shelly replied. "She's going to be thrilled when she hears the news about the baby, but we don't want to tell her just yet. We need to get used to the idea first, and..." She paused, and her smile faltered. "The internet tells me I'm now of advanced maternal age—that's the nice term for a geriatric pregnancy. Anything could happen, right?"

Ivy knew that, but she didn't want Shelly to hold such negative thoughts. "You and your baby are going to be healthy and fine."

"I hope so. Guess I'll have to do maternity yoga now. Maybe I could teach a class on that."

"See? This is going to be fun. Are you ready to call Mom and Dad now?"

Shelly nodded, and Ivy placed the call. Although Carlotta and Sterling had a dozen grown grandchildren, there hadn't been a baby in the Bay family in a long time. As the youngest child, Shelly had always felt behind. When their eldest sister Honey had her baby, she was still a child, so Elena and Shelly weren't that far apart in age.

The phone rang a few times before their parents answered.

"It's so good to hear from you, Ivy," Carlotta said. "We're

at a market getting fresh fruits and vegetables. Did Forrest tell you we called?"

"He did," Ivy said. "But Shelly has some news for you." She passed the phone to her sister.

Shelly clutched the phone and grinned. "Mom, Dad, by the time you get back, you're going to need to set an extra place at the table."

After a brief silence on the other end of the line, Ivy could hear a loud cry of exclamation, and then their parents started talking at once.

"When? How far along? Have you been to the doctor? What does Mitch think? How are you doing?"

Shelly held the phone from her ear, laughing. "I've got a little morning sickness, but we're doing fine."

"Do you need me to come home, *mija*?" Carlotta asked earnestly. "I will."

"No, Mom. Enjoy yourselves. Ivy is taking good care of me. She's feeding me eggs and dry matzos and ginger ale. We've got this."

"We'll be sure to fly back for the big event," Sterling said.

"Before you give birth," Carlotta added with a wistful note in her voice.

"Don't interrupt your trip for me," Shelly said. "I want you to have a great time. You've earned it."

Ivy saw a tinge of sadness on Shelly's face, and she recalled what it was like to be thousands of miles away from her mother when she was pregnant. At the time, Jeremy had been extremely attentive, so that helped, but when her mother flew out to see her, she'd been ecstatic to see her and very much in need of mothering.

By the time Shelly had finished her conversation, the color had returned to her cheeks, and she seemed to have more energy.

"Now that you're feeling better, I'm going back to the

house," Ivy said. "They'll be ready for the paint soon, though I doubt if that smell will agree with you."

"I'm okay now," Shelly said. "It comes and goes, but I can stay outside. The fresh air will be good for me, and I can check on those tomatoes. You guys did a good job of keeping up with the garden, but my plants need me."

After tidying the bathroom for Shelly, Ivy packed a few slices of matzo crackers and an extra bottle of ginger ale just in case. She'd have to add some bland items to her shopping list to have in the house for Shelly. Most of all, she resolved to have more patience with her sister now that she knew she was pregnant.

When they arrived at the house, Ivy went down to the lower level to see how it looked, and Shelly followed her. Ivy was amazed at the transformation that cleaning and organizing could bring. Her energetic nieces and nephews accomplished more in half of a day than she could have in a month. Every surface was clean and, with decades of grime scrubbed away, the wood floors had depth and sheen again.

Everyone was busy. Poppy and her sister Coral were taping edges to prepare for painting, and her cousins Skyler and Summer were unfolding drop cloths they had used to paint the upstairs last year.

Bennett and Forrest were working on a light fixture on a table. Seeing them together made Ivy smile. Bennett had been friends with Forrest and Flint before she returned to Summer Beach, so her brothers immediately welcomed him into the family. They looked up when Ivy and Shelly came in.

Bennett looked at Shelly with a heartfelt smile. Instantly, Ivy knew that Mitch had taken him into his confidence.

"Wow, what a difference," Shelly said, turning around to take in all the changes. She took out her phone to snap photos. "People love to see before-and-after and in-progress photos on the blog." She lowered her voice. "At least I can do that today," she whispered to Ivy.

"I'll pitch in here," Ivy said. "Why don't you check on your garden and talk to Mitch? I think we have everything under control here."

"I can probably watch the front desk, too."

"Only if you're feeling up to it."

After Shelly left, Ivy made her way to Bennett, who wore a frayed, white knit shirt with paint splatters dotted across it. Forrest and Flint left to check on Reed and Rocky and the other cousins who were working on repairs.

"Nice shirt," Ivy said. She liked how it stretched across his broad shoulders. She kissed him lightly.

"This is my painting gear," he said. Pausing, he added, "Mitch spoke to me. Do you know about Shelly?"

She nodded. "I checked on her when I went to pick up the paint. When I got there, she was looking pretty green."

"Are they going to tell the family yet?"

"We called Mom and Dad before we came. Give them a chance to catch their breath about this."

"It's better that they take things at their own pace." Bennett jerked a thumb over his shoulder. "Did you have a chance to look in the storage area?"

"Poppy and I sorted through some of the furnishings and boxes stored here, but we haven't seen everything. We got busy upstairs with guests."

"I found a couple of crates of books," Bennett said. "You might want to shelve those in your library or on the bookshelves down here."

"We'll do that," Ivy said. "I'll decorate with old books to create a cozy ambiance. I once saw an old neighborhood library in Los Angeles artistically converted into a wine bar. We're going for a similar feeling to work well for a variety of events, from book club meetings to business retreats."

"That sounds unique," Bennett agreed. "This is an out-of-the-way location that some companies might like for planning sessions. I can imagine people creating strategy on the beach or in the wine nook."

"I like that idea," Ivy said. "Where are those books you found?" She wondered if some might be part of Amelia's coveted library.

"Over there." Bennett gestured toward a couple of old crates.

She followed him and stood by while he removed the lids. "Oh, I recognize these," she said, mildly disappointed. "The encyclopedia set. Shelly and I saw these when we first opened this level."

"Anything of value in there?"

"Not unless the internet crashes," Ivy replied. "Someday, my future grandchildren won't even know what these are."

"I don't think my nephew does."

Ivy smiled up at him. "Does that make us old?"

"Not at all. I prefer to say we're at the crossroads of old and new." He took her hand. "Personally, too."

Bennett's words touched her. "I couldn't agree more," she said, thinking of the decisions they still needed to make.

*T*he next day after the paint had dried, Bennett hefted one end of the rolled-up rug that had been stored on the lower level for decades. "Can you get the other end of this?"

"Got it, bro," Mitch replied, lifting the other end of the carpet with the enviable ease of youth.

Dust puffed from the fibers as they hauled the rug toward the bookshelves. While this was hard work, Bennett enjoyed helping Ivy organize this space. He glanced around. There was still a lot to clean up. Even though the area had been sealed, fine sand and silt had managed to filter through the cracks after years of constant sea breezes.

The area smelled of fresh paint and salty sea air now, a welcome change from the musty odor that had greeted Bennett just a few days ago.

This past year, Bennett had maintained his ridgeline house that he'd rented to a family, and the inn had become his home. He'd never dreamed he would ever live in this old house, but neither had he imagined he'd fall in love again after Jackie died. If there was one thing life had taught him, it was that you couldn't predict the future. Just as he'd resigned himself to singlehood forever, here he was crossing off items on Ivy's endless to-do list.

He smiled to himself. Not that he minded. He knew he was right where he was needed.

Still, the offer that Diana was dangling before him was tempting. The amount of money the other municipality was offering was frankly staggering. The position of City Manager came with a generous paycheck, plenty of perks, and the chance to be a big fish in a bigger pond. It could even launch a more impactful political career if he wanted.

As a younger man, he would have jumped on it. Still, he wasn't *that* old.

However, he knew what Ivy would say about this. While it fed his ego to think about the possibilities, Ivy nourished his heart and soul. He wasn't sure if he could satisfy one responsibility without jeopardizing the other.

Yet, Diana had been relentless.

"Hey, drop it here," Mitch said, shaking his end of the rug. "Earth to Bennett. Where are you, man?"

Bennett reeled in his thoughts and looked at Ivy. "Right here?"

"That's perfect," Ivy said, gesturing to the spot. "Roll it out so I can vacuum, please."

He and Mitch kicked the carpet, sending it across the wood floor before smoothing it out. The intricate, handwoven Persian rug was still stunning. With a good cleaning, the dusty colors would become vibrant again.

"Beautiful," Bennett said, glancing back at Ivy. He noted how the sunlight from the high windows illuminated her face with a sunny glow. He could lose himself forever in the depth of her green eyes. "How's this, sweetheart?"

She must have caught his silly smile because she planted a kiss on his cheek. "I appreciate everything you're doing." Glancing over her shoulder, she added, "You, too, Mitch."

"Comes with the gig," the younger man replied, dusting his hands on his jeans. "This is family business now."

"I suppose it is," Ivy said. "How's Shelly feeling?"

"Still queasy this morning, but she'll be in here as soon as she can. She has some essential oils she's trying out—ginger and cardamom—and is working on a yoga routine to ease the morning sickness." Rubbing the back of his neck, Mitch added, "We went to see the doc yesterday. I never knew being a woman was so complicated."

Bennett looked at Ivy, and they both chuckled.

"She'll feel better soon," Ivy said. "She's doing all the right things."

Memories of Jackie and her pregnancy sprang to mind—part of the painful things he'd blocked and hadn't recalled in years. "You might want to get some ginger and peppermint tea, too."

Mitch raised his brow. "Already got it. How'd you know about that?"

Bennett could feel Ivy's gaze on him, and he knew that she understood. Mitch was so wrapped up in the newness of marriage and fatherhood, he'd forgotten. Bennett said lightly, "I hear folks talk. I'm really happy for you."

Mitch ruffled his spiky blond hair. "I didn't realize everything about a person's body could change so fast. But I've got no regrets, man. Creating a new life is pretty cool."

"That little one will have plenty of cousins and aunts and uncles."

"I never had that," Mitch said. "Being part of the Bay family is awesome. Man, can those big kids eat. I had the grill going nonstop yesterday."

Bennett chuckled. "Especially when they're working hard."

Mitch dusted his hands. "If that's all you need, I've got to check on my crew at Java Beach."

"Go ahead, and thanks for your help—as always." Ivy

unwound the cord on the vacuum cleaner and turned to find a plug.

Catching her hand, Bennett said, "I'll do that for you."

"You don't have to," she said, raising her eyes to his.

"Actually, I do. I can't stand idle and watch you work. It's damaging to my frail male ego."

"I don't believe that for one second," she said, smiling. "But I won't argue. I'll plug this in, and you can take over. I want to arrange some books on these shelves anyway. At least the leather-bound encyclopedia relics will look nice."

"And be a good conversation starter."

Bennett was glad that Forrest had sent his electrical team to inspect and repair the system down here early this morning. Old wiring could cause fires, and that was the last thing Ivy needed after working so hard.

THE NEXT DAY after working at City Hall, Bennett wheeled into the car court behind the inn. Ivy waved and strode toward him across the terrace. Sunlight accented the highlights in her glossy brown hair, and the skirt of her creamy linen sundress brushed her calves. His heart quickened at the sight of her.

Behind her, the afternoon wine and tea event was in full force, and piano music filled the air. A group of older, well-dressed guests were chatting and laughing on the terrace, but he didn't feel up to joining them this evening. He'd had a draining day working on budget items.

"Hi, honey," Bennett said wearily. He stepped from his vehicle.

"Hi, sweetie," she said, sliding her arms around him with a kiss.

"I could sure use more of that," Bennett said, managing a grin for her. "Would you like to have a private wine and cheese event at my place?"

"I'd like that."

They climbed the stairs to his apartment. While Bennett opened the wine, Ivy opened the refrigerator and began to assemble a platter of appetizers.

He poured two glasses and carried them to a sofa that he'd positioned to look out over the ocean. She swung open a pair of French doors to let in the cool evening breeze.

Ivy placed a plate of Havarti cheese, crackers, and sweet peppers from Shelly's garden on a low table. Slipping out of her shoes, she sat beside him, curling her legs under her.

"You're awfully nice to come home to," Bennett said, kissing her again. He handed her a glass and touched his wine goblet to hers. "Here's to coming home to you for the rest of our lives."

"I'd like that," she said softly.

He pulled her close. "You know, we should choose one room or another. We *are* married."

Ivy smiled a little at that. "I know you have your routine in the morning during the week." She hesitated. "So do I."

"Everyone does. We don't have to wait for special occasions."

Ivy glanced around the apartment. "I want to talk about this, but does it have to be now? It's been a long day, and I have the new book club meeting tomorrow. We still have a lot to do tonight."

From her guarded tone, Bennett knew they wouldn't make any headway on the issue tonight. "Have you heard from Misty lately?"

Ivy shook her head. "Misty is doing voice-over auditions and working with the director of the television series that she's going to do once her broken leg heals. I'm so proud of her, and I love having both my girls on this coast."

Bennett couldn't help the words that tumbled from his weary lips. "Is that why you're hesitant about us?"

Ivy pulled away and took a sip of wine. "It does feel a little awkward. They've known me only with their father."

"They were pretty supportive at our ceremony."

"I know. It's me, not them." Raising her eyes to his, she added, "I'll get there. Just be patient with me."

"I'll do my best." Bennett wrapped his arms around her. "How about we watch the sunset from the balcony?"

Ivy smiled, looking relieved. "I'd like that."

Swallowing his pride, Bennett stood and held his hand to her. With her in his world, life made sense again. He had a purpose, one that wasn't tied to a large salary or a demanding position. Pushing Diana's offer from his mind, he tilted Ivy's chin and kissed her softly. "I'm glad you're here."

"So am I."

If there was one thing Bennett had learned, it was that love could be fleeting. He'd never dreamed that his wife and unborn child could be stolen away in an instant. They hadn't even suspected the complications of her pregnancy. Life had no guarantees, and all he could do was love the woman who stood before him today.

Yet, that didn't mean he didn't want more from their relationship.

"*W*elcome to the new book club," Ivy said, greeting each guest as they arrived in the newly renovated literary section. Upstairs, Poppy was directing people to the lower level.

Shelly stood beside her, offering guests a cup of mint tea or a Sea Breeze Cooler. Some guests had brought bottles of wine or plates of appetizers.

"I wonder if they come for the food and drinks or the books," Shelly whispered. "Only a few guests are abstaining. And me, of course."

"Put me down for tea as well," Ivy said. "I should keep my wits about me tonight."

Ivy didn't want to tell Shelly what happened when she came down to open the windows earlier this evening. Not that she saw anything—it was more of a feeling of being watched, crazy as that seemed. She didn't have a sense of foreboding or evil or impending disaster. No, it was more of a mixture of relief, approval—and furniture placement.

Odd, she knew.

But there it was. Ivy shivered. She'd moved the chairs several times, but it took a sudden gust from an open window and a spider launching from a Russian chandelier for her to realize that a particular chair was better placed elsewhere.

Maybe that had been Amelia's favorite chair.

Not that she believed in any of that. However, she did put that chair in a spot that had the best view of the room.

Just in case.

Footsteps sounded on the staircase. Looking up, she saw Celia arriving.

"I'm so glad you could make it," Ivy said. Celia had stayed at the inn last year after her home was damaged in the Ridgetop Fire. Her friend's sleek black hair was swept off her face into an elegant chignon, and she wore a simple, black silk tunic with low heels. "How is Tyler?"

"He has a couple of friends from Silicon Valley visiting, so they're having a poker party on the boat. I'm so glad you called about the book club. After working with children in the music program all day, I need some grown-up time." Celia sniffed. "And I'm not counting my husband and his friends in that. They're so boastful and prideful. Like unruly teenagers."

Ivy detected displeasure in Celia's expression. She and Tyler had been separated for several months last year when he refused to join her at the inn while their house was being rebuilt. He'd taken off on his yacht and didn't tell her where he was going.

Ivy gave her a sympathetic smile. "My mother always said that a good marriage is created through the art of compromise." As the words left her mouth, she couldn't help wonder where she fell on that spectrum.

"That should work both ways," Celia said pointedly.

"Wine or Sea Breeze?" Shelly asked, interceding with a selection of vintage stemware and glasses from a tray she'd prepared.

Gratefully, Celia accepted a wineglass. "At least I can still count on good friends."

"Always." Looking around at the crowd that had gathered,

Ivy realized how many new friends she'd made since moving from Boston.

As Celia sipped her wine and perused the old leather-bound books Ivy had arranged on the shelves, another resident, the enigmatic Ginger Delavie, made her way imperiously down the staircase. Even in a simple, crisp white shirt and pencil-thin black slacks and flats, the older woman looked regal. Her collar was turned up, and a silk scarf framed her face.

"What a marvelous space," Ginger said, surveying everything from the Russian crystal chandeliers to the Persian rugs and hastily slip-covered chairs. "I love the old-world ambiance. I feel like I should have worn Bertrand's old smoking jacket. It was a gift from the Czar, his godmother's second cousin by marriage—quite a tenuous connection if you ask me. Still, she treated it like a treasure and never let us forget it."

Ivy smiled. Ginger was the real treasure. As a young couple, she and her late husband, a career diplomat, had moved into a nearby beach house they christened the Coral Cottage. Ginger had taught advanced math at the local high school, and she had a particular fondness for codes and storytelling. Her granddaughter Marina was one of Ivy's closest friends from years ago. She couldn't wait to hear what sort of books Ginger would suggest.

A couple of guests from the inn made their way downstairs, too. One was Bettina, the young nurse Ivy had sent to Pages for beach books. She stopped to talk to Ivy.

"I saw Paige at the bookshop, and you were right about her," Bettina said. "She suggested a book I would never have thought to pick up, but it was just what I needed—sassy, funny, hysterical. It was fun to laugh out loud again."

"We all need that," Ivy said, thinking about Paige's quite different book recommendation for her. *Pride and Prejudice.* What was the meaning behind that?

Geena stood awkwardly beside another guest, her eyes scanning the downstairs area. "You cleaned up the place over the weekend. Did you find any more loot?" She had a smile on her face that seemed more like a smirk, but Ivy tried to give her the benefit of the doubt.

"Not this time," Ivy said, forcing a smile.

"Where was the art when you found it?"

Ivy nodded across the room. "Over there. We sent everything back to the rightful owners."

Geena shot her a look without replying. She took a chilled cooler and strolled toward the rear chairs.

Ivy shook her head. *It takes all types*, her father used to say.

Before long, everyone had arrived. Jen, the proprietor of Nailed It, had come with Leilani from the Hidden Garden nursery. Leilani had brought white chocolate and macadamia nut cookies. Darla, Paige, and Louise, who ran the Laundry Basket, settled in, too. Bennett's sister, Kendra, who worked as a scientist, arrived with a cheese tray and a book.

Gilda had joined them from upstairs. She sported Pixie in a glittery pink, faux-fur-lined doggie backpack that nearly matched Gilda's hair. "It's for her protection," she explained. "Little dogs can be trampled in crowds, and she'll yap all evening if I leave her alone."

"Pixie is welcome," Ivy said, scratching the feisty Chihuahua behind the ears.

Imani Jones, wearing her latest rainbow-hued, tie-dyed sundress, arrived with Maeve, the City Attorney for Summer Beach, who pressed another bottle of wine into Shelly's hands. The two women were engrossed in a legal discussion as they strolled in.

Maeve paused to accept a glass of wine. "Thank you, dear. And what gorgeous arrangements. Roses are my favorite flowers, and those frilly petaled lavender ones are divine." She glanced at Imani. "Are these from Blossoms?"

Shelly beamed while Imani smiled and shook her head. "I

suspect Shelly grew these. She has quite the garden here and creates stunning arrangements."

"Simply lovely," Maeve said. "It's always such a pleasure coming to the inn. I have a family reunion in October, so I'll suggest they stay here. Perhaps we could have Ginger's granddaughter cater dinner in the dining room. Marina, isn't it?"

"That's right," Ivy said. "Marina would have been here tonight except that she is catering a party. We'd be happy to accommodate your family." Ivy noticed Shelly grinning at her.

"You were right," Shelly said as the other two women moved on to greet others.

"About what?"

"Sometimes, you have to give before you get."

"Often true." Ivy bumped Shelly's shoulder. "As I look out over these new friends of ours, I realize we're the lucky ones. Let's circulate before we begin the meeting."

Conversation filled the room, and everyone seemed to be enjoying themselves.

Even Darla. For now, anyway.

Ivy didn't think she'd ever had such a nice group of women friends. When her daughters were young, she'd barely had time to keep up with the few acquaintances she had in Boston. As for the socializing she and Jeremy did, it was always with his friends or business associates.

Ivy moved among the gathering, thinking about how interesting each woman was. The women they had first spoken to —Jen, Darla, and Celia—said they preferred a night to themselves. After talking to Bennett, he'd offered to organize a book club night for the men in town.

Turning to Paige, Ivy asked, "Would you like to speak to the group tonight about ordering books for the club?"

"I'd appreciate that," Paige said. "That way, I can make sure everyone gets the books they want in time." A mysterious little smile played on her lips. "But of course, there is much more to a book club than reading. We'll talk about that."

After everyone was seated, Ivy started the meeting. "I want to welcome you to the inaugural book club meeting at the Seabreeze Inn. We've heard stories about how the former owner, Amelia Erickson, held grand soirees and intimate salons with some of the foremost artists and intellectuals of the day." The chandelier overhead flickered, and Ivy paused as people noticed.

Shelly laughed and winked at her.

Ivy held up the old guest book she'd found. "This is a guest log of her book club." She slipped on a pair of leopard-print reading glasses. "Amelia called it the Literary Society of Summer Beach."

"We're continuing an important tradition," Ginger said. "To read and share our thoughts is much more productive than an evening spent in front of a television. Not that I have anything against that, mind you. I'm quite fond of my friend Julia Child's old cooking shows. Still, we need variety and intelligent discourse."

Ivy smiled. And so it was beginning. She yielded the floor to Paige, who knew everyone except for a couple of curious inn guests who had just wandered in. Paige's bright blue eyes sparkled behind her lapis glasses, and her wavy silver hair fell softly around her narrow shoulders.

Geena stood at the rear of the room, refusing to take a seat even when Ivy motioned to her. She got up and took a chair to the stubborn younger woman.

Paige began. "Historically, reading and literary clubs were vehicles for women to gather, educate themselves, and even influence policies. Years ago, the women's right to vote was a hotly debated topic, and grass-roots organization efforts often sprang from literary meetings."

A murmur of interest and approval rippled across the crowd.

Paige went on. "Besides activism, women also read as a means to broaden their world view and escape narrow societal confines. Stephen King once wrote that 'Books are a uniquely portable magic.'"

"Transporting one like the magic of music or art," Celia added.

"Very similar," Paige agreed. "When people enter the magical portal of pages to read deeply and discuss shared human experiences, a transformation occurs. It's nourishment for the mind, the heart, and the soul," she said, touching a graceful hand to her temple and chest. "Through your love of books, you'll gain deeper insights and elevate your understanding of our journey—why we make the choices we do and the eventual outcomes and impacts on our life paths. Because what are books but inner journeys?"

She smiled. "If that seems too deep now, you'll come to appreciate it. Most of all, the heart of a book club is its members. How we share and support each other will strengthen the bonds between you." She paused in reflection. "I've seen this beautiful transformation so many times."

Ivy glanced around the gathering and saw people nodding in agreement. Even Geena listened in rapt attention. Perhaps this experience would bring out a different side to her.

Paige spoke of the wonder of storytelling, walking among the group as she did. Lithe as a fairy, she still moved with youthful energy. "This is true for fiction as well as nonfiction. As a book club, we might also enjoy stepping into a real person's shoes. Reading biographies is a good way to experience another person's fascinating life."

"Like the *Real Housewives* series," Darla suggested with a wry expression, and everyone laughed. "Or not."

"Some people have brought reading list suggestions," Ivy said, trying to keep the group on task. "Maybe we can share those."

"I always like to take the temperature of a room," Paige said. "Let's see a show of hands from those who like serious literature, such as the classics." She counted a few hands. "And for fun, popular reads?"

More hands shot up.

"Very well, then," Paige said. "I would love to see and hear your book suggestions for the club, so pass them around to me. While we're doing that, let's go around the room and find out what we all enjoy reading." She turned to Ginger. "What do you like to read, or what books have made an impact on you?"

Ginger sat erect in a tapestry wingback chair. "I've always thought Leo Tolstoy's *War and Peace* is quite entertaining—it's a grand Russian soap opera. But I also love a good international espionage thriller."

Imani was next. "My taste is pretty varied. I like domestic and legal thrillers. And of course, anything by Maya Angelou or Beverly Jenkins—she writes marvelous romantic sagas."

Seated next to her, Maeve nodded. "I've read every book John Grisham has written, but I've also reread Jane Austen's books quite often."

As Ivy took that in, she thought she saw a slight smile curve on Paige's face.

Maeve continued. "In many ways, Austen's books and characters are timeless. Human nature hasn't changed that much—we still have disagreements between women and men —and societal issues." She paused and smiled. "As to what book made the most impact on me, it had to be when I was a girl. *My Friend Flicka* by Mary O'Hara. How I loved horses, and that book introduced me to reading."

Paige nodded. "All the young horse lovers adored that story."

Jen was next. She picked at a thread on her blue jeans as she spoke. "I have French heritage, so I love the work of Colette." A mischievous smile bloomed on her face. "But I also have a secret vice—cowboys and Navy Seals. Lots of steamy romance."

"Oh, la la," Shelly said, and everyone laughed.

Paige nodded. "Many women adore their hot book boyfriends."

"Oh, I'd never cheat on George in real life," Jen said, blushing slightly. "But sometimes I pick up a few ideas to spice up things."

"Hear, hear," Shelly said, raising a bottle of ginger ale. Laughter rippled around the room.

Leilani raised her hand. "I love family sagas, and I've learned more about my native Hawaii from novelists than I did from history books in school. I've recommended several authors on my list."

"I see that," Paige said, holding up a card that Leilani had given her.

Next up was Darla. "I'll read anything. Mysteries, cozies, sci-fi, historical, and beach series. I usually read several books a week, and I belong to an online book club with friends. There's nothing better than a new book and old Scotch."

Ivy smiled as she pictured that. As she listened, she wondered what Paige would do with all these varied preferences.

Finally, Geena shot up her hand. "I like true crime," she said in a challenging voice. "I like to see how much people can get away with."

That comment made Ivy uncomfortable. Geena seemed to have an ulterior motive, but Ivy couldn't imagine what it was. Maybe she was starved for attention, and being contrary was the only way she knew how to get it.

Shelly nudged her with the toe of her sandal as Maeve and Imani traded looks.

"The darker side of real life can be fascinating, too," Paige said smoothly.

Geena nodded, her eyes sparkling in a way that unnerved Ivy. Or maybe she imagined that.

"Part of being in a book club is gaining exposure to books

you might not find on your own," Paige said. She handed several print outs to Poppy to pass around. "This is a list of ideas I had. Put a mark beside the ones you like—choose as many as you want, and recommendations are welcome. Next week, we'll talk about which books you'd like to read. Once we decide, I'll prepare a list of discussion questions so that when we meet, we can delve into the deeper issues that book presents."

"Are we reading any books this week?" Celia asked.

Paige smiled. "If you'd like, choose one you've been meaning to read or an old favorite. We can talk about what you liked or learned. And I'm happy to recommend books to anyone." She paused. "Ivy is planning to read *Pride and Prejudice.*"

Ivy grinned. She was committed now.

A murmur rose across the gathering. "That's a good book to start with," Imani said as others nodded. "But I'd like to hear what others might want, too."

"That's settled then." Shelly stood. "While that list is going around, who'd like a refill?"

"I'll help you," Ivy said. Upstairs in the kitchen, she pulled another cork from a wine bottle.

"What's up with that criminal-in-training down there?" Shelly asked.

"I have no idea," Ivy said. "Maybe Geena was just trying to get a rise out of us."

"Some people," Shelly said, shaking her head.

They didn't have many guests that made Ivy feel uncomfortable, but this one did. Geena had a sharp edge about her that others noticed, too.

"There's something about her," Ivy said. "I can't quite work out what. But I'll be watching." At least Geena wouldn't stay forever.

After everyone left, Ivy and Shelly saw everyone out. They returned downstairs to tidy the space.

Shelly plumped a few pillows before picking up the old guest book. "Maybe we should start using this again."

"Let's get another one," Ivy replied as she collected used glasses. "That one belongs to the past."

"The meetings seemed to have great importance in their lives," Shelly said as she opened the cover. "The Literary Society—looks like they were a lot more serious than we are."

"I'm sure there was some laughter along with their spirited conversations." Ivy paused to glance at a page. "I love how they wrote back then—the ink they used and the way they signed their names with such intent and elegance."

Shelly flipped through the pages. As she did, a thin, folded paper fluttered to the floor.

Ivy stooped to pick it up. After unfolding it with care, she lowered herself onto the sofa and scanned the old-fashioned script. "It's a letter from Gustav to Amelia, asking her to look after someone named Marta. He wrote, 'I trust you will see to her in her time of need and remember the pledges I made to her.'"

"Marta. Didn't we see that name in the front? I think she was one of the guests." Shelly peered over her shoulder.

"If it's the same person."

"A pledge," Shelly said. "I wonder what he meant by that?"

Ivy gazed at the letter for a long moment. "We might never know. The answer is lost to time." Yet, she couldn't help thinking that the past seemed ever present in this old house.

The following day, after assisting with the weekend breakfast crowd at the inn, Bennett set out for the marina to work on his boat. A boat owner's work seemed endless, but he loved puttering around his craft and being out on the water. It was a good way to relax at the end of a week.

He also needed to clear his mind about Diana. She had been persistent in singing the praises of the new position—from the team he'd be working with to the prestige, generous salary, and expense account. He gazed over the water, watching boats in the distance.

A siren's song, perhaps.

Taking out his supplies, he thought about the offer. If not for Ivy's hesitation, he probably wouldn't be considering this position, he told himself. But what if Ivy could find a bed-and-breakfast to run in this new community? Would she be willing to join him? Anything was possible.

He wondered if Shelly and Poppy could run the Seabreeze Inn on their own. After all, once the business was running, which it was, it was just another business.

Ivy wouldn't even have to work. She could stay at home and paint.

He paused. Was he kidding himself?

While he was applying a final coat of sealant to the hatch, a young woman in a skimpy swimsuit sauntered toward the boat. "Hi," she called out in a friendly voice. "Are you the mayor?"

Bennett looked up, shielding his face from the sun. "Sure am."

"Bennett Dylan?"

"At your service. What can I help you with?"

She held out a large envelope. "You just did. You've been served. Have a great day!"

Bennett sighed and took the papers, and then she spun around and hurried away. "Probably city business," he muttered to himself. Why couldn't this have waited until Monday morning?

He rested his brush on the can of sealant and opened the envelope. It was a lawsuit, all right. But not for the city. It was against him as a real estate sales professional.

For selling Las Brisas del Mar.

He passed a hand across his forehead in disbelief. His first inclination was to disregard it as a frivolous lawsuit, but he knew he had to answer it. He'd talk to Maeve and Imani about this. Perhaps they could help him or recommend someone who could.

This was the last thing he needed.

Just then, his phone buzzed. He glanced down, recognizing the number as the trustee for the old inn. "Hey, Joel. Funny you should call right now."

"Not funny at all. I just got served with a lawsuit."

Bennett squinted against the sun. "So did I." Bennett could hear Joel flipping through papers on the other end of the line. He lived in Los Angeles.

"You're being sued, too? Incredible." Joel let out a sigh. "It's from someone purporting to be an heir to Las Brisas. Any idea who this could be? I see the name, but it means nothing to me. Has anyone contacted you or the buyer?"

"That would be Ivy Bay. She's operating it as an inn now."

"I hope that's going well for her. Well, this is unfortunate, but we'll have to go along with the process. I assure you that we searched for heirs. Even if we missed one—and I don't see how we did—they had years to come forward."

"Is this the unknown niece that disappeared during the war?"

On the other end of the line, Joel shuffled pages. "I can't tell, but she would be quite old by now, so maybe it's a child of hers. The house was in trust for years to allow for possible heirs to come forward. I'll give this to one of our associates at the firm to review and research. I'll let you know what we find."

After Bennett hung up, he immediately thought of Ivy. *Has she received anything?* He tapped his phone to call her, but his call went straight to voice mail.

Worried, he tossed the documents aside and quickly cleaned his brush and stashed his supplies. The rest of this job would have to wait.

*W*hen Ivy walked into the kitchen, her daughter was already preparing the breakfast platters. Today, she had tamed her strawberry blond mane into a pony-tail and wore a cute watermelon-printed sundress. "This early rising of yours is becoming a habit. And you look really nice."

Sunny grinned. "I'm still covering for Shelly. We worked out a deal."

Ivy wondered what that might be. Whatever it was, Sunny was motivated, and that was a pleasant change.

Sunny lifted the platter of muffins. "Did you know Geena was going to check out so early?"

"She's gone?" Ivy hadn't had time to speak to her about all the printing and copying.

"She was on her way out when I came in. Left her key on the desk and walked out." Sunny rolled her eyes. "I hope we don't get many like her."

"Most of our guests just want a quiet place by the beach to relax." Fortunately, they had Geena's credit card on file. "I'll close out her bill and send it to her after breakfast." She sighed, feeling lighter now that Geena was gone. Still, Ivy felt sorry for her. Even though Geena had been abrasive, it seemed like an act she put on when she felt uncomfortable or threatened. Ivy wondered why she felt so vulnerable.

Just then, the door to the downstairs creaked on its old hinges until it stood slightly ajar. Ivy crossed the kitchen to shut the door. She flipped the lock on the knob. "I thought I'd locked this after the book club. Did you go down there this morning?"

Sunny shook her head. "Maybe it's Aunt Shelly's friendly ghost."

"Not you, too," Ivy said, laughing it off.

For the rest of the day, Ivy was busy crossing off tasks on her to-do list. She still had a lot she wanted to do with the downstairs, such as adding window coverings. She was sure she could figure out something inexpensive that would look nice.

To her surprise, Tyler had called, asking about renting the space for a casino night fundraiser for Celia's school music program. He wanted to surprise her, which Ivy thought was an encouraging sign. She hoped they'd make a go of their marriage, even though she imagined Tyler must be a challenge to live with. He asked to see the space later in the week.

By mid-afternoon, Ivy was back at the reception desk. Sunny was going to school, Poppy was showing new guests to their rooms, and Shelly was tending to the garden. Now that Ivy knew what was going on with her sister, she was more forgiving because she remembered her own difficult pregnancy.

Shelly's excitement was nearly palpable. She and Mitch didn't want to tell many people their news yet, but she'd had to share her secret with Poppy and Sunny after they'd shown concern for her health.

"Thank you for visiting us," Ivy said to a young couple who were checking in. They couldn't have been much older than Poppy or Sunny. A thought struck her. Someday, she would have to let her niece and daughter go when they were ready to move on. But for now, she loved having her family nearby.

The young woman twirled her hair. "Can you recommend a good restaurant in town?"

Ivy smiled and rattled off a list. "Java Beach for breakfast and lunch on the beach, the Coral Cafe for supper—also on the beach—and Rosa's for the best fish tacos." She brought out a list that Poppy had prepared to hand out. "You'll find more on this list."

Just then, she noticed her cell phone was buzzing. "Excuse me, one moment." In reaching for it, she pressed the wrong button and sent Bennett to voice mail. She'd have to call him after checking in the guests.

She answered a few more questions and sent the young couple on their way to explore the village. As they were leaving, another young woman in a beach coverup strode in.

"I'm looking for Ivy Bay," she said pleasantly.

"That would be me. How might I help you?" The cute young woman reminded her of Sunny and Misty.

The woman smiled sweetly at her and handed her an envelope. "You've been served. Have a good day."

"What does that mean?" Ivy asked, looking down at the brown envelope in her hands. Yet, her question hung in silence. When she looked up, the young woman had bolted and was trotting down the pathway to an idling car.

Ivy would never catch her. Besides, she had a fairly good idea of what had just happened.

With a sigh, she opened the envelope and began to read the first page. Ivy could hardly believe what she was reading. Legal terms seemed to jump from the page, whirling like a dark tornado into her consciousness and blotting out the sunshine of what had been a pleasant day. *Egregious, disregard, liable…*

As she lowered the papers in shock, Shelly strolled in, her arms full of freshly cut roses for the arrangement in the foyer.

"Why the frown, Ives?"

"Looks like I'm being sued."

"By a guest?"

"No," she replied, drawing out the word. At once, a cold sweat formed on her chest, and she labored to breathe normally. Pressing a hand to her hammering heart, she said, "It seems Amelia Erickson had an heir after all. Someone named E. E. Erickson."

Shelly's mouth formed an *O*. After a long moment, she spoke. "That can't be right. Jeremy paid cash for this house. So all this initials-only person, E. E.—probably some greedy guy—has to do is ask Amelia's estate or trustee for the funds, right?"

"I don't think it's that easy. Bennett told me the proceeds of the sale were donated to charities Amelia had named."

Shelly spread her hands. "So, he should ask those charities. Not you."

"Wait a minute." Ivy scanned the documents, her heart racing as the scenario at hand took shape. "It's not about the house." As she grew light-headed, she leaned against the check-in desk for support. "This lawsuit is charging that I had no right to give away the items we found." Dizziness washed over her, and even her limbs tingled.

"I don't understand," Shelly said. "The paintings and jewels—those were originally stolen during the war—but not by the Ericksons. All Amelia did was shelter them for the rightful owners."

"As far as we know." Ivy squeezed her eyes shut. "There has to be a way out. This lawsuit is asking for millions." She couldn't even fathom such a number, and she'd certainly never have that much.

"So, what are they trying to get at?"

"They want the artwork and jewelry we found. This could cost me the house."

"Oh, Ivy," Shelly said, her expression crumpling with pity. "That's not right."

"No, it isn't." Still, as waves of anguish and anger crashed over her, Ivy brushed away sudden hot tears that sprang to her eyes. Just when she thought she couldn't be hurt again, this happened. What had Imani once said? *Anyone can file a lawsuit, but not everyone wins it.* Still, the funds to defend such a suit were not in her budget.

"I need to think," Ivy said, turning to head for the kitchen. "I am not going to stand for this. We did the right thing in returning the property."

By the rear door, she switched her shoes for her flip-flops, grabbed her sun hat, and strode outside toward the beach. She was so upset and confused she was shaking.

The roar of the waves and the squawk of seabirds were welcome, but none of that could drown out the torrent of thoughts that rushed through her mind. Turning away from the crowded visitor beach, she headed in the other direction.

Striding angrily through the surf's edge, she considered her options. First, she had to find an attorney. Imani had helped her before, but would she be willing to this time?

Gritting her teeth, Ivy kicked a patch of sand. How could someone do this to her? And just when she was finally weaving together the frayed ends of her stretched-thin budget. Thankfully, the house was paid for, but it had been neglected so long that repairs were costing a fortune, not to mention the taxes that were accruing.

While the former trustee had kept up with essential repairs on the ground floor, none of the guest rooms had been touched in years. She and Shelly had become quite adept at late-night plumbing fixes, but at some point, the system needed an overhaul.

Her husband had bought a lemon of a house, and she was stuck with it—and all its hidden problems. Problems—and questions—were surfacing like a whack-a-mole game at a carnival.

Was she in over her head? And was this the proverbial final straw? What on earth was she doing to attract this kind of negative energy into her life? She had to be honest with herself about this—as well as her new marriage.

Suddenly, an unexpected rush of water around her calves threw her off balance, and she cried out as she began to fall.

"Got you," Bennett said, gripping her arm and pulling her up to safety.

Where did he come from? Ivy whirled on him, ready to pour out her frustrations, but the grim look on his face told her that he already knew.

Ivy clung to him. "Shelly told you."

"I got served, too."

"No," she wailed. "You're in this mess because of me."

"I was in it long before you or Jeremy," Bennett said, flexing his jaw. "If you remember, my partner Claire took the original listing. She's above reproach, and she checked out the legalities. She and the trustee go way back. So I'm not concerned for us—only for you."

Ivy blinked away angry tears. "My case isn't about the house—it's about what we found in it. All the artwork and jewelry." She threw up her hands. "We did the right thing, and now I'm being penalized for it. I know the world isn't fair, but this is downright despicable. I don't believe that lawsuit for one minute. I'm willing to bet that so-called heir—E. E. or whatever his name is—doesn't have a drop of real Erickson blood in his veins. You told me the trustee waited years to sell the property because of it. Isn't that right?"

"That was my understanding. And Claire's. I don't think the trustee would lie to us."

"Then why, why, *why?*" Ivy smacked her forehead in frustration.

Bennett narrowed his eyes. "The publicity from the discoveries probably drew out the crazies—and a lawyer who smelled a payday."

"But what if they're right? And I'm at fault for giving away the loot?"

"I don't know," Bennett replied slowly. "But we have to have faith in the system."

Expelling a puff of air between her lips, Ivy folded her arms and turned toward the sea, disgusted at the thought of wasting time and energy to defend herself—even if she was in the right. There was only so much she could do. She didn't have any actual proof about ownership claims one way or another. Yet, surely the FBI would back her up. The German crown jewels had been on the list of stolen goods.

Still, a chill crept over as she thought about the master-piece paintings that Hitler had termed *degenerate art*. Perhaps the provenances on those pieces were not clear—and there had been so many of them.

She hated to admit it, but she could have some liability. Above all, Ivy wanted to do right by people, but when would she have her chance? She glanced back at the inn, almost wishing she'd never seen it. When could she stop worrying about this mess of a place and just live her life?

Biting her lip, Ivy turned back to Bennett. "I'm afraid that this time, I'm going to need a miracle."

"Sometimes you have to make your own miracle," Bennett said, wrapping his arms around her. "I'll support you any way I can."

Later that afternoon, after Bennett had left to meet his tenants to make a few repairs at his house on the ridgetop, Ivy returned to the inn. She was deeply troubled over the lawsuit, but she still had work to do.

While Shelly had been away on her honeymoon, Poppy had set up a new, automated guest registry. The two of them were leaning over a screen at the reception desk in the foyer. When Ivy walked in, they looked up with worried expressions.

"Did Bennett find you?" Poppy asked.

Ivy nodded. "I hope you're feeling up to helping more," she said to Shelly. "I'm going to have to tend to this legal mess, which will probably take a lot of time. I've already put in a call to Imani."

"I am, and I will," Shelly said with a solemn expression. She motioned to a bottle of ginger ale. "This phase won't last forever, but I'm here for you."

"Me, too," Poppy added.

Just then, the front door swung open, and Imani bustled in carrying a bundle of sunflowers. She wore a vivid orange ruffled sundress and had swept her long sister-locks back with a matching scarf.

"I bought too many of these for Blossoms, so I thought you might like them here," Imani said to Ivy. "And I got your call."

"Such happy flowers," Shelly said. "We can sure use those today." She rose to take the flowers. "I'll find a vase and put those in water." She cast a look back at Ivy and Imani.

Fixated as she now was on the lawsuit, Ivy had lost her joy in one fell swoop. In its place was a jumble of feelings she thought she'd gotten past after she'd finally cast Jeremy's transgressions out to sea. He couldn't have known about these liabilities, but he was the one who'd sent her careening down this slope. And now she felt like she'd landed in a heap of mud and muck at the bottom.

After Shelly left with the flowers, Imani smoothed a hand over Ivy's shoulder. "Do you want to talk here or somewhere else?"

"I'll watch the front desk," Poppy offered.

Ivy smiled at her niece and turned to Imani. "Let's sit on the terrace. I need more fresh air." She slid out the thick envelope of legal documents from under the desk and tucked it under her arm, even though she felt like shredding those wretched papers. "Would you like tea or a glass of wine? And we have a new inventory of ginger ale and ginger tea. Peppermint, too."

"I'll take you up on that offer later," Imani said. "I'd like to get started while it's still quiet around here. I know how quickly that can change."

They made their way through the house to the terrace outside, chatting until they came to the fire pit. If guests had their windows open, Ivy knew the sound of the ocean would drown out any discussion. After settling into a pair of marine-blue Adirondack chairs, Ivy pitched forward on her knees and began to tell Imani about what had happened.

"It's so frustrating to be in this situation," Ivy said as she showed Imani the legal documents. "I feel like every time life starts to go my way, someone blasts a shot over the bow of my little lifeboat, and I have to start bailing like one of those old cartoon characters to keep my head above water."

"Now that's a visual," Imani said with a slight smile. She angled her head toward the house. "Although that's more like a yacht." She began to read the documents.

Ivy gazed up at the old house and sighed. "I know I'm blessed to have this home, but it's not like I didn't work twenty years for it. I spent all of my adult life having babies, raising the girls, cooking, shopping, and overseeing repairs of all sorts —generally making Jeremy's life easy so he could focus on his work. I thought we were partners—until he drained our retirement accounts to buy this with Paisley."

Imani looked up from the papers. "Judging from all you've done around here, I'll bet you worked just as hard—if not harder—than he did. You certainly made better choices."

"Yet, here I am," Ivy said, raising her hands before she let them drop. "I felt a kinship with this house the first time I saw it. We'd both been cast out of use. Slated for demolition or destined to be forgotten because we'd gotten too old. I love this grand, quirky old house—we're like relics from another era, keeping each other afloat. But it's a lot to handle."

"Oh, please," Imani said, shaking her head. "You're hardly a relic. Bennett thinks he married a hot woman—and you still are. As for the house, it's given you and your family a livelihood and shelter. To all of us who lost our homes in the fire, too."

"How is your house coming along?"

Imani allowed a small smile. "Axe's construction team is nearing completion now, so Jamir and I will be moving back in once we have the flooring in place."

"I'm happy for you, and I know you're looking forward to having a home again, but you'll be missed here."

"You'll still see a lot of me," Imani said, chuckling. "Between the book club and Shelly's yoga, it might seem like I never left."

"I hope so," she said, taking Imani's hand. This dear, accomplished woman had become a close friend over the past year. Ivy would miss seeing her and her son at breakfast every morning, but she was happy that Imani had a new home. She gave her friend's hand a little squeeze before letting go.

"This house hasn't been without its problems," Ivy said, continuing her story. "And this one might be the worst yet. The nerve of this man—"

"Excuse me," Imani said, holding up a hand. "How do you know that's a man?"

Ivy ran a hand through her hair. "I guess I don't. There was no first name on the documents—only initials. Shelly made an assumption, and I suppose I did, too."

"Don't assume anything," Imani said. "Now, go on." Steepling her fingers, she leaned back to listen.

Against the sound of the ocean, Ivy went on, explaining. When she finished, she asked, "So, what do you think of this mess?"

Imani shook her head. "It might seem like a disaster, but not everything is as it seems." She stood and rapped the sheaf of papers with her knuckles. "I can help you bail out your yacht—you haven't sunk yet. Just be careful what you say to anyone about this. This might be legitimate, or it could be a shake-down. We'll soon find out."

As Imani left to go to her room, Ivy spied Geena sitting in a chair fiddling with some sort of electronics. Why had she returned? Ivy strolled past the pool and across the terrace toward her.

Stopping near Geena, she asked, "Back so soon?"

Geena looked up, seemingly taken aback. "I forgot something," she said, averting her gaze. "Mind if I sit here for a little while?"

Ivy forced a smile. "Let us know if there's anything you need." As she walked into the house, Ivy suppressed a shudder. Although Geena had been a guest, something about her still didn't quite add up.

*A*s Ivy furrowed her brow at the laptop computer, Poppy looked up from her work at another desk in the library. "Isn't Tyler coming by soon to look at the space for the casino party?"

"Is it that time already?" The number of emails, documents, bank statements, and photos Ivy had to organize for Imani was overwhelming. She had to prove she hadn't profited from the sale of any of the items they'd found.

Stretching her arms overhead, Ivy said, "Could you or Shelly show him around?"

"I can, but Shelly is helping Mitch with a birthday party at Java Beach. Someone from out of town rented the whole place. I thought she'd told you."

Ivy removed her leopard-spotted reading glasses and drew her hands over her face. "She did. I just forgot that it was today."

"I think Tyler would prefer to talk to you." Poppy's expression softened. "A break might be good for you, Aunt Ivy."

Poppy wasn't the only one to suggest that. Bennett had mentioned several activities to get her away from her computer and clear her mind. Yet, she would feel better if she finished this work. She pressed a key on her keyboard.

Nothing. Ivy sighed. "Could you check the internet connection, Poppy? It seems to have gone down."

"Maybe that's a sign."

Ivy looked up at her niece. "That's usually my line."

"Where do you think I learned it?"

Ivy tapped the keyboard again, but there was no response other than a tiny spinning wheel. "Maybe I wore it out today. Guests are going to be upset."

"I'll check it, but most of them are out having fun."

That was true. Ivy pushed away from the keyboard and shook her hands to get some energy flowing. "Let's go," she said, shifting her attitude. "Tyler is going to love what we can do for their event."

Ivy left Poppy in the kitchen and started downstairs. Tyler would be here in ten minutes, so she didn't have much time to tidy the space. She didn't think anything of the door standing open, but as she descended, she saw Geena—of all people—at the bookcase, rummaging through old books. She held her phone in her hand, hovering it above a book.

"Excuse me, can I help you?" Slightly irritated, Ivy thought about an old rock 'n roll song, *Hotel California.* Geena had checked out, but would she ever leave? How fitting, she thought wryly.

Geena put a book back on the shelf. "Just looking."

But Ivy knew what she had seen. "And taking pictures?"

Geena shrugged. "I'm a book lover."

Ivy pressed her lips together. She could think of only one reason Geena might be doing that. "If you're looking for reading material, you're welcome to borrow any of these books. But if it's rare or valuable old books you want, you won't find any there."

Imani appeared on the stair with a book tucked under her arm and approached them.

A flush filled Geena's face. "I wouldn't want——"

"Oh, really?" Imani stepped beside Ivy and nudged her in warning. "You would, or you wouldn't be trying to fleece my client for everything she has."

Ivy's mouth dropped open; she could hardly believe what she was hearing. "Geena is behind the lawsuit?"

"You had no right to give all that loot away," Geena sputtered. "There has to be more stashed here, too. Just look at this place. My mom says the family is owed something."

"I suggest you pack up and get out," Imani said.

"She checked out a long time ago," Ivy said icily, restraining herself.

"Then you can clear out in thirty seconds," Imani said smoothly. "We can talk later with your counsel."

Geena picked up her backpack and stormed past Ivy, but Imani stepped in front of her. "Contrary to my client's generous offer a few moments ago, if you have any of her books in that heavy backpack, you should leave them here. Otherwise, she'll have a reason for action against you."

With a huff, Geena tore off her backpack and unzipped it. After withdrawing three old books, she tossed them onto the floor. "Happy now? I was only saving you the trouble of having to deliver them to me later." She pulled on her backpack and took the stairs two at a time in her rush.

Ivy picked up the books and collapsed onto one of the old barstools that Mitch and Bennett had found in the storage area, along with a vintage bar of ornately carved mahogany. She had just ten minutes until Tyler arrived.

Imani eased onto the stool beside her.

Scrubbing her face with her hand, Ivy asked, "How did you know who she was?"

"I asked my old research assistant to see what she could find about E. E. Erickson," Imani replied. "She discovered that Eugenia Elizabeth Erickson and Geena are one and the same."

"Did she say where the Bellamy name came from?"

"Geena recently did a legal name change."

"So she came here to check out everything," Ivy said, tapping her nails on the bar in thought. "She's not what I would have expected of an heir of the Ericksons, even though they'd lost contact with the niece decades ago. I've heard it was sometimes difficult to trace people after the Second World War, but it still seems like her parents would have tried."

"You never know what might have transpired."

"I guess not." As unpleasant as Geena was, Ivy felt a little sorry for her. Who knows what her family had been through? Still, what Geena wanted wasn't something that Ivy could surrender. Or was it? Paige hadn't thought the books had much value, but Geena might have thought a few of them did.

Ivy opened the book on top. Henry James. *The Golden Bowl*. Under that was Leo Tolstoy's *War and Peace* and F. Scott Fitzgerald's *This Side of Paradise*. Ivy opened each one, but she couldn't see anything special about them other than the name recognition. Maybe that's what Geena had been after.

Poppy appeared at the top of the stairs. "Excuse me, Aunt Ivy. Tyler is here about the casino night."

"Come on down." Ivy checked her attitude. She needed to make a good pitch for Tyler. And that meant getting Geena out of her mind. Lifting her chin, she smiled and greeted Tyler.

"I'll be upstairs," Imani said, sliding off the stool with a wink. "Hi, Tyler. Take a look at this bar. Pretty classy for events, don't you think?"

AFTER TYLER AGREED to the cost Ivy had quoted and left, Ivy slid onto the couch, mentally exhausted but thrilled to have booked their first paying event.

On the coffee table in front of her sat Amelia's old literary society guest book, which reminded her that she wanted to buy one for their group, too. Or maybe she'd make one and paint the cover and hand-design the pages. If she weren't dealing with this silly lawsuit, she'd have the time to do that.

She ran a hand over the vintage cover, appreciating the artistry of another time. As she did, a distinct chill wafted over her.

Had she imagined that? Swiftly pulling her hand back, she rose and made for the stairs. She'd been working too hard. What she needed was fresh air to sort out her thoughts.

Stopping to switch her shoes at the back door, she headed for the beach, welcoming the constant roar of the waves and the fine spray on her face.

After nearly losing the inn last year, she still harbored fears about hanging on to it. But thankfully, her family was helping. She appreciated the work that Forrest and Flint and the cousins—especially Poppy—had done this summer, and now it was poised to pay off.

In addition, Misty was supporting herself, and even Sunny had just landed a part-time job at an animal rescue organization.

Her youngest daughter had always loved animals, but her father couldn't bear the thought of fur in his pristine home— that Ivy kept that way for him. At the time, she had thought remaining pet-less was just as well because she'd be the one to clean up after the creatures, but now she realized that Sunny craved the company of animals.

Ivy smiled to herself. Especially the unpedigreed strays that a year ago, with her spoiled friends, she would have shunned—but only because of their opinions. Sunny loved animals. Maybe they gave her the nonjudgmental love she needed.

Ivy understood that. Jeremy's love had been full of conditions.

Fortunately, Sunny was changing. Maybe Poppy and Jamir were having a positive influence on her. Without a car, she'd even been begging Jamir to go to a public library in a neighboring community. Many college students gathered there because it was larger than the quaint public library in Summer Beach.

While Ivy suspected that her daughter didn't spend as much time studying as she said, at least she was putting forth more effort than she had in the past.

A wave rushed toward Ivy, and instead of dodging it, she let it swirl around her ankles, enjoying the brisk chill on the warm sand. Although it threatened to dislodge her, she stood firm in the dizzying rush until it swept away.

For the past year in Summer Beach, she had stood firm, too. She'd had to rely on her creativity and skills. With any luck, this lawsuit would fold, although she wasn't sure how. She reminded herself that she'd come this far without disaster striking. So many of the things she worried about had not come to pass. She hadn't lost the house, and guests had actually come and paid her to sleep in an old house that was far from perfect. Sunny hadn't disappeared in Europe with her wild group of friends.

And she wasn't alone or lonely.

Could Bennett understand why she didn't want to give up her newfound freedom, emerging identity, and recent achievements for him just yet?

She hugged herself and faced out to sea.

As the sun warmed her shoulders, a thought dawned on Ivy. Her mother had often ignored traditional roles, working alongside her husband even when her children were young. They divided business accounts, so Carlotta often went on trips alone to see their retail partners, leaving her husband to tend to the children—or vice versa. Sterling had become as adept at laundry, grocery shopping, and meal planning as Carlotta had been.

They were partners in love and in life—doing it their way.

With such role models, why had Ivy taken up the more

traditional role with Jeremy? But she knew the answer. He'd wanted it that way. Yet, after reeling her in with murmurs of love, his voice became louder and stronger than hers. He earned the money, so he wanted everything his way.

Everything.

And Ivy instinctively knew that to keep her husband, she had to follow his plan. Some of their friends had divorced, though she hadn't wanted that.

She picked up a weathered branch and threw it out to sea. In the end, she had been forced to tackle the new and unknown. But, by doing so, hadn't her actions brought the life she loved today?

Squinting, she wondered if behind her hesitancy to commit to Bennett lurked a fear of the unknown. Or worse, of the known?

Watching the waves engulf the driftwood, she thought about her dilemma. What if there was another way to live their lives? Only one way to find out, she thought.

For that, she'd need an extra dose of courage. She would have to get over her fear of the unknown, the *what-ifs* that often plagued her. She'd faced that before in taking charge of her future and creating a new life, but this time, the decision involved her heart. Still, she was determined to live the life she wanted *and* have the partner—and freedom—she desired.

Once more, she stopped and faced into the brisk breeze off the ocean. She'd get those purple shoes she desired— without permission or guilt. They might even have glittery bits all over them.

Smiling, she turned and strode back toward the inn, her head held high.

*B*y the next week, chatter about the book club was circulating through town, and most everyone who could was eager to meet again. Ivy was glad that Paige had whetted people's appetite for books.

That afternoon, Ivy had dressed in a new pair of white jeans and snake print loafers. She'd added a thin, beige mock turtleneck with a zebra print denim jacket. Turning back the cuffs, she added several bangle bracelets. Satisfied with her look, she made her way to the kitchen.

As she was preparing for the meeting, Bennett strolled into the kitchen. He wore a white polo shirt and khakis—his frequent beach mayor attire—and his closely cropped hair was growing more streaked in the summer sun.

"Another gathering tonight?" he asked, giving her a quick kiss on the cheek.

"The book club has been the talk of the town," Ivy replied, warming to his touch. She was arranging appetizers on a platter—grapes, sweet peppers, an assortment of cheese and crackers, and homemade banana nut bread. "I'm already fielding questions about the availability of the downstairs for special events," she added with pride. "Tyler booked the area for a fundraiser."

Bennett gazed at her with admiration. "Sounds like your plan is working."

"We'll see." Still, she felt good about the prospects. "I missed you at this afternoon's gathering."

Bennett eyed the cheese platter. "I stayed a little later to talk with Maeve about Geena's case."

"Imani has an interesting idea; I can tell you about it later." She gestured toward the platter. "If you're hungry, help yourself."

"Thanks. I'll replenish your stock when I visit the cheese shop in the village." Bennett helped himself to a small wedge and a handful of crackers. "Have you finished that book you were reading for the book club?"

Ivy shook her head as she brought out a hummus dip she'd made. "Between new guests and Imani's questions, I didn't make much progress on *Pride and Prejudice*, other than to think less than charitably toward Mrs. Bennet with one *t*."

"Mrs. Bennett. I like the sound of that," he said between bites.

"Not unless you answer to Mr. Ivy." Ivy laughed. "I'm not taking any part of your name—you're welcome to keep it all. It's a lot of trouble to change your legal identity these days. Look at what Shelly is going through." Her sister had been complaining about all the paperwork after her marriage.

"Will you answer to Mrs. Dylan socially?"

Ivy paused with the hummus in mid-air. "I haven't thought about that, but I suppose I will. Even though we're not quite legal."

"It's legal where it counts." A smile spread across Bennett's face, and he pointed heavenward. "I'm mighty proud to be your husband. Unless you've changed your mind."

Ivy had applied for a new driver's license and passport, so if they wanted to legalize their marriage, they could. Still, she was hesitant. Was this normal? Or was it somewhat akin to buyer's remorse? Except this wasn't a car or a house; it was the rest of her life. Could she ever be one-hundred-percent sure?

Was there even such a thing?

"We need to talk about that," Ivy said. She glanced at the large round clock in the kitchen. "But people will start arriving soon. I'd better finish this and get downstairs. Poppy is already setting up."

"I'll be in the room going over some business for the city." Bennett trailed a finger along her arm. "Would you like to join me for a glass of wine later? We can talk then."

Despite her uncertainty, her pulse quickened at his touch. "I'd like that," Ivy said, ignoring her practical side. When she was around Bennett, her heart took over. Still, they *were* married, however gray that area was.

A little while later, the same crowd as last week gathered, only this time, they'd all brought their favorite books. Everyone was immersed in conversation. Imani and Maeve, Celia and Jen, Gilda and Nan, and a few new guests. Even Bettina, the nurse, had returned. She and her husband were nearing the end of their vacation, and she looked rested and cheerful.

Paige stood by, smiling with satisfaction. Her silver hair glinted in the light of the freshly cleaned chandeliers.

Ivy greeted her, and Paige turned her bright eyes toward her. "Books bring out the best in people, don't you think?"

"I do," Ivy said.

"Will your sister be joining us again tonight?"

"I don't think so. Shelly is feeling a little under the weather."

Paige slid a knowing glance at Ivy. "She needs her rest. Now more than ever."

"She does," Ivy said, wondering if Shelly had confided in Paige. "Did she...?"

"Tell me?" Paige finished. "Dear heavens, no. But she has such a lovely glow about her." She lowered her voice. "And she had to bolt for the ladies' room when she was in the shop buying her books. But unlike many people in this town, I can keep a secret." Paige cast a look at Darla and pressed a finger against her lips.

"We appreciate that," Ivy said, relieved. "It's very early, and Shelly and Mitch want to make sure that all is well."

"I understand."

And yet, just before the meeting began, Shelly appeared, tapping Ivy on the shoulder.

"You made it," Ivy said, happy to see her.

"I rallied," Shelly said, toting a bottle of ginger ale. "Mitch wanted to see Bennett, so I came along."

"I'm so glad you did." Ivy hugged her. As she did, she could feel that Shelly had lost weight. Ivy was worried about her gaunt appearance, but Shelly assured her she was feeling better.

Poppy nudged her. "Look who is coming down the stairs."

Ivy sighed. *Geena.* Of all the people Ivy didn't want to see, Geena was at the top of that list. "She fooled me. I didn't peg her as a con artist. A troubled young woman, perhaps, but not an outright liar."

"She thinks she's justified," Imani said.

Poppy drummed her fingers on her drinking glass. "I wonder what she wants?"

"Cash," Imani replied. "That's pretty clear. In her mind, she's already taking possession. And she wants to irritate you."

"I could kill her with kindness," Ivy said.

Shelly leaned in. "Or just ki—"

"Really?" Ivy cut her off. "You could be more creative."

"Hey, you have to admit my New York attitude comes in handy when you need a heavy." Shelly struck a pose, flexing a bicep. "Mitch told me he saw her at Java Beach. The word in town is that she moved into the Seal Cove Inn when you kicked her out."

"What?" Ivy was appalled. "I didn't kick her out. She left on her own."

Poppy leaned in. "That's the gossip at Java Beach, Aunt Ivy. Geena sure has a lot of nerve showing up here again. I can ask her to leave."

"Let's wait and see what she's up to," Imani said in a thoughtful tone. "Could be useful."

Just then, Geena looked in their direction.

"Shh," Ivy said. It was all she could do to bite back another comment. On this level, the acoustics carried sound well.

Poppy lowered her voice. "If only there were a way to take a DNA sample on Amelia and Gustav."

As Ivy swung her gaze toward Geena, a thought occurred to her. "Maybe there is," she said slowly, her mind whizzing around a new idea. "Wouldn't it be interesting if someone in her family had submitted DNA somewhere?"

"I think I know what you're talking about." Imani narrowed her eyes. "Recently, some old criminal cases have been solved through familial connections from online genealogy sites."

"Exactly," Ivy said. "What if we could find other family members and follow the DNA trail?"

"Perhaps," Imani said. "But don't get your hopes up. There might not be anything to find."

"But there could be," Ivy said, grasping at the idea. She didn't have many options. "A lot of people are doing DNA research for genealogy."

"Or, what you find could confirm what you wish wasn't true," Imani said.

As Ivy realized the validity of that statement, her hope fell. "But we did the right thing in returning the treasures we found here."

"Of course, I agree with you, but there are always at least two sides to an argument," Imani said. "Still, it could be worth a try."

Poppy's eyes widened with excitement. "I'll research that for you, Aunt Ivy. And I'll find out if she has any family around. I'll check online."

Geena took an old book from the shelf. Then, with a pointed look at Ivy, she placed it back on the shelf with an exaggerated movement. "*Voila.*"

"Let's start the meeting," Ivy said, trying to ignore her.

Everyone found a chair and, scooting close together, sat down.

"We can start by sharing our favorite books," Paige said. "Ivy, why don't you begin and tell us what you thought of the book you read."

Ivy held up the copy of *Pride and Prejudice* that Paige had given her. "I'm still in the early chapters, and I'm not too fond of Mrs. Bennet, who is determined to marry off her daughters. Still, given the era—more than two-hundred years ago—and the fact that Mrs. Bennet has two-and-a-half times the number of daughters I have, I'll give her a pass," she added, grudgingly extending a measure of forgiveness toward the character. "She probably didn't have time for much introspection." A laugh rose around the room. "As for Lizzie, I believe she is searching for herself, even though she might not realize it yet."

Paige nodded. "The search for oneself is a frequent theme in Austen's works. Why do you think that might be?"

Maeve raised her hand. "In the nineteenth century, women's roles were narrowly defined. And yet, they searched for meaning and often found ways to follow their passions, just as Jane Austen did with her writing."

"That's an interesting observation," Paige said, inclining her head.

"As for Lizzie, I think her subconscious attraction to Mr.

Darcy annoys the part of her that wants to remain independent and self-actualizing. Although she also yearns for love and acceptance."

A small smile tugged a corner of Paige's mouth. "And do you think she will find a resolution?"

Ivy rubbed her temple in thought. "It's a struggle, but I like to think she will." As Ivy caught Paige's eye, it seemed as if the older woman might have insights Ivy hadn't shared with her.

"In this novel," Paige began. "Jane Austen wrote, 'Till this moment I never knew myself.' For those of you who had read the novel, what do you think she meant by that?"

A lively discussion ensued, and as Ivy listened, she began to understand why Paige might have suggested this book for her.

A book whisperer, indeed. Ivy exchanged a nod of gratitude with Paige. She would keep reading this novel.

Sitting next to her, Jen swept her long brown hair over her shoulder and rested her chin in her hand. "This book sounds more interesting than I thought it would. And I could really go for a Mr. Darcy."

As each new member of the book club talked about *Pride and Prejudice* or a favorite book, the conversation rose and carried along for the next two hours, which seemed to pass quickly.

Geena kept to the rear of the room and declined to speak. Ivy couldn't figure her out. Oddly, she looked interested in what other women had to say—as if she was starved for connection. *What a dichotomy*, Ivy thought. Geena didn't seem to have the personality to draw people to her.

After deciding on the books to read for the first quarter of the club meetings—with *Pride and Prejudice* as their first selection—the women continued chatting. Poppy poured more wine and tea for those lingering.

"Looks like they're enjoying the company," Ivy said to Shelly.

"I can understand why. This place has good vibes. Even with Geena here."

Ivy sighed. "She has to leave sometime."

Just then, Mitch joined them. Sliding his arm around Shelly, he said, "How are you feeling, babe?"

Shelly beamed at him. "Great, but a little tired."

He kissed her forehead. "I thought you might want to leave early. How about a bubble bath in that big old clawfoot tub?"

"I'd love that," Shelly said.

Standing next to them, Paige turned and smiled. "It's getting late, but you know book lovers. We like nothing better than to talk about our favorite books."

"And drink wine," Poppy said, emptying another bottle. "Aunt Ivy, I can stay here if you want to turn in as well."

Bennett had invited her for a glass of wine, and she looked forward to relaxing with him. She had been waiting until after the meeting to enjoy a glass. "I'd appreciate that."

Ivy walked out with Shelly and Mitch. She stood by the kitchen window, watching them as they strolled arm in arm to Mitch's car, and he helped her inside. His gentle way touched Ivy's heart. Blinking back her emotion, she thought of all that Shelly had gone through in the effort to live her dream. And soon, if all went well with her pregnancy, they would be welcoming a new little life into the family.

Ivy leaned against the doorjamb and waved as they pulled out of the car court. If there was one constant in life, she decided, it was change.

Turning away from the lights of the car, Ivy considered the dishes in the sink. Usually, she would have tended to them before going to bed, but Poppy had offered, and Sunny would be back from studying with Jamir to help her soon. Ivy would gladly leave the dishes to the girls tonight.

Across the car court, a window glowed in the old chauffeur's apartment. On the balcony, a silhouette stood against the light.

Bennett was waiting for her.

She smoothed her hair and tucked it behind her ears before making her way outside. The night was balmy, so she took off her denim jacket and draped it over her shoulders.

As she crossed the car court, Bennett's deep, gravelly voice floated down to her. "I was hoping you'd come."

"The book club is still going on, but I ducked out."

Bennett gazed across waves that looked surreal in the moonlit sky. "How about a walk on the beach with a to-go glass?"

"I'd like that," she said, smiling up at him.

Bennett leaned over the railing. "I'll be right down."

Moments later, Bennett descended the stairway carrying two glasses of wine. He gave her one and slid his hand into hers. "Not a bad way to end a day, is it?"

Thinking of Shelly and Mitch and the love they shared, Ivy touched her glass to his. Despite the doubts and second-guesses swirling in her mind, she felt at home when she was with Bennett.

Was that her heart speaking? If only she could tune out the noise in her brain. Raising her gaze to his, she resolved to do just that tonight. "Here's to ending each of our days together."

"Nothing better." He tapped her glass again. "To a perfect evening and to our future."

After taking a sip, they strolled toward the ocean. As they walked, the bright moon cast shadows of swaying palm trees across the sand. A distant rumble filled the night, and the waves rolled in with such thundering power that Ivy leaned into Bennett to steady herself. She breathed in the salty aroma, feeling cleansed and relaxed.

But beneath her feet, the sand shifted, pulling away and

then rising again. Her wine sloshed, and she clutched his arm. Something was happening. "That's so weird—" Slipping again, she paused, rocking on her feet.

"Look," Bennett cried. He jerked back toward the inn, where they could see the water sloshing in the pool, illuminated by underwater lights. In every window from the basement to the second floor, lights flickered once, twice, three times, and then, the house went black.

"An earthquake!" Ivy clung to him, trying to keep her balance, but together they stumbled to their knees, their wine glasses tumbling from their grasp and spilling onto the sand. Ivy scrambled to stand, but grains of sand seemed to liquefy beneath her feet. Seconds seemed like an eternity, and a thousand thoughts roared through her mind. Where were Sunny and Misty? Shelly and Mitch?

They had to reach the inn.

Above the roar of the ocean, Ivy could hear screams from the house, and her heart sank. As her pulse shot up, prayers formed on her lips. What had her brother just said?

Flailing about, she slipped as the sand beneath her hollowed out.

"I've got you," Bennett called out, lifting her in his arms. He struggled to stand as the earth shuddered. "Hang on!"

Ivy flung her arms around his neck. Yet the beach still rippled, tossing them to their knees again. She clawed at the sand, trying to get a grip. Looking behind her, she cried, "Look out!"

Just then, a wave crashed onto the shore, enveloping Ivy with an icy blast of water that robbed her breath.

*B*eside her, Bennett sputtered and coughed as he took on saltwater. As the surf receded, Ivy clutched him around the chest. Using her weight as leverage and relying on her lifeguard training, she shifted him higher onto the shore and turned him over.

Bennett raised his hand, motioning to her. With a great cough that seemed as if it turned him inside out, he shoved himself to his knees.

The liquefied sand beneath them once again became *terra firma*.

"Don't try to talk," Ivy said, shivering in her wet shirt and jeans. Her slip-on loafers were gone, as was the jacket she'd draped over her shoulders.

With a great, hacking cough, Bennett pulled himself up. "I'm okay—" He stopped as another great cough seized his chest. "Let's get in there…make sure guests are okay." He glanced behind them in the dark. "Could be a big wave coming."

A terrible thought seized Ivy. "A tsunami?" She knew it was possible; giant waves could sweep thousands of miles across the Pacific Ocean, but local quakes could also trigger them. If the plates had shifted under the ocean, that action could generate high waves.

Bennett nodded grimly. "In 1960, the Valdivia earthquake in Chile sent a tsunami to Hawaii—my parents survived that." With Ivy's help, he crawled to his feet. "We have to get people to higher ground. The city has trained for this."

"I need to call the girls, too." As they raced toward the house, Ivy patted her pocket, but her phone was gone, ripped away in the waves—just like her shoes and their wine glasses. "Do you have your phone?"

"In my room," he said. "We need to get people out first. Summer Beach has an evacuation plan, which Chief Clark and others are probably putting in place."

They hit the terrace, which was wet. The water in the pool was still sloshing back and forth over the edges as if a great unseen hand were shaking it.

Bennett jerked open the kitchen door. Darkness enveloped them, with only shafts of moonlight through the windows lighting their way.

"Flashlights are under the sink," Ivy said, pausing to slip her bare, sandy feet into Shelly's garden clogs by the rear door.

"I'll get them." In the dark, Bennett rummaged in a cabinet. "Here we are. Torches, as Arthur and Nan say." Flicking one on, he swung a beam around the kitchen.

Ivy crossed the room, dripping water as she went, glass crunching beneath her feet in the sturdy clogs. A commotion rang throughout the house. Taking a flashlight, she opened the door to the lower level. Pricks of light pierced the darkness. She shone the light down the stairwell.

"How is everyone down there?" Ivy called out. "Anyone hurt?"

Pixie's frantic yaps greeted her, and Poppy's nervous voice floated up to her. "Mostly okay, I think. Just shaken."

Directing the light onto the stairway, Ivy gingerly made

her way down, testing each step for stability. Bennett was right behind her. Poppy met them at the base of the staircase, her face a mask of shock.

Ivy glanced around the dimly lit space. Books had fallen, a plant had toppled over, and assorted items were strewn across the floor. She saw Paige on the couch with Geena beside her. One of their guests, Bettina, knelt beside Darla with her fingers on the older woman's pulse. Ivy recalled that she was the nurse on vacation.

"Paige fell, but we have her sitting down now," Poppy said in a shaky voice. "Darla had some chest pains, and Bettina is looking after her." Poppy paused, taking in Ivy's wet, bedraggled appearance. "What happened to you?"

"We got caught in a wave," Ivy said, her hair dripping on the stairs. Her white jeans were filthy with sand and dirt, but that no longer mattered. She lowered her voice. "Not to alarm you, but we need to get everyone upstairs in case a larger set of waves rolls in. And I have to check on guests upstairs."

"Do you mean a tsunami?" Poppy's eyes widened.

"Bennett said it's just a precaution. We don't want anyone to panic." Ivy looked out across the worried faces of the women who had become like an extended family to her. In the dim light, she couldn't tell if there had been any damage, aside from books tossed from the shelves. On one side of the stairwell, a few bricks had fallen from a wall.

Ivy shone her light and raised her voice. "We need everyone to come upstairs now. We have more flashlights up there for you."

"We shouldn't be in the basement if there's an ocean surge," Paige added. "A lot of us are old-timers around here." She patted Geena's hand reassuringly. "The ridgetop is where we need to go. Right, Mr. Mayor?"

Bennett nodded. "Everyone should meet in the car court behind the house, and we'll begin evacuating from there."

"Historically, there have been a few small tsunamis in this

area," Nan said, rising. "But you never know when the big one might hit. It's better to be safe." She held a hand out to Paige.

The bookseller rested on Nan's arm, and Geena assisted her on the other side.

The big one. Ivy shivered at the thought. People in California often talked about that in terms of earthquakes. This temblor had been significant, although it wasn't the *big one.* Or at least, she didn't think so. It all depended on where the epicenter was. For all they knew, Los Angeles or San Diego might have been hit harder. Still, a tsunami could be a huge secondary threat.

Ivy would have to make sure every guest got out. *But what about Shelly? And Misty and Sunny?* Ivy bit her lip. And Forrest and Flint and their families. *Surely they're safe,* she told herself, refusing to think the worst. Forrest and Flint had built their homes as strong as possible to withstand significant earthquakes, although even that caution would be fruitless against a rare major quake.

"My house on the ridge is almost finished," Imani said, kneeling beside Darla. "You and anyone else are welcome there."

"Be careful about driving up there," Bennett said. "There could be power lines down." He hurried down the stairs. "Paige, I'm going to carry you upstairs and make you comfortable. Sorry that I'm a little soggy."

"Reminds me of my younger days," Paige said, attempting a smile.

Ivy touched Poppy's shoulder. "Can you see if you can reach Sunny and Misty? My phone is gone—I lost it in the waves."

Poppy shook her head. "I don't have any service. None of us down here do."

"Might have lost the cell phone tower," Bennett said in a grim tone. Turning to Ivy, he added, "We don't have much time. Fifteen, maybe twenty minutes. We'll have to move swiftly to get people out. Clark and his team will be making sure the roads are safe to pass, and we'll need every car. You'll need your keys." He paused. "While you're getting everyone, I'll turn off the gas."

Ivy sucked in a breath. There was a lot to do, and she could only trust that her loved ones were okay. She turned to the guests of the inn. "For those of you who are visiting, Bennett is the mayor of Summer Beach. He's a volunteer fire-fighter with disaster training. Let's all listen to him and start moving upstairs."

Guests and local residents began trudging upstairs. Gilda was soothing the nervous Pixie, who was huddling in her pink doggie backpack. Imani and Maeve began taking charge of their friends.

"This way, ladies," Imani said, training the light from her phone on the steps. "Easy does it. No more accidents on our way up."

"There's glass in the kitchen," Ivy called out. "We'll sweep it up, but be careful where you step."

At last, Bennett picked up Paige, who winced but didn't complain. She looked small in his arms, and he carried her swiftly upstairs. Ivy pressed a shivering hand against her chest, touched by the sight of her husband.

After all, that's what he was.

Trailing Paige and Bennett, Geena seemed to have been stunned into silence. She looked worriedly after Paige.

Ivy didn't have time to wonder about Geena. She hurried upstairs, where she brushed aside toppled floral arrangements and decorations. Something overhead creaked, and she looked up. The chandeliers were still swaying on their long chains in eerie, slow-motion swirls. Quickly, Ivy stepped aside.

"Look out above for the chandeliers," she called back to Poppy. Forrest had checked them last year, but it was still spooky. Ivy tested the staircase before going up to the guest room floor. It seemed solid and sturdy enough. Upstairs, she went from door to door, asking people to bring jackets and meet downstairs. She met with some resistance from one young couple.

"It's over," the young man said, holding a flashlight that Ivy had left on each bedside table. "We'll be back at the beach in the morning." His wife, barely wrapped in a slinky negligee, was reclining on the bed.

Ivy smelled alcohol on his breath. "I know you've been having a great time, but we need to evacuate. There is a tsunami warning."

The young man rolled his eyes. "Who says?"

She needed to impart a sense of urgency. "The state emergency commission and our mayor. He's downstairs evacuating guests." Just then, a loud siren split the night. "And that's the tsunami warning," she added, fairly certain that's what it was.

Ivy remembered hearing a siren years ago when she was a little girl at her parent's home. Fortunately, her family home was on a promontory, so they had been high above the beach below.

"And you might want to bring warm clothes," Ivy said. "It can get cool at night with the ocean breezes on the ridgetop."

After they agreed somewhat grudgingly, Ivy hurried to the next door. She didn't have much time, so Poppy had agreed to notify guests in the sunset suites.

Ivy tore into her room at the end of the hall and peeled off her wet clothes in record time, hopping on one foot as she struggled with damp jeans. She pulled a hoodie over another pair of jeans and stepped back into Shelly's clogs.

Car lights pierced the night, and she peered from the window. Bennett was filling his SUV with guests, and Imani was doing the same. Other guests were piling into the cars they'd brought. Ivy grabbed the keys to her old Chevrolet convertible and raced downstairs.

Outside, she gazed out over the ocean, holding her breath.

No discernible change was evident, but that didn't mean the motion hadn't been set into action.

"Glad you changed," Bennett said, stepping beside her. "I was worried about you in those wet clothes. I grabbed some of mine for you." He had also changed haphazardly.

Ivy tilted her head toward the sea. "What do you think the chances are?"

"I don't know," Bennett said, frowning. "In '64, we lost the Summer Beach marina to big waves from the Alaska earthquake. I don't like to roll the dice against Mother Nature."

As the last of the guests climbed into Bennett's SUV, Poppy said, "Everyone is accounted for, Aunt Ivy. Except for Jamir and Sunny."

"I'm not going without them," Ivy said, still trembling from the ocean chill. "They were at the public library—the larger one down the coast—but it shouldn't take long for them to get back." The neighboring community wasn't that far— maybe fifteen minutes away. "I can't risk Sunny returning and not knowing what to do."

"These other people need to get out of here now," Bennett said, anxiously flexing his jaw.

"Jamir knows what to do," Imani called out from her car. "He's been through the city's disaster planning course. Sunny is safe with him."

"What if they're not?" While Sunny had told her she was going to study with Jamir, Ivy knew that Sunny had skipped out with friends in the past. "I'm staying."

"I can't let you do that," Bennett said, his words firm and measured.

"You can't *let* me?" Ivy intoned. Her pulse pounded in her ears, making it hard to think straight. "You need to reconsider your words. That's my daughter. I'd never forgive myself if anything happened to her."

Bennett swept a hand across his chin. "I'll help you tape signs to the front and back doors telling her where to go."

"Thanks for understanding," she said, touching his shoulder. "But just so we're clear, don't tell me what to do. Explain it, and let me decide."

As the siren continued to shriek, Bennett handed the keys to Poppy. "I'll stay with your aunt. If you're okay to drive the SUV, you can take it up to the ridgetop."

"I had only one glass of wine," Poppy said, looking alert. "And that quake released a lot of adrenaline in me."

"Good." Bennett continued, speaking efficiently and motioning in the direction of the ridgetop. "Chief Clarkson will have a person at the base directing traffic, and he'll be at the top telling people where to go. Look for him. Be careful to avoid any downed power lines on the way. We'll take Ivy's car, and we won't be far behind you."

Poppy nodded solemnly, and Bennett turned back to Ivy. "We don't have much time."

"Be sure our other guests follow you." Ivy hugged Poppy. "I promise we'll see you soon."

She watched her niece climb into Bennett's SUV and ease from the car court behind Imani. They led the way for guests who didn't know where to go.

Ivy clutched her hoodie around her. *Had Los Angeles suffered the big one?* She recalled a prayer and sent it up for her daughters. *Sunny and Misty, be safe.*

"We have to hurry," Bennett said, taking her hand.

They rushed into the kitchen, and Ivy pulled a tablet of paper from a drawer. "We need two—one for the back door and one on the front. Not just for Sunny, but for anyone who might come by." A strange feeling of foreboding passed over her. "I also want to make sure Shelly is okay."

"Mitch knows where to go," Bennett said, touching her shoulder. "Shelly is in good hands."

"What if he doesn't?"

"Mitch knows not to underestimate the sea. He'll get Shelly to higher ground."

"I have to go by their place."

"Ivy, we might not have time."

"It's not far. I could practically run there."

Bennett pushed his hands through his hair and nodded. "Okay, where's the tape?"

"In that drawer." Using a flashlight, she scrawled a note, and Bennett made another one.

"I'll put this one on the back door and meet you in front," he said.

Ivy raced to the front door and taped the note to the door. With her hair whipping around her face in the ocean wind, she ran toward the old Chevy. Bennett opened the door and as soon as she was in, he took off.

They'd left so quickly that neither of them had thought to put up the convertible top. Ivy shivered and rubbed her arms, troubled about her extended family. How long would it take to reach them all?

Bennett turned on the heater. "Let's knock off this chill."

"Thanks." Ivy leaned back against the red leather seat and drew in several deep breaths to calm her racing pulse.

Another siren sounded ahead. Seconds later, an emergency vehicle passed them, going the other way. Ivy sent up a little prayer for whomever the emergency personnel were on their way to help. Her grandmother had always done that.

As Bennett drove, Ivy fidgeted with a hangnail. If only she could reach her children. She was worried about Jamir, too. And all their friends in Summer Beach.

"Are you okay?" Bennett slid a look of concern toward her.

Ivy nodding, trying not to fidget. "Even though I grew up here, earthquakes are unnerving. And I never recall fleeing toward higher ground."

"Summer Beach is taking more precautions these days. Everyone saw what happened in Thailand. A family from Summer Beach was vacationing there when the sea rushed in.

Fortunately, they survived, so they stayed to work with the rescue effort. When they returned, they helped us set up the city's disaster drills for potential tsunamis."

"Always better to be safe," Ivy murmured, glancing back at the ocean, not that she could see much. The lights of cars behind them were blinding, and the sea was dark except for the white, moonlit break of waves rushing onto the shore.

As they drove, she saw a line of cars snaking up the ridge-line road in the distance. Emergency lights flashed through the night. Ivy gripped the leather edge of her seat. Seeing the town plunged into darkness was unsettling.

"We should check on Kendra and Dave and Logan, too," Ivy said, thinking of Bennett's family. Kendra hadn't come to the book club meeting because Logan had a swim meet. She wondered if they were even home. "Do we have time to go by there?"

"We'll take a shortcut," Bennett said. "It's good of you to think of them. We're all family now."

He turned at the village and wove through an alley. Slowing in front of his sister's darkened house, he peered in. "The house looks fine, and their car is gone. Dave is fairly prepared for disasters, so I'm sure they're okay. I'll call them when I can." He continued toward the beach where Mitch and Shelly lived.

Ivy peered over the car door. "There's seawater spilling onto the street."

"The water level is rising," Bennett said, his face grim. "We don't have long." He reached for her.

Clutching his hand, Ivy thought about her daughters. She chewed the inside of her mouth as she watched water flooding into the street. Had they taken too long in leaving the house?

Bennett pressed his mouth into a narrow line, and Ivy feared the worst. She could read the worry on his face as he gripped the steering wheel and rolled cautiously through the water. The old Chevy convertible wasn't as high or as safe as Bennett's large SUV.

Finally, he wheeled into Mitch's gravel driveway, where Shelly's old Jeep was still parked. Mitch's car was still in front, too. Light from a lantern filled the front window.

"Let's go." Taking her flashlight, Ivy swung from the car and pounded toward the cottage. Bennett followed her. Bursting through the front door, she called out for Shelly and Mitch. Another dim light shone from the bathroom. She rounded the corner.

Shelly sat on the edge of the tub, looking pale and sick.

"Where's Mitch?"

"Getting supplies from the shed. He wants to drive up to the ridgetop." She shook her head. "But I don't feel like going anywhere."

"You've got to." Ivy jerked a thumb toward the ocean. "The ocean is pouring into the street. You have to leave now."

"Listen to your sister," Mitch said, striding up behind Ivy. "I don't care if you throw up in the car. We're going now."

Shelly's face grew even paler in the lantern light. "You can't be serious. I'm not getting sick in my car. It might be old, but I'd never get that smell out."

"Then I'll open the door for you," Mitch said. "Babe, we have to go. I won't let anything happen to you or our baby. But we're running out of time."

"I'm not going. I grew up in California, and we never had to evacuate." Shelly clenched her jaw and glared at Mitch. "This is all your fault, by the way."

"Come on, Shells," Ivy said. "The reason we never evacuated was because we lived on a high promontory."

"No," she spat out. "If you want to leave, I'm not stopping you."

Mitch threw up his hands in exasperation.

Time was running short, and Ivy had to get Shelly out. Her sister could be awfully ornery when she was feeling bad.

Ivy put the lid on the toilet down and sat across from Shelly. "I know you feel rotten. I know the sickness comes and goes. But right now, you have to think of your baby. You want it to have the best chance at life, don't you?"

Shelly's stubborn countenance crinkled, and her eyes glistened with quick tears. "Of course, I do. But I hardly have the strength. I've been sick since we got home."

"I understand, and I know what you're going through."

"*He* doesn't," Shelly said, flinging a hand toward Mitch.

"Babe, that's not true," Mitch began, but Bennett shot him a look, nodding toward Ivy.

Arguing wouldn't help—Shelly seldom backed down from a fight. Bennett nodded silent encouragement, and Ivy tried again. "Your child is going to have a wonderful life here, but you'll have to stick up for it like Mom did for us."

Shelly blinked. "She always did, didn't she? I wish she were here now."

Ivy took her hand. "You'll soon tell her about tonight. Right here, right now—this is the first time you're going to stick up for your child. You might feel like you can't, but I know you. You're going to do it anyway."

Tears spilled over her sister's eyelids. Nodding, she cast an apologetic look toward Mitch. "My legs are really rubbery."

"I got you, babe," Mitch said, rushing to her side. As tough as Shelly could be, his love for her was evident. He slid his arm around Shelly's waist and helped her up, mouthing the words *thank you* to Ivy as he did.

Ivy let out a sigh of relief. "We evacuated all the guests, and we're driving the Chevy." She quickly gathered Shelly's purse. "You can come with us or follow." She picked up her sister's phone from the edge of the sink.

"That's not working," Shelly said. "I tried to call you."

Bennett blew out the lanterns as they hurried out.

Supporting Shelly, Mitch said, "I'll help you into the Jeep."

Shelly nodded. "We should pick up anyone who needs a ride."

Outside, Ivy and Bennett sloshed through water and slid back into the car. Ivy turned to Bennett. "I'm awfully glad we came. Thank you for humoring me. I know how Shelly is when she's sick and upset. Her stubbornness comes out, and I don't know if Mitch could have budged her."

"You did good in there," Bennett said, shifting the car into gear.

They waited until Mitch pulled out behind them, then they drove slowly toward the ridgeline. As water filled the streets, Ivy could feel the car hydroplaning, its rear end fishtailing around corners.

Bennett kept his grip on the wheel and steered through it. Glancing out as he drove, he said, "Chief Clarkson's team has probably been combing the village and homes close to the sea, but if you see anyone out, let me know. We can fit people in."

"I will." As Ivy watched for signs of life, her heart ached for the damage she saw. While the earthquake wasn't as destructive as it could have been, many older homes and businesses appeared to have sustained damage.

Still, the threat was a long way from being over.

Ivy glanced at the gaping hole where Bennett had pulled out the radio. She wished they could at least hear the news.

He followed her gaze. "I meant to put in your new sound system this weekend."

"We'll find someone who has a radio."

Around them, the village was dark. Some shopkeepers had hastily boarded front windows and laid sandbags in front of their doors. She realized she hadn't been prepared, but at least her house was slightly above sea level. A few feet…she tried to calculate. Would that be enough? Biting her lips, she realized the lower level might not fare well. Or the foundation.

Yet, there was little she could do. At least she had cleared

the guests from the inn and talked Shelly into leaving. She had
no idea when guests would be able to leave.

Ivy peered behind them at the ocean swells, black and
ominous as the night. As she grasped the dashboard, she
barely recognized her hands—pale and quivering in the
moonlight. She caught sight of herself in the rearview mirror
and quickly looked away, drawing a hand over her damp hair.
It was sticky with saltwater and plastered back.

She was glad to have Bennett beside her. He had let the
town in disaster preparations. But more than that, she could
feel his love and concern for her—and for her family.

As the car planed across a lane, Ivy tightened her seatbelt
and looked out the window. Some shop windows had cracked
in the earthquake, an awning had come down, and displays
had toppled.

Bennett slowed. "Look at Paige's shop. That old building
could be a complete loss."

Ivy gasped. The roof of the bookshop had caved in, and
the front windows had shattered. The headlights shone on
fallen bookshelves, their wooden planks jutting like bones from
mounds of books, which wouldn't stand much of a chance in
the rising water. Ivy shook her head at the sight. "We'll have to
help her rebuild."

"There will be plenty of clean-up to do in town," Bennett
said, keeping his attention on the road. When the car lost trac-
tion again, he frowned and flicked his gaze toward her. "You'd
better hang on. This old car wasn't built for this."

*B*ennett tightened his grip on the oversized 1950s steering wheel. As cool as the night air was, nervous perspiration gathered around his torso. From what he could see, many residents and shops in Summer Beach had sustained damage. Beside him, Ivy fidgeted with the hem of her sweatshirt.

"Clark can put out a call for officers to be on the lookout for Sunny," Bennett said, taking her hand.

"And Jamir," Ivy said. "They're together. Or they're supposed to be. And I still wish I could reach Misty. She told me she would be in a recording studio doing a voice-over for a commercial today. She was going out with some other actors afterward."

"They're probably okay," Bennett said, trying to reassure her. He hoped the kids were all right. "Once communication is working again, we'll try them. Depending on where the epicenter of the earthquake was, Los Angeles might not have even felt this."

Or it might have been worse there. He didn't want to alarm Ivy, but from the look on her face, she might have been thinking the same thing.

People in California often talked about the *big one*. Sooner or later, paradise might have to pay. Bennett wondered if it would be in their lifetime, but no one could say.

Glancing in his rearview mirror, he tried to gauge the rising water, but it was too dark to see much besides the headlights behind him. This could be the disaster he and his team at City Hall had prepared for, although he hoped it wasn't.

Every year, city employees staged a practice drill for various disasters: flood, fire, earthquake. Ahead, he could see a firetruck hosing a blaze that had erupted.

The earthquake wasn't the worst he'd ever been in, but that could often be just the beginning.

Ivy's gaze was transfixed on the fire, too. "After San Francisco's 1906 earthquake, fires erupted, and the city burned for days," she said. "Are you sure you turned off the gas at the inn?"

"Absolutely," Bennett said. Seeing the worry on her face, he added, "I taught people how to do that in the city's disaster planning seminar. Everyone in the city has been training for this."

Watching the water swirling through the darkened streets, Bennett gritted his teeth. As beautiful and compelling as the ocean was, it could also turn into a snarling, threatening menace—sometimes with little warning. This time, the only notice had been the low rumble far beneath the earth as ancient plates heaved against their burdens. A second or two was all they'd had.

Ivy's grip on his hand intensified. "My dad said that huge Alaska earthquake caused a tsunami that wiped out much of Crescent City in northern California."

He couldn't tell her that wouldn't happen here. The goal was to save lives; everything else could be rebuilt. "Try not to think of all that now. We've planned for this, and we're going to make it through, no matter what."

Knowing that Ivy was a strong swimmer and had been

trained as a lifeguard gave him a measure of comfort, though he hoped her talents wouldn't be needed.

Feeling Ivy's pulse pounding in her wrist, Bennett brought her hand to his lips and kissed it. He'd finally found the woman he wanted to spend the rest of his life with. He would do everything in his power to ensure her safety—and that of every other person in Summer Beach. If only he could reach her daughters.

"No one in this town will be left behind," he added, determined to follow through on that promise.

As if punctuating his words, a loudspeaker along the beach crackled with a warning to head to higher ground.

Bennett slowed the car. A trail of red tail lights wound up the road, with traffic to the ridgetop snaking along.

"This is like hurrying in slow motion," Ivy said, frowning.

Alongside the road, people were walking—mostly young tourists with backpacks from the beach campground. When Bennett saw a man in a Hawaiian shirt, he called out to him. "Hey, Arthur. Nan is with our group ahead. Can I give you a ride?"

"Very much obliged to you," Arthur said, relief evident in his voice. "I was worried about her. I went to the inn, but no one was there. I saw your sign on the door, so I started off."

Bennett took a backpack from him and put it in the back seat. "We got everyone out as fast as we could. All our phones are out, or we would have called."

Arthur climbed into the back seat. "What a day for my car to be out of commission. After taking Nan to work at City Hall, I delivered the car for service and planned to pick it up tomorrow. I was so knackered, I'd gone to sleep watching *Doctor Who*. What would you say that earthquake measured? Think it was a seven-pointer?"

"Not even close," Bennett said. "I'd say a little more than a six on the Richter scale. If that. The Northridge quake was a 6.7. I was visiting Los Angeles when that one occurred, and that was big enough for me."

"Guess it depends on where the earthquake is centered as to how much it's felt," Arthur said, nodding.

Bennett noticed that Ivy was looking almost as pale as Shelly, and she'd gone very quiet. "We'll be there soon," he said.

Nodding, Ivy gave him a wan smile.

Bennett eased forward in the line of cars. "How is your house, Arthur?"

"Not too bad, but the chimney crashed down," the other man replied, running a hand over his cleanly shaven head. "It's a pile of bricks now. I hate to think about the antiques at the shop."

"Did you have things secured?" Ivy asked.

Arthur gave a wry laugh. "We're all exceedingly careful after an earthquake, strapping tall pieces and sticking earthquake putty under crystal vases. But after a while, we become lazy and forget to take precautions." He took a bottle of water from his pack. "At least I picked up my earthquake kit from the kitchen on my way out. Would you care for a bottle of water?"

"Thanks, but I have a case in the trunk," Ivy said. "Forrest dropped it off just a few days ago."

"Just in time," Bennett said. "We might be up there for a while."

"Don't you have tenants in your house?" Arthur asked.

"I do," Bennett replied. "I'll check on them, then we'll find a place to wait it out." He turned to Ivy. "What else did Forrest put in the trunk?"

"I'm not sure." Ivy lifted a shoulder, and let it fall. "He told me, but I had so much on my mind with guests. Some sort of supplies, as I recall."

"I don't think we'll be camping out," Bennett said. "But

some of that might come in handy. Where are you heading, Arthur?"

He pushed his glasses up on his nose. "No idea, other than up." From his bag, he drew a portable transistor radio that crackled when he turned it on.

"A radio," Ivy exclaimed. "Can you get news from Los Angeles?"

"I'll try." Arthur tried to tune in stations. As he fiddled with dials, a screeching sound filled the car, and he made a face. "Sorry. Woke you up, though, right?"

"I don't know when we'll sleep again," Bennett said in an attempt at levity.

Pausing on a faint channel broadcast from Los Angeles, Arthur held the radio toward the front seat. A news report was in progress.

"South of the city, an earthquake along the coast measuring—"

Static overtook the broadcast.

"No," Ivy cried. "Try to get that back."

Arthur shook his head. "Maybe I'll get better reception on the ridgetop."

Bennett touched Ivy's hand. "Doesn't sound like the earthquake impacted Los Angeles very much."

Ivy let out a breath, though a frown still creased her forehead. "Misty is probably okay—as long as she was there. But I don't want her to worry. I wish I could reach her."

Soon, they were passing the flashing lights from Chief Clarkson's patrol car. Bennett pulled to one side, just past where an officer was directing traffic. "Wait here for me," he said. "I'll check in with Clark."

The police chief was on an emergency satellite phone the city had just acquired. "Good to see you, Mayor," Clark said. "I'm glad you helped evacuate the inn. I've had my team going door to door on the beach checking on folks."

"Is everything under control?" Bennett asked.

"All is going according to plan."

"I have a favor to ask of you."

Clark raised his brow. "As long as it's legal, Mr. Mayor."

Bennett told him about Sunny and Jamir and asked if anyone had seen or heard from them. "Could you help us locate them?"

Drawing a hand over his chin, Clark nodded. "Where is his mother?"

Ivy walked up behind Bennett. "I saw Imani take her car. She should have been ahead of us. She offered to take people to her house up here."

"My officer must have waved them through. Her house is nearly finished." A cloud of concern filled Clark's face. Leaning over, he lifted his communication device in the police car and gave instructions to his people in the field to be on the lookout for Imani, Jamir, and Sunny.

"We'll find them," Clark said, grim-faced, as he took Sunny's phone number in case cell signals started working again.

"I know you will," Bennett said, putting his arm around Ivy. This was personal; he knew how much Imani and Jamir meant to Clark. "What can I do to help?"

Ivy lifted her chin and glared at him. "He means, what can *we* do to help? That's my daughter."

"I stand corrected," Bennett said, throwing her a look of apology. How could he have been that macho or that insensitive? Ivy was a force on her own, and he'd have to respect that more.

The police chief rubbed his chin. "You can help with the flow of traffic. That will free up me and others to find out what we can. Folks need to know where to go. They can park on the street and in the empty field at the top of the rise."

Ivy nodded. "Let's get to work."

Arthur stepped out of the car. "This is my town, too. Count me in, and tell me what to do."

Bennett grinned. "Looks like you have three more reporting for duty, Chief." He could always count on Arthur and Nan to do whatever they could to support the community. After easing the car off the road, he stepped out and went to work.

Just then, a fancy golf cart with a golden hood ornament whizzed along the side of the road from the opposite direction. Carol Reston—a Grammy Award-winning singer and local celebrity—was at the wheel with her husband. They looked like they were dressed for a party.

"We heard what's happening in the village," Carol said. Her signature fiery-red hair was swept under a coral scarf, and layers of coral jewelry graced her neck and wrists. "Hal and I are opening Shangri-La to anyone who needs shelter."

Her husband leaned out of the golf cart. "What's the use of having an estate if we can't put it to good use?"

"That's generous of you," Ivy said, hugging Carol and Hal.

"Last year, when we had that dreadful fire here, you put up everyone at the inn," Carol said. "And you hosted Victoria's beautiful wedding on short notice. It's karma, darling. What goes around comes around, and now it's our turn."

"We were having a dinner party with friends from Beverly Hills when the earthquake hit," Hal said. "As soon as we heard the tsunami siren, we knew everyone would be heading our way. So we all decided to do what we could."

"If you're sure it's not too much trouble," Ivy began.

Carol made a face and waved a hand. "Come stay with us at Shangri-La. We're all pitching in. Besides, we could use your hostess skills—you have a natural way of making people feel at ease."

"She sure does." Bennett saw Ivy brighten at that comment. She had to work hard at making her job as a host look easy. When she'd first opened the inn with Shelly, he'd be the first to admit they hadn't really known what they were doing. More than a few people in town wondered if the sisters were up to managing the old landmark house. Yet, he'd watched Ivy and Shelly rise to the challenge. Even when Ivy was stressed, she managed to make others feel comfortable and welcome.

"Our chef is cooking for anyone who is hungry," Hal added. "The housekeeper and our friends are making up beds and putting cots wherever they can."

"I appreciate that," Bennett said, deeply touched at their efforts and immediacy in stepping up to the challenge. "So will many others."

"Mitch and Shelly are right behind us," Ivy said, gesturing to the Jeep. "Mitch will probably help in the kitchen."

"He'd be welcome." Carol touched Ivy's arm. "Is your family okay? And the inn?"

"I don't think there's much damage to the house, but we won't know until daylight." Ivy went on to tell her about Sunny and Jamir and the trouble she was having reaching them and the rest of her family.

"Maybe we can help locate them," Hal said. "Because we travel so much with Carol's shows, we've got satellite phones you're welcome to use."

Hope flared in Ivy's eyes. "Thank you for that." She turned back to Bennett. "Once we find them, I'll come back to help."

Bennett kissed her cheek. "You stay there and help out."

"I can go with Shelly and Mitch," she said, gesturing toward the Jeep. "Keep the car if you need it."

"I'll put the top up," Bennett said. "I'll see you later."

Hal turned to Chief Clarkson. "We also have a high-quality satellite communication system in the house. We've been tracking the seismologist reports from Caltech and the Coast Guard reports. You and are your team are welcome to our command center if you need it."

Carol leaned over. "And we'll bring food back for everyone. Might be a long night."

"That's mighty nice of you folks," Chief Clarkson said, touching his forehead.

"I'll run back and forth in the golf cart," Hal said. "Happy to shuttle people to our place or deliver messages."

Bennett looked back at the darkened sea. The sound of the waves—a constant in everyone's life in Summer Beach—seemed different tonight, as if the currents were gathering with ominous force. He could almost feel the power of the waves drawing nearer.

Or was he imagining that? He tried to shake the feeling of dread. Turning to Ivy, he said, "Arthur and I will send people your way. And I'll be on the lookout for the kids."

"I hate to leave you," she said, pressing a hand to his chest.

Ivy's simple movement calmed him, but it also renewed his determination to ensure the safety of her family—*their* family now. "We're safe as long as we stay up here. Watch out for aftershocks—they can be nearly as bad as the first quake, especially in weakened structures."

"We will." She slid her hand into his and squeezed it.

Hating to let her go, he brought her hand to his lips. "Let me know the minute you hear anything from Sunny and Jamir, and I'll do the same. And your family. I want to know that they're all safe. We can send messages through Hal."

When Bennett wrapped his arms around Ivy, he felt her heart beating as fast as his. He couldn't imagine how distraught he would have been if he and Ivy had been separated during the earthquake. As much as he wanted her to stay with him so he could look after her, she was needed elsewhere. He stroked her still-damp hair, but he had to let her go.

Bennett tilted her chin up. "Don't forget how much I love you," he murmured, touching her lips with his. He worried about her loved ones, too, and prayed that Sunny was safe.

*I*vy climbed into the Jeep behind Shelly, who was clutching a paper bag in her lap. As they drove away from Bennett, Ivy wished she could stay with him, but they were both needed elsewhere. At least she was with her sister and Mitch.

As the Jeep swayed over fallen debris in the road, Shelly groaned. "I feel like I'm on an airplane with a motion sickness bag. Who knew morning sickness could last all day?" She brushed wisps of hair from her face. "I don't know how our mom went through this four times. At least she hit a double with Flint and Forrest."

"Maybe you will, too," Ivy said with a slight smile. At least she could help Shelly, and lightening her sister's mood would help.

Picking up on that, Mitch laughed. "One and done, and we get the two we wanted. Hey, that would be great."

Shelly looked horrified. "No more preggy jokes. You two have no idea what it's like to be inside my skin right now."

Ivy couldn't help chuckling. "Think of how cute they'd be, Shells. They could have matching surfboards."

Shelly lifted a corner of her mouth. "Could you imagine

having two—or even one—right now and going through all this?"

"Look around," Ivy replied. Outside, people had little children with them. Some were pitching tents in front yards, others were rocking kids to sleep on porches, and still others were trudging along with little ones in their arms or beside them.

"Here are some little tykes that might need some help." Mitch pulled beside a young family. The woman carried a sleepy toddler while a boy slightly older clung to his mother's free hand. An older boy tagged behind, shuffling his feet. Mitch leaned across Shelly and called out through the open window. "Need a lift?"

"Where to?" the woman asked.

"We're going to help out at Shangri-La, Carol Reston's house." Mitch pointed ahead.

The woman's face was a mask of relief. "You have no idea how much I'd like that. Come on, kids." She herded them into the Jeep. They crowded into the back with Ivy while the teen climbed into the rear compartment.

"I'm Jessica," the woman said and introduced her two boys. "And this is Gracie."

Mitch looked in the rearview mirror. "I think we met at Nailed It. Aren't you Jen's sister?"

"I am," Jessica replied. "We just moved here. My husband is deployed out of San Diego."

"Marines?" Ivy asked.

"Navy. While he's gone, it's nice to be near Jen and George, especially with the kids." The toddler in her arms began to get fussy, and Jessica wiggled a small stuffed bear in front of her. She sighed. "I wish he were here now."

Ivy remembered what it was like juggling two children close in age. "Want me to hold Gracie?"

"Would I ever," Jessica said, passing the little girl to Ivy. "Do you have children?"

"Two grown girls," Ivy said, trying to keep her composure. Not knowing where Sunny and Misty were was hard to manage, even if Misty was out of harm's way.

Shelly must have heard the catch in Ivy's voice because she launched into a friendly conversation with Jessica.

Ivy noticed that each of them was studiously avoiding the topic of the earthquake or pending tsunami. That might scare the small children. For the most part, they were above the threat here. At least, Ivy hoped that was the case.

A few minutes later, Mitch eased the Jeep toward a walled estate. A bronze plaque by the gate read *Shangri-La*. The gate was open, and Hal had already returned. He was a commanding sight with his tall, trim stature and silver hair.

"Come on in," Hal said as he waved people into the car court. "We made better time in the golf cart than you did."

"We took on some extra passengers along the way," Mitch said. "Hope that's okay?"

"You're all welcome," Hal replied. "You'll find Poppy with a crew from the inn on the deck."

When Ivy stepped from the Jeep and walked inside the house, she was immediately entranced. The modern décor was stunning—shimmering shades of sapphire and teal accented the modern, cream-and-white expanse that was open to the ocean behind walls of glass. Candles flickered everywhere, filling the room with soft light.

"Wow," Shelly said, pausing beside her. "Could this look any more like a Hollywood set?"

"They're serious art collectors, too," Ivy whispered.

Even little Gracie stared at the artwork. "Pretty," the toddler said, pointing.

"I like it, too," Ivy said, kissing the child's soft hair.

All around them, large pieces of artwork, splashed with color, lined the walls. In the shadowy candlelight, Ivy spied an Andy Warhol pop art piece, a Tamara de Lempicka art deco painting of a group of women, a Frida Kahlo self-portrait, and a Cindy Sherman persona photograph. She could only imagine what these looked like when they were properly lit. As much as Amelia and Gustav Erickson had been collectors in their day, so too were Carol and Hal today.

Beneath these rare works of art, groups of bedraggled people lounged on pillows and blankets spread on the white marble floor, chatting about the earthquake. They looked well, though shaken.

On a bookshelf behind glass doors stood several golden award figurines that Carol must have won for her music. Ivy wondered how everything had escaped damage in the earthquake, but they had probably secured valuables.

"Check out her Grammys," Shelly whispered, shining a flashlight she carried on the awards.

"She earned every one of them," Ivy said softly. Carol's songs had often provided the soundtrack to Ivy's life. Carol still toured and performed, and Hal managed her career and that of others on the music label he owned. They were a power couple in the industry.

Yet, Summer Beach was their refuge from the world, a place they'd lived for years where they could unwind and walk the beach in their flip-flops and sun hats away from the prying eyes of paparazzi. Locals treated Carol and Hal like regular folks, not the celebrities they were elsewhere—although they still attracted attention from tourists who recognized them. Ivy could hardly imagine having to go through life that way.

"Come in," Carol called out from the bar, where an assortment of people had gathered.

It was easy to tell who had been the dinner guests. They wore elegantly casual evening attire and were perched on stools at the granite-clad bar. Ivy thought she recognized some famous faces, but she couldn't quite place them. Other Summer Beach residents wore jeans and T-shirts and flip-flops. They were avidly sharing earthquake experiences. A sleepy child fussed in its father's arms.

Still holding little Gracie, Ivy stepped down into the sunken living room. Shelly and Mitch followed her, and Jessica trailed behind with her other two children. To one side was a formal dining table laden with silver and china. The meal looked as if the earthquake had interrupted it, as partially finished desserts were still on the table.

Carol's chunky bracelets jingled as she hugged each of them. "I'm so glad you're here—especially these little ones." She knelt to greet the children. "I have a brand new playroom that I think you'll love. I designed it for my grandbabies with everything that they might like."

"Does that mean Victoria is pregnant?" Shelly asked.

"She is, and we're all thrilled," Carol said. "You'll find others in the playroom, too. Maybe you can help there. The children were upset when they arrived. They had been jolted from sleep and whisked away from home. We're setting up a quiet place so they can sleep."

At that, little Gracie yawned and tucked her fist under her chin. She turned into Ivy's shoulder.

Shelly's face softened. "I'll take Gracie to the playroom." As she took the child from Ivy's arms, she whispered, "I need the practice."

Jessica took the other child by the hand while the older boy followed them.

Carol motioned to a middle-aged woman in a dark dress. Her dark hair was wound into a thick, shiny bun. "Ms. Miranda, would you please show our guests to the playroom?"

"With pleasure," the woman said in a soft southern drawl. "And would you young-uns like anything to eat? Chef Raul is in the kitchen, and he can whip up almost anything you like. His gourmet grilled cheese sandwiches are amazing."

Jessica looked grateful. "They'd like that, even though it's late for them."

"Is that my sister I hear?" Jen rounded the corner. "Jessica, I was so worried about you and the kids."

Jessica fell into Jen's open arms, and Jessica's children piled in to hug Jen. "Am I glad to see you," Jessica said with relief.

Jen and Jessica and the boys caught up with Shelly, who was carrying Gracie to the playroom. When the little girl heard her aunt, she blinked and cried out for her. With some reluctance, Shelly passed Gracie to her aunt and stayed with Mitch.

Seeing Jen and Jessica together with the children reminded Ivy of her relationship with Shelly.

"Miranda has been making up beds and cots," Carol said. "No one should trek back down until the all-clear signal sounds. Waves can be hours apart and increase in strength. So we're going to stay put and keep everyone safe. Fortunately, we have enough supplies to feed everyone for quite a while." Carol winked at them. "And Hal has a fully stocked wine cellar."

"I can't thank you enough," Ivy said.

"Shelly, if you're okay with Ivy, I'll look for Raul," Mitch said.

"Go help," Shelly said. "I'm fine, and there's a big, hungry crowd here."

"I'm sure Chef Raul will welcome your help, especially at breakfast," Carol said. "We're going to make a night of it."

Carol introduced her guests at the bar, and Ivy soon found herself chatting with a film producer and a costume designer. Although she would have loved to talk about costuming, she excused themselves. "We should see if Mitch needs help in the kitchen."

"Thanks," Shelly said, breathing out a sigh of relief after they walked away. "I didn't want to be rude, and they were interesting, but I can only take so much. It's shocking how tired I get."

"Just wait," Ivy said, smoothing her arm across Shelly's shoulder. "You still have months to go."

"Were you like this when you were pregnant?"

"With Misty, I was like you. I thought she'd never arrive. But with Sunny, I had plenty of energy, not a bit of nausea, and she was an easy, early delivery. She was kicking to get into the world. But don't worry. This will pass."

Shelly gave her a weak smile. "Promise?"

Ivy nodded. "Then the real work—and the joy—begins. You're going to be a great mother, Shelly. Keep that in mind."

"I try to, but it's hard when I'm gagging at the toilet. I keep wondering—where's all that motherhood bliss I see in photos online?"

Ivy laughed. "Anyone can look blissful for a few seconds. With a new baby, I was thrilled just to find time to shower."

They walked into the gleaming, white-and-gray marbled onyx kitchen, where Mitch was already building grilled cheese sandwiches and toasting them on an enormous, stainless-steel cooktop with red knobs. Mitch grinned at them over his shoulder.

"He's in heaven," Shelly said, smiling at her husband. "Look at all this gear in the kitchen. He's never cooked in a place like this. His kitchen at Java Beach is the size of a closet."

"Need help with anything?" Ivy asked.

Chef Raul looked up from a plate of appetizers he was preparing. "We sure do. Can you take these out to people? Miranda is needed with the children."

"I'm happy to do that," Ivy said. She felt more comfortable throwing herself into work than lounging around. "Will you be okay here, Shells?"

Just then, Mitch slid a cup of ginger tea across the counter to Shelly. "I thought my wife might need this," he said with a wink.

Shelly picked up the tea and smiled. "Who loves you?"

He folded his arms on the counter and gazed at Shelly with love in his eyes. "Sure hope you do." Grinning, he turned back to the grill. "Let me know what you think you can eat. Special orders for you."

Shelly beamed at him.

Ivy watched the exchange and smiled. She was truly happy for Shelly. All her dreams were coming true.

Ivy picked up a platter of sliced vegetables, dip, nuts, and cheese. As she started for the living room, a tremor shook the house, and screams erupted.

"Just an aftershock," Mitch called out, steadying himself on the counter as Shelly did the same. "Nothing to worry about, folks. It's the way we rock 'n roll in the golden state."

The chef steadied pans swaying on an overhead rack. "I've already locked down everything that's breakable."

Teenagers were giggling in one corner, and in another were a pair of older women with worried frowns. Others began chattering about the size of the earthquake.

Ivy stopped by the two women she recognized as Darla's friends from Java Beach. "It might help to have something to eat."

"I don't think I can swallow a thing," one woman in a plaid flannel shirt buttoned askew said. "I'm too nervous, and I think I ought to have stayed at home."

Her friend looked skeptical. "And what if a giant wave came through?"

"I'd climb on the roof."

The other woman snorted. "With your knees? You're staying put, Madge. There's not a darn thing you can do there."

"There you go being bossy again," Madge said, pulling her flannel shirt around herself. "If I want to go back, I will, and I'll tell you another thing—"

"I'll leave a few nibbles if you change your mind," Ivy said, cutting in. She put some goodies onto paper plates she'd tucked under her platter. "It's been quite a night—an unscheduled slumber party, right?" She couldn't let anyone go back to their homes until she heard from Bennett or Chief Clarkson.

The women looked at each other and grinned. "Remember when we used to have those?"

With their attention diverted, they began sharing stories. Ivy left them, glad to have given them something else to think about.

Remembering that Poppy was here—somewhere—Ivy threaded through the expansive house. She'd heard how large the home was, and the inn was certainly a good size, but this was a sprawling estate that hugged the ridgetop. She stepped onto a patio and looked out, breathing in the faintly salty night air.

Across the grounds, guest cottages and outdoor pavilions were tucked between palm trees swept into graceful arches by perennial sea breezes. She scanned the horizon for any signs of a swelling sea. Although she couldn't see much except the glimmer of waves in the moonlight, she imagined the daytime views must be spectacular. As it was, without the lights of the village dimming the sky, the stars overhead blazed in the velvet night.

Far below, Ivy spied the rooftops and grounds of the inn. A sudden image of herself watching waves crash through her home and the village beyond from this perch flashed through her mind. She blinked against the image, yet it was so vivid and overwhelming that her pulse raced and her breath constricted.

Ivy pressed a hand against her forehead, willing away the feeling—even though that wouldn't stop a tsunami. Like everything else she'd experienced, she would face it if it came. Until then, the only thing she could do was to help where needed.

When she and Bennett had stopped to speak to Chief Clarkson, she'd overheard a few people grumbling about having to evacuate. Bennett and Clark were concerned about people returning before they gave the all-clear signal. As much as people complained, Bennett said that it was better than fishing them out of receding waters.

She'd do her part to keep people here and out of harm's way.

From a balcony above Ivy, voices floated down on the breeze. Lifting her platter, she marched up a flight of stairs at Shangri-La. The view was even more astounding from this level.

"Aunt Ivy," Poppy cried, rushing to her. "I've been so worried about you. What took you so long to get here? And have you seen Shelly or Sunny?"

Ivy told her about Sunny and Jamir and how worried she was about them. "On the way here, Bennett and I stopped to make sure Shelly and Mitch were coming."

Glancing at a crowd of people behind Poppy, Ivy saw Gilda seated in a lounge chair clutching the shivering Pixie. "How are the guests you brought doing?"

"Darla is feeling better now," Poppy said, looking over her shoulder to where their neighbor was seated. Darla was talking to Paige and the nurse, Bettina. "Many guests have their books from the meeting. Talking about them seems to soothe people."

"This will certainly be a book club meeting to remember," Ivy said, resting her tray on a table. Bonding over books had another interpretation this evening. "How are our other guests doing?"

"Everyone understands the situation. Even Geena." Poppy raised her eyebrows in surprise.

Geena's presence was troubling, and at a time like this, Ivy didn't want to think about that unpleasant young woman. Still, Ivy had a feeling that she was the one who needed the most help. Whatever was behind her motives probably stemmed from some deep-seated dissatisfaction. While that wasn't Ivy's problem, that issue might have pushed Geena to pursue her action against the inn.

Like it or not, Ivy felt she should check on Geena. "Where is she?"

"She was sticking close to Paige for a while." Poppy nodded toward the living room. "The last time I saw Geena, she was checking out the artwork around the house. I sure hope Carol and Hal have it locked down."

"I don't think she would tear paintings off the wall."

Arching a brow, Poppy looked doubtful. "I wouldn't put it past her, Aunt Ivy."

"She must honestly think that she is entitled to what we found at the inn. We need to find out why." Eager to change the subject, Ivy said, "Did you see Imani after we left the house?"

"She went to her new place, but I think we should check on her and the others that went with her."

"We could take some food to them," Ivy said. "Mitch is cooking in the kitchen, and there is plenty to share. Still, there's plenty of room here for them. They'd be more comfortable than at Imani's partially finished house. I'll find Carol and ask her."

"I can pass that tray around if you'd like," Poppy said, nodding toward the tray Ivy had put down. "Let me know when you want to go."

Ivy handed the platter to her. "Thanks. I'll talk to Mitch

and tell them what we need. We can take Bennett's SUV because he stayed with Chief Clarkson to help out, and he has my car anyway. I'll call you when we're ready."

Before leaving, Ivy visited with the guests. Darla looked calmer, and Bettina assured Ivy that she was doing fine. The two women were immersed in conversation about their favorite mysteries.

Ivy returned to the kitchen and spoke with Mitch, who agreed to pack food for the group at Imani's house. With all that was on her mind—Sunny and Jamir, Shelly, and Bennett—Ivy fought against the worry that would consume her if she let it. To keep her mind occupied, Ivy hoisted another tray of appetizers. She wanted to check on other book club attendees and guests.

That included Geena.

Ivy wondered if she learned more about her if there would be a way to diffuse the situation without resorting to costly legal battles. Imani would want to know how valid her claim was. It couldn't hurt to talk to Geena, as long as she didn't make any promises.

Ivy set off to look for her.

It wasn't long before she found Geena, standing before a painting next to a flickering lantern on a desk. As Ivy drew closer, she saw that Geena was frozen in front of the darkened painting, staring into mid-space.

Composing herself, Ivy approached her. "It's going to be a long night, and I thought you might be hungry."

Stunned from her silence, Geena blinked. Drawing the heel of her hand against her eyes, she asked with some irritation, "Why are you even talking to me?"

"We might have our differences, but I still care about you," Ivy replied, speaking as gently as she could manage. "That was a good-sized earthquake. I don't know if you've ever been in one before."

"I haven't," Geena said, her voice catching.

Ivy saw a crimson flush spread across Geena's neck and face. Maybe she could reach her now. "The first one can sure blindside a person. Everything you thought was solid seems to wobble in front of your eyes—even the floor seems to liquefy. It's a shock to the system, so your equilibrium might feel off for a while."

Geena dipped her chin and swept a hand across her cheeks. "My grandmother told me my grandfather had a heart attack during an earthquake."

"I'm sorry. That must bring up sad memories. Were you close to him?"

Geena averted Ivy's gaze. "I never met him," she said in a barely audible voice.

At once, Ivy suspected who Geena was talking about. It had to be Gustav. After a hesitation, she asked, "Did your grandmother ever visit him in Summer Beach?"

"No, but my mother..." Her voice trailed off.

While Ivy waited for Geena to finish her thought, she put a miniature Florentine quiche, an empanada, and a vegetarian meatball onto a small paper plate. The chef had clearly been raiding the appetizer shelves in the freezer. Carol and Hal often entertained on a grand scale, so she wasn't surprised. She handed the plate to Geena. "Mitch made these. You might need some energy."

Geena took the offering and picked at the empanada. "Ever since Mom read that article about everything you found in the house, she's been after me to do something about it." Still unable to look Ivy in the eye, Geena poked the empanada until cheese and green chiles oozed from the corner. "She has a point, right?"

"Maybe so," Ivy said, intent on drawing out more from Geena. "I take it this wasn't your idea?"

"You don't know how tough she is."

"Then why didn't she file the lawsuits?"

"She says I'm a lot smarter than she is. She hates talking to attorneys and complains that they never understand her."

"That's a lot for your mother to ask of you," Ivy said thoughtfully. "You must love her very much. And your father?"

"Never knew him. Mom said he split before I was born, just like her father. Took his name with him, too." She let out a breath.

Geena darted a look at Ivy. "You should settle with her. That's all she wants. Then she'll stop nagging both of us."

Ivy shook her head. "I don't have what she wants. What we found in the house wasn't ours to keep."

"My mom told me that Gustav Erickson made promises to Granny and broke them. He was supposed to divorce his wife and marry her. Mom is always mad thinking about the life-style that was stolen from her."

"Do you mean, as the daughter of a wealthy man?"

"She's smart, you know." Geena sniffed. "So am I. Sure, Gustav left a trust to pay for her schooling, but Mom wasn't the academic type. After Gustav died, Mom called his wife right up—only she acted like she couldn't remember anything."

"No, Amelia probably wouldn't have," Ivy said softly.

"Because she was greedy."

"She had Alzheimer's disease. It was probably called dementia back then."

A look of realization flashed across Geena's face. "Any-way," she continued, shrugging off the thought. "If he'd recognized Mom and given her his name, then she could've been introduced to society and married a friend of the family or something. As it was, she decided to change my name later. Gustav never had any other children, so he wouldn't have missed any of that money." She paused. "You can see her point, can't you?"

Ivy couldn't answer that. "What I don't understand is why she waited so long to do something about it."

"Mom figured Granny didn't have the money to fight for what should have been hers. My attorney said it was too late to go after the will, so Mom decided to do this."

Geena seemed eager to unburden herself, but her story didn't seem to add up. Imani had reached out to the estate trustees, and they'd never had any knowledge of Geena or her family. "Maybe you have other relatives on the Erickson side of the family. Have you ever looked into that?"

Geena rubbed a hand over her mouth. "I haven't actually pursued it," she mumbled, glancing away.

Ivy was unaware of other relations anyway. "It seems like your mother's opinion means a lot to you."

In the dim light, Ivy saw a tear spill over Geena's lower lid before she brushed it away. "We have only one mother. Mom says we're supposed to honor our elders and do what they ask, right?"

When Ivy didn't answer, Geena blinked and swung her gaze back to the painting. "I wish I could learn to paint."

Ivy's heart softened toward this woman. It was just a guess, but the relationship she had with her mother didn't sound healthy. "You could if you wanted."

Geena shrugged. "I used to draw a little."

While the other woman talked about how much she had enjoyed art in school, thoughts of Sunny crowded Ivy's mind. "I'd like for us to talk more later, but I have to check on others here."

Another tear spilled over Geena's eyelid.

Ivy glanced toward the doorway. "I don't think you should be here by yourself—in case of a big aftershock. I saw some refreshments in the kitchen, and I think Carol is bringing out some good wine. You might like to relax with others in the book club." Ivy recalled seeing them together right after the earthquake. "You and Paige can look after each other."

Geena sniffed and nodded. "That would help my nerves."

"Let's find Paige together."

As the women made their way back toward the crowd of people, Ivy watched Geena. Gone was the bravado she'd arrived with at the inn. Her mother must have goaded Geena into taking action, but there was still something off about her story. However, Ivy couldn't think about that now. She left Geena with Paige, who immediately began asking her about the books she liked to read and making suggestions for her. That was a safe topic that seemed to spark life in Geena, and Paige was a patient listener—she was a book whisperer, after all.

Ivy set off down the hallway. Turning with her tray, she saw a flickering light from another room and heard what sounded like a television. Ivy reached out to try a light switch, but it was still dead. She hurried toward the room. Inside what looked to be Hal's office, young people were huddled around a screen watching a news broadcast.

Ivy put down the platter, awestruck at the images. A neighboring community had sustained more damage, and everyone was moving to higher ground. Ivy blurted out, "I thought the electricity was out."

Hal walked in behind her. "Not with these young engineers around."

A younger woman smiled shyly. "The power is still out, but we connected this screen to Hal's satellite phone and hooked it all up to a portable gas generator for power that my friend had in his truck. Now we can stream this. Cool, huh?"

As Ivy passed the platter around, she watched the screen flicker. Seismologists from Caltech in Pasadena and emergency personnel were monitoring the situation and reporting. She listened while the younger people talked about more ideas for the generator. Perching on the edge of a desk, she tried to hear above the excited chatter beside her.

A reporter continued on the screen. "The risk of an

underwater landslide remains large. However, not all earthquakes cause tsunamis. Scientists say four conditions contribute to such a situation after an earthquake in Southern California. First, earthquakes occur beneath the ocean, causing a slide…next, a magnitude of at least 6.5…"

Ivy wondered what this quake had registered on the Richter scale. It must have been close to that unless the temblor occurred close to the surface or was very nearby. They would have felt it more then.

"Shallow depth," a scientist on the screen added. "As well as vertical movement of the seafloor. Those are part of the conditions for a tsunami."

The reporter went on. "Coastal communities remain at risk. If you are in such an area, be wary of rising water and seek higher ground at once."

The show cut to a reporter standing near a beach with a crowd of people in the background.

Ivy passed a hand over her forehead. How would she find Sunny? Just as she stood to leave, a familiar figure flashed on the screen behind the reporter.

Sunny.

"That's my daughter," Ivy cried, pressing a hand to her chest. Looking closer, she saw Jamir standing beside Sunny before the broadcast cut out. "Does anyone know where that was?"

"Somewhere on the coast," one girl said. "I didn't catch it."

"I recognized the signs behind them," Hal said. "They're on the other side of the ridge, not far from here."

"Is that anywhere near the public library?"

"Not too far," Hal replied. "We'll keep watching for you."

"I need to get to her." Ivy twisted her hands.

Hal frowned and drew a hand over his chin. "Have you alerted Chief Clarkson?"

"He's doing what he can." Ivy bit her lower lip, worried

that Sunny and Jamir were stranded. If only she could get to them.

She wished she could call Bennett. He'd promised to send word if he heard anything. As she thought of him, she ached with regret over her indecision with him. Maybe because it had been so long since she'd had a real partner at her side—if ever—that she hadn't fully appreciated him or the life they could have together.

Guilt over her hesitation with him coursed through her. After Jeremy's sudden death, she knew how fast life could come at you.

What if she'd lost Bennett in the earthquake?

What if he never really knew how much he meant to her?

Once they got through this situation, she vowed to make changes. In herself, in their relationship.

"That satellite cell phone you have," Ivy began, addressing Hal. "Could I use it? I'm trying to reach my daughter."

"Of course," Hal said, turning to one of the engineers.

Just then, the screen went dark, and collective dismay filled the room. "The battery on the phone is dead," the younger engineer said.

"Use the generator," another one said.

"This might take a while," Hal said. "If you'll wait a little bit, I'm sure we can accommodate you."

Ivy blinked back the dismay and disappointment she felt. As a sense of urgency coiled within her, she felt the grief of precious minutes slipping away. Somehow, she knew she didn't have much time to find Sunny.

After excusing herself, she rushed to find Poppy, who was in the kitchen bundling up the rye bread and croissant sandwiches Mitch and another volunteer had made for them to take to Imani's house.

Poppy picked up a box of sandwiches. "I'm loading everything in the SUV, Aunt Ivy. We should be ready to go in a minute."

"I think Sunny and Jamir are stranded nearby," Ivy said, telling Poppy what she'd just seen. "We have to see Imani and figure out how to reach them." She turned to Mitch. "Will you tell Shelly I'm leaving?"

"Sure will," Mitch said, feverishly building sandwiches while he spoke. "While you were gone, she came in here with a couple of the kids to get some food."

"Is she feeling any better?"

"A lot," Mitch said, looking relieved. "Being with the children probably takes her mind off her bad stomach. The feeling comes and goes, too."

"This is just a phase, and it will pass soon enough." Ivy picked up another box packed with crackers, peanut butter and jelly, sardines, and bags of apples. "Thanks for doing this, Mitch."

Ivy and Poppy hurried to the vehicle. On the way, they met Carol in the car court, and Ivy quickly explained what they were doing. Before she could ask Carol about bringing the people at Imani's here, the other woman's eyes clouded with concern.

"They're all welcome here," Carol said. "Imani's new home is adorable, but she hasn't furnished it yet. Be sure to tell them to come over. Hal can help ferry them if needed, and we'll make room."

"I'll let them know," Ivy said.

Poppy had already loaded the rear cargo area, and Ivy slid her box next to the others. Taking the keys from Poppy, she stepped into the large SUV.

When they arrived at Imani's new, still unfinished home, their friend met them at the door. Behind her, Ivy could see other guests from the inn, along with friends and locals. They were gathered in a circle on the concrete floor of the living room with the glass doors open to the sea breezes. Maeve was reading aloud from a book while others listened, their faces etched with weariness and worry, trying to remain calm.

"At least the plumbing is working now," Imani said, waving them in. "Maeve decided to continue the book club to keep everyone's mind occupied." She knocked on a wall. "Good to know this place is strong enough to withstand an earthquake."

"It's nice here, but——" Ivy felt like she was bursting. "Imani, we have to reach the kids."

"I'd like to," her friend said. "I'm worried about Jamir. Have you heard anything from Sunny?"

"I caught a glimpse of them," Ivy said, her words tumbling out. While Poppy unloaded the food, she told Imani about seeing the kids on the screen in Hal's office. What she'd learned this evening from Geena could wait. "We've got to find them. I've got a strange feeling."

Imani frowned, and a conflicted look filled her face. "We're not supposed to go back down toward the village, and Clark is busy with the evacuation."

"Bennett is helping him." Ivy flexed her jaw. "These are our children—and I need your help."

Nodding toward Bennett's SUV, Imani said, "We can take that. Maeve and Poppy can stay with the folks here."

"Carol invited everyone to Shangri-La," Ivy said.

After finishing her sandwich, Maeve pushed herself from the floor. "Imani, I appreciate your hospitality. But I think everyone would be more comfortable there."

After explaining the change of plans to Poppy, who agreed to drive guests to Shangri-La, Imani and Ivy climbed into the large SUV.

As they drove, Ivy peered down at the hillside. "There's a steady stream of cars creeping up here." She angled her chin toward the road that hugged the shore. "The coastal route is standing still."

"Must be because of the threat down the coast," Imani said, frowning. "Can't blame folks for coming up here. I've been worried about Jamir and Sunny being able to get through in time."

Ivy swallowed against the panic that seized her chest. If they headed down the ridge, they might not be able to reach higher ground again. If they had to, they could climb to the attic at the inn and ride out the weather. But they had to find the kids first.

"We have to try," Ivy said, sharing her thoughts about what to do.

"That could be risky." Imani thought for a moment and then touched Ivy's arm. "I have another idea. Turn around and head for the backside of the ridge."

With Imani directing her, Ivy reversed and turned toward the end of the street that lined the ridgetop. Following Imani's direction, she turned onto a dirt road. As the vehicle bounced across the uneven terrain, Ivy's feeling of urgency increased.

"This is a seldom-used fire road," Imani said, touching the dashboard for balance. "People hike up here from the Summer Beach side to meditate because the ocean views are amazing. This is one of Ginger Delavie's favorite spots. It's not an easy hike from Summer Beach, but it is practically inaccessible from the other side." Imani scanned the landscape. "Go slowly."

"We don't have much time." Ivy flicked on her bright lights and rolled down the windows to see better.

The ocean breeze was stronger up here, and it whipped through the cabin. The ocean roared beneath them, but it did little to calm the tension that gripped Ivy's chest. She prayed that Sunny would stay with Jamir, who was fairly leveled-headed. While she loved her daughter, Sunny often acted on impulse.

"Let's get out," Imani said.

Making sure to leave the vehicle's headlights blazing, Ivy stepped from the SUV. She gazed out over the coastal village below, her heart hammering as waves crashed onto the shore.

Imani motioned toward the far end of the ridge. "Down the back of this cliff is an old wooden staircase. Since it hasn't been used or maintained in years, it's perilous. The wood is rotten, and people have had bad falls, especially at night. Even though it's blocked off, kids sometimes go exploring."

Ivy heard the concern she felt in her friend's voice. "Do you think Jamir would have taken this route?"

"It's the fastest way from the other side. If the streets are clogged, he might think of this as a shortcut." Imani quirked up a side of her mouth. "I'm trying to think as he would."

Ivy managed a laugh. "Sunny would just hitch a ride."

"They could, but I don't think Jamir would take a chance on not making it to safety—especially with Sunny."

Ivy gripped Imani's hand. "I'm glad you're here. I'd be out of my mind with worry."

Just as Imani began to speak, a scream pierced the night.

The scream hurtled up to Ivy from the side of the cliff. Fear surged through her like an explosion. *Sunny*. Without thinking, Ivy acted, sprinting toward the edge of the ridge.

From the earliest moments of her daughter's childhood, that cry of peril had always sent her running.

"Be careful," Imani yelled, running behind her. "The cliff isn't stable."

Having grown up at the beach, Ivy knew that. Yet, she had to reach her daughter. She swung her flashlight ahead, seeking a solid-looking path.

"Sunny," she called out. "Are you two there?"

Beside her, Imani cried out, too. "Jamir, Jamir. Are you here?"

Ivy crept to the edge through brush and rocks. Falling to her knees beside an old sign that read, *Danger - No Trespassing*, she shone her light into the dimness and looked over the edge.

Jamir turned his face up to the light, squinting against it. His voice floated up to them. "We're down here. Sunny lost her footing, but she's hanging in there."

Only fragments of the wooden steps remained on the

nearly vertical path, and there were none at the top of the cliff. Jamir grappled rocks that jutted out from the side.

Beneath him, Sunny's sandal-clad feet slipped on the rocks. She scrambled to hold on. Watching her, Ivy held her breath, hardly able to bear it. "Hang on, sweetie. We'll get help."

Sunny landed on the remains of a broken step. "Mom," she cried out.

"I'm here, baby. With Imani. We're going to help you." Ivy cast a furtive glance at Imani. "How are we going to do that?" she whispered to her friend.

"I don't think we can get down there," Imani said softly.

Ivy lifted her eyes toward the heavens and squeezed back hot tears that threatened to spill from her eyes. She could not watch her daughter fall to her death. Whatever it took to save Sunny, she would do. She prayed for the strength she barely felt.

"Sunny slid down past me," Jamir called out. "I tried to stop her."

"Don't either one of you move," Imani said. "Hang on, and we'll figure out something." She turned a determined face toward Ivy.

"We need something to reach them."

A thought occurred to Ivy. She propped up the flashlight at an angle to cast light over the edge before easing back. "Bennett keeps equipment in the vehicle." If only he was here now.

Ivy raced to the SUV and flung open the rear hatch. A black utility bag was strapped to the side of the rear compartment. Opening it, she rifled through it to find several rolls of webbing, hooks, and other items that might help them. Looping it over her shoulder, she started back toward Imani.

"Bennett has some gear we can use," she said when she reached Imani. She plopped it down. "We can use this webbing. I've seen Bennett do safety and rescue demonstrations for the city." She'd watched him, but she'd never dreamed she might have to replicate his actions.

"I wish we had help," Imani said, looking doubtfully at the gear.

"I don't want to leave the kids, but I can stay with them if you want to try to get help." Ivy's heart pounded; time was of the essence.

"That might take too long," Imani said. "Sunny sounds worn out."

Suddenly, Ivy remembered something her father had once taught her. "Maybe we can call for help."

Imani pulled her phone from her pocket. "Mine is still dead."

"I mean with the flashlight. Point it back down the road and use the S.O.S. signal." Taking Imani's flashlight, she pressed her thumb on the button to demonstrate. "Three quick flashes, followed by three long flashes, and then three more short ones. Rest and repeat." She peered back into the inky blackness. "Many people around here sail, and they'll know that signal if they see it."

"I got it," Imani said. After calling out reassurances to Jamir, she turned toward the ridgetop community and began to flick the light.

Ivy ventured back to the rocky edge. "How are you two holding up?"

"I'm okay," Sunny said, but her voice was weak.

"I can get down to help her," Jamir added.

"Sunny, can you hang on?"

"Yeah, I think so. I'm just afraid to move."

"Stay right where you are." Ivy opened the bag. "Jamir, I can toss a length of webbing down to you. Do you think you can catch it and loop it under her arms to steady her and pulled her up?"

Jamir looked down the slope. "If I miss it, we'll lose it."

They couldn't afford that. Ivy sat back on her haunches,

thinking. She could pull the SUV closer and attach one end of the webbing to the vehicle somehow. If the webbing were long enough, she could toss it down to them.

She rushed to the vehicle and cranked the engine. After pulling it as close as she dared, she jumped out and bent down to look at the front bumper. With dismay, she remembered bumpers having space between the car—like her old Chevy—but this one was molded against the front of the car. Still, there had to be something.

Looking under the car, Ivy saw a tow hook. She was working on securing one end of the webbing to it when she heard Imani cry out.

When she turned around, she saw headlights gaining ground toward them. Imani was jumping and waving her arms.

An emergency vehicle from the fire department came to a stop, and Bennett bounded from the passenger side and raced toward her. "What happened?"

"It's Sunny and Jamir," Ivy said, grabbing his hand. "They were trying to climb the old stairs, and Sunny got stuck. Jamir is in a section where there aren't any steps, and it's a steep slope. He's trying to get back to her, but it's dangerous."

The fire chief, Paula Stark, stepped from the rescue vehicle. "We saw your signal," she said. "That was smart."

Ivy led Bennett and Paula to the edge, where they assessed the situation. After conferring, the pair decided on a course of action.

"Keep talking to them while we get ready," Bennett said as Paula returned to the rescue vehicle. He caught Ivy's hands and squeezed them. "We'll get the kids, but are you okay?"

Ivy swallowed a sob of fear that rose in her chest. "I'm just so glad you're here."

"So am I." Bennett folded her in his arms. "I see you found my gear. You would've figured something out." He pulled back. "But right now, we need to keep the kids calm and confident."

"I can do that. Imani, too."

While Bennett hurried to help Paula, Ivy and Imani eased back toward the rocky edge and called out to Sunny and Jamir again.

"Hold on," Ivy yelled. "Bennett and Chief Stark are here. They're coming to help you."

"Tell them to hurry," Sunny said, her voice sounding weaker and frightened. As she shifted, rocks clattered down the cliff. "Mom, I love you. I'm sorry if I haven't been a very good daughter."

"Sweetie, you're perfect as you are. I love you so much." Ivy lay flat and clutched the rocks at the edge, her fingers digging into the dirt. "We're going to get you up. Hang on, and stay as still as you can."

"I'm trying."

Jamir shifted toward Sunny, but as he did, his toehold slipped. Scrambling at the rocks, he slid down a little more.

Instinctively, Imani cried and reached out, teetering on the edge.

Behind her, Bennett gripped her arm. "Got you," he said. "Ease back."

"I'm okay, Mom," Jamir called back.

Ivy watched as Paula retrieved a harness from the rescue vehicle, and Bennett stepped into it. She and Imani stepped aside as the other pair worked quickly. Once secured, Bennett backed over the edge of the cliff and stepped his way down the side like a mountain climber.

Ivy could hardly bear to watch as those she loved clung to the edge of the cliff. However, bit by bit, they all worked their way up.

After what seemed an eternity, Sunny finally crested the top. When she saw her mother, she burst into tears. "I'm so sorry, Mom. And Imani. I never meant for Jamir to have to come after me. But after the earthquake, he did. I know I shouldn't have gone off and left him at the library."

Ivy wrapped her arms around her trembling daughter. "You're both safe—that's all that matters right now." Filled with gratitude, she reached out to Bennett and brought him into their circle. "How can I ever thank you?" she choked out as she embraced her husband.

"You never have to," he said, comforting her.

"Thanks," Sunny said, hugging Bennett. "You're the best."

Beside them, Imani threw her arms around Jamir. Tears of joy sprang to her eyes.

"How did you know to come up here?" Jamir asked.

Imani swept her hands along either side of his face. "I thought about what you would do, calculating the shortest distance between two points."

"We almost made it," Jamir said. "But more steps are missing now than a couple of years ago."

"Never do that again." Imani spoke sternly, but her expression quickly softened. "But thank heavens you both made it."

As Bennett and Chief Stark were putting up their equipment, house lights on the ridgetop blinked on, although the village was still dark.

"Hallelujah," Imani said, pressing her palms together.

"People still need to stay put," Paula said. "The threat below hasn't diminished." She turned to Bennett. "I've got to head back."

"Thanks, Chief," Bennett said. "I'll go with you." After promising Ivy he'd see her soon, he walked back to the emergency vehicle.

Ivy helped Sunny into the SUV, and Jamir climbed into the back seat with her. He put his arm around her while she wiped her grimy, tear-streaked face. Both kids were scraped and dirty, but they were safe. Ivy was so grateful, yet she hated to think what might have happened if she and Imani hadn't found them.

As she walked around to the driver's seat, she met Imani. The two women embraced, each of them overcome with emotion.

"That was too close," Imani said, wiping away tears of joy. "I was terrified for them."

Ivy smiled with relief. "So was I. Thank goodness you knew where Jamir would be."

"And that you knew Morse code." Imani grinned. "We make a pretty good team. I'm awfully glad you landed in Summer Beach."

"You've kept me out of a lot of trouble," Ivy said, suddenly remembering Geena. But right now, it wasn't about that. She glanced back at her daughter and Imani's son. Tonight was about keeping family and friends safe.

As Ivy approached Shangri-La, lights blazed in every window. When they arrived in the car court, Poppy and other friends rushed out to welcome Jamir and Sunny. They listened to the pair tell the story of how they'd tried to scale the back-side of the cliff.

Just then, Sunny's phone rang. "I've got phone service again," she cried as she pulled it from the pocket of her jeans. "It's Misty."

Ivy's heart thudded with relief. "Put her on speaker."

Sunny tapped her screen. "Mom is here with me. Are you okay?"

"I am, but I've been worried to death about all of you," Misty said. "When the earthquake hit, I was just finishing a late recording session for my voiceover at the studio. We've been watching the news about what's going on in and around Summer Beach. I hope you're not at the house anymore. Did you know there's a tsunami watch?"

"We know," Ivy said. "We got everyone out of the house and went up to the ridgetop. We're at Carol Reston's home. She and her husband Hal have opened their doors to everyone." Sunny looked like she wanted to talk to her sister, so Ivy added, "I'm so happy you're all right. I think Sunny has something she wants to share with you."

Sunny broke away from the group, choking on emotion as she told her sister what had happened. "I was so stupid for leaving Jamir at the library, but he came and found me. The people I'd gone with all took off and left me. I'm never speaking to those jerks again."

Ivy was glad to hear that. Maybe Sunny would learn something from the ordeal.

"Come inside when you're through talking," Ivy said. "Mitch is in the kitchen if you're hungry, and you can clean up if you'd like."

Weary and emotionally exhausted, Ivy went inside. Imani joined her, and as they entered the living room, more faces turned toward them. Friends and guests were curled on the sectional sofa or lounging on the thick rug. Some held wine glasses while others clutched cups of coffee or tea. And at the center of the group was Paige, who held up *Pride and Prejudice.*

"After the others from Imani's arrived, we decided to continue the meeting," Paige said.

"That kept us all from worrying," Darla added, who was sitting next to Bettina and her husband.

On another couch, Maeve was sitting with Nan and Gilda, who was stroking Pixie beside her. Jen and her sister Jessica leaned against each other, and one of Jessica's children was asleep in her lap. It was long after midnight now.

Bettina looked up. "This is the most memorable vacation we've ever had. I might have to move here just for the book club."

"You're welcome anytime," Paige said. "When we return

to the village, I'll put together those books you wanted. I always keep Jane Austen's books in stock."

Ivy realized that Paige didn't know that her shop had been so severely damaged. Ivy hadn't told her what she and Bennett had seen on their way to the ridgetop. But now wasn't the time to tell Paige that. The older woman was fully engaged in her role, encouraging thoughtful discussion among the group. Ivy would tell her later or in the morning.

Bennett had told her that no decisions would be made tonight, so Hal and Carol were making sure that everyone had a place to sleep, whether it was a guest room, a sofa, or a cot. They'd unrolled sleeping bags for the children, most of whom had already nodded off.

The conversation shifted back to *Pride and Prejudice* and the disaster of Lydia's elopement. Paige was nodding as Maeve drew a comparison with the present day. "The story is timeless because marriage between classes and cultures can still be a highly charged topic."

As the group continued discussing the plot of the story, Ivy made her way into the kitchen. Mitch was cleaning the kitchen with Chef Raul while Shelly dozed in a chair at the table, her head resting on her folded arms.

When Ivy eased into the chair next to her, Shelly woke. "Did you find Sunny? Poppy told us you and Imani went searching for her and Jamir."

Ivy smoothed a hand over her shoulder. "She's fine. I think she'll turn in soon, but you'll hear all about it in the morning."

As Shelly yawned, Mitch dried his hands and made his way to her. "Carol has given us a guest room. Ready to come with me?"

Shelly smiled sleepily and looped her arms around his neck. "Lead the way, my wonderful husband."

Mitch grinned, though he looked worn out, too. "Carol said that you and Bennett are in the room next to ours. Their dinner guests are in the bungalows."

"I'll wait up for him." Ivy had no idea how long that might be, but she knew Bennett wouldn't leave his post until everyone was safe. "Goodnight, you two."

Mitch slid his arm around Shelly, helping support her as they made their way through the hallway. Watching her sister and Mitch, Ivy was struck again by how much their lives had changed since she and Shelly had arrived in Summer Beach.

With Shelly's pregnancy, she and Mitch seemed to be growing ever closer, and Ivy couldn't be happier. She'd been married long enough in her life to know that difficulties could bring a couple together or drive them apart.

A little while later, after a spirited discussion that shifted from books to personal situations, Paige finished her wine and closed her book. "Even alert minds require rest. I can't promise our next meeting will be as exciting as this one has been, but this is an evening we'll never forget."

As Paige rose, Carol returned to the gathering. She touched the bookseller's arm and smiled. "I have a special guest room reserved for you, my dear."

Carol looked around the circle of people who had become new friends and closer friends through the course of the evening and nodded toward her housekeeper. "Miranda and I made up places for everyone to sleep tonight—or what's left of the night. She'll show you to the accommodations."

As others made their way to the temporary sleeping quarters, Carol sat next to Ivy. "Has Bennett returned yet?"

Ivy shook her head. "I'm sure he'll be late. He'll want to make sure that everyone in Summer Beach is safe."

"We've had Bennett to ourselves in this town for a long time," Carol said, inclining her head. "Someday, we'll have to learn to share him."

Just then, the rear door banged open. Hal slipped off his wet athletic shoes by the back door.

Carol hurried to her husband. "You're half-soaked, darling."

"Only the lower half," he said with a grin. "I helped place sandbags to protect some of the structures down below. Of course, those won't help against a massive wave, but we're all hoping for the best." He looked up at Ivy. "Bennett was directing the crew, so he should be along soon. We've done about all we can do."

"I'll wait up for him," Ivy said.

After Carol and Hal turned in, Ivy brewed a cup of green tea to wait for Bennett. She thought about what Sunny and Jamir had faced this evening, trembling as she realized that tonight could have ended tragically. Would she and Imani have been physically strong enough to pull Sunny and Jamir to safety as Bennett had?

While she couldn't answer that, she knew that what Bennett had done was not without risk to himself. Undoubtedly, he would have done the same for anyone in trouble—and that was another reason she loved him—but tonight, he'd saved her daughter's life. She was beyond grateful to him.

She sat at the kitchen table, sipping her tea. The house was quiet, but she would wait for her husband. He had waited long enough for her.

hen Bennett returned to Shangri-La, the property was dark, save for a sole light in the kitchen. Through the window, he could see Ivy at the kitchen table.

He was bone-weary, but he and other Summer Beach residents had done all they could. He barely had time for a break before sunrise when he'd need to be available again. After parking, he walked inside, and Ivy rose to greet him with a hug.

He saw her tea on the table. "You waited up for me?" The thought eased the aches in his body. However, he didn't have long to rest.

"Of course," she replied, her eyes shimmering with emotion. "I've been thinking about us—and about what you did for Sunny and Jamir tonight. I'm so grateful you came to help. If you hadn't…" She blinked, her voice trailing off.

"But you knew how to signal for emergency help," he said. "Give yourself credit for that."

He was thankful that he'd managed to help Sunny and Jamir to safety, and he dared not even think of what the alternative might have been. Pulling Ivy close, he welcomed the warmth of her body. They were both exhausted.

After everything that had happened today, Diana's employment offer—as attractive as it sounded—no longer held the same appeal. He was needed in Summer Beach, and this is where his family was. Still, the other city wasn't that far away. He thought of what he could do for Ivy and her children with his salary increase. Was he passing up what might be the best career opportunity of his life?

Ivy turned her face up to his. "Did everyone make it to safety?"

"All that we know of," Bennett said, pulling his thoughts back into the moment. "Everyone who could get a vessel away from the docks went out. That keeps boats from being smashed in the marina or washed onto the shore. Chief Clarkson's team and other volunteers went from door to door checking to make sure folks got to higher ground. Have you been able to reach Misty?"

Ivy's face relaxed with relief. "She called on Sunny's phone when the service came back on, and she's safe in Los Angeles."

Bennett kissed her forehead. "I'm so glad."

"Your boat is still in the marina, isn't it?"

"I've had other priorities," he replied.

"But you worked so hard to restore it."

He placed his hands on her shoulders. "Ivy, the tsunami watch has been upgraded to a warning. As much as I loved that boat, it's the least of our worries." Mentally, he'd already let it go.

Ivy's lips parted as she grasped the meaning of this. "Heaven help us if a big wave hits."

"Actually, it could be a series of waves with increasing intensity. We have to be ready for each one and try to keep people in place until we're sure the threat has passed." He clutched her hand between his.

"Are they sure a tsunami is coming?"

Bennett shook his head. "Nothing is for sure. Maybe we'll get lucky, and the waves will dissipate before reaching the shoreline."

Ivy touched a finger to his furrowed brow, smoothing it. "How long do you think it might be until people can return to their homes?"

"I can't say," he replied, turning his face into the softness of her palm. "Emergency teams all over Southern California are monitoring the situation. We have to watch and wait for the all-clear signal." As the adrenaline that had surged through him earlier waned, extreme fatigue filled him, and his speech faltered.

"Carol prepared a guest room for us," she said, looping her arm around him.

"I wish I could rest, but this is a critical time," he said. "Hal said he'd leave out some dry clothes for me. I've got time to refill my coffee, and that's about it."

"Did you get some of Mitch's sandwiches we sent over? While we were gone, the book club pitched in and helped him make food for others, too. Hal has been delivering in the golf cart."

"I handed them out to other people, but I didn't have time to eat."

"If you're not going to sleep, at least you need sustenance," Ivy said, putting a hand on her hip.

"Yes, ma'am," Bennett said, summoning a smile for her. Steadying himself with her support, Bennett stepped out of his wet shoes, leaving them next to Hal's. He glanced around the well-appointed kitchen.

Hal could have relaxed here and stayed dry, but the award-winning producer was working alongside everyone else to take care of the community. Bennett had a lot of respect for that.

While Bennett checked in with his sister and her family,

Ivy brought out a platter of sandwiches the book club women had made with Mitch. "Looks like tuna, lobster salad, or roasted chiles and cheese."

"Two of the latter, please." While Ivy slid the sandwiches onto a plate and poured a fizzy Italian soda for him, Bennett eased onto a stool. Outside the kitchen window, the moon was high in the sky. The fronds of tall palm trees whispered in the ocean breeze, casting shadows across the expansive gardens and paths that wound through the property. On any other night, he would have admired the view, but tonight it was all he could do to stay alert.

"Is there any coffee left over?" he asked, eyeing the clock above the professional stovetop. It was two a.m., and he had many hours to go yet.

"I'll put on a fresh pot."

"I can do that," Bennett said, not wanting to sound like he had expectations of her. "I wasn't asking you to do it."

"Really?" Ivy turned to him and made a stern face. "Eat. I've got this. You have to fuel up for the next round out there. And take some of this food back to the others. If I know Clark, he probably gave away his share, too."

"Pretty sure he did. There were a lot of families who grabbed the kids and fled. The children were tired and cranky. Some people were in the middle of preparing dinner."

"That's why I don't eat fashionably late," Ivy said, raising her eyebrows. "This is California. You never know when an earthquake will cancel your reservation."

He appreciated her sense of humor, even at a time like this. Not that he'd seen an earthquake like this in more than twenty years. When she put the plate before him, he wrapped his arms around her. "Thank you, sweetheart. I promise I'll make this up to you."

"As if you could have controlled Mother Nature? Please. Not even you can do that, Superman." She dropped a kiss on his cheek. "Now eat up and get back to work."

"Not before I have a coffee chaser."

"Coming right up."

Bennett wolfed down everything she'd put before him, filled a thermos he found in a cupboard, and packed a bag of food and supplies.

"Can I come and help?" Ivy asked as he was getting ready.

"You could, but we need a place to send people," Bennett said, thinking out loud. "If you can stay here to meet them and see that they find a place to lay their heads, that would be a big help."

"I'll do that," she said, sliding her arms around him.

With food and supplies, Bennett returned to the emergency staging area he'd help set up by the road leading to the ridgetop. As the moon traversed the sky, he passed out meals and bottles of water and hot coffee to Clark and others aiding people.

In between helping people figure out where they should go and receiving updates from the state emergency department, Bennett kept an eye on the ocean. The full moon illuminated roiling whitecaps, and the tide was higher than normal, but he couldn't see any massive, towering waves yet.

He prayed he wouldn't.

As the eastern sky grew lighter, the thread of traffic slowed. The last of Summer Beach and surrounding residents had sought shelter and were safe.

Clark clamped a hand on Bennett's shoulder. "There isn't much else to do right now, and it might be a long day ahead. Why don't you grab a few hours of rest, then I'll follow you? It won't do any good for both of us to wear out. I can last a little longer, but you look awful."

"Hey, thanks for that." Bennett bumped fists with the chief. "I'll take you up on it, but be sure to wake me if anything happens. I mean it."

Clark promised, and Bennett started back to Shangri-La, where he'd sent so many people tonight.

Ivy was still up, making people as comfortable as she could. Bennett told her the plan.

"I'm pretty exhausted, too," she said. "I'll join you."

In the guest room, Ivy helped Bennett peel off his clothes. She started the shower for him, and he stepped under a stream of hot water from a state-of-the-art waterfall shower. It felt so good, but with his legs giving out, his momentary bliss came to an end.

As she handed him a towel and turned down the bed, he watched her every move. She took his breath away. To him, his new wife was the most beautiful woman in the world.

"This must be what heaven is like," he murmured, embracing her. "I only wish I had more energy. If we make it through this, I want us to go somewhere—just us."

"*When* we make it," she whispered. "And we will."

After collapsing into bed, Ivy snuggled next to him. This was the love—and the woman—he'd needed in his life. He thanked the universe for sending Ivy to him, and after a few breaths, he fell fast asleep.

It seemed as if only minutes had passed since his head touched the pillow when a rap sounded on the guest room door. Hal's deep voice reverberated through it. "Good morning, Mr. Mayor. Clark is here with some news."

Bennett blinked and shot out of bed, his heart hammering. Had a tsunami come ashore? Was Summer Beach still standing? "Be right there."

Ivy was curled next to him on the silkiest sheets he'd ever slept on. He hated leaving her, but she needed rest. There was no need to wake her until he knew what was happening. After kissing her smooth cheek, he grabbed his phone, pulled on the fresh clothes Hal had left for him, and stepped into the hallway.

"Did you get any sleep?" Bennett asked his friend.

"A little," Hal replied, though he looked remarkably rested. "I never slept much when I was younger and even less now. Chief Clarkson is in the kitchen, and Chef Raul has coffee going for us."

"Good morning," Chief Clarkson said as Bennett walked into the large kitchen. "I've got good news."

"Could sure use some," Bennett said, feeling hopeful.

Clark explained that he'd received a call from the department monitoring the potential for a near-field tsunami. "As the data is coming in, the risk for Summer Beach is decreasing. Although we had a series of smaller waves that flooded the streets and some low-lying sections of town, we escaped the larger, destructive waves."

"Thank goodness," Ivy said from the doorway.

Bennett turned around. She was wrapped in one of the white terry-cloth robes that Carol had left in the guest room. "Come join us." He rose and pulled out a chair for her, admiring the way her hair curled around her face first thing in the morning.

Continuing the discussion, Bennett said, "This is the best outcome we could hope for. Once we have the signal to return, we can begin releasing people to re-enter the village area."

Clark nodded. "I'm receiving reports that most houses came through the earthquake pretty well, but a few older structures are badly damaged. I hate to report that Paige's shop is one of them. She also lives above the store in the old apartment that the original owners built."

"We saw that on the drive up here last night," Bennett said, reaching for Ivy's hand.

"Does Paige know?" Hal asked, frowning.

"No, Paige rode with Poppy last night," Bennett said. "They wouldn't have taken that route, but we did because we went to check on Shelly and Mitch."

"I planned on breaking the news to Paige this morning," Ivy said. "We can make room at the inn for her." She reached for Bennett's hand.

"You're going to have a full house again," Clark said. "I don't imagine there will be too many displaced, but there might be a few who will need longer-term lodging."

Ivy pushed her tangled hair back from her forehead. "That's what we're here for. Send them over, and we'll find a place for them. I imagine we'll have a few cancellations from people who are wary of aftershocks."

Bennett squeezed her hand. Ivy didn't have to step up like that for the residents of Summer Beach, but he was pleased that she was. This community meant a lot to him. Neighbors had cared for him after Jackie died; in return, he would do everything he could for them. To see Ivy doing the same brought a warm feeling to his chest.

Surely he could help Ivy work out any doubts she still had. This is the woman he loved. If only she could realize how much.

"ere's to an unforgettable night," Ivy said as she raised her glass of orange juice over the breakfast table.

People who had spent the night at Shangri-La gathered in the kitchen. Mitch and Chef Raul had turned out a breakfast of eggs and bagels, yogurt and granola, and fresh fruit and juice. Poppy and other book club members had helped Ivy set up a buffet similar to what they usually did at the inn.

"Thanks to each of you for pulling together in this effort to keep us all safe and sane," Ivy said, gazing around the large table at Sunny, Shelly, Imani, Nan, Maeve, and others. Gilda clutched a shivering Pixie. Even Geena had joined them for breakfast, staying close to Paige. "And special appreciation to Carol and Hal for opening their home to us."

Everyone in the kitchen broke out in cheers and applause.

"We made it through an earthquake and a tsunami threat," Shelly added, raising her glass high. "Woo-hoo to us!"

"Good neighbors work together," Carol said. She executed a slight bow while Hal pressed his hands together in appreciation to those gathered. "We haven't had a slumber party like this in years."

Carol had also committed to attending book club meetings, and Ivy was glad to see that everyone there treated her as a real friend. Carol had turned out to be more modest than Ivy had imagined. Instead of ordering her household staff around, Carol had worked beside them making up beds, serving food, and helping people shelter in any way they could.

"And to all of our new friends," Paige said, putting her arm around Geena, who smiled uncertainly at the people around the table. "Bettina and her husband would like to remain in Summer Beach after their vacation, and I'm trying to talk Geena into staying, too."

Imani shot a look across the table at Ivy, but she refrained from comment.

Inwardly, Ivy groaned at the thought. Geena was troubled, and while Ivy agreed that the woman needed a break, she wasn't eager to have her as a neighbor. Geena's mother seemed to have a strange influence on her daughter—even though Geena was old enough to exercise judgment.

Or did Geena see Paige as a new mark? Ivy hated to think that, but she didn't know much about Geena. Could her story last night have been an act to gain Ivy's sympathy? That's what Imani would say.

"I'm proud to be a part of the renewed literary tradition at the old Las Brisas Del Mar," Paige said. "I've attended many book club meetings in my time, but I've never held one by lantern and candlelight. Amelia Erickson would be proud."

Sitting beside Ivy, Shelly nudged her under the table. Ivy dreaded telling Paige about the damage to her bookshop and home, so Shelly had promised to share the task.

Ivy wished Bennett was here because he'd known Paige so long. But after an early breakfast, he had gone with Chief Clarkson into the village to begin assisting people returning to their homes. Once Ivy went back to the inn, she would make room for the displaced, too.

Everyone around the table and seated at the kitchen bar looked exhausted from the ordeal, but they ate hungrily. Without being asked, Sunny and Jamir took charge of washing dishes after everyone had finished.

When Shelly saw Sunny putting an armload of dishes into soapy water, she whipped out her phone to take a photo. "I have to record this momentous event—Misty won't believe it."

"Go away or come help," Sunny said, flinging soap suds toward her aunt.

Wiping bubbles from her face, Shelly laughed. "I'm off to the playroom on diaper duty. Who knew babies were so poopy?"

"They're worth it." Ivy chuckled. Shelly would have to get used to that soon.

As people cleaned up the areas where they'd spent the night, Ivy approached Paige. "Before you leave, Shelly and I would like to talk to you. It's important."

"Why, of course," Paige said, her eyes twinkling with energy. "We had quite a book club event, didn't we? One of the most memorable, I'd say."

Ivy could just imagine the shock of seeing everything she owned in a state of rubble. While Paige chatted about books with others, Ivy helped dry dishes. Soon, Shelly joined them again after assisting in the playroom.

Outside, the three women strolled to a gazebo that looked out over the sea and sat down. Ivy began. "Paige, I have some unfortunate news for you."

After Ivy broke the news of the earthquake damage, the older woman heaved a deep sigh and gripped her hand. "My home *and* my business? What on earth will I do?" Tears gathered in her wide blue eyes.

Ivy's heart went out to her. "We're here to help in whatever way we can."

Paige blotted her eyes with a handkerchief she drew from her pocket. "I don't know if I'll be able to deliver books to my customers now. And just when your book club and literary salon were looking so promising."

"Shelly and I have been talking about that. Since we'd like to keep that going, we have a proposal for you that we hope you'll accept."

"I'm not one to take charity if that's what you have in mind," Paige said, twisting a strand of silver hair. "I've built a good business here in Summer Beach. Over many, many years." Her voice caught on the last word.

Ivy heard the desperation in her new friend's voice. It hadn't been too long ago that Ivy had felt that same sense of loss. Without her husband and the home in which she'd been so secure, she'd felt rudderless.

"We know how you feel," Shelly said. "We both had to start over last year. It wasn't easy, but the people of Summer Beach supported us. Now it's our turn to do that for you."

"But you're both younger women." Paige raised her hands and let them drop. "Maybe I'm just too old to start over."

"Absolutely not," Ivy said. She flicked a glance toward Shelly. She had an idea, although she hadn't discussed it with Shelly. "We've got so much room on that lower level, and we've been trying to think of ways to fill it. The book club doesn't meet that often, and it seems a shame to waste all that space."

"Especially when we could have a charming bookstore there for everyone to enjoy," Shelly added.

Conflicting emotions crossed Paige's face. "You're opening a bookstore?"

Ivy smiled and shook her head. Shelly had read her mind. "I don't know the first thing about running a bookstore. No, everyone would want Pages bookshop there."

"I certainly couldn't impose," Paige said.

"It's no imposition," Shelly said. "Think of the fun we'll have. We'll put up new signage, and our guests can shop there. Soon, all your regular customers will know where you are."

Paige looked doubtful. "I don't know that I can afford the rent. You see, I owned my building outright. My inventory is probably destroyed, too."

"You'll bring all your valuable customers to the inn," Ivy said. "We wouldn't dream of charging you rent because you'll be doing us a favor. If you have insurance, we can help you sort through the paperwork to replace your inventory."

Paige's shoulders shook, and she pressed the handkerchief to her mouth. Unable to speak, she simply nodded.

Ivy stroked the woman's hand in comfort. This development was a shock to the older woman—not that Paige wasn't still quite capable. Ivy recalled her nimbleness on the ladder and her instant recall of books, authors, and quotes.

After a few moments, Paige drew a breath ragged breath. "My apartment is above the shop to one side on the second floor. What a grand old place it is. Lovely high ceilings, ocean views, and built-in bookcases in every room. I have no idea where I'm going to live."

"We thought about that, too," Ivy said. "I'm reserving the best room at the inn for you."

"I don't know how I'll ever thank you for this," Paige said, her face brightening with the light of hope.

"We're all in this together," Ivy said as the three of them hugged.

AFTER RETURNING to the main house, Ivy saw people gathering their belongings as they prepared to leave. Paige joined Maeve and Darla, and Ivy overheard her telling them what had happened. Both women embraced Paige in comfort.

Ivy knew the community would support their beloved book whisperer. She began to help people to their cars.

Imani and Jamir paused by the front door. "We'll see you back at the inn," Imani said. "But it won't be long before Jamir and I will be returning to our home on the ridge." She put her arm around her son and smiled. "As for today, I'm thankful my son is still in one piece."

"We'll miss you," Ivy said. "But I hope we'll still see you at the book club."

"I wouldn't miss it." A thoughtful look filled Imani's face. "We had a lively conversation last night. Even though we've all known each other for a long time, we learned a lot more about what makes us tick. Our friends shared some of their innermost feelings."

"You sure stayed up late." Jamir paused and grinned. "I heard you had some real ground-shaking revelations."

"Oh, that's bad," Imani said, laughing and swatting his shoulder. "Just for that, you're driving." She tossed the keys to him. "Keep that up and see if I drag your sorry you-know-what off a cliff in the next big one."

"I hope that's the last one for a long, long time," Ivy said, chuckling with relief. "But that was quick, sharp thinking, Jamir. If a big wave had surged in, you'd have saved yourselves."

"See?" Jamir said. "I could have been a hero."

"Don't let that go to your head," Imani said, hugging her son.

While a couple of small aftershocks had shaken the timbers, they were nothing like the strong jolt and sway of the original quake. The threat of a larger earthquake and a tsunami had passed, and most of Summer Beach would return to normal. Still, judging from what Clark had said about the street flooding, Ivy expected damage to the grounds and gardens. Suddenly, a thought occurred to her.

Her niece and Sunny were talking nearby. Ivy turned to them. "Did anyone happen to close the windows in the lower level before leaving?"

Poppy clamped a hand over her mouth. "I'm so sorry, Aunt Ivy. I didn't even think about it. And I was the last one out."

"It's all right," Ivy said, mentally preparing herself for a messy clean-up job. After witnessing seawater rushing through the streets when she and Bennett were driving to check on Shelly and Mitch, she was sure that water must have poured through the open windows just above the ground level on the exterior of the building.

"We might have some standing water, but it's nothing a mop brigade can't handle," Ivy said. With a wink at her daughter, she added, "Right, Sunny?"

While Sunny gave a mock groan, Imani nudged Jamir, who was grinning. "You think you're getting off easy?"

They all laughed now, and Ivy smiled. She could worry about what might have happened at the house, or she could accept whatever had swept her way and trust that they could put it right. "We'll crank up the music and make the clean-up fun. Nothing like an earthquake and tsunami threat to put things in perspective."

"Or getting rescued from a cliff," Sunny said with a shy glance at her mother. "I promise I'll never try that again."

"Just be careful," Ivy said, putting her arm around her daughter. "No more sneaking off and leaving. Your best friends are right here."

Sunny nodded and bumped fists with Jamir. "I won't leave you at the library again."

"You better not," Jamir said with a good-natured grin. "Because that's the last time I go looking for you."

As Imani was leaving, she pulled Ivy aside. "We still need to address that other issue," she said softly, inclining her head toward Geena.

Ivy followed her gaze. Geena was helping Carol and her housekeeper fold up the cots and blankets that guests had used. "I had a conversation with her last night," Ivy said. "We need to talk—I have a feeling about her."

"So do I," Imani said. "She's greedy and overreaching. Don't let her exhibition of helpfulness sway you. The inn is all you have." She paused. "You haven't found anything else in the old house, have you?"

"Nothing of any monetary value," Ivy said. "Although Shelly is still searching for the pot of gold."

"You're creating that every day by building your business," Imani mused. "And that's what we have to protect."

WHEN IVY RETURNED to the inn with the rest of their guests and book club members, the landscaping was as she'd expected. Seawater had formed pools on the lawn strewn with kelp, seaweed, and debris. Although the purple and pink petunias along the walkway had been bent flat or uprooted in the surge, the palm trees still stood.

"Look how high the water was," Poppy said. A water line at the front of the house marked the level above the windows on the lower story. "Our book club space is probably a disaster."

"We'll sort it out as fast as we can for Paige's new bookshop," Ivy said with conviction. They'd told Poppy about it on the way home, and she'd been excited at the new prospect.

On the house, the lower front windows were closed, but Ivy recalled that others were open. She'd done that to air the lower level for the meeting. Now, all the work her family did had been for naught. Ivy had no choice but to face it. That was the only way she knew to move forward.

With resolve, Ivy climbed the stone steps to the front door. Water puddled on the terrace, probably from waves that had crashed against the home. The exterior doors were closed, but they were old and drafty. The main level could be flooded, too. Ivy thought of all the beautiful parquet wooden floors that might be damaged beyond repair.

Dreading what she would find, Ivy turned the key.

*I*vy pushed open the door and stepped inside the house. Glancing around, she let out a sigh of relief. The wood floors were dry in the foyer, but Ivy feared the extent of the lower level damage. She turned to her niece. "I'm going to check the ballroom for leaks. Would you have a look at the other side of the house before guests return? Then we'll face the downstairs together."

"Will do," Poppy said, hurrying toward the parlor, library, and music room.

Holding her breath, Ivy stepped into the ballroom and made her way toward the tall Palladian windows and doors that opened onto the front terrace.

Except for paintings that were slightly askew on the wall, the room was as they'd left it. Ivy picked up one of Amelia's silver candlesticks that had toppled and rolled onto a rug. That the old house had survived the earthquake relatively unscathed was a testament to its architect and builders. She opened the doors to the sunshine. While the old wooden frames were damp around the edges, they would dry.

Outside, guests were making their way to the door, so she returned to the foyer to greet them. After making sure that everyone had what they needed—most were going to their room to rest or clean up—Ivy met Poppy in the kitchen.

"All clear on that side of the house," Poppy said.

"Thank goodness. Ready to face the downstairs?"

The back door banged open, and Shelly stepped inside. "You're not doing this without me." She plopped her purse on the kitchen counter. "Our cottage was fine—we're on a rise—so Mitch went to check on Java Beach and the rest of the village. Jen and George are planning on brisk business at Nailed It."

"We'll probably be visiting soon, too," Ivy said as she greeted her. "Although we might need a boat to start bailing water down below. How are you feeling?"

"A lot better," Shelly said. "It helps to stay busy."

Ivy hesitated at the door to the lower level. "We'll have to clean quickly to get Paige's shop situated, or put it in the ball-room—except I've promised that to the wedding party. However, I want to make sure she's comfortable."

"As we were leaving Shangri-La, I saw her with Darla," Poppy said. "They were going to look at the bookshop and her quarters on the way back."

"If they can get in," Ivy said. "It might not be safe." She paused and turned to Poppy. "If it is, would you rally the cousins to go over there and see what books and displays might be salvageable for her store downstairs? And her personal effects. We should have room for it all, though we might need to store her things in the ballroom until the down-stairs dries out."

"Which guest room are you going to put her in?" Shelly asked. "I thought you were full."

"We are," Ivy began. "But Bennett also asked us to make room for others that might need lodging. They're still assessing damage in town. Some houses might be condemned. We've always got the attic rooms if needed."

Shelly turned to Poppy. "Why don't you stay with us? The

couch folds out into a bed large enough for two. Sunny could come over, too, if you don't mind. That will free up a couple more rooms for a few nights."

"Another slumber party would be fun," Poppy said. "I'll clean my room for Paige."

"Are you sure Mitch wouldn't mind?" Ivy asked.

"He's let a lot of friends stay with him when they needed a place to land for a while," Shelly said. "He'll probably understand, but I'll make sure."

"That would help," Ivy admitted. Poppy and Sunny were accustomed to switching rooms to accommodate guests. While that wasn't what Ivy had in mind this time, she appreciated the offer. And there might be others arriving at the inn. "Since Paige is away, let's have a look below."

Expecting the worst, Ivy opened the door and flicked on the lights. The three of them started down the stairs.

Ivy's lips parted in surprise. "It looks dry." She glanced up at the high windows, which were all closed. After inspecting them all, she turned to Poppy. "I thought you forgot to close the windows."

"I did." Poppy squinted up. "I was the last one out—unless someone else closed them. I wasn't thinking about tsunamis, only about getting everyone out and up to safety. I don't think anyone would have stayed behind to shut windows."

"I was nowhere around," Shelly said. "So by process of elimination, I think we can all agree on who did this."

"Who?" Ivy and Poppy asked in unison.

Shelly picked up the old guest book from a side table and opened it. "Amelia Erickson, of course."

As much as Ivy hated to admit it, she was inclined to agree with Shelly this time. Although she made a face at the remark, she still sent up silent appreciation—just in case.

Poppy laughed. "Maybe she did."

Shelly put her hands on her hip and glanced around. "Now, where are we going to put that bookshop you committed us to? Not that I'm against it. In fact, I think it's a brilliant idea."

"How about that side of the room?" Ivy gestured to a vacant area. "We can use some of the old furniture and rugs to demarcate the space for Paige. She probably won't have the same amount of inventory she had, but even if she does, we can accommodate it."

After pacing off the area, they returned to the section where the book club had met. Ivy scooped up a pen and notepad that had fallen, and Poppy repositioned a potted orchid that had slid to the edge of a table.

Shelly angled her head as she stared at a back wall beside the staircase. "Hmm. That looks odd." She crossed to the wall, stepping over a couple of bricks that had fallen nearby.

"What?" Ivy asked.

Shelly reached up to a brick that was jutting out. "This mortar is pulverized like dust." She shoved the brick back in, perhaps a little too hard.

"Wait—" Ivy cried, but it was too late.

The brick dropped through, clattering onto something behind the wall. Startled, Shelly jumped. A couple of bricks above the now larger vacant space teetered, then tumbled after it, leaving a gaping hole in the wall. She peered up at the other bricks.

"Get away from there," Ivy said. "That whole wall could come down." She grabbed a book and wedged it into the gaping hole. "There, that might hold it for now."

"That's a hazard," Shelly said. "There's nothing behind it."

Poppy cleared her throat. "Then why would someone build a wall there?"

Ivy met Shelly's eyes. "I wonder if that was constructed at the same time as the wall upstairs that sealed off this place?"

"Would you like to knock it down, or shall I?" Shelly asked, grinning.

"Let's all demolish it together," Ivy replied. "That was so much fun."

Poppy held up a hand. "But there's probably something of value behind it. Otherwise, why would it be there?"

Ivy nodded. "You've got a point. And I don't want anyone to get hurt." A small aftershock swayed the light fixture as she spoke, and she touched a chair for balance.

Shelly stepped farther back from the brick wall. When the tremor stopped, they all looked at each other and let out a collective sigh.

"We should have someone disassemble it before it collapses in an aftershock," Ivy said. "I'll call Forrest to see what he suggests. For now, let's pull some furniture over here so that no one goes exploring."

"I'll make a *Danger* sign," Poppy said.

Shelly put a finger to her chin. "Maybe we'll find my pot of gold back there."

"We might," Ivy said. "Or maybe Amelia simply changed her mind and sealed off the entire level. She hid a lot down here. The paintings, rugs, furniture. That little space under the stairs was hardly enough."

"Then why not just stop building it?" Shelly asked.

"Amelia was sensitive to design," Ivy replied. "She wouldn't have left this half-finished, even if she was in a hurry."

"Unless the dementia was kicking in," Shelly said.

Ivy shook her head. "This would have predated the upstairs wall. While she was becoming a little forgetful, as we saw in that old film we found, the disease was not yet full blown. She lived here through the war and was still a force to be reckoned with."

As Ivy stared at the wall, she wondered what, if anything, was behind it.

. . .

LATER THAT AFTERNOON, after Ivy had directed a pair of guests to the children's beach, Poppy bounded from the library. Her eyes were sparkling with excitement. "I think I found something online about Geena's family. Come with me, and I'll show you."

In the library, Poppy pointed to her computer screen. "I found this post on another person's social media profile that was linked to Geena. Her name is Rebecca Bellamy. And look at this photo."

Ivy slipped on her leopard-spotted reading glasses and leaned toward the screen. "That's Geena, and the woman beside her looks like a relative."

"Read the post," Poppy said. "It's her long-lost sister. Rebecca found Geena through a DNA search. It says here that their mother gave up Rebecca for adoption as a baby."

Intrigued, Ivy sank into an armchair. "So we should find Rebecca and talk to her." Hope for a DNA solution surged within her.

"We don't even have to do that," Poppy said. "Rebecca posted an entire album of photos about her reunion with Geena, as well as her newly found mom and grandmother. She also posted about her grandfather, who never married her grandmother. It seems Rebecca was the first child. Geena was the second, and her mother insisted on keeping her."

Ivy sat back in her chair, thinking. "Did they have different fathers?"

Poppy looked like she was about to burst with the news. "Not according to the family tree, which would be the same for both sisters. I've got it right here." Poppy tapped a key, but the computer screen froze. "There goes the internet connection again."

"Still, that wouldn't matter because their maternal grandfather would have been the same," Ivy said, tapping her fingers as she thought. Seeing Poppy's expression of excitement, she ventured a guess. "Not Gustav?"

"Not even close," Poppy replied. "At the grandparent level, my guess is that the father either didn't know about the baby or wouldn't marry the grandmother, so she passed off the child as Gustav's in order to get money. Or maybe the father was in on it, too. Like a con job to extort money." She tapped the keyboard again, but the screen remained frozen. "I wish I could show you the family tree."

As Ivy considered this, disappointment set in. "But for Gustav to have fallen for that story, he must have been having an affair with the grandmother."

Even though that had taken place decades ago, she felt terrible for Amelia. Ivy had wanted to believe that they had a strong marriage. From all that she had read and heard, the couple shared many common interests and were dedicated to artists and their work. "Back to the parent level. Did Rebecca say why her mother gave her up for adoption?"

"She says here that her mother had her out of wedlock." Poppy cringed at her last word. "I hate that phrase. I always think about someone throwing away the key."

"It's not like that today," Ivy said, rising from her chair to pace as she pieced together details. Geena's family was more complicated than she had imagined.

"It still sounds like old-fashioned imprisonment," Poppy said. "Marriage is a contract. I took business law in school. It's only fair that if someone breaches the contract, it should be up for renegotiation."

"It often is." Ivy paused and gave her a wry smile. It sounded simple—until the heart was involved. "Had I known about Jeremy's indiscretions, we would have had some serious talks."

Poppy beamed. "But it's cool that you and Bennett are each doing your own thing. So it's possible to be in love and still give each other a lot of space."

"I suppose," Ivy said softly, although she was now having second thoughts about the status of their relationship. Maybe they didn't need quite as much space as she'd imagined. In reconsidering, she wondered if her actions were hurting their relationship.

Lately, Bennett seemed to have something on his mind that he wasn't sharing with her. It was just a feeling, and she could be wrong, but she sensed an odd shift in their relationship.

"When you fall in love, you might feel different. Ideally, you become true partners in life." As her last words hung between them, Ivy thought about that. *True partners in life.*

"Maybe I will." Poppy's cheeks turned pink. "I'd like to find out."

Ivy continued pacing as she recalled the conversation she'd had with Geena at Carol's. "Geena told me she didn't know who her father was."

"Maybe she didn't—until earlier this year."

"That makes sense," Ivy said, sorting information in her mind. "I would guess that after Geena's mother gave one child up for adoption, she didn't want to give up another baby."

Poppy laced her fingers behind her head. "So if Geena knows the truth, why does she think she's entitled to anything we find here?"

Ivy thought about that. Geena had said that her mother was adamant that she file the lawsuits. Had her mother or grandmother—or both—been perpetrating a lie all these years? Or was Geena simply trying to con them?

"Maybe Geena's mother felt she had to act fast with new information from Rebecca," Ivy said. "That might explain why she was pressuring her daughter to file the lawsuits."

Poppy's eyes grew wide. "Her mom did that? Wow, that's mean. And pretty cowardly."

"Thanks for researching this, Poppy. It looks like I have some things to do." She strode to the door. "Could you and Shelly take care of the afternoon wine and tea event? Especially today, it will help calm people's nerves about these little aftershocks."

Poppy grinned. "You bet."

"And please be sure not to turn anyone away who needs a place to stay. We'll manage." She paused. "The same goes for breakfast. Let's open the doors to the inn. Like Carol and Hal, we can make room for anyone."

Ivy marched upstairs to Imani's room and knocked on the door. When her friend answered, she asked Ivy in. They sat at a small table by a window in the beach-themed guest room.

Quickly, Ivy told her what Poppy had found. "I might have a shot at resolving this. Can you give me a day to try to sort this out in my way?"

"Do you want me to talk to Geena with you as your attorney?" Imani asked.

"I appreciate that, but I think she is more apt to open up to me," Ivy said, thinking about the conversation at Shangri-La.

Imani folded her hands on the table and nodded. "Give it a try, but don't commit to anything." She grinned and added, "You're a fierce woman when you know what you want."

Ivy chuckled. "Fierce. I like that. I don't think I've ever been called that."

"No? Surely you've been called persistent."

Ivy arched an eyebrow, recalling what Jeremy used to say. "Stubborn is more like it."

"Same thing. Women are stubborn; men are persistent." Imani rolled her eyes. "Forget that. Just go forth and be fierce. And good luck."

AFTER LEAVING IMANI, Ivy fired the engine on her old Chevrolet and started for another bed-and-breakfast in the village. The Seal Cove Inn didn't look like it had sustained any damage. After parking in front, she climbed the front steps of the old Victorian home. Inside, exotic orchids flowered against a breezy shabby-chic interior of white slipcovers and dark, polished wood. Ceilings were high, and fans swirled lazily above.

A woman about Ivy's age at the front desk smiled. "Hi, Ivy. What brings you here today?"

"Hi, June," Ivy said, stepping up to the desk. "I thought I'd stop by and see how you fared through the earthquake."

"Not too bad. This house is pier-and-beam construction, so the floors are a little uneven anyway due to shifting over the years. This old grand dame swayed through it with grace, although we lost a few wine glasses and decanters in the honor bar. How about you?"

"A little landscape damage, but the house came through it fine. I think Amelia Erickson was watching after her home." Although Ivy spoke lightly, there was a kernel of truth in her words. Shelly and Poppy sure thought so.

"These old homes have their share of spirits." June folded her arms and leaned on the desk. "The earthquake freaked out a couple of guests, who checked out immediately. Actually, that was fortunate because I just filled those rooms with the owner of a boutique in the village and her family. Their cottage tilted and flooded, poor folks. It's a good thing they're insured."

"We're standing by to help people, too." Ivy drummed her nails on the desktop. "I was wondering if Geena Bellamy might be around. I heard she's staying here."

"She sure is. She's a good kid once you get to know her, though I understand you have your differences. Do you want me to ring her room?"

"If you would, please."

June picked up the phone, but before she could dial, Geena came down the stairs. She'd showered and changed. Her hair was still damp, and she wore black jeans and a matching denim jacket. When she saw Ivy, she raised her brow in surprise.

"Oh, hi," Geena said to Ivy. She paused by the front desk. "June, I'm going out for some groceries for the room. Do you need anything?"

"Glad you asked. I'm out of my favorite tea." June told her what type she wanted, and Geena agreed to buy it at the market.

"Mind if I walk there with you?" Ivy said to Geena. "I just ran out of bread."

Geena shrugged. "Suit yourself."

The two women set off toward the store. As they walked along the sidewalk, Ivy saw a couple clearing their yard of water-logged items.

"I'm glad the sun is out," Ivy said, making an attempt at small talk.

"I suppose so." Geena fell quiet again.

Instead of leading with the DNA evidence Poppy had found, Ivy wanted Geena to come to a decision on her own. Otherwise, she might become defensive and dig in. She ventured again. "You talked a lot about your mother last night. I couldn't stop thinking about that."

"I guess I did." Geena kicked a small pebble on the sidewalk.

"I got the feeling that you're doing this—these lawsuits—for her."

Geena pursed her lips and sighed. "She's my mom, so it's my duty."

"Is that what she told you?"

"Like I said, it's complicated." Geena hesitated. "If I do this, then she won't need me to look after her and Granny anymore."

"Are they ill?"

"No, it's nothing like that," Geena said. "Mom just wants to have some fun, go to Las Vegas, stuff like that."

"Does she gamble a lot?"

Geena shot a wary look toward Ivy. "Probably too much. Granny won't give her any more money."

A picture was forming in Ivy's mind. "Not that I'm suggesting it, but what would happen to your mother if you moved away?"

Geena didn't say anything for a little while, and the question hung between them. Her lips quivered, and she brushed a hand impatiently over her cheeks.

Ivy waited.

Finally, Geena expelled a breath. "I have a sister I didn't know I had. Rebecca. Earlier this year, she called me and then came to see us. My mom was pretty affected by it all because she'd been forced to give her up. My granny regretted insisting on that, but at the time, she thought it was for the best. She knew how hard it was to raise a child by herself."

That seems to fit, Ivy thought. "And how did you feel about meeting Rebecca?"

Another small silence ensued before Geena spoke again. "This is going to sound awful, but I sort of wished Mom had given me away, too. My sister says she has the greatest parents, and she has the life I always wanted. She went to college, and she's married to a great guy—she even has two sweet children and a dog." She paused for a moment. "Even though my mom is hard to live with, I feel like I have to look after her."

"Why do you feel that way?"

"Mom is always talking about how old she is, but I know people older than her that do a lot more." Geena shook her head. "I don't know how long I can take the stress she heaps on me. At this rate, she'll probably outlive me."

Ivy studied Geena from the corner of her eye. "So, what keeps you there?"

"I don't know if I have what it takes to make it out there on my own." Geena forced a wry laugh. "I didn't have the best grades in school. But my granny still believes in my ability."

Ivy felt sorry for Geena—she needed someone on her side. "I think your grandmother is right," she said with conviction. "You need to give yourself a lot more credit."

Geena kicked another pebble. "Mom told me that if I do this for her, she'll give me enough money from what we get to buy my own place. But I know her. She'll find a high-stakes game and lose it all overnight. It's happened before."

"Stop waiting on her," Ivy said, daring to touch Geena's shoulder. "You're a smart woman. Do you have friends you could stay with until you got on your feet?"

Geena gave her a half-smile. "June offered me a room if I handle the evening shift. I also heard Celia say she's looking for someone to oversee a new art program for kids in the Summer Beach schools." She twisted her lips to one side. "I probably wouldn't be any good at it, though."

Celia had told Ivy all about the program and asked if she knew anyone to work it. If Geena was as passionate about art as Ivy imagined, that could work for both for them. "I think you'd be perfect. You could join my art classes if you want to brush up on your technique. No charge."

Geena stopped on the sidewalk and stared at her. "You'd do that for me?"

"Why not?"

"But, the lawsuits…."

Ivy held Geena's gaze. "Do you really want to continue pursuing them?"

Geena shook her head. "But Mom…." Her voice trailed off.

Ivy placed a hand on Geena's shoulder. "You've spent your life doing what your mother wants. What about your dreams? This is a chance for you to get out and pursue them."

Geena bowed her head into her hands. "She'd kill me if I did that."

Ivy frowned at her choice of words. "Literally or figuratively?"

"She threatens me all the time, but she doesn't mean it. I hate to leave Granny, but I know she'll understand."

"Think about it. And I'm not saying this because I'm trying to talk you out of the lawsuit—well, maybe I am a little —but you need to look out for yourself. For your life. You can still have the life you've dreamed about, maybe even one like Rebecca has."

Geena's mouth lifted at the corners. "My sister told me things about my family I didn't even know. She did the DNA research."

"And?" Ivy held her breath.

"My mom doesn't believe in DNA."

"But isn't that how Rebecca found you?"

Geena rolled her eyes. "Mom thinks it's right sometimes, but not always."

"What do you think?" Ivy was curious to see how Geena thought.

"I don't know if you can have it both ways. Rebecca found our real grandfather through DNA. Mom didn't want to hear anything about him. When we tried to tell her, she insisted she was an Erickson and stormed out of the house." Geena paused. "I don't want to sue you or anyone else. I wish I'd never listened to her. Do you think I can call it off?"

"I think you should explain all of that to your attorney— without your mother around."

Geena faced the sea and tipped her head back. "I don't care if there are earthquakes here. I'd like to stay."

Ivy quirked her mouth to one side. "They don't often happen—if that helps."

"It does," Geena said. "I've already made more friends here than I had back home. June, Paige, Celia—even you. The book club is cool, too. Listening to all those smart women is so interesting." She dipped her chin. "I know it seemed like I had a chip on my shoulder. But I'm not really like that."

"No, I don't think you are." Ivy paused. "It's never too late to rewrite the story of your life."

The two women neared a market on the corner. Inside, they shopped together for a few items, and Ivy helped Geena carry her bags back to the Seal Cove Inn.

Although Ivy couldn't tell Geena what to do, she wished the other woman would make the right decision for her life. If she continued on the path her mother had set for her, it would be a costly fiasco for all of them.

But sometimes, people had to hit bottom before they changed.

Ivy hoped this wasn't one of those times.

"*P*ack anything you see that can be salvaged," Bennett called out to those who were helping sort through the inventory at Pages. He placed a stack of unharmed books from an upper shelf into a box destined for new shelves at the inn.

"Only books that are in new, saleable condition," Ivy added. "Put the rest of them in the donation pile. Or if they're waterlogged, toss them. If you have any questions about items, ask Paige."

"Wait," Paige said, holding up a hand. She sat on a chair at the center of the old bookstore with an odd assortment of mementos on her lap. "If it looks old or valuable or is signed by an author, please save it. Many of these books are like old friends. Even if they're wet or dirty, they'll dry."

As Bennett finished packing the box, he called out, "Did everyone hear that?"

"Got it," Ivy said, which Poppy and her brothers Rocky and Reed echoed. Shelly was looking after the inn while they were here, an activity that didn't require any heavy lifting.

"We should have this done in a few hours," Bennett said. "Want to grab dinner in the village tonight?"

Ivy grinned. "Is that an invitation for a date, Mr. Mayor?"

"It can be." Brushing his hands against his worn jeans, he rephrased the question. "Would you like to dress up and go to Spirits & Vine tonight? I heard they came through the earthquake pretty well. They have special cabinets and displays, so they didn't lose anything but a few glasses."

"I would," she said, smiling. "But I have to get Paige settled in her room."

He tried again. "We can unpack most of this in the afternoon."

"I still want to make sure she has everything she needs," Ivy said. "Last night was terribly rushed. This is traumatic for Paige—decades of her life on display and all of it being sorted into piles and boxes."

Bennett hadn't thought about it that way, but Ivy was right. Had he been insensitive in his drive to clean up the town? He brushed against her and squeezed her hand. "You're right. Another time, then?"

"Of course, silly." Ivy smiled at him. "Thanks for understanding."

"We still have to eat," Bennett said. "How about I fire up the barbecue and cook for everyone?"

"That's a good idea," Ivy said, folding another box. "I have a lot of burgers and shrimp in the freezer that we could make, along with some vegetable kabobs."

Bennett was pleased to have Ivy working beside him to help dig out Summer Beach residents who had been affected by the earthquake and partial flooding. Fortunately, without major waves, flooding had been minimal. Much of Summer Beach was slightly above sea level. Every bit of elevation helped, and they were out of danger now.

Between the clean-up efforts in the village and the marina and helping to relocate vulnerable residents, he'd hardly had time to think about the travel plans he'd been considering before the earthquake. The glossy travel brochures were still in his desk drawer at the office. He wanted to surprise Ivy with a magical, memorable trip—just the two of them.

Aside from the few times they'd slipped away for a weekend, Ivy had worked nonstop ever since she'd arrived. At the very least, she deserved a break. Most of all, he hoped a longer trip would solidify their relationship.

From now on, they would have to make life decisions together, too. Bennett cleared his throat. "Listen, there's something I've been meaning to ask you," he began.

Just then, his phone buzzed. Holding up a finger, he pulled the phone from his pocket. "Bennett here."

"Hi, it's Diana. I'm calling to see how you fared in the earthquake." The head hunter's chirpy voice projected from his phone.

Ivy slid a glance toward him.

Feeling self-conscious for not having shared this career decision with Ivy yet, Bennett rubbed a hand across the neglected stubble on his chin. Adopting his mayoral tone, he said, "The community didn't sustain any major damage. Right now, we're cleaning up and taking care of people who've been impacted."

"That's exactly what I would have thought," Diana said. "I hope you've had a chance to think about the offer. I'll be driving through Summer Beach from Los Angeles to San Diego this week. Are you free for lunch or dinner so that we can talk more? I still think a change could do you good."

"Could I call you later?" Feeling Ivy's eyes on him, Bennett stepped away. He needed to discuss this with her before accepting or rejecting the offer, but he hadn't had the chance.

As painful as it was to think about it, Ivy might suggest another option. He'd been worried that she hadn't made an effort to move into his quarters or invite him into hers. He

wanted to have a full married life, not just when it was convenient for her.

He had to brace himself for the possibility that Ivy hadn't
been ready to marry. Had he been deluding himself all along?

"Looking forward to seeing you soon," Diana said.

After he hung up and pocketed his phone, Bennett turned
around. Ivy had moved to another part of the store.

Realizing why she'd left, he ran the back of his fingers
across his jaw. If this relationship didn't work out, he wasn't
sure his heart would be strong enough to keep seeing Ivy
around Summer Beach. But where else would she go? Her
home and business were here. While he'd been in this community a long time, he could always return to visit his sister. That
wasn't a decision he wanted to make, but maybe he shouldn't
be too quick to reject Diana's offer.

He made his way toward her. "Sorry, I had to take that."

"City business, I'll bet," she said in a cool tone.

"Sort of like that."

Without adding anything else to the conversation, Ivy
picked up a box and began sorting more books into it.

Feeling awkward, Bennett hitched up his jeans. "Business,
anyway."

"You don't need to explain, Mr. Mayor." Ivy didn't even
look at him. "Unless you feel you need to."

Bennett felt his face warm.

Paige lifted her hand, interrupting them. "Ivy, dear. Could
you make sure those boys aren't throwing away anything of
value? They work so quickly."

Ivy dropped the box she'd just packed onto a stack.
"Happy to help." She started toward Reed and Rocky.

Bennett sensed he was in some sort of trouble. That wasn't
the first headhunter call he'd received, and it wouldn't be the
last. All kinds of people reached out to him in his position. Ivy
would have to understand that.

Shaking his head, Bennett picked up another box. If they

didn't make it, whose fault would it be? Immediately, he chastised himself for that thought. He'd been married long enough to know that a good marriage depended on shared goals and fair compromises.

He felt they were reaching a decision point, yet he wasn't entirely sure which way it would go.

*A*fter dinner, Paige eased into a chair in the guestroom. "Your Bennett is such a good cook. His grilled Portobello mushrooms were delicious. What a treat that was."

"We're glad you enjoyed it," Ivy said, fluffing the downy-soft pillows in Poppy's old room where she had settled Paige. With orange blossom-scented potpourri and freshly laundered linens, the room was a comfortable respite for their new guest. Ivy had also brought some of Paige's favorite books for the white-washed bedside table.

Paige reached for the books. She picked up one by Pearl S. Buck, *Pavilion of Women*. "This classic novel set in China might be interesting for the book club," she mused. "Or *Rebecca* from Daphne du Maurier. Have you read that?"

"Long ago," Ivy said, smiling. "You have quite a collection."

"And each of them like an old friend."

As Paige looked through her books, Ivy unfastened the shutters and opened a window to the evening breeze. Outside, Bennett was heading toward his quarters.

Ivy rested her fingertips on the glass, thinking about the

phone call he had received earlier. Ever since, he'd been acting odd, as if he was keeping something from her. She'd overheard part of the call from a woman named Diana, but she hadn't been able to make out much of it. As mayor, Bennett received many calls from people in Summer Beach.

However, this one was different.

Diana didn't seem to be from Summer Beach. Ivy heard that much before Bennett turned away. She wouldn't have cared who Diana was, except that Bennett seemed to be hiding something about the woman.

Her pulse quickened as thoughts of different scenarios raced through her mind. Bennett's actions reminded her of Jeremy. Once, when she had questioned her husband's behavior, he told her she was imagining things. So she'd dismissed it —and even felt terrible for accusing him.

What a fool she'd been to believe his lies.

Ivy wouldn't make that mistake twice. As she angled the shutters for Paige, she thought about the overnight bag in her room she had already started packing to surprise Bennett.

Was she too late?

The salty ocean breeze cooled her heated face. Forcing a smile she didn't feel, she turned back to Paige. "I hope you'll be comfortable here."

The older woman looked up from her book and beamed at her. "Hosting me—and my bookshop—is extraordinarily kind of you, my dear. Maeve promised to help me sort through my insurance policy to file a claim. She says it should cover my lodging and rent for the shop. So I won't be a freeloader for long. I can't imagine what happened to my purse in the melee. I must have left it at Carol's home or in a car."

Ivy turned down the bed, patting the soft, white-cotton duvet cover. "Regardless, you're welcome to stay as long as you need to."

Paige drew in her lower lip. "I still feel like I'm imposing."

"Not at all. As I told you, having you here is good for business," Ivy said with a wink. "People are thrilled that you're opening your shop at the inn."

"Do they already know?"

Ivy laughed. "Word travels fast at Java Beach—and through the book club. Poppy is already dreaming up a re-opening party for you. We'll invite the whole town if you wish."

"What fun that would be," Paige said, brightening.

Ivy glanced around the guestroom. "I think you'll be comfortable here for a few days, but I would like to move you to that nicer room I mentioned."

"Nonsense," Paige said. "I wouldn't want you to go to the trouble of preparing another room."

Ivy walked to the door. "It's something I've been meaning to do." *And need to do.* Before Paige could ask another question, Ivy shut the door behind her.

As much as she enjoyed having her freedom, she loved Bennett—and she had taken a vow. It was time that she committed fully to him. As it turned out, the occasional evening or weekend she managed to carve out for him wasn't enough for either of them. He'd made his desires known; she was the one who'd wanted to ease into the marriage.

Now, she needed to commit. As much for herself as for him. Seeing how Shelly's marriage was evolving with Mitch brought to Ivy's mind those critical early days in her first marriage.

She and Bennett needed that.

Pausing at the kitchen window, she saw lights in Bennett's apartment and started for the back door. Maybe she could surprise him tonight.

The lights flicked off, and Ivy sighed. She'd missed her chance, but she could try again tomorrow.

Downstairs, she heard Reed and Rocky, their youthful

energy still going strong at this late hour. They were disman-
tling the brick wall, which had grown more hazardous with
each mild aftershock. It wouldn't take much of an aftershock
to bring it down, and that could injure someone.

Ivy made her way toward the lower level to check on her
nephews.

After they finished, she would clean the area again before
unpacking the boxes they'd brought from Paige's shop. The
boys were bunking in the attic rooms tonight to set up the new
bookshop tomorrow morning. Ivy was excited to see how it
would look, and it would surely lift Paige's spirits.

Halfway down the stairway, Reed waved to her. "Aunt Ivy,
we found something you'll want to see."

Eagerly, Ivy picked up her pace. She skipped off the last
step to face Reed and Rocky through dust plumes rising in the
air. The two brothers looked so much like their father had at
that age. Reed was working with Forrest in the construction
business while Rocky had decided to go back to school for a
master's degree in business.

"Good thing we opened those windows," she said, waving
dust from her face.

Rocky stepped toward the partial opening under the stairway. "We're being careful taking down this wall. We should
finish tonight or in the morning."

"I'm so grateful for your help," she said, passing the stacks
of bricks they'd made. She peered through the opening they'd
made into the dimly lit area. At once, she gasped and turned
back to them. "Can you help me get these boxes out?"

"Sure, but let us do it," Reed said. "It's pretty dirty back
there. The mortar between these old bricks broke down over
the years. Between some of them, it's mostly grit and dust."
He stepped inside the enclosure and began to pass boxes back
to his brother.

"Think there might be more treasures in here?" Rocky

asked as he placed the boxes outside of the opening for her to see.

"We never know," Ivy said.

Rocky opened a flap on one. "Looks like a lot of old books."

"There are a lot more of those in here," Reed called out.

"It's Amelia's celebrated library," Ivy said. Her heart quickened at the thought. As she'd read through the guest book, she noted the names of many authors who had visited the literary society. Maybe she'd find some of their signed books.

"Here's a box that's lighter," Rocky said.

Holding her breath, Ivy opened it. "It's old letters."

She thumbed through boxes of correspondence that had been packed for decades. Postmarks ranged from all over the world. The envelopes were addressed to Amelia Erickson, and the return sender on most of them was Gustav Erickson.

Ivy pressed a hand to her heart and sighed. Amelia had saved her husband's letters. "What treasures these are, although they're not what you might think of as valuable."

Her friend Megan Calloway was working on the documentary of Amelia Erickson in between other projects. She would be excited to see these letters, too.

Reed and Rocky peered over her shoulder with interest.

"Wow," Rocky said. "Imagine writing all those."

"That's what people did before we all carried phones." Ivy smiled wistfully. She still had to order a replacement. "Letter writing is a lost art."

She ran her fingers over letters carefully tied with an assortment of dusty pink and green grosgrain ribbons. Some had little notes tucked under the bows. "No one saves emails like this."

"I'll put that box on the coffee table if you want to look through them," Reed offered.

After he did, Ivy sifted through the letters, reading the notes Amelia had affixed to each stack to keep them organized. One read *Berlin*, others, *New York* and *San Francisco*. Some were from friends, and their names were attached to the front. She stopped at one. *Marta.*

The name was familiar.

Ivy reached for the guest book and opened it. Marta Mueller's name was written on a guest log page. Flipping toward the back, she found the letter she had tucked in and opened it.

A pledge to Marta, it read.

Returning to the box of correspondence, Ivy brought out the *Marta* stack of letters. The early dates matched, although the letters in the stack contained some from much later. With extreme care, Ivy opened the earliest letter.

Her lips parted as she read.

As Marta has been a fine and faithful scribe for our collection, I insist that we aid her. She wrote to me that her dire predicament advances. While she remains hopeful, I am substantially less so. Perhaps I am jaded, but I know men, even though I never met this one.

We are in a position to help her, my dearest, and so we must. Will you arrange a midwife or private physician for her? She will not ask for one as she insists on discretion. Should I not return from this dangerous situation, I trust you will honor the financial pledge I made to her. In the absence of a father, I pledged that we would provide for her child until it reaches the age of majority and gains a profession. Marta has kept our confidences, and so we will keep hers.

Ivy lowered the letter with a flood of relief.

Gustav wasn't having an affair; he was shielding Marta. She scanned the letter and rifled through others, eager to know the story.

All were from Gustav, replying to Amelia's letters about Marta's evolving pregnancy. Evidently, Marta was staying with Amelia in their San Francisco home. Then the letters stopped.

Perhaps Gustav had returned, eliminating the need for continued correspondence about the situation.

She lowered the letters. As a thought occurred to her, she made her way upstairs to the phone at the front desk. It was late, but this was important.

"*I* was going to call you," Geena said, absently folding and unfolding a napkin into a triangular shape. She'd just arrived on the beach with a smoothie from a nearby cafe.

Sitting on a broad flat rock that looked out over the ocean, Ivy slid the Jane Austen novel she'd been reading into her striped canvas tote bag and breathed in the fresh ocean air. Lizzie and Mr. Darcy would have to wait.

"I hope I didn't wake you last night," Ivy said. "But we need to talk."

Geena shifted self-consciously beside her. "I made a decision."

Ivy touched the younger woman's hand to still her nervousness. "There's something I have to tell you, too."

Geena shook her head sharply. "I need to say this first. I called my mom this morning and told her that I'm staying in Summer Beach. And I'm dropping her stupid lawsuits. In the beginning, she made it all sound so easy, but legal issues are a lot more complicated than I realized. After what Rebecca told me, I don't believe Mom's claims anymore."

Before Ivy could speak, Geena continued. "She spouts all

this stuff about respecting your elders, but she doesn't respect me or she wouldn't have put me up to all this. Still, I'm kind of glad she did because I've found a different way of life here."

"I'm sure she loves you in her way," Ivy said. Geena didn't look like she'd slept much, and her heart went out to her.

Geena sniffed. "She loves gambling more. Whenever Granny would cut her off, she'd use me."

"Gambling is an addiction, as sure as alcohol or drugs," Ivy said gently. Geena's harsh words were rife with anger, but under them were probably years of hurt, lies, and broken trust.

"That's for sure."

Ivy continued. "When a pastime becomes excessive, those who've become addicted hurt those they love the most—often without meaning to. Your mother is lost, too. Could you suggest treatment or a support group for her?"

"Maybe I should," Geena said, clasping her knees. "My granny has sheltered my mom forever. Mom started going to the horse races with a guy—our dad, I figure. Later, she discovered online gambling, and that really hurt her. Thank goodness Granny is good with money—what little she has left."

"Does your grandmother have enough to support them?"

Geena dipped her head. "My grandaddy's wife invested the money in something called annuities. Or, the man I thought was my grandaddy." She looked at Ivy with doleful eyes. "He wasn't, was he?"

Ivy couldn't answer that. Instead, she asked, "Is your grandmother's name Marta?"

Geena raised her eyebrows. "How did you know?"

Ivy reached into her canvas bag. "When the earthquake hit, it shook loose an old brick wall under the stairs on the lower level. The old mortar between the bricks had cracked and disintegrated. It was dangerous, so it had to come down right away."

Withdrawing a stack of letters bound with a pink grosgrain ribbon, Ivy went on. "I found these letters behind the wall in some boxes. I think you should have them. The answers you're looking for are in them."

After giving Geena the old correspondence, she ran a hand over Geena's shoulder. "I'm glad you're staying. I believe you're right where you belong."

Geena crinkled her brow in doubt. "You do? I thought you'd be upset with me after everything."

"I'll admit I was, but that was before I knew the whole story." She angled her chin toward her house. "That old home has been waiting for all of us to return, in one way or another." Smiling at Geena, she said, "Go ahead, open the letter on top."

As Geena read, Ivy gazed across the beach toward the inn. Maybe Shelly and Poppy were right to believe Amelia's spirit still inhabited her beloved Las Brisas del Mar. If so, Ivy couldn't help but wonder if Amelia's work was complete. Or, perhaps they were both caretakers of a home that continued to offer compassion, comfort, and second chances to so many —as it had for years.

Herself included, Ivy realized, lifting her face to the breeze.

As she considered this, she was confident that it was time for her to accept her second chance—with Bennett.

Beside her, Geena lowered a letter and wiped her eyes. "Having grown up without a father, my mom wanted to believe he'd been someone important. Her friends had fathers, but she didn't even know who her dad was. When Mom learned who had left money for her schooling, she convinced herself that Gustav Erickson was the one. My granny started working for him when she was a teenager fresh from Europe —doing translations from German and writing the history of pieces in their art collection."

"She was a translator?"

"For a long time, she did English-to-German—and vice versa—translations for business. Even for books." Geena smiled shyly. "That's where I got my love of reading, which helped me deal with my mother."

Ivy drummed her fingers on the rock in thought. Her friend Megan would surely want to speak to Marta about Amelia for the documentary film. Ivy did, too.

Now curious about Geena, she pressed on. "Does Paige remind you of your grandmother?"

Smiling, Geena nodded. "But I'll still see Granny. I talk to her every day, and she supports my decision. She said she'd take care of Mom now that I want to move on. Granny is the strong one, even though she's soft-spoken. Her mother lived to be more than a hundred, and she probably will, too. She's a lot like Paige."

Clutching the letters to her chest, Geena slid off the rock and deposited her smoothie cups into a nearby trashcan. "I want to finish reading these right away."

"If you have any questions about the Ericksons, I can probably answer some of them. We're still discovering more about who they were."

As they walked back toward the village, Ivy noticed a lightness in Geena's step that hadn't been there before. "Will I see you at my art classes soon?"

"I'd like that," Geena said, darting a shy look of gratitude at Ivy. "I'm starting work with June tonight for the rest of the summer. I'm also going to tell Celia that I'll accept the position she's offered me. Between those, I can start building my life here."

Ivy saw fresh hope flickering in Geena's eyes. All she had needed was a chance to escape her mentally abusive mother —and people who believed in her. Geena was lucky; Ivy knew some people didn't have that chance to escape. She felt the pleasant, companionable weight of the book she carried in the canvas bag on her shoulder and adjusted the straps.

Maybe that's what books were for, she thought. *A welcome mental reprieve.*

As dusk set in, Ivy entered her room and turned around, taking it all in. This lovely space—with its honeyed hardwood floors, chandeliers, antique furniture, cavernous closet, and clawfoot tub—had given her shelter when she'd needed it the most.

This had been Amelia's innermost sanctum, where she had hidden her birth mother's delicate ring. Ivy touched the vintage garnet ring on her right hand.

She walked into the large dressing room and turned on the lights. The chandeliers cast a glow in the room and reflected in the mirrored closets. She ran a hand over a closet door.

When the war threatened her and others, Amelia built a secret passageway behind this closet to the attic. And she'd even created a hidden dressing room for those she had sheltered here, where Ivy had found Amelia's first wedding dress.

Remembering how lovely Shelly had looked at her wedding, Ivy smiled. That had been the happiest day of Shelly's life; her dream of finding her life partner had finally come to pass.

Soon, Ivy hoped they would be welcoming the child Shelly and Mitch both wanted. Ivy wondered if it would be a girl or a boy. A child would brighten their winter, and Ivy was looking forward to helping Shelly.

Life went on, whether you were ready for it or not.

With a quick breath, Ivy made her decision. Opening a closet door, she selected a favorite dressy sundress that she seldom had a chance to wear.

Ivy turned on the radio. Humming to soft jazz, she shed her clothes and dipped into a refreshing bath. Afterward, she brushed her hair, slid the white linen dress over her sun-dappled shoulders, and finished with a light brush of blush, lipstick, and a spritz of Bennett's favorite perfume.

She glanced at herself in the mirror, sure of what she wanted. She was ready.

It was time for her to leave this comfortable nest for the adventure of a new life with the man she had come to love. She laughed to herself; she wasn't going far, but the distance, however short, was symbolic of her readiness to share her life again. She'd proven that she could make it on her own. That had been vitally important to her.

As she stood here today, she was sure of her feelings; she wasn't caught up in the sudden excitement of the unplanned weekend wedding, rushing before her parents embarked on their long sailing voyage.

She stepped to the window and looked out toward the former chauffeur's quarters that Bennett now occupied. Built over four garage stalls, it was large enough for both of them, with comfortably sized rooms: kitchen, living and dining room, and bedroom. A balcony with an endless view of the sea made the unit seem larger than it was.

The apartment was the ideal place for them to relax, with a cozy fireplace for winter, fresh sea breezes, and the steady low roar of ocean waves. Even the nearby happy chatter and music of guests by the pool or on the terrace made Ivy smile.

Touching her fingers to the windowpane, she saw lights on in Bennett's living room. She wasn't going far; her commute to work was mere steps to the house. Yet, she was crossing a major bridge in fully committing to a new life.

Peering into the closet, Ivy thought about what to take. Bennett could help her move the rest tomorrow. She would clean and prepare the room for Paige to move in then. Ivy thought warmly of how spoiled and cherished Paige would feel here. She wanted to do that for the woman who had given so much of herself to Summer Beach over the years.

She brought out her half-packed tapestry bag and placed it on the bench at the foot of her bed. After opening a drawer, she brought out a change of clothes, including a silky ivory gown with lovely lace insets that she'd bought on a whim and had never worn. After tucking those items into the bag, along with a few toiletries and pieces of jewelry, she zipped it closed.

Ivy was excited and ready to see her husband, imagining the surprise and delight he would feel. She slid a special bottle of champagne she'd been saving into the side pocket of the bag, along with a letter she'd written to Bennett to commemorate the date—inspired by the letters between Amelia and Gustav. With a last look, she shut the door behind her.

As she climbed the stairs to Bennett's, a rush of excitement welled within her. Strains of jazz filtered through the open windows. She tapped on the door and opened it. "Anybody home?"

Bennett strolled from the bedroom, tucking a dressy white shirt into a pair of slacks she had never seen him wear.

"Oh," she said, momentarily confused. "You look nice. Are you going somewhere, or did I forget something?"

"I'm sorry, I won't be gone long," Bennett replied hastily. "I didn't expect you. I thought you were working downstairs on Paige's new bookshop."

"Poppy has that under control." She waited, but he didn't elaborate on where he was going so dressed up—for Summer Beach, that is.

He seemed flustered at her presence. "I have to finish dressing, and I've lost my belt. You can wait, or I'll see you later. After dinner." He paused. "You look nice, too, by the way."

His behavior seemed odd, but then, she had surprised him. She hadn't thought he might be going out by himself, which was unlike him.

While Bennett hurried back into the bedroom, Ivy set down her bag. As she did, she spied a yellow notepad on the coffee table by his phone. Curious, she glanced at the pad. Bennett had made several notations on it. *Diana.* And, presumably, her phone number.

Beneath that were the words *City Manager* and *salary range*, followed by an admirable six-figure number. And beside that was the name of a city that was quite a drive away.

Ivy's mouth went dry.

Bennett was looking for another job. Why hadn't he told her?

A chill swept through her.

The name of a fancy, romantic restaurant in the neighboring community was jotted to the side. This was a place people went to celebrate—or be alone. She'd heard that Jeremy used to take Paisley there.

Next to that were several glossy travel brochures. Ivy ran her fingers across them. *Paris, Hawaiian Islands, Nordic Tour, African Safari.*

Bennett had never mentioned such a trip to her.

Her pulse raced, and she felt dizzy at the realization that something she wasn't supposed to know about was going on.

As Bennett rushed from the bedroom, still buttoning his shirt sleeves, Ivy whirled around. Her tingling limbs began to shake.

"When were you going to tell me you were leaving?" she asked, pointing to the notepad.

Bennett held up his palms. "Wait, I haven't committed to anything."

"How about me?" she asked, pressing a hand to her chest. "Didn't we commit to each other? I should have known about this." A waft of cologne floated in the air, and Ivy pointed toward the notepad. "You're meeting Diana?"

His face colored. "Yes, and I'm running late. Look, I know I should have told you, but the last few days, what with the earthquake and all…" He hesitated, rubbing his neck. "Can we talk about this when I get back?"

With her throat closing with anger and disappointment, Ivy strode toward the door. She felt like she'd been punched in the stomach. All the confidence and certainty she'd felt had been knocked out of her.

"Don't go like that," Bennett said. As he reached for her, he stumbled over her tapestry bag. "What's this?"

"Nothing," she choked out, her hand on the doorknob. He could have it all—she didn't want any reminders.

"Champagne? Were we celebrating tonight? If we were, I'm sorry I forgot."

Ivy waved her hand, dismissing his words. How long had he been planning this? The thought that he'd kept such an important decision from her was too much to bear. "Just forget it. I was clearly mistaken about our relationship."

"Ivy, no," Bennett said, his voice cracking. He reached for her, turned her into his arms, and brought her hand to his lips. "Please, you're my wife."

"Obviously not for much longer." She jerked her hand away.

Looking as if he'd been wounded, Bennett took a step back. "Is that what you really want?"

"Maybe there was a reason we hadn't taken this next step," she spat out, hating every word she was uttering but unable to stop.

Bennett held up a hand as if repelling her words. "Your choice, not mine."

"You couldn't wait until I was sure? Or at least ask what was bothering me?" She squeezed her eyes against angry tears that threatened to spill over her lids. "No, you just went and accepted a job somewhere else."

"I thought you were sure about us," Bennett said, his words eerily flat. "Maybe your driver's license was out of date, but I thought you were ready to commit to our life together."

"Even if I had been, what about that?" She flung out her hand toward the notes he'd made. "Committed couples share everything. What am I supposed to do—leave the inn now? Shelly can't run it by herself, especially in her condition."

"I'm not asking you to leave it."

At that moment, Ivy realized what he meant. That explained the travel brochures. Blinded by angry tears, she flung open the door and raced back to the sanctuary of her room.

Bennett didn't follow her.

a tap sounded at her door, but Ivy ignored it. In the darkened room, she sat in a chair by the window, watching the tides of the ocean beyond and trying in vain to numb the wound in her heart.

"Can we talk?" Bennett asked in a low voice. "I cancelled my dinner for you. I know what those notes looked like, and I'm sorry. It's not what you think."

The ache in her soul was so deep that it robbed her breath, and she couldn't respond.

Bennett knocked again. "Are you there?"

Maybe he'd go away if she didn't answer. He was moving away from Summer Beach anyway. She bit her lip to repress her sobs.

The door creaked open, and a slash of light from the hallway illuminated the room. Ivy shook her head, chastising herself for not locking the door.

Bennett stepped inside and moved toward her.

"You don't have to explain," Ivy said in a sharp tone. "The picture is quite clear."

"I don't think it is. Diana is a headhunter, and she's quite persistent."

Ivy folded her hands and angled herself toward the window. "Seems like it worked."

Bennett knelt in front of her, his hand on the chair. "I don't have any interest in Diana or in taking that position."

"Then why skulk off like a coward who had something to hide? Why even meet her at all?"

"Okay, I'll admit that I was flattered—but by the offer, not her. A man likes to know what he's worth on the open market, even if he doesn't have any intention of taking another job. But then, I didn't know why you were hesitating so much. I wondered if you'd had second thoughts about us."

Ivy turned to him. She started to deny that but realized he might have a point. She swallowed against a growing lump in her throat.

"Maybe I needed to know I had a way out if you dumped me." He ran a hand over his closely cropped hair. "If you had, I don't know if I could have stayed in Summer Beach. You're everywhere, and everyone here loves you." He took her hand in his. "Me, included."

Ivy swallowed her emotions so she could speak. "I wanted to be sure that we loved each other, that we weren't caught up in the mad rush of that wedding weekend and my parents' departure."

"I thought about that, too." He stroked her hand. "I wouldn't have left without you—unless you wanted me to."

Ivy went on, needing to say everything to him now. "I thought my desires didn't matter, that you didn't care about the inn or my painting or the life I've been building here—you simply expected that I would drop everything and follow you. I don't know which was worse."

"I would never think that. We make decisions like that together."

"We have to." Ivy recalled her commitment to herself. "I love you, but I want this marriage to be far different from the one I had before. I have a busy, active life with a lot of responsibilities. If you expect me to do all the housewifely duties that Jackie might have done for you, then you need to know that I'm past that phase."

Bennett curved a corner of his mouth. "I know what I'm getting into. If I wanted someone to fawn over my every need, I could have had that. But it gets boring. And if you fall into that trap, I'll be the first to let you know."

So far, so good, Ivy thought. Still, she had to know everything upfront. "And then there's Diana. I'll bet she's attractive."

"She is. But not to me." He kissed her fingertips.

Weakened by the torrent of emotions that had flooded through her, Ivy felt herself respond to him. She'd come through an earthquake and threat of a tsunami, supporting everyone around her, and yet the thought of losing Bennett had nearly devastated her. Did she love him too much? Or was she still traumatized by Jeremy?

"Seeing that note—combined with the fact that you hadn't mentioned it—really shook me." She drew a breath. "You should know that I have some triggers. I'm not proud of that, and as much as I like to think I'm over everything that happened with Jeremy, I'm not yet that fully confident woman you might want. I'm close, but I still have my moments of weakness."

"You're exactly who I want," Bennett said, stroking her hand. "None of us is one-hundred-percent confident or perfect all the time. We're all in the process of becoming better versions of ourselves—as long as we're working toward it."

She arched an eyebrow. "Even the mayor?"

"Definitely. I just make the best decisions I can at the time." Reaching behind her, he turned on a leaded-glass lamp that threw a soft amber light around them.

His eyes gleamed with emotion. "I know how long it can take to heal after a tragedy. It's natural to think about those we lost. And it's all right to react when things trigger you. All that is part of who you are and the resilient woman you are becoming. I get it."

"Do you?" Ivy searched his eyes for the truth she desperately needed to see. "I can't bear the thought of us having secrets from each other. I didn't even realize it would affect me like that. I try to control those feelings."

"I know you do." He caressed her arm as he spoke. "And I also know it's difficult. I couldn't listen to piano music for several years because Jackie used to play. It made me sad and angry that she was taken from me just as we were starting our family. But now, I can feel the joy in music again."

Bennett pressed his palm to her cheek and went on. "Ivy, we have to live in the now. We could have been lost in a freak accident of nature the other day."

"I've been thinking about that, too," she said softly. Life was so tenuous.

Bennett shifted onto the other knee. "Nothing in life is certain—but I hope that what we feel for each other remains in our hearts until our last breaths. I love every one of your quirky imperfections, and I hope you'll put up with mine, too."

A smile grew on Ivy's face. "Perfection is overrated. A messy life can be far more interesting."

Bennett returned her smile. "You should share that with the ladies of the book club."

"I believe I will." Leaning forward, she embraced him. "Thanks for waiting for me—and for understanding." As he drew his hands along her back, she warmed to his touch. "If I didn't love you so much, I wouldn't have blown up."

"You had every right to," he said. "I was an idiot for not sharing that with you, even though I didn't want to take the position. It appealed to my ego, but that was all. I did recommend a friend of mine, though."

"Then it's settled?"

"All except for this." Blinking with emotion, Bennett pulled her letter from his pocket. "You've expressed your feelings so beautifully—this read like a painting of words. I will cherish this, and I will love you forever and beyond."

"And I will love you." Satisfied at last, Ivy drew her hands along his face and kissed him with every bit of love in her heart.

"May we start the evening over?" Bennett asked. "We could go for a walk on the beach to clear our minds, and I'll make dinner in our new place. Ours, together."

"Dressed like this?" Ivy looked at his crisp white shirt and her white strappy sundress.

"I think you look incredible." Bennett grinned and rolled up his pants legs, revealing gray socks dotted with colorful fish. "Ready when you are."

She laughed. "At least take off your socks and shoes."

Lifting the edge of her dress, she took his hand and led him down the rear staircase through the kitchen and across the terrace. Leaving their shoes at the edge, they stepped onto the beach.

The top layer of sand was still warm from the sun's rays. As Ivy strolled beside Bennett, her toes dug into the cool sand beneath. She shivered slightly in the salt-tinged evening breeze —not from the chill but from the exciting prospect of their new life ahead.

Bennett unbuttoned his collar and draped his arm around her. "I put that champagne you brought on ice for later."

"That's awfully presumptuous of you," she said, teasing him.

"Hopeful is more like it." He kissed the top of her head. "I don't even want to think what might have happened to us."

"Neither do I," she said, raising her gaze to his. "It helps to clear the air between us. Maybe we should have a rule. No major decisions—no matter how angry we are—for at least a day until we cool down."

"At least," he agreed. "You know, we're going to be angry with each other from time to time. Sometimes I overcommit, or I might forget to call, or—"

Ivy stopped him with a kiss. "Sometimes, I'll do the same. It won't mean that we don't care."

"All we can do is try our best." He kissed her back. "I love you more every day, Ivy Bay."

"Me, too." Yearning for the warmth and feel of his body, she swept her arms around his neck.

As the ocean roared behind them and the moon gleamed above, Ivy gave into the passion that flared within her. Tonight held the promise of a magical ending to a tumultuous week.

Framing her face in his hands, Bennett gazed down at her. "I think that champagne might be ready for us."

With their arms linked, they made their way to their private quarters above the garage. Ivy hesitated at the door, wanting to remember this night. Despite their earlier disagreement, it was turning out even better than she had hoped.

On the beach, they'd talked openly about their hopes and desires and plans for the future. This was the relationship— and the marriage—she wanted.

Bennett pushed open the door and swept his hands around her waist, lifting her lightly across the threshold.

As her toes touched down, she laughed and kissed him. "I didn't expect to be carried over the threshold."

He grinned self-consciously. "At our age, a modified version of that was in order. Let's pour the bubbly. I have some cheese and crackers that could hold us for a while unless you're famished."

"I'm famished only for you," Ivy said, encircling his neck. His breath was hot on her neck as she guided him toward the bedroom.

"In that case…" Bennett began, loosening another button.

Ivy pushed a strap from her sundress, and Bennett kissed her shoulder. They tumbled onto the bed, losing themselves in each other. As the moon climbed high in the night sky and waves burst onto the sand, they drank from the wellspring of each other's love long into the night. Ivy had never felt so loved—or loved so much.

Ivy stretched in the new bed, delighted at the shadows the surrounding palm trees cast over the tangled white sheets. She tickled Bennett's shoulders until he rolled over. "Good morning, my love. Is it always this sunny in here?"

"Only when we forget to close the shutters." He wrapped her in his arms again. "I have to check again to make sure I wasn't dreaming. You're really staying?"

"For as long as you'll have me," she said, smiling at his sleepy eyes. "Or as long as you feed me. Are you as starving as I am?"

Just then, Bennett's stomach rumbled, and they laughed.

"We forgot dinner last night," he said. "And the champagne."

"How about we make breakfast together? With mimosas," she added playfully.

"Mmm, I like that idea. But what about your breakfast buffet?"

Raising herself on one elbow, Ivy glanced out the window into the inn's kitchen just beyond the car court. "I see Poppy and Sunny inside. They can manage without me for one breakfast."

"Do you want to let them know?"

She shook her head. "They've got this. I don't have to micro-manage anymore." She stretched again. "Maybe I'll even give up my list-making habit."

"Don't go too far all at once," Bennett said, laughing. "Race you to the shower. And this time, I'm well-rested."

They kicked off the covers and bounded into the bathroom, giggling like teenagers. It struck Ivy that she had first fallen in love with him when they were teens, even if she hadn't understood the fullness of what that meant at the time. Being with Bennett felt like she was coming home—and becoming the person she had always truly been.

He loved her as she was. Just the way she loved him.

After their shower, they padded to the kitchen with their wet hair slicked back, wearing matching white terrycloth guest robes.

Ivy made coffee, sliced fruit, and spooned yogurt into bowls while Bennett sliced mushrooms and zucchini for an Italian frittata. After enjoying coffee, Ivy opened the champagne and poured it into a pair of crystal flutes she found, along with a splash of orange juice.

"Taking the day off?" Bennett asked.

"I think I will. I'll text Sunny and Poppy." She glanced at her tapestry bag, untouched by the door. "We have a lot more than that to move in here."

Bennett swept her into his arms. "I couldn't be happier."

Breakfast on the balcony with Bennett felt like such an indulgence—and the beginning of their life together.

As she and Bennett were lingering over breakfast, Mitch and Shelly pulled into the car court in the old Jeep. Mitch brought out a carton of baked goods from the back while Shelly looked up at them.

"I didn't expect to see you up there, Ives," Shelly said, shading her eyes.

Ivy took Bennett's hand. "Just me and my husband having breakfast."

Shelly and Mitch looked at each other and smiled.

"I'll check on the guests," Shelly said. "You two take your time. All the time you want."

Ivy laughed and blew her a little kiss. "Thanks, Shells."

Beside her, Bennett chuckled. "How fast do you think news of this will zing around Summer Beach?"

. . .

AFTER REARRANGING Bennett's belongings to make room for hers, Ivy and Bennett packed her room later that afternoon. As Bennett began to carry boxes to her new quarters, Imani appeared in the hallway and volunteered Jamir.

Not to be outdone, Mitch pitched in, too.

When the upstairs fell quiet, Ivy checked downstairs. Shelly had planned to help Poppy and Sunny shelve books under Paige's direction. Pausing on the last step, Ivy took in the busy scene.

"What a magnificent new shop," Paige exclaimed. Seeing the surfboard that had been made into a bookshelf and other creative fixtures she'd had in the shop had clearly given Paige a new level of exuberance.

Shelly had fashioned an entrance to the shop, framed by an arched trellis. A hand-painted sign, probably painted by Paige's talented daughter, read:

"A reader lives a thousand lives before he dies. The man who never reads lives only one." — George R.R. Martin

So true, Ivy thought, thinking about the story she was reading. She joined Shelly in the new bookshop. "I love what you've done here."

"The cousins have done most of the work," Shelly said. "Poppy and Sunny shelved and decorated. Rocky and Reed finished moving the salvaged fixtures into place, and now they're picking up another load of Paige's personal belongings."

With most of the guests at the beach, they were all making quick work of moving. Ivy peered at Shelly. "How are you feeling today?"

"Only one queasy episode today," Shelly said cheerfully. "If all goes well, this little one will be joining us early next year."

"I can hardly wait," Ivy said, fervently hoping Shelly

would have a smooth, healthy pregnancy going forward. She wondered if their parents could return for the event.

Shelly slung her arm around Ivy. "This is definitely one of your better ideas. Paige is ecstatic."

"I can feel that. Her happiness is filling the room." Ivy smiled as she watched Paige putter around the shelves, giving instructions and turning books this way and that. "Giving someone hope is a beautiful thing. I'm glad we could do it."

Shelly's eyes widened. "Speaking of that, guess who is coming back to the book club?" Without waiting for an answer, she plunged on. "Geena, of all people. She found work in town, and she dropped the lawsuits. You wouldn't have had anything to do with that, would you?"

Ivy thought for a moment. "Actually, that was all Amelia's doing. Geena seems like a good kid beneath her tough-act exterior."

"Yeah," Shelly said slowly. "She's got that New York vibe —in a small-town sort of way. I can respect that."

Ivy grinned. "Maybe she'll turn over a new page in the book club."

"Oh, that was bad," Shelly said, poking her in the side as they both laughed.

Satisfied that Paige's new bookshop was coming along, Ivy returned to her old room. She was pleased that the space had been emptied so quickly so that she could clean it for Paige. Bennett, Mitch, and Jamir had whisked away her boxes and clothes in a fraction of the time it would have taken her.

After changing the sheets and cleaning the bedroom and bathroom, Ivy brought in a vase of pink roses that Shelly had clipped for Paige and placed it on the dresser.

She poked around Amelia's former bedroom to see if there was anything she had forgotten. She loved this spacious room, but the apartment offered more privacy. Besides, Paige would be thrilled, and the room was large enough to hold most of her belongings from her apartment. It would probably take months to rebuild her shop and the living quarters above.

Ivy retrieved her jewelry box from the closet and tucked it under her arm. The case held some of her mother's precious pieces that Ivy shared with Shelly, including turquoise, coral, and jade necklaces and bracelets. Carlotta had collected these from artisans around the world during her travels with their father.

Just holding the jewelry case made Ivy feel closer to her mother, and she could hardly wait to tell her about this important move. After taking a last glance at the room she'd grown to love, she took the back stairs to the kitchen, where she heard laughter.

"Hi, everyone," Ivy said, walking in.

"We're taking a break," Shelly said, looking up.

Her sister stood at the counter mixing cranberry and pink grapefruit juices. Poppy, Sunny, and Imani had gathered around the long center island on stools. Gilda held Pixie tucked in the crook of her arm. All of them were grinning at Ivy.

Even Paige hid a smile behind her hand. She sat on a stool with an open book before her.

Shelly glanced outside at the men carrying Ivy's boxes up the stairs to Bennett's quarters. "We thought this called for a Sea Breeze celebration."

"And why is that?" Ivy asked. "I'm only moving in with my husband."

Poppy dissolved into laughter with Sunny while Imani and Gilda traded knowing looks.

Ivy put her hands on her hips in mock annoyance. "Now, what's wrong with that?"

They all gathered around Ivy, enveloping her in a huge group hug.

"It's just that we've never seen you look so happy," Imani said. "You're absolutely glowing."

"Seriously," Sunny added.

Gilda chuckled. "And the mayor, too."

Feeling slightly embarrassed, Ivy felt her face redden. "Can't people have a little privacy around here?" she asked, trying to frown, but she was so happy she couldn't.

"At the Seabreeze Inn?" Imani arched an eyebrow for emphasis. "Not likely, unless we don't know someone."

"Or care about them," Gilda added.

"No, then we talk about them more," Shelly said.

Poppy laughed. "That's so true."

Putting a hand to her forehead, Ivy groaned. "Please tell me the gossip level here isn't as bad as Java Beach."

"This is a small town," Paige said. "People have to have something to do." Her eyes shimmered with mischief. "Or as Jane Austen wrote, 'For what do we live, but to make sport for our neighbors, and laugh at them in our turn?'"

Shelly chuckled and held up a glass pitcher of her coral-hued cooler. "Sea Breezes are ready—virgin or fully loaded?"

From her perch at the end of the counter, Paige closed her book and peered over her lapis-blue reading glasses. "Well, definitely not the former for Ivy," she said, her blue eyes twinkling with mischief.

Ivy's mouth fell open, and she whirled around as everyone else broke into laughter. Giving up, she joined in. "Guess I finally recognized my Mr. Darcy. What a book club this is going to be."

Paige winked as she tucked a hand demurely under her chin. "It's never too late to rewrite the stories of our lives."

Imani laughed. "Who knew this book club would bond over an earthquake and *Pride and Prejudice* at Carol Reston's Shangri-La?"

"And gain new residents for Summer Beach in the process," Poppy added. "Besides Geena, I heard Bettina already found a nursing position."

"When I first arrived, I knew I'd found home, too," Ivy

said, smiling at the memory. "Life is better in Summer Beach."

Ivy turned to Shelly, who was pouring juice. "Just a splash of vodka. It's barely cocktail hour, even at the beach." She was still feeling pleasantly lazy after the breakfast mimosas.

After filling each person's glass as they wished, Shelly held her virgin concoction high. "Here's to the newlyweds, together at last. Can I get a woo-hoo for my sister?"

Everyone clinked glasses, shouting, "Woo-hoo! Go, Ivy!"

Just then, Bennett opened the rear kitchen door. "What's all the commotion in here?"

Ivy laughed and hugged him. "Just another day at the Seabreeze Inn." She gave Bennett a glass. "Let's sip these by the pool," she said as the laughter continued.

Outside, she and Bennett settled on a chaise lounge. Touching her glass to his, Ivy said, "The pool looks so inviting. We should have a swim to cool off after all this moving."

"I like the sound of that," Bennett said. The edges of his eyes crinkled in a grin.

She stretched her legs in the sunshine. "Even though I know challenges are inevitable, I feel pretty good about us."

"So do I, sweetheart." Bennett gazed at her with admiration. "This summer and the year ahead will be a time to remember."

Ivy kissed her new husband. "Let's make them all like that."

AUTHOR'S NOTE

Thank you for reading *Seabreeze Book Club*, and I hope you enjoyed the book club meetings at the Seabreeze Inn. Be sure to read the next story in the Summer Beach series, *Seabreeze Shores*. Find out what happens as Ivy helps Shelly prepare for a new baby, and new guests arrive at the inn with unexpected surprises.

If you've read the Coral Cottage at Summer Beach series, join Marina and Kai and the rest of the Delavie-Moore family as the cafe expands and the performing arts center debuts in *Coral Holiday*.

Keep up with my new releases on my website at JanMoran.com. Please join my VIP Reader's Club there to receive news about special deals and other goodies.

MORE TO ENJOY

If this is your first book in the Seabreeze Inn at Summer Beach series, I invite you to revisit Ivy and Shelly as they renovate a historic beach house in *Seabreeze Inn*, the first book in the original Summer Beach series. In the Coral Cottage series, you'll meet Ivy's friend Marina in *Coral Cottage*.

If you'd like more sunshine and international travel, meet a group of friends in the *Love California* series, beginning with *Flawless* and an exciting trip to Paris.

Finally, I invite you to read my standalone family sagas, including *Hepburn's Necklace* and *The Chocolatier*, 1950s novels set in gorgeous Italy.

Most of my books are available in ebook, paperback or hardcover, audiobooks, and large print. And as always, I wish you happy reading!

ABOUT THE AUTHOR

JAN MORAN is a *USA Today* bestselling author of romantic women's fiction. A few of her favorite things include a fine cup of coffee, dark chocolate, fresh flowers, laughter, and music that touches her soul. She loves to travel, and her favorite places for inspiration are those rich with history and mystery and set against snowy mountains, palm-treed beaches, or sparkly city lights. Jan is originally from Austin, Texas, and a trace of a drawl still survives, although she has lived in Southern California near the beach for years.

Most of her books are available as audiobooks, and her historical fiction is translated into German, Italian, Polish, Dutch, Turkish, Russian, Bulgarian, Portuguese, and Lithuanian, and other languages.

Visit Jan at JanMoran.com. If you enjoyed this book, please consider leaving a brief review online for your fellow readers where you purchased this book or on Goodreads or Bookbub.

Made in the USA
Columbia, SC
12 December 2023

28277977R00157